FINAL ARGUMENT

ALSO BY CLIFFORD IRVING

NOVELS

On a Darkling Plain
The Losers
The Valley
The 38th Floor
Autobiography of Howard Hughes
Death Freak (co-author)
Sleeping Spy (co-author)
Tom Mix and Pancho Villa
The Angel of Zin
Trial

NON-FICTION

The Battle of Jerusalem
Spy
Fake!
Project Octavio
Daddy's Girl

Clifford Irving

FINAL ARGUMENT

A NOVEL

HAMISH HAMILTON · LONDON

HAMISH HAMILTON LTD

Published by the Penguin Group
Penguin Books Ltd, 27 Wrights Lane, London W8 5TZ, England
Penguin Books USA Inc., 375 Hudson Street, New York, New York 10014, USA
Penguin Books Australia Ltd, Ringwood, Victoria, Australia
Penguin Books Canada Ltd, 10 Alcorn Avenue, Toronto, Ontario, Canada M4V 3B2
Penguin Books (NZ) Ltd, 182-190 Wairau Road, Auckland 10, New Zealand

Penguin Books Ltd, Registered Offices: Harmondsworth, Middlesex, England

First published in the United States of America by Simon & Schuster 1993
First publisned in Great Britain by Hamish Hamilton Ltd 1993
10 9 8 7 6 5 4 3 2 1

Printed in Great Britain by Clays Ltd, St Ives plc

A CIP catalogue record for this book is available from the British Library.
ISBN 0-241-13436-6

THANKS

NO ONE NAMED Eric Sweeting has ever been executed at Florida State Prison, although for the most part the details of his electrocution mirror what happened to Jesse Tafero on May 4, 1990.

Many people helped my research. I particularly thank William Sheppard, defense attorney in Jacksonville; Hope Tieman Bristol, assistant state attorney in Fort Lauderdale; Maurice Nessen, who escorted me to Raiford; Cyra O'Daniel and Pat McGuinness of the Florida public defender's office; George Katsikas and Rentie Weston, Jr., of the Department of Health and Rehabilitative Services; Brian Davis and Henry Lee of the state attorney's office; Senior Judge Arthur Franza; Professor Michael Radelet of the University of Florida; Pam Daniel, editor of *Sarasota;* Kathy Blum, editor of *Jacksonville;* Ernest Downs; Pat and Stephen Weinbaum; Robert Johnson for his kindness in allowing me to use material from his extraordinary books, *Death Work* and *Condemned to Die;* Jack Slater; Holly Nadler; and Maureen Earl.

And Jeannie Repetti at Kramer, Levin in Manhattan, for years of generosity and friendship.

I have taken a few liberties with the geography of Duval, St. Johns, and Sarasota counties. If the citizens of those counties will forgive me, I'll be grateful.

C.I.

San Miguel de Allende

With gratitude
and with love
this book is dedicated to my aunts and uncles

Beabe Hamilburg
Bess & John Norman
Ruth & Albert Prago
and, in memoriam,
Mabel Rosenthal
Flo Schwartz

and, with the same sentiments,
to my loyal friend and agent

the amazing Frank Cooper

Therefore was one single man created first, Adam, to teach you that if anyone destroys a single soul from the children of man, Scripture charges him as though he had destroyed a whole universe—and whoever rescues a single soul from the children of man, Scripture credits him as if he had saved a whole universe.

—MISHNAH, SANHEDRIN 4:5

1

A TIME CAME when my wife and my law partners were convinced I was going crazy, and the best I could reply was, "I hope not." That was a year ago. I was forty-eight years old, I had worked hard, I had almost everything I wanted, and once the economy recovered I would achieve the rest. Or so I believed.

In the late afternoon of a golden winter day, I gazed out my office window at the warm waters of Sarasota Bay and, beyond it, the Gulf of Mexico. The bay spread itself before me like an enormous billowing blue skirt . . . a skirt I would have loved to dive under. But the pink message slips were piling up.

With the light waning, I turned on a brass lamp. I was reaching for a copy of *Florida Rules of Court Service* when the intercom buzzed with the call that would change my life.

"Ted"—the nasal voice belonged to my secretary, Ruby—"a guy named Elroy Lee is on the line, collect. From the jail. He's in there on a possession charge. Says he met you up in Jacksonville years ago, but from the way he talks, it doesn't sound likely. Shall I pass him along to one of the associates?"

I looked again at the bay, where a few homebound sailboats had spinnakers set before a light breeze. My vantage point was a fifth-floor office at the downtown firm of Royal, Kelly, Wellmet, Jaffe & Miller. (I was Jaffe.) The floor of the office was soft Spanish cork, the walls oatmeal-colored burlap. The teakwood desk was shaped like a boomerang. Azure light bled through hurricaneproof glass into

13

an interior coolness. Twelve years earlier, when I joined the firm, I'd designed all this: custom-built stereo, Florentine leather chairs with hidden steel supports for the lower back, even an Italian espresso machine in a corner under my diplomas and awards and the Frida Kahlo oils I'd bought in Paris. It was the office of my dreams.

I was senior litigator at Royal, Kelly, one of the best and priciest firms on the west coast of Florida. But two years before, we had invested heavily in one of our clients' luxury condos on Longboat Key, the sandy sliver of high-priced real estate where my wife, Toba, and I lived. In the gloomy depths of what we still called the recession, the rentals dried up like old leather. At last week's partners' meeting to split up the pie for fiscal 1990–91, Harvey Royal had announced that after the basic draw, which guaranteed each of the five partners a salary of $200,000, there would be no pool money to split.

"We're hurting," Harvey said, "and we need clients. Bear that in mind, gentlemen and madam, when you think about taking off early to the golf course."

Apropos, Barry Wellmet told a new lawyer joke. "What can a duck do that a lawyer can't?"

Heading for the door, I growled, "Shove his bill up his ass." My son had told me that one.

So when my secretary buzzed through to me that an unknown man named Elroy Lee was on the line from Sarasota County Jail, I said, "I'll take the call, but hang on a minute. Tell me why you think it's unlikely that this guy knows me."

"Sleazebag," Ruby said succinctly.

I had known a lot of sleazebags during my ten years as a state prosecutor in northern Florida. Come to think of it, I still did, except now they were executives of corporations. But sleazebags need lawyers too. Maybe more than most people.

"Put him through, Ruby."

In a few seconds a hard-edged southern voice came on the line. "Mr. Ted Jaffe?"

"Yes, Mr. Lee, and what can I do for you?"

"For starters, you can get me out of jail."

"Seems like a reasonable request. What's the charge?"

"Possession of cocaine in my vee-hicle. Third-degree felony. I got one or two prior convictions."

"And what made you call *me*, Mr. Lee?"

"I'm from Duval County, right? I remember you from up there

when you were top dog with the state. I had this bad luck down here, so I'm looking through the yellow pages for a lawyer, and there's your name. Recollected it right off the bat."

"You're sure that you don't want the public defender?"

"Sure as hell's hot and a Popsicle's cold. Don't worry, Mr. Jaffe, I can pay you."

I looked at my watch. "I'll be over to see you between nine and ten o'clock tomorrow morning."

"You can't make it now?"

"No, I really can't. Sorry."

"What's so danged important you can't help a man out who's got real serious asthma and a pulse bladder, and he's scared to death of what might happen in a cell with a buncha bad people he don't know?"

"Nothing, except that my wife and I are invited to a lobster barbecue in exactly one hour. What've you got to offer me that's better?"

The truth made him chuckle. "You don't have thirty minutes, for chrissake? Your danged lobster's more important than a man's health and welfare? What kind of a lawyer are you?"

"A realistic one. And one who loves lobster. This isn't crayfish, Mr. Lee. This stuff's flown down from Maine. You'll get through the night. You've had practice."

But then I glanced up. Above the shelf of books that contained *Moore's Federal Rules of Criminal Procedure* and *West's Florida Criminal Laws and Rules*—what we called the Bible—was a framed cartoon that I'd clipped from a law journal. It showed a shark about to chew up a grouper, which in turn was about to swallow a minnow, which in turn was about to gobble up a worm. The shark was saying, "There's plenty of justice." The grouper was saying, "There's some justice." The minnow was complaining, "There's no justice," and the worm was crying, "Help!"

I had a flare-up of compassion for the downtrodden of the species. So to the worm who called himself Elroy Lee, I said, "Tell you what I'll do. You remember what we used to say up in Duval County?"

"What might that be, sir?"

" 'When you're up to your neck in shit, pardner, don't open your mouth.' You keep yours shut for another twenty minutes, and I'll drop by and see if I can get you off the hook."

Elroy Lee chuckled. "I hear you, Counselor."

. . .

I met him in one of the lawyers' visiting rooms at the Sarasota County Jail. He was a lean white man in his early forties, with thinning sand-colored hair and cold green eyes. A gap between his two front teeth made him look like a squirrel, and he had a rodent's alert expression and quick, furtive movements.

The charge against him was possession with intent to deliver, a second-degree felony—a little more serious than he'd suggested over the telephone. Truth behind bars is as rare as snow in the Gulf of Mexico.

Elroy said, "This is a weird town. I got here like about a week ago? You want to hear what happened?"

"If it's got to do with your case, yes. My lobster's getting colder by the minute."

He ignored my plea. "I get to town, I gas up my car at an Exxon, the self-service part, and on the other pump is an old guy wants to save a few nickels. Except his wife's at the wheel of this '69 Mercedes and she backs up, maybe get it more into the shade, who the fuck knows—she doesn't see him, she drags him fifteen feet. And he's *dead*. It's the first fucking thing I see when I get to Sarasota!"

"Elroy," I said sharply, "let's talk about possession with intent to deliver."

"Then I see on TV that an eighty-four-year-old guy at the airport plows his Caddy into a bunch of people getting their suitcases—he kills a woman, puts three more in the hospital. What is this place, a war zone for senior citizens?"

I explained to Elroy that in some parts of geriatric Florida you were in the greatest danger stopping for a red light or going through a green light, and he brayed a laugh.

"Tell me what happened to you," I said, my patience about to flee.

A few days ago, he explained, he was riding along on Route 41 in his Olds Cutlass, and at a stoplight two cops waved him over to the curb. They searched the Cutlass, found cocaine in the trunk. Not crack cocaine, just powder.

"Were you speeding?"

He didn't think so.

"Did they ask your permission to search?"

Hell, no.

"How much cocaine?"

"A paper bag, with twenty-eight little plastic Baggies inside it. Each Baggie's got a gram, so that's twenty-eight grams."

"You're lucky. One more gram and it would've been trafficking, and that's a first-degree felony. The bond would have been fifty thousand dollars, and they could have added up your priors and given you a habitual-offender classification. The deep weeds, Elroy. As it is, it's still possession with intent to deliver."

From my client's studied silence at the receipt of this information, I deduced that he was a veteran and knew all that I'd told him and plenty more. You couldn't call it luck that he was carrying one gram less than was required to merit the graver accusation of trafficking.

I was already regretting having taken the call. This was the kind of man I used to prosecute with some degree of pleasure.

"Elroy, I'll want to know where that car's been for the last seventy-two hours and exactly when it's been out of your sight and control. And I'll need to know if any reliable witnesses can confirm what you tell me. Reliable, like church deacons and schoolteachers. My fee is seven thousand five hundred dollars, and my firm's policy on collection is simple. You pay it in full up front. Then neither of us has to worry about it later."

He looked unhappy. "Mr. Jaffe, I haven't got that kind of money."

I could smell his sweat and the sweat of a hundred other men who had sat in his chair. Elroy dug an asthma inhaler from the pocket of his jailhouse khakis and puffed on it twice. I was meant to feel sympathy, I realized. Criminals just never could figure out why lawyers didn't trust them.

Elroy's pale eyes narrowed. "I can't do any more time. I told you, I got a pulse bladder. It's like a cyst, but it's choking the artery to my balls, and it hurts most all the time. That's from getting kicked by cops, catching the clap and herpes and shit like that."

I may have edged my body slightly away from him.

"You think a pulse bladder is infectious, Counselor? You think if I breathe on you, maybe you'll get herpes?"

"I can think of better ways of catching it than getting breathed on by you," I admitted. And I kept my distance. You never knew what horrible discovery you were going to read about next week in the medical section of *Time* or *Newsweek*.

"So what about it, Mr. Jaffe? Am I gonna do time?"

17

Did he think I was Nostradamus? The system had so many holes that anyone could slip through it. A good lawyer made a major difference, and in a simple criminal case I received what was known as a "former prosecutor discount" when it came to the sometimes tasteless sequence of plea bargaining with the state attorney's office.

"You might do a nickel," I said. "The way they're jammed up at the state prison you'll be back on the street in ten or twelve months. That's a bargain, my friend, for twenty-eight grams of white lady."

"What if I take my best shot at digging up the fee and it don't work out?"

"Back to the yellow pages, Elroy."

I stood and walked across the room to the barred window. No law or canon required that a lawyer like his clients; my obligation was to tell them the truth and do the best I could to minimize their exposure to legal grief.

From behind my back, Elroy asked slyly, "Can't we work something out like before?"

I turned to him; now it was my turn to frown. Before what?

"Like up in Jacksonville," he said.

I could see the butter on my lobster congealing and growing cold. "I don't follow you."

"I told you I had a couple of priors—three or four, come to think about it. Couple's under my real name, which happens to be Jerry Lee Elroy, not Elroy Lee. You know me now?"

"No, I don't." But I was already uneasy. I *did* know him. I just couldn't place him in the proper context.

"Jacksonville."

"All right," I conceded, "the name's familiar. Refresh my memory."

"Ten years ago, in Duval County. You were on the other side of the law then, Counselor."

"Not quite," I said. I had been chief assistant state attorney in Jacksonville and Duval County, but a lawyer, no matter what side he was on, was always an officer of the court, bound by the canons of ethics and his conscience, such as they were. Mine had always been pretty well anchored in place. I'd never done anything I was ashamed of. As a lawyer anyway.

Then it struck me; I remembered the cute gap between Elroy's teeth. It was twelve years ago, not ten. "The Morgan trial?"

"Right!" He looked immensely pleased.

"You were a witness, is that it?"

"For the state. For *you*. I snitched on this guy, Morgan." He gave a shy, toothy smile. "You got it now? You remember the deal? Okay?"

I still hadn't the slightest idea what he was getting at. "Okay *what*?"

"Work something out like we did before."

"Listen carefully," I said. "I don't read minds. *What* did we do before?"

Elroy sighed and rolled his ditch-water-green eyes in their sockets as if he were dealing with a backward child. "I was just thinking . . . I help out this here sheriff the same way I helped you out back then, and then these guys could drop the charges on the cocaine. Then my case don't take up so much of your time, and maybe you'll see your way clear to less cash."

I walked back across the stuffy little room and sat down once more at the table. I tapped with my pen on my yellow legal pad.

"What the hell are you talking about, Elroy? What did you do in Jacksonville back in 1979 that I'm supposed to remember? Run it by me nice and slow."

Elroy concentrated for a minute. "Nigger killed a rich Jew, you remember that?"

Now I had other reasons for wishing I were with my wife and my promised lobster. Under the table, where he couldn't see, I balled my fists. "I remember very well," I said coldly. "A black man named Darryl Morgan shot a white man named Solomon Zide."

"Out at the beach, right?"

"Yes," I said, "at the Zide estate. After a big party."

"That's it. It just so happens I was in the same cell with the nigger that did it. Big nigger, too dumb to pour piss out of a boot before he put it on. Cop took me up on the roof of the Duval County Jail. He asks if this nigger talks to me, and I say, 'That's not likely.' Cop wants to know, 'How about on the telephone? You ever hear him say, "Yeah, I did it"?' I go, 'He could have.' 'Well, he *did* do it,' the cop says, ' 'cause he told *me* he did it, so he might just as well have told someone else, like on the telephone here in jail, right?' And I say, 'What's in it for me?' Cop tells me he can cut a deal for me on my case, get me time served and probation. Hell, if the nigger told the cop he did it, he's a dead nigger already, right? So I go, 'Okay, now I recollect on it, I heard him say he done it.' "

19

I remembered how the issue arose in Judge Eglin's court twelve years ago. As in all Florida criminal cases, there had been full disclosure during discovery, and Gary Oliver, Darryl Morgan's lawyer—the names had not been in my mind for a decade, but they rose up now like jagged rocks at low tide—had made a pretrial motion to suppress the testimony of Jerry Lee Elroy. Even if Darryl Morgan had said on the jailhouse telephone what my witness would testify to, Oliver claimed, it was still intended to be a private communication and therefore privileged.

"No," I'd argued to the court, "if there's one phone per cell, and you know three other men are standing around, where's your expectation of privacy? That doesn't wash, Your Honor."

The judge nodded, and I had continued my direct examination: "And so what did Morgan say, Mr. Elroy?"

"He said, 'I'm in deep shit because I was robbing this house and I shot some Jew . . . then his wife come running out, and we had to take care of the bitch too.' "

Judge Eglin had ruled that the witness would be allowed to testify before the jury.

Now, twelve years later in Sarasota, I was finding out that this redneck worm who had been my witness in a capital murder case—my last case before I went into private practice and moved down here to the good life on the Gulf of Mexico—had perjured himself at a police officer's request. He had lied first to me, and then to the judge, and finally to the jury. He'd lied about a man who was facing the death penalty. I hadn't known he was lying, but that didn't change the fact. And it didn't make me feel less disgusted with myself —or less apprehensive.

"What was the charge against you in Jacksonville, Elroy?"

"Aggravated battery. Beat up on a woman, no big deal."

I could have throttled him.

"You recall the name of the cop who talked you into remembering what you didn't hear?"

"Hey, maybe I *did* hear it."

"*No, you scumbag, you didn't hear a fucking thing!*" I crashed my fist on the metal surface of the table with a force that startled him and me both.

"Take it easy, Counselor . . ."

"Don't get cute with me," I snarled. "Not unless you want to do twenty years on the concrete at Raiford. Who was the cop?"

Elroy turned a little pale, and he concentrated for a minute. "On the stocky side. Had a mustache. Nasty as catshit."

I tried to remember which Jacksonville Homicide sergeant fit that description. Unfortunately, many.

"Lew Harmon?" I suggested. "Marty Girard?"

"One of them two, I think. Was a long time ago. What about it, Mr. Jaffe? You got good connections here with the sheriff—can you arrange it?"

I dropped my voice as though someone might be listening. "Are you sure you can make bail?"

"I got a friend coming over from Miami tomorrow afternoon. He'll have the money. But I don't know a bondsman over here."

I made up my mind. Something had to be done, and I had to keep this man under my control no matter what the cost. "I'll find a bondsman for you," I said, "and we'll be here together at three o'clock tomorrow afternoon. I'll get you out of here."

Elroy seemed surprised. "You'll take my case?"

"Yes, I'll take your case."

"What about the fee?" he asked slyly.

"We'll work that out. Don't worry about it. I need to think about this for a while."

When I left the jail, the sun was a squashed blood-red ball quivering on the horizon. A chill wind had sprung up to ripple the bay. I hurried to my car, but there was no way to avoid that wind. As it struck me, I had the feeling that it blew out of the past.

2

I N EARLY DECEMBER, over twelve years earlier, Solomon Zide and his wife sponsored a benefit performance by the Florida Symphony Brass Orchestra. The concert took place at the Zide estate at Jacksonville Beach on what would come to be memorialized as the night of Solly Zide's death. It was a black-tie affair, part of a tour sponsored by the Jacksonville Mental Health Association. Buffet dinner was $250 a plate.

I received one of the engraved invitations in the morning mail at my office on the fifth floor of the Duval County Courthouse. The envelope was addressed in blue ink, in a flowing feminine hand, to Edward M. Jaffe, Esq., Chief Assistant State Attorney for the Fourth District of Florida.

I was a public servant, a prosecutor, not a lawyer who could afford to spend $250 for dinner. I didn't own the Frida Kahlos then, and the only decent espresso I'd ever had was when I was backpacking through Italy the summer before law school at the University of Florida.

But the invitation included a handwritten note from Connie Zide, a note that read: "Please come with Mrs. Jaffe. You will be our honored guests."

When I arrived home that evening I showed the note to my wife. I told her that I'd called Connie Zide's secretary and accepted.

"Why did you do that?" Toba said. "You could have called me first. Why did you assume I'd want to go?"

FINAL ARGUMENT

We were in the kitchen, where I was opening a bottle of Gallo
Hearty Burgundy. Toba, slim and black-haired, her long neck grace-
fully curved like that of a Modigliani model, stood at the butcher-
block table, chopping onions to go with calf's liver. She was wearing
a hand-printed batik sundress that looked to me as if someone had
thrown fried eggs and soggy hash browns over it. In the living room,
Cathy and Alan bickered over the volume level of the television. It
has always amazed me how women manage to ignore the endless
squawks of their children.

"Since when did you have anything against a party?" I asked.

Toba glanced up, trying to look at me, but the sting of the onions
blurred her vision.

"Ted, are you attracted to Connie Zide?"

Radar. Women are born with it. I forced what I hoped would
come out as a smile of amused, warmhearted indulgence.

"Connie's an attractive woman," I replied with extreme care. "But
no, I'm not attracted to her. Not the way you mean. I admire her.
Solly Zide's supposed to be a hard man to live with."

At the time I was thirty-six years old. Connie Zide was forty-seven.
Connie and I had been involved in a court case after she had been
mugged by a Cuban thief, and later we had served together on the
boards of two North Florida Jewish charities. I wasn't lying to my
wife; I wasn't attracted to Connie any more than I would be to a
scorpion that had stung me after I'd walked blindly into the bathroom on a dark, damp night.

But I was prevaricating; Connie and I, until recently, had had an
affair. As a result, I'd learned things about myself that even now,
closing in on the age of fifty, I still find difficult to accept. We are
what we are, said Theseus back in the Golden Age. But I wonder
now if that's as true as it sounds.

My child bride, as I liked to call her—she was five years younger
than I—seemed to bow to my denial. "Ted, you hate these big fancy
parties."

"I usually do. But they're going to play a Mozart horn concerto.
That's hard for me to resist."

"The last concert we went to? In summer? You fell asleep in the
middle of Wagner."

I remembered that debacle, which included a few snores and
nearly falling off my chair. "I'd been in trial all week, I was tired,
and Wagner's not my cup of tea. Besides, this is business tonight."

She raised an eyebrow. "Business? What's that mean?"

But then, at last, she had to yell into the living room for the children to stop scrapping and reduce the volume.

"Come with me to the party," I said. "I have a surprise for you."

On the fateful night, I strolled about the grounds of the Zide estate with my wife. Our hosts lived in a fourteen-thousand-square-foot pink palace fronting the Atlantic. The two-story entrance foyer was dominated by a curving Ferrara marble staircase, which soared from the middle of formal drawing and dining rooms crammed with Louis XIV furniture. Hanging on the red Chinese silk walls were a matched pair of blue Chagalls, a Dufy oil of the paddock at Longchamps, a series of Picasso bullfight sketches, and some god-awful paintings of French court scenes by Forcella. The bathrooms were purple onyx, with the requisite heavy gold fixtures. Parrots sat in cages in each corner of the rooms, squawking a cacophonous tropical medley.

This outrageous structure was set behind ornate iron gates on a lawn roughly the size of the field at the Gator Bowl, where Toba and I went every November to see our alma mater's University of Florida Gators battle the University of Georgia Bulldogs. The Zides also had two clay tennis courts and two Jacuzzis, one outdoors and one in the master bedroom suite. The six-car garage housed a Ferrari Mondial, a pearl-gray Mercedes 500SL convertible, a Stutz Blackhawk, and a chocolate-colored Cadillac stretch limo. The entire junglebound estate was edged by massed flower beds under crape myrtles and palm trees.

"Have you ever been here?" Toba asked me.

"No," I lied. We were approaching the buffet tables. "Let's pig out."

Besides the usual cold meats and local shellfish, smoked Nova had been flown down from Zabar's in New York. The champagne was Moët & Chandon. I could hear the rumble of the ocean surf and smell the fragrance of mimosa. Palm fronds clicked in the darkness. Toba's black hair shone in the spotlights that illuminated the pool area. I'm a lucky man, I thought, and life is good. And with a little more luck and some patience, soon it will be even better.

Connie Zide, surrounded by a group of men, passed by and thanked Toba and me for coming. At a party, Connie's attraction worked collectively. She seemed to hum silently, like a nuclear-powered reactor. No matter where she moved on the grounds of the estate, the center of the party shifted with her. When she excused herself to go to the powder room, people relaxed and felt more at ease. Other women seemed to become more attractive; men's laughs became more natural. Tonight she was wearing a necklace of pearls and emeralds and a diamond ring with a center pearl so large it gleamed like a small, iridescent ice cream cone. I knew that the jewels were fake.

Until just two months ago this woman had held me in thrall. On the edge of this very lawn, in the cloaking darkness of a September evening, we had copulated like dogs in heat until I fell away from her with sore knees and weak loins and the fear that I had lost my mind. I was her prisoner then, but now I was free. At least, paroled.

Toba squeezed my arm. "Are you having fun?"

"Because I'm with you." I meant it; no one in my life has ever seemed as comfortable to be with as my wife.

"So what's the secret, Ted? Why are we here?"

I smiled as if I were about to tell my kids a particularly thrilling bedtime story.

"Some of Solly Zide's pals in Sarasota want me in their law firm. They need a litigating partner. Therefore, in the sense that I didn't say no to the party invitation, I'm kissing Solly Zide's ass. Is this the beginning of the end of my integrity?"

"Sarasota? Tell me more!"

In our view, Sarasota—halfway down the opposite coast of Florida, on the Gulf of Mexico—was where people tended to migrate in order to live the good life. No serious crime, no pollution, no hassle, and not much hustle. And usually no jobs. We were northern Floridians. Toba was from Daytona Beach; we had met at Gainesville when I was in my second year of law school. Neither of our families came from the old Sephardic stock that had emigrated south from the Carolinas during the early nineteenth century, but neither were they arrivistes in red golf pants or ash-blond coiffures and harlequin sunglasses with sparkle frames. They were business folk. They settled and worked and bred.

I slipped an arm around Toba's waist. "Did you think you'd always be a prosecutor's wife? That you'd never travel on the Concorde?" When the puzzled look didn't quite fade from her eyes, I said, "Something happened on the beach last Sunday."

I had been jogging, I told her, wearing a T-shirt that advertised in gold letters the Duval County State Attorneys Athletic Association. I

25

played shortstop for the prosecutorial nine in the Merchants Softball League. "Good field no hit" had always been my label, but this year in the annual game against the defense attorneys I had singled in the winning run with the bases loaded, and the *Times-Union* had run my photograph with the caption: Ted Jaffe Comes Through. I wasn't an athlete, so no accolade could be sweeter; I'd framed it and hung it on the wall next to my law diploma.

But that Sunday on the sand, two skinny black teenagers passed by and glanced at the logo on my sweaty chest. One boy said, "Fuck you, man."

I kept on jogging.

Who had I convicted? A brother? His father? The boy himself? Unknown faces tend to blend into other faces, and when they were of another hue they blended much more easily. I knew that a black sixteen-year-old could hate a honkie assistant state attorney as much as he could hate a white cop. He could hate both because both possessed the power and the potential to harm him, and probably would.

Toba listened to the story, then shook her head wisely. "That wouldn't make you turn tail. You get rid of scum, Ted. You feel good about it."

Bugs grated against the immense screen covering the pool. The scent of jasmine drifted through the air, and several people passed by, laughing. I drank my second glass of champagne.

"I guess I'm just a little bit tired of putting people in jail," I said. "Even scum."

"You want to keep them *out* of jail?"

Once I had, yes. In the early sixties I'd been a history major at FSU in Tallahassee, where the last Confederate victory of the Civil War had taken place. I led protest marches for civil rights. One night in my final year of law school I was helping the other editors on the *Law Review* finish off a case of iced Chihuahua beer. My friend Kenny Buckram, another Jacksonville boy, threw out a question to the gang.

"What's your deepest ambition?"

Those were wonderful years: questions had simple answers. "To argue a case successfully before the Supreme Court," I said. "And to save an innocent man's life. If possible, at one and the same time."

Most of our little group wound up in civil law, where the money was. A few, like Kenny, joined the public defender's office, but he had a private income from a doting grandmother. And I, for the sake of courtroom experience, joined a clinic program offered by the state attorney's office. I took four misdemeanor cases to trial before six-person juries in Gainesville, winning all four. I loved winning. It was a kind of aphrodisiac.

Shortly afterward, Beldon Ruth, chief assistant state attorney in the Fourth Circuit, invited me up to Jacksonville for lunch. Beldon was in his late thirties at the time. Immaculately dressed in a navy blazer, with yellow polka-dot tie and elephant-hide boots, he was "not fat," as he explained when I knew him better, "just a little short for my weight." A black man in power: unusual enough in the late seventies, even rarer then, in the sixties. He had been a police sergeant down in Dade, then completed a law degree at Florida Atlantic. A few years later some good ole boy who went up against him on a capital murder case in Jacksonville said, "That nigger could pick your pocket with his tongue."

Beldon Ruth and I ate conch fritters and catfish at The Jury Room, a private club in the Blackstone Building, across the street from the courthouse. I explained to him that I had always pictured myself as a defense attorney.

"You want to help people who are guilty?"

"Why was I under the impression," I fired back, "that under American law they're considered innocent until proved otherwise?"

"You can consider them whatever you fucking well like," he said, slathering hot jalapeño sauce on his catfish, "but if we indict them, you can bet your ass they're guilty. In my bailiwick, a prosecutor doesn't go to trial unless he has the facts—but a defense attorney goes in there because he has to eat. And before he eats, he has to cozy up to the slimy bugs who rape our sisters and sell smack to our twelve-year-old kids. A prosecutor gets to put those people where they can't do any more harm. And that dog'll hunt."

We were southerners and spoke the same language. This was not a visiting lecturer in jurisprudence but a man in the trenches. Suddenly I wanted to be there with him, under fire. I shook Beldon Ruth's hard hand, and I took the job he offered me. When I passed the bar exam I married Toba, and we moved into an apartment on Neptune Beach, forty minutes from the courthouse in downtown Jacksonville.

Five years later, in a panic to ensure his getting the black vote in the next election, the governor over in Tallahassee called Beldon and asked him if he wanted to be state attorney for Duval County and the Fourth District: that was Jacksonville. The current incumbent had been elected to the state senate.

Beldon replied—so the legend went—"Governor, would a two-ton hog make a lot of bacon?"

He considered me his brightest young prosecutor and appointed me to take his place as chief assistant. And that's who I was on the night my wife and I strolled the moonlit lawn at the Zides' party and I told her I had a better offer from a Sarasota firm.

"This firm," I said, "represents a string of Solly Zide's luxury condos over on the Gulf. The litigating partner accepted a judgeship. They need an experienced trial lawyer. Someone really good."

I wasn't modest about my skills; when I went to trial I had a ninety-eight-percent conviction rate. My peers had named me Florida Prosecutor of the Year in 1970 and for two years in a row after that kept me as president of the statewide association.

"Sarasota's lovely," Toba said. "But it ain't cheap, my lad."

"The firm's offered me a draw of eighty-five grand a year against fifteen percent of the profit."

Toba's eyes widened, just as mine had; that was more than double my current salary. But my wife wasn't an impetuous woman. "You think it would be good for the kids?"

Alan was eight, a dreamy boy who had trouble paying attention in class. Cathy was ten, a straight-A student. Sometimes it seemed that there weren't enough books in the Jacksonville library system or local bookstores to satisfy Cathy's lust to read.

Toba plucked a fresh glass of champagne from a silver tray. She answered her own question. "Well, maybe. God knows there's no decent safe high school here in Jacksonville. Not even out at the Beach. You know just what I mean."

"Too black is what you mean," I said.

"I hate to say things like that. Or even think them. But yes, that's what I mean. Black means more violence. More drugs."

"It would definitely be whiter and safer in Sarasota."

We heard the musicians warming up beneath the peppermint-striped tent: first the French horn, then the deep moan of the bassoon, like the wail of a stricken mythical beast.

"Ted, what do *you* want to do?"

I hadn't lost all my youthful idealism; I still wanted to be involved, to be proud of what I did. But beyond that, I wanted wines smoother to the palate than Gallo. I wanted a little sailboat of my own, and a car for my wife that didn't break down every other season. I wanted my kids to go to a decent college without my having to pinch pennies and give up the trip to the Soviet Union and the East African safari that Toba and I had talked about for years.

However mundane all that seemed, I was tired of making small sacrifices. I wanted to be comfortable—maybe quite a bit more than comfortable.

When I told all that to Toba, she smiled. Her dark eyes were luminous from the wine, and perhaps also because prospects of more gracious living had opened to her.

"It's no crime, darling. You say it as if you're ashamed of it. That's what everyone wants."

"I used to think I wasn't like everyone else," I admitted. "That seems to have turned out to be an illusion."

"I love you, Ted," she said.

I fingered her thick black hair. "So let's think about it, although not for too long. They need an answer by Christmas." Out of the corner of my eye I saw Connie Zide dancing on the grass to the beat of a steel drum. I thought of her naked, of how her heels beat a wild tattoo on that September night when she'd come underneath me on this immaculate lawn, right there by the swimming pool. I dropped my hand to my wife's hip and said, "Let's go into the bushes."

Toba's eyes picked up an even deeper sparkle. She flushed a little. "What's got into you?"

Oh, Toba, if only you knew.

If she knew, if she ever found out, would she be able to handle it? Please God, let me never know the answer to that question.

"It's your tits, Toba," I said seriously. "I love the way they slide around under silk. They bounce like little kittens. Come on."

"You're serious?"

"Who'll miss us?" And there was a spot I knew, not twenty yards away in a grove of banana trees, where no one could see us.

Her flush deepened. "If they knew downtown what you were really like, Ted, they might not let you practice law. Not even in Sarasota."

Toba and I excused ourselves from the party a little after ten o'clock.

Much of what happened I learned later. I was trained at asking questions and listening for significant details. I snoop. I have a good memory when it suits me.

JSO, the Jacksonville Sheriff's Office, determined that the last guests left the Zide estate by eleven-twenty. The caterers and other staff finished cleaning up around one o'clock in the morning. All the cigarette butts, giant shrimp heads, dirty napkins, and broken champagne glasses were swept up, bagged, pitched into a truck, driven off to the dump.

And then a silence settled over the Atlantic coast, a silence that was barely touched by the distant rumble of the surf. White tendrils of lightning crackled on the horizon. An occasional night bird flew by, croaking its melancholy song of alarm.

Some days later, on December 10, 1978, in Room 208 of Baptist Medical Center, Connie Zide made the following tape-recorded statement to Detectives Floyd J. Nickerson and Carmen M. Tanagra of the Homicide Division of JSO:

> ... We went to bed as soon as the caterers left, because that musicale, our party, had been tiring. But I couldn't sleep, and Solomon, my husband, is—was—a real night owl. He'd read in bed sometimes half the night, so around one-thirty in the morning I got up to make him a cup of camomile tea. And he followed me downstairs to the kitchen. We wound up playing backgammon—that was in the yellow drawing room. Then Neil, our son, came home from a party and sat down with us. It was probably 2:00 A.M., perhaps a little later. Right after that we all heard a sound from the patio, as if an urn had tipped over and crashed. Our electronic security is state-of-the-art. There's an armed night watchman at the gate—Terence is not young anymore, but he's a former Orlando police officer—and Paco, the Doberman, poor thing, was supposed to be down at the beach cabanas. So none of us was particularly alarmed by this crash. We didn't think of burglars at the time. It was late, we were tired. My husband just said, "I'll go look." He got up from the backgammon table and went off to do just that. I followed him, sort of trailed behind at a distance, not really concentrating, talking over my shoulder to Neil. Then I heard shots. Three, four, five in a row, I couldn't tell—I still don't remember. I went nuts, ran outside. Solomon was lying there on the terrace with blood all around him. Two men were standing there on the grass. One had a gun—a young black man, looking very frightened. I recognized him as one of our employees, al-

though at the time I couldn't put a name to the face. I was in no state to think. And then the other man, who I believe was closer to me, yelled something and raised his hand and slashed at me with something. I imagine it was a knife, but I never saw it. I must have fallen down . . . and I hardly remember anything else until I woke up here in the hospital. I assume I went into shock. . . .

Solomon Zide had been shot twice in the chest with a .38-caliber revolver. A third bullet had been found lodged in the Swedish oak paneling on the far side of the room. Connie Zide had been slashed twice, once in the upper arm and once in the face. Neither weapon was ever found; they were presumed to have been thrown into the Atlantic Ocean or the Intracoastal Waterway. Minutes later young Neil Zide, unhurt but close to hysteria, called the Jacksonville Beach police and then a man named Victor Gambrel, the head of security for Zide Industries. When Gambrel and the law and the paramedics all came storming up the driveway and into the house, Neil had recovered and was able to describe the murderer of his father. "Young, black, wearing sneakers, jeans, and I seem to remember a dark T-shirt. There were two of them. I didn't get a decent look at the other one who cut my mother. They were obviously clumsy, they didn't expect anyone to be awake at that hour. . . . My father surprised them, and they panicked. No, I don't know how they got onto the property. They ran off that way." He pointed in the direction of the beach.

By the time the JSO Homicide team arrived on the scene, the entire estate was locked in the hard yellow glare of its own floodlights. Detective Tanagra found the dead Doberman—poisoned by a piece of meat. She also found imprints of two pairs of sneakers in the wet sand near the beach cabanas. From the spacing and the gouges in the dunes, it looked to her as if two men had been running. One of them wore size fourteen or fifteen shoes.

"Let's cruise around," Floyd Nickerson said to her. "Pair of bayou coons, where can they go? Feet like that you can't hide."

The team of detectives drove off in their unmarked Plymouth and left the tech squad to do its work. Tanagra, at the wheel, headed south on A1A, then veered off to Marsh Landing before taking Roscoe Boulevard along the Intracoastal, while Nickerson broadcast an APB throughout the county. The detectives stopped at various bars and icehouses, then angled west and then north on Southern

Boulevard. Over the mossy bayous and highways hovered a jungle darkness. They stopped at bars with pickup trucks out in front, talked to bartenders and waitresses. Black men drinking beer and rye whiskey peered at them with stoic dread. Nickerson, in his late thirties, was burly, mustached, his pockmarked white skin shiny with sweat; he was made instantly as a cop. Carmen Tanagra was thin, flat-chested, good-looking, often taken for a junkie.

The detectives turned east on Atlantic Boulevard, back toward the beaches and in the direction of the naval air station. They passed gas stations and car dealerships and pizza joints, empty lots overgrown with weeds, supermarkets, a Discount Auto Parts, intermittent Lil' Champ food stores. A big sign on an abandoned warehouse said GO GATORS. At nearly 5:00 A.M. the air was cool but still humid.

Nickerson had a nose for finding people. "Turn in there. . . ." He pointed across the highway to a Lil' Champ, with its plastic statue of a kid standing with one gloved fist raised.

Tanagra slowed the Plymouth. "You need something?"

"Smokes."

They both smoked red Marlboros. "I've got an extra pack," she said.

With a blunt finger, Nickerson pointed again. "Just turn in, Carmen."

A blue, salt-pitted '68 Ford pickup, which had been smacked in the rear and had a caved-in panel behind the passenger's side door, stood isolated in one of the parking slots. A Pink Panther hung from the rearview mirror. The front bumper was broken. A small puddle of leaking oil glistened in the blurry glow of a streetlamp.

"Nigger truck," Floyd Nickerson said.

Two young men came out of the Lil' Champ, carrying a carton of milk, a six-pack of Miller High Life, and several bags of potato chips. One of them, William Smith, was lean and tall. He wore a gray sweatshirt and sported an Afro. The other youth, Darryl Morgan, wore faded jeans and a black Nike T-shirt. He was huge, probably six feet six, could have been a basketball player from U. of North Florida, except that as he ducked his skullcap of black crinkly hair to move through the door, he moved awkwardly, not the way an athlete would move. Nickerson glanced down at Darryl Morgan's sneakers. Feet like boats.

By the time the detectives stepped forth to be seen, William Smith had climbed behind the wheel of the pickup and slammed the door behind him. Darryl Morgan, the big-footed one, moved more slowly.

"*Poh*-lice! Hold it right there!" Nickerson flipped his gold shield, which said JACKSONVILLE SHERIFF'S OFFICE. He made sure the crackling fluorescent light above the Lil' Champ shone on it. "Let's see some ID, boys."

No one moved. Moths struck and sizzled on the fluorescent tubes.

"He over twenty-one," Morgan said, indicating Smith in the truck. Smith had carried the beer. "I jus' along for the ride."

Nickerson said, "If I wanted to hear from an asshole, I'd have farted."

Smith turned the ignition key, starting the engine so that the pickup rattled violently.

Nickerson tugged at the Saturday Night Special in his waistband.

Tanagra yelled at Smith, "Hold it, hold it right there, hold it!" She reached for her own pistol. "You hear me? Right there!"

Morgan backed his huge frame against the building. His eyes were wide as eggs.

Nickerson dropped to one knee and fired what he would later describe in the official police report as "two warning shots when the suspect Smith attempted to escape." One of the shots struck a nut on the front left wheel of the pickup, flinging sparks into the night like angry fireflies. The other passed through the old metal of the driver's door and into William Smith's left thigh. Smith yelped in pain and fell forward. His left foot lifted off the clutch; the weight of his right leg was thrown onto the accelerator.

The pickup hurtled backward in a screeching curve. Before Smith could shift his weight and lift himself up, the rear end of the truck smashed into a pair of concrete posts on the edge of the highway. The pickup tilted over, as if a dozen men had shoved it, and fell on its side with the sound of a thousand nails being dropped on a counter. Then it bounced and settled. The engine died. A shower of glass fell.

Silence slowly filled the damp air outside the Lil' Champ. Metal creaked for a minute or so. Until Darryl Morgan, his back still pressed flat against the building, said, "Lord Jesus . . ."

"Go take a look, Carmen," Nickerson told his partner.

After a couple of minutes, Carmen Tanagra walked back from the wreck. The way she walked, hips undulating in tight slacks, a distinct space between her upper thighs, often made men stare and calculate. She was not unaware of it.

"Boy seems to have a bullet in his leg. Definitely has a sliver of windshield in his throat, and it's sticking out the back of his neck. He's looking poorly."

"You gonna stand around talking, Carmen? Or call an ambulance?"

"No rush for that, Nick."

"What are you saying?"

"Graveyard dead, that's what I'm saying."

Nickerson's eyes rolled in his head. He wheeled on Darryl Morgan, who towered over him but looked as frightened as a rabbit dumped into a swamp teeming with alligators.

Nickerson said angrily, "You and your dead pal been out to the beach tonight, right? Looking to score a few TV sets, or maybe better. Got caught in the act and lost your cool, and you shot a man. Big fella, don't pop my cork by telling me it ain't so! Let's just hear about it. And then I'll tell you how you got the right to remain silent, and all that other shit."

3

T EN DAYS AFTER the murder of Solly Zide I accepted the job with the Sarasota law firm. Then it was called Royal, Kelly, Green & Wellmet—Green was the one leaving, and Jaffe was about to insinuate himself into the letterhead. I gave three months notice to the state attorney's office in Jacksonville and celebrated by buying a case of château-bottled Bordeaux.

But I was basically a sober fellow and still had work to do. One of the places to do it was the Lawyers Lounge on the fourth floor of the Duval County Courthouse. The voices drifting through its smoky blue air might have been those of men and women chattering in a singles bar, except that the subject was time served, deals offered, the hairpin curves of criminal law.

One morning I sat on the sofa there with a young assistant public defender, plea-bargaining a drug case. She said gravely, "Mr. Jaffe, the last offer you made was a straight eighteen. Would you consider coming down to maybe twelve years, with a substantial fine?"

I swallowed more coffee; I knew this was going to be a long day. "Eighteen is bottom line," I said, "and if your client had the brains of a pissant, she'd take it. Better yet, she'd hightail it back to Colombia."

"But I can't tell her to do that, can I?"

That was true. That would break the canons of ethics. But it would certainly simplify matters. Sometimes I wished that lawyers could do what any other practical person would do—like, in this case, tell the client to jump on the next plane and go home.

"Yes," I said, "she's got to be smart enough to figure that out for herself. What's her bond?"

"Fifteen thousand dollars."

"She's a mother, right? She's got two children down there in Medellín?"

"You're telling me . . ."

"I wouldn't think of such a thing. You do whatever melts your butter. Just remember how poor the State of Florida is, and that we could use the bail money."

Most prosecutors, if they hadn't chosen the law, might have opted for law enforcement or the church. I wasn't one of that majority.

The telephone by the coffee urn rang, and one of the hovering defense attorneys snatched it up. "Your lord and master," he said, waving the receiver in my direction.

A moment later the gruff voice of Beldon Ruth said in my ear, "Get your ass upstairs, Ted, if you're not too busy and you're still working for me."

I took the stairs two at a time to the fifth floor and soon sat squeezed between two potted purple azaleas on the window ledge of the state attorney's office, the only space available for any visitor to sit down. Beldon's legal files for current cases were spread on the floor in semicircles in front of his desk. They were also piled on the sofa and on three chairs.

"What a fucking mess," I said. "How are you going to survive when I'm gone?"

"I'll do just fine. It's you I'm worried about." Beldon rocked back and forth in his creaky swivel chair. "I know Sarasota—I took a vacation there once with Laurette. Lost my watch in the sand and didn't give a rat's ass. Screwed a lot, drank a lot of Tennessee sour mash, walked into a lot of art galleries, watched a buncha beautiful sunsets. I was sure glad to get home and go to work again. But come to think of it, I guess that was the good life."

"I'm betting that it still is," I explained.

Beldon laughed, the deep rumble of a man twice his size.

"What's Toba going to do while you pace the wall-to-wall carpet of your office, wondering whether to trade your Honda for a Porsche or a Mercedes?"

How well he had come to know me. I wondered if he liked what he now saw.

"Real estate. She may be the one winds up driving the Porsche. You going to hang out here for the rest of your life, Beldon?"

He sighed theatrically. "Bare work and poor pay sort of suits me."

"I won't be doing just civil law," I said, feeling a little defensive. "There'll be criminal cases."

"Hell, yes! You're gonna argue for leniency when rich folks' kids get drunk at the wheel or buy dope from a lady cop. You're gonna rack up thousands of hours of community-service sentences. But meanwhile you still work for the State of Florida. So listen up for a bit."

He picked up the bulkiest of the brown accordion folders piled on his desk.

"The Zide case," he said.

I had assigned it to Dale Settels, an eager young prosecutor who had moved last year from Boston to Jacksonville.

"A slam-dunk for the state," I told Beldon.

"It's for sure a slam-dunk for the newspapers and the TV," he grumbled. "Could go national, and sure as hell it'll go southern. Two black perps, and one gets shot by a trigger-happy JSO Homicide asshole while the kid's trying to escape."

"Or so the asshole says," I pointed out.

"Got the ACLU poking their nose into that, and more power to 'em. So we're left with one live black defendant in a big murder trial, and wouldn't you know it, he's come up with a black lawyer."

I hadn't heard about that. "Who is it?"

"Guy named Gary Oliver."

"I don't know him."

"But you see where I'm heading? Constance Zide knows you, likes you, seems to trust you, and she's asked me if you'll prosecute."

I made no comment. This was quicksand.

"An old dog for a hard road," Beldon said. "You're not old, and you're on your way out the door to greener pastures. But you're the man for the job. Will you do it, Ted?"

My affair with Connie Zide was defunct—Beldon didn't know about it; no one did—but it was still something for me to consider. Beyond that, however, was an even more worrisome factor. Seven years earlier, in *Furman v. Georgia,* the Supreme Court had declared the death penalty unconstitutional. Florida's state legislature in Tallahassee was the first to fashion new law to get around that edict. Now in 1979, first-degree murder carried with it the possibility of electrocution, a spectacle that seemed to grip Floridians almost as much as that of a man jerking at the end of the hangman's noose had once excited the English. Schoolchildren in our state built model electric chairs. The governor had already earned the nickname "Barbecue Bob."

This case, for many reasons, was not for me.

"Tell me about Gary Oliver," I said.

"Used to be a good private investigator. Then he got uppity and went to law school, like some other dickheads we know. But he's got a problem the others don't have. Down in St. Augustine last winter he was so shitfaced he was pulled over for drunk driving, and he hands the cop his fishing license. Guy's favorite drink is the next one."

"Why didn't Darryl Morgan go to the public defender?"

"He did, and Kenny assigned a white woman lawyer. Morgan didn't trust her—he fired her. She didn't protest too much: I heard she didn't like him or the case. So his mother managed to come up with whatever it took to hire Gary Oliver. Actually, I heard that Oliver's doing it for just his expenses."

Not that it mattered, Beldon explained. Forty-eight hours after his *Miranda* rights had been read to him, Darryl Morgan confessed the murder to Sergeant Floyd Nickerson of Homicide. A few nights later he repeated the confession in front of his cellmate at the Duval County Jail. And Connie Zide identified him positively as the man who had shot her husband during the attempted burglary. Neil Zide confirmed the ID at a police lineup.

"This Morgan kid's six foot six," Beldon said. "A fucking giant. Hard to mistake him for anyone else."

"So the jury will convict."

"You can bet the family jewels on it. But not on part two."

In Florida a murder trial was divided in two parts. In the first part the jury heard evidence, then voted as to guilt or innocence. If the verdict was Guilty, in part two of the proceedings the same jury voted on a recommendation for sentencing. The final decision was up to the judge.

"Let me tell you what I'm feeling," I said. "Until '72 you did all the death penalty cases. That suited me fine. I've never done one, and this doesn't strike me as the time to start."

"So you'd want someone defending Morgan who'll give you a decent battle when it comes to sentencing."

"If I had the case, yes."

"You're asking me is Oliver capable of doing that, the answer is fuck no."

I hadn't asked him a damn thing. "Well, there's my answer too."

"It won't come to that, Ted. Take the case. Handle the media people. Cut a deal up front with Oliver."

"Why can't Settels do that?"

Beldon studied me for a few moments. "Is there some other reason you don't want to prosecute?"

"No," I said hurriedly, fiddling with the lock on my briefcase. I looked up. "If I cut a deal, you'll approve it?"

"Hey, white boy, you think I want blood? A twenty-year-old dumbass black boy's blood? We got a white cop who got trigger-happy, and some unhappy black folks out there all over the county and the state. I don't want a riot. I don't even want a trial. I want it smooth, Ted. That's your specialty. Do it as a personal favor to your old Uncle Beldon."

He had me where he wanted me, and I nodded. "For you," I said, puckering my lips.

"Bless your little cotton socks," he said. He threw me a kiss and handed me the case file.

When the grandfather clock in my office chimed the morning hour of seven, I settled behind my state-issue metal desk and read the rap sheet on Darryl Morgan, who for a month prior to the murder had been an assistant handyman on the Zide estate. (Mowing that stadium-size lawn was a day's work for a man on a Toro, and it was done twice a week.) He was the third of five illegitimate children born to Marguerite Little, who cleaned white people's homes in Jacksonville Beach. His biological father was unknown. Marguerite's common-law husband, A.J. Morgan, was a groundskeeper at the Palmetto Country Club and a part-time Baptist preacher, who had been heard to cry, "I'm here to do God's work, whatever the hell it is."

Marguerite's other living children were Dwight, a heroin addict who had left home at seventeen and was doing time in Illinois for armed robbery; and Gull, twenty-two, illiterate, churchgoing, narcoleptic, the mother of four children by various fathers. After two abortions, she had been sterilized by a local midwife. Gull made a living as a prostitute, charging ten dollars, singing Christian hymns, and sometimes falling asleep while she worked. The family lived in a four-room wooden shack on the edge of a rat-infested palm grove west of San Pablo Road, half a dozen miles from the beach. No cooling Atlantic breezes reached that grove.

Since his fourteenth birthday Darryl Morgan hadn't known two straight years of freedom. Banished to reform school for breaking school windows and hoisting a tape deck from a parked car, he had then done time on a penal farm for jackrolling drunks and in Clay County Jail for grabbing money from a Burger King cash register. Finally he had been sentenced to a branch of FSP for burglarizing an auto parts warehouse. He was eighteen then. He did nineteen months on that seven-year bit, then was released, because in the crowded Florida prisons a man usually served less than a fifth of his sentence.

Gary Oliver, his knight in the lists, arrived at my office at 8:00 A.M.

I poured coffee from the Silex into two chipped mugs. We both took it black without sugar, a coincidence that seemed to please Oliver, for he beamed and made comment. Lifting a pack of Winston Lights from the pocket of his suit, he offered one to me. I shook my head.

"You a nonsmoker, Mr. Jaffe?"

"No, sir, I'm an addict who quit." I didn't mention that I still puffed at the occasional Havana smuggled in by friends flying back from London or Mexico City.

Oliver clucked his tongue. "That tells me you're a man of character."

"At times, yes."

There it was, the raw truth. I was proud of myself. I could have accepted Oliver's compliment without comment and probably gotten away with it.

My portly visitor got right to the point; he said to me, "Mr. Jaffe, I'm from Georgia. Why are you people in Florida so in love with killing black folks?"

He may have been my adversary, but he deserved a straightforward answer.

I told him that all over the country people were fed up with the way the prisons let men loose before they'd served their full term of punishment. These men went back into the community, took drugs, and did the crimes all over again. And most of these men were black. Down here in Florida, retired white folks were fleeing not just the wind-chill factor but the specter of drug-crazed primitive Afro-American men invading their old neighborhoods. They wanted safety in the sun. Get rid of the scum . . . especially the black scum.

Kill them.

Oliver seemed shocked that I would lay things out so bluntly. He would have been happier, I thought, as a country lawyer in some small Georgia town.

"You believe in the death penalty, Mr. Jaffe?" This was not a challenge; he was more probing than Beldon had implied.

"What I believe," I said, "is beside the point. I believe in upholding my oath as a state attorney, and that requires me to apply the appropriate law. However"—I eased up—"I have some leeway. If you convince your client to plead out to first-degree murder, the State of Florida will accept a life sentence."

"With a mandatory twenty-five years?"

"That's the law. You know that."

But maybe that wasn't true. I was constantly dismayed at how many things lawyers *didn't* know, how ill-prepared they arrived for trial. What did you call the man or woman who graduated last in the class at medical school? *Doctor.* The same held true for lawyers.

Oliver's large moist eyes narrowed. "I'll put it to him," he promised.

The following week, on a warm February morning, he returned to my office. Settling into a chair, he wiped his forehead with a damp handkerchief.

"This Morgan boy's crazy as an outhouse rat. Wants to take it to a jury. Claims he's innocent."

"I'm sure he does. But you've seen the evidence."

"Evidence don't mean a damn when you're young and full of piss and vinegar."

"You know a jury will find him guilty, Mr. Oliver. There are two eyewitnesses and two separate confessions. He's got a prior criminal record that includes violence. Morgan's black and the murdered man was white. That alone could kill him. I'm giving him a good deal. I'm giving him air to breathe."

Oliver sighed. "He says black folks will see he didn't do it."

"No," I said sharply. "Black or white won't matter. And you can't tell a Baptist juror that your client reads a chapter of the Bible every day. When she sees what Morgan and Smith did to Mrs. Zide's face, she'll get mean. Your responsibility, sir, in a case like this, where the evidence is strong, is to keep your client alive."

Oliver said, "I don't think this particular client has both oars in the water."

I shifted position, swiveling to look at the river. I wished I were out there sailing—it was difficult to kill anyone at the helm of a sailboat.

Turning back, I said, "Tell him this. If he goes to trial and he's found guilty, I'll do my best to put him in a coffin. He panicked that night at the Zides'—I can grasp that. But he had a weapon in his hand. He was prepared to use it, and he used it. A jury could reach up and bite off his big black dick. Tell him that'll hurt."

Oliver looked glum. "You think that boy's quiet and repentant," he said. "I'm here to tell you he's got a mouth on hinges. He'd argue with a signpost, he doesn't know 'Sic 'em' from 'Come here.' He says to me, 'Fuck you, and fuck this Ted Jaffe. Whup his Jew-boy ass.' "

Oliver wasn't bargaining; he was turning me down. No smooth road.

Still I didn't quite believe it was going to happen. I waited a week. It had to be that Darryl Morgan's nerve would break first, and he would cop out and take the offer of life.

I called Gary Oliver at his run-down office over on Poinciana Boulevard.

"Has he changed his mind yet?"

"No, he wants a trial."

"I don't believe this."

"Believe it, sir."

That was how I was trapped into going to trial in a capital murder case—my last case as a prosecutor in Jacksonville. I wondered if Beldon had known all along that it was going to happen, but it took me twelve years before I gathered up enough anger to ask.

4

"**R**UBY," I YELLED, flying by her desk on the way out. "I'm going to the beach."

"Are you serious?"

But she knew I wasn't. In Sarasota, at the time when Jerry Lee Elroy called me from the jail, I was working on four cases. All seemed headed for trial unless the parties could agree to settle out of court.

In one, a Longboat Key real estate developer was suing a contractor for major construction errors and failure to deliver on time. In another, a pro football player with the Tampa Bay team had become involved in a dispute with a local transvestite hooker—"Man, she was wearing a bikini, she had tits, and down in the crotch you couldn't see any bulge at all!"—and he had cut her up so badly she required forty-five stitches. In the third case, after a local savings and loan had been taken over by the government, its former CEO was being sued in a class action for fifty million dollars. The last case involved alleged price-fixing by Manatee County milk distributors.

I drove across the causeway for lunch at the Colony Beach & Tennis Club with Harvey Royal, senior partner of our firm, and our client, the condo developer who was suing the contractor. A few yards from the Gulf, while a fresh sea breeze rustled the palm fronds, we discussed trial strategy and a list of witnesses to subpoena. The food was gourmet, the air unpolluted. I lived five minutes away. This was definitely the good life, recession or not.

When the client left, Harvey and I spent another half hour over coffee, continuing to develop a theory of defense in the S & L case. We discussed nonperforming commercial loans, *quid pro quo* transactions, FDIC pleadings, the appearance of growth at the expense of long-term health.

Harvey called for the check. "Any new business coming in?"

"Two-bit stuff."

"We can't afford two-bit stuff these days, Ted."

"Keeps me off the streets," I said.

Harvey offered a watery smile.

I drove back across the causeway that spanned the calm blue waters of Sarasota Bay, thinking about Jerry Lee Elroy.

A state's witness had lied. Common enough. We lawyers lived in a jungle of lies. I couldn't recall any case that had gone to trial in which some surprise revelation hadn't popped because of a damning fact that a client had overlooked, or conveniently misremembered, or lied about. But this was different. Elroy, my witness, had lied because he'd made a deal with a cop, Floyd Nickerson.

I finally remembered the name. . . .

Darryl Morgan had confessed to Nickerson, who had shored up his position by suborning false testimony from a jailhouse snitch. If that had come to light during the proceedings, Nickerson would have been booted out of the sheriff's office and Elroy would have been charged with a felony. There would have been a retrial.

Dumb, because the case was good enough already. In fact, airtight. So why had Nickerson done that?

I had no satisfactory answer.

For the last dozen years I had banished from my conscious mind the murder of Solomon Zide and the memory of Darryl Morgan. My unconscious mind was a different story. I had had nightmares. Those nightmares were of a man's head bursting into flames. But they never visited me more than twice a year, and I had learned to live with them.

At three o'clock I appeared once again at the Sarasota County Jail. With Jerry Lee Elroy, I stood before the judge who had drawn bond duty. Elroy handed me a certified check drawn on a Miami bank, and I passed it along to the bondsman.

By 4:00 P.M. my new client was a free man. While I waited by the wire cage, he collected his red nylon windbreaker, gold wedding ring, asthma inhaler, money, and Miami Dolphins key ring. He wore a baseball cap that said DAMN FLORIDA SEAGULLS and had fake bird droppings all over the top.

"Lookit here." Elroy waved a bulging wallet made of alligator hide. "They never give it back to you in the same currency. I had three hunnerd-dollar bills and three twennies—now I got enough fives and ones you can stuff a turkey. Suppose some guy with AIDS had all this shoved up his asshole? You mind waiting while I try and get my hunnerds back?"

"Yes. Let's get the fuck out of here," I said. I grabbed his arm, more roughly than I'd intended. But he got the point. That was a language he understood.

In my office, seated in a Florentine green leather chair and looking out at the bay through the tinted plate glass, Elroy was more subdued. He was impressed by the opulence. (And so he should be; it had cost more to furnish that office than most men make in a year.) It promised staying power and clout, which were usually more desirable than justice. Except that now a fly had managed to sneak into the office, buzzing not around Elroy, who stank, but around me.

I leaned forward across the expanse of polished desk and said, "What you told me before about what happened up in Jacksonville. I can chew it, Elroy, but I can't swallow it. You follow?"

The damned fly landed on my nose. I brushed it away.

"Hey, it was a long time ago," Elroy said. "Maybe nine, ten years."

"Nearly twelve. And the first thing I want to know is, back then, did you think I *knew*?"

Elroy just shrugged.

The fly was back, droning around my left ear. This was not adding to my dignity. "Listen to me carefully," I said. "I would never have let you testify in the Zide case if I'd known you were lying."

Elroy said, "Oh, sure. Well, I mean, how'm I supposed to know who knew what? I only knew what the cop and the other lawyer told me." He was watching the fly. "I'm talking about that state chick who was out to get me on the battery charge."

"She and Floyd Nickerson came to you and made the proposition?"

"Who? Oh, yeah, right, the cop. I told you, he talked to me on the roof and asked me to do him this favor. Then later the state chick says, 'Okay, we're waiving the bail bond, we'll cut you loose on your own . . .' What's it called?"

"Your own recognizance."

"Right. On my own . . . on that. 'All you gotta do is show up in this other court, repeat what you told this detective. If not, your nuts'll wind up in a sling.' "

"You ever talk to Morgan about the shooting?"

"The fuck is Morgan?"

I kept my tone even. "Darryl Morgan was the man in your cell, the one you swore confessed in your presence that he'd murdered Solomon Zide."

Elroy smiled shrewdly. "Yeah, he talked to me. Four guys in a cell, hard not to talk to the next guy. And these other two, they was real swamp rats from over in Columbia County. Morgan was a tree nigger, know what I'm saying? He goes, 'I's in here for a bad reason, 'cause I don't kill no one and they says I do. I's in deep shit.' And I go, 'Hey, man, tell me about it.' So he did—like he thought I really meant *tell* me about it. So he does it. He *told* me."

"What exactly did he tell you?"

"Like how he and his dumb-assed pal tried to rob this fancy house, and they make a real mess of it. Someone comes running after them, so they run away. I go, 'Hey, dude, you're up for first-degree murder, that story ain't worth a milk bucket under a bull. You gotta turn it into: they try to shoot you, you shoot back—like it's self-defense, see?' He goes, 'I never had no gun. That don't be true.' "

Elroy stopped, rose from the leather chair, took a manila folder from a pile, and swatted the fly against the lemon-smelling teak surface of my desk. With one blackened thumbnail he flicked it to the carpet. He smiled thinly, then sat down again. "Counselor, I ain't learning nothing when I'm doing all the talking. When are we gonna discuss *my* case?"

There was no way out of it; that was my job. And it was a way to get where I had to go.

"Tell me everything that happened."

He had run a stoplight, he said, at Route 41 and Beach Avenue. He had an outstanding warrant for failure to pay traffic tickets, and when the traffic cops flashed him over he'd cut through a bank parking lot and tried to lose them on the back roads before you get to the interstate. But then he took the wrong turn down a dirt road and came up against a chain-link fence at the end of a cul-de-sac. They nailed him.

In the back seat of the car they spotted a triple-beam balance scale. Probable cause. They held him by the side of the road and radioed in for a drug dog. A cocker spaniel jumped straight to the trunk of the Cutlass and went nuts.

"They're going to want to know who you got the cocaine from," I said. "If you decide to be a stand-up guy and keep your mouth shut, you can forget about the five years I was talking about yesterday. You're looking at ten to fifteen."

"You mean if I get convicted."

"Pay attention, Elroy. If you go to trial and get convicted, the judge will classify you as a habitual offender, stick it to you on three separate counts, and run the sentences back-to-back. That could add up to half your life. I'm talking about getting it down to ten to fifteen if you make a deal."

"That's what you call a *deal*? Where are we, Red China?"

"It's the best you can get unless you snitch."

Elroy wasn't the kind of man who had to think that over for more than a few seconds. "What do I get if I snitch?"

"Five years, maybe. You might even walk away if you convince them your cooperation is sincere."

"I can be plenty sincere. But I have to tell you, Counselor, these other people they might want to know about, these are heavyweight dudes. These people are from Miami. You snitch on these people, they inch you. You know what that is?"

"Yes."

Elroy glanced around at my plush office, with its rows of classical CDs and bound *National Geographic*s. "You sure you know what that is?"

I leaned back in the jade-green leather chair and said calmly, "They cut off your fingers. And then your hands, and then your feet. And then your cock. Inch by inch. With a machete. Right?"

Elroy nodded solemnly. "It ain't just a bedtime story, amigo."

"You ever hear of the witness protection program?"

"I saw a movie about it on TV. This guy's ex-wife's boyfriend snitched and got into it, so she and him took the guy's kids to another state. Got a new name. Poor guy didn't see his kids for years, and he hadn't done nothing at all."

"Well, Elroy, you haven't got kids and an ex-wife, have you?"

He laughed bitterly. "I do, but I don't know where the fuck they are."

"Then think about it. I'll talk to whoever's handling this in the state attorney's office. I'll see what they've got on you that you haven't told me about. Meanwhile, don't leave town."

Ruby was printing out the day's letters on the LaserJet, stacking the revisions of legal briefs and collating whatever parts of the copies the big Xerox hadn't collated: getting ready to hit the singles bars on the Quay. I came out of my office at ten past five.

"Just a few things, Ruby, if you don't mind. And if you haven't got a hot date . . . "

Ruby was a divorced woman in her late thirties who answered ads placed in the local magazines. But she still blushed.

"What is it, Ted?"

"Book me on a late-afternoon flight to Jacksonville the day after tomorrow. Then get in touch with the sheriff's office up there. See if there's a Homicide detective named Floyd Nickerson still on the roster. Find out his shift and his days off. If they give you a hard time, call Kenny Buckram at the PD's office—he'll help. Then call the state attorney's office, Fourth District. There was an aggravated battery case nolle-prossed back in '79. The accused was our client, Jerry Lee Elroy. I need to know the woman ASA who prosecuted and dropped the case. See if she's still around."

Ruby looked up from her shorthand pad. "Will you need a hotel room?"

"Yes, in town, not the beach. And I'm not finished. Call FSP in Raiford. There was a man named Darryl Morgan committed to death row in April 1979." I took a deep breath. "I need to know what happened to him."

"What do you mean?" Ruby asked.

"Was he executed or not. And who handled his appeals." Even if Morgan was dead, I was obligated to set the record straight.

"Did you say '79 or '89?"

"*Seventy*-nine, Ruby."

"That's twelve years ago. Why wouldn't they have executed him?"

"Just find out," I said, and turned away.

At six o'clock I was still reviewing the file when Ruby bounced in, clutching her steno pad and a sheet of yellow legal paper.

"I booked you on two flights on Wednesday—USAir 456 at three forty-five and Delta 1088 at five. Confirm with your credit card number two hours ahead of time. You do that, you can just show up and run on board. You're in the Marina Hotel, eighty-nine dollars with a king-size bed. That's a corporate rate. Did you want a rental car the other end?"

"Yes, if I go."

"I reserved National. A compact. You get mileage on your One Pass frequent flier program." Pleased, she looked back at the steno pad.

"The prosecutor in the Elroy case was named Muriel M. Suarez. She's still there. Floyd J. Nickerson left the Jacksonville Sheriff's Office in 1980. They didn't choose to tell me where he is now, or maybe they really don't know. I put in a call to Mr. Buckram at the public defender's office, but he was in Tallahassee for the day. I left a message with his secretary for him to call you at home tonight up to eleven P.M. Was that okay?"

"Fine," I said. My heartbeat was accelerating. The worst for the last. She was torturing me because I'd made her stay in the office so late.

She read from her notes. "Darryl Arthur Morgan entered FSP 24 April 1979. Appeal to the Florida Supreme Court in June 1981— that was denied. Court of Appeals, Second District, filed on the basis of previous incompetent counsel—also denied. That's 1983. Public defender handling it all. Appeal to the Eleventh Circuit in Tampa, denied in 1985. Atlanta, Federal Court of Appeals, application denied. We're up to 1988. Application for cert with the U.S. Supreme Court—naturally, denied. The governor signed the death warrant on October 2, 1990. Scheduled for execution, assuming no relief in the trial court, on April 11 of this year, 1991. One more appeal for postconviction relief to the trial court in Jacksonville. Original trial judge no longer on the bench, case will go to another judge. Decision pending."

I said quietly, "You're telling me that Morgan is still alive."

Ruby said, "He better be, because if they find out a dead man's making all these appeals, they're going to be seriously pissed off."

5

BEFORE WORLD WAR II, my father had been an insurance sales-
man in the Bronx. He spent the war as a clerk at a naval base in
Virginia, and in 1945 his insurance company asked him to start a
branch office in Jacksonville.

Sylvia Jaffe, my mother, said, "Miami would be acceptable, Leonard. But Jacksonville? Who ever heard of it? Where in Florida is this
place?"

"An industrialized city, in the north of the state," he reported.
"On the beach. A short drive anyway."

"Did you know," he said to us on the train ride down, "that once
upon a time there were Indians in Florida, just like in the Tom Mix
movies?"

Neither my younger sister, Rhoda, nor I had known that.

"And that they had thirty movie studios! But there were so many
car chases and mob scenes that in 1920 the city fathers got fed up to
the gills and kicked them out. Can you imagine? They lost *all that*."

I asked my father if there were still Indians.

"Where?"

"Where we're going," I said impatiently. It may have been my first
cross-examination.

"Maybe," Leonard said.

The Timucuans had been wiped out by the French Huguenots,
and what was left of the Seminoles and the Mikasukis lived far to
the south in the Everglades. As a boy I never quite grasped that; I

was sure they were nearby because someone in authority had told me so, and from the age of seven onward I roamed the banks of the St. Johns River in search of any indigenous population I could find: a Jewish Tom Sawyer. Rhoda asked to go with me, but I left her at home. Girls couldn't do that sort of thing, I told her, with the wisdom of my youth and of those straitjacketed times.

In the environs of Jacksonville, whose rutted trails and bogs I explored on a single-speed Schwinn bicycle, what I found (instead of redskins) were Florida crackers who skinned possum and ate deep-fried turtle and marsh hens. I came upon old men in the cypress strands who took me fishing for sheephead and snapper and who taught me that different animals' eyes shine different ways: a coon's green, a gator's persimmon red, and a deer's eyes golden red like a coal of fire. I learned to say "a mess of" when I meant a lot, "a tad bit" when I meant a little.

In junior high, however, and at home, when I used such cracker language, eyebrows were raised. And Rhoda, eager for revenge, laughed at me. I hated her for that.

I had a secret relationship with Rhoda. When we were younger and traveled in the back seat of the family Chrysler, Rhoda often complained, "He's *touching* me." Neither of our parents saw evidence of this, but it was true. I don't believe there was anything sexual in what I did to her; I was just trying to annoy her. I was not innocent, not truly good. I knew I had to work at being good, and it often seemed like too much trouble. Rhoda would get up from the TV and say, "He's making noises at me. He's breathing funny." She didn't whine these complaints, which lent some credence to them; but no one except me understood what she meant. I was being driven by forces just a hair beyond my control.

Eventually the tormented Rhoda would go upstairs to her room and read. As a result she was better educated than I and later was offered several graduate scholarships when she left FSU cum laude as a psychology major. She moved to La Jolla, California, became a psychotherapist, and married a man in the bagel business.

Her relationship with me now was friendly but distant. She, more than anyone, suspected that I wasn't truly good. She would not have been surprised by what happened between me and Connie Zide.

I first met Connie Zide almost a year before the night of the musicale and the murder of her husband. Driving home from work one afternoon, I decided to stop at the Regency Plaza Mall to buy a tie. The dark-red foulard I had bought two years before at Dillard's was my favorite to wear in court, but I had spilled turkey gravy on it at lunch a few days earlier. The stain refused to come out.

I nosed the Honda toward an empty slot in the mall parking lot, and at that moment a tall, tawny-haired woman emerged from Dillard's, moving from cool shade into the glare of sun. She wore a tailored gray suit. She was not young. That woman, I thought, can't be as beautiful and as elegant as I believe she is—there's no one like that in Jacksonville. There may be no one like that in North Florida. Palm Beach, New York, the cover of *Vogue*, that's possible. Shadow and artifice were ganging up to trick the senses of an overworked man.

A young fellow in blue jeans and a white sleeveless T-shirt stepped from behind a Datsun. Gold chains jangled around his neck and glittered in the slant of hot light. Quickly, with peppy strides, he closed the distance between himself and the elegant woman. I hit the brake and threw the car into Park. I wanted to yell, "Watch out!" but I was too far away.

Alejandro Ortega, born in Santiago de Cuba nineteen years earlier, son of a *marielito*, expert broad-daylight jewelry thief, got rapidly to where he was headed—face-to-face with Doña Constancia—and slipped his hand through the big gold necklace dangling from her white throat. He yanked hard. As he expected, the connecting link snapped.

Connie Zide gave a tremulous cry. A bone at the back of the neck, a cervical vertebra, was bruised.

Alejandro clutched the necklace in his hand and wheeled, ready to sprint through the parking lot to his souped-up Trans Am, which faced the exit in the shade of a royal palm, driver's door open a few inches, motor idling.

Connie Zide owned a lot of jewelry. Most of it was expensive. She'd once filed a claim with her insurance company for a two-and-a-quarter-carat white diamond that had slipped out of its setting. It took more than a year to collect, and even then it wasn't payment in full. After that she had copies made of her best jewelry, and she wore the copies on shopping trips or to luncheons where there wasn't tight security. So what Alejandro Ortega snatched from her lovely white neck was fake.

She was wearing low black heels. She took one quick step, and as

Alejandro started to bolt, with her red-tipped fingers she tore one of the gold necklaces from his neck.

Later she said, "Why did I do that? Because I felt violated, Ted. People think they can do anything they want with a woman who's on her own. And most of the time they're right. But I hate that feeling. You're just a target for these little shits."

"You weren't frightened?"

"There wasn't time."

"Did you mean to yank the chain off his neck?"

"I didn't *mean* anything, for heaven's sake. It was all adrenaline."

"And weren't you frightened that he'd retaliate? They do that, Connie."

"I had a pistol in my handbag. And a license to carry it."

"You'd have used it?"

"If I had to . . . *quien sabe?*"

Alejandro's necklace was a gift from his girlfriend Luisa, who brokered a little three-card monte game down in Coral Gables, where Alejandro lived most of the time when he wasn't touring the better shopping malls of the southern United States. He got four or five quick running steps away from his mark before he realized that the feeling he'd experienced of something wrenched from his skin was genuine; it had signaled the disappearance of the 24K gold chain draped with much affection about his neck by the beloved Luisa. Inscribed too, with tender sentiments. He whirled in the air like a basketball guard about to launch the ball to the hoop. The bitch had scoffed his necklace!

He snaked toward her, lips curled in a smile of acknowledgment, the way a torero contemplates a bull who's made a thrust of his horns into the torero's territory. He extended his hand in mute, eloquent demand. At that point he became aware of a presence growing larger by the millisecond, but it was too late to do anything about it. That presence was me.

I'd decided that if this unknown beautiful woman could do what she'd done, then I, the male of the species, could get off my butt and lend a hand. I weighed one hundred and sixty-seven pounds and hit that fellow broadside, on the run, with a bent shoulder. One hundred fifty pounds of Alejandro flew backward, striking the radiator of the Datsun with such force that the wind left his lungs. He wound up on his knees, visibly amazed, huffing. I had twisted his right arm high up behind his back.

I looked up at the woman in the gray suit and said, "Would you mind, ma'am, going back into Dillard's? Ask someone to call 911. Don't take too long."

And to Alejandro I said, "Don't even think about fighting back. I'll snap your arm like a twig. Then I'll break your neck. I'm a karate black belt. *Cinturon negro, comprendes?*"

There wasn't a word of truth in any of that.

Pale but thrilled, Connie Zide said, "My hero." It didn't sound at all sarcastic.

I'm almost positive that the serious expression on my face didn't alter, but some other sea change took place in me, some upheaval of the senses in keeping with my braggadocio. Latin people have a name for it, which translates into English as the "thunderbolt." You cannot evade its effects.

After the cops arrived and wrote down Mrs. Solomon Zide's name, address, and telephone number, and bundled Ortega off to the Duval County Jail, Connie slumped against the side of her car and said, "My God, what a thing to happen! I need a drink. Can you indulge me just a bit more than you already have?"

We went to the first bar we could find on Atlantic Boulevard: a quietly lit place called Ruffino's Kitchen, which served thin-crust pizza. She ordered a double Johnnie Walker Black on the rocks with a twist.

We talked, but there was a roaring in my ears, and half the time I wasn't able to listen with the required concentration. I had known a few beautiful women before. Toba, when she was in her twenties, would have been considered beautiful, or close to it. A young assistant public defender who had been Miss Florida and had an M.A. in penology hit on me for an entire winter, and I patted her cheek and said, "You're lovely, Angie, and I'll bet it would be great fun, but I don't need the complication."

Connie Zide's blue-green eyes, set in the perfect oval of her face, were large and clear, her lips ruddy and full, her teeth even and white. Her body was richly sculpted, with a slender neck, round breasts, and long legs. All of this was topped by an affluence of silky light-brown hair that fell halfway down her back unless she piled it on top of her head, which is what she normally did in public. (Most southern women then, I'd observed, had hair that looked fried and dyed.) If you got past the dazzle you noticed that she was deep into her forties but looked ten years younger. That was because her bones were prominent and also because she'd had periodic work done on the skin and musculature by a world-class cosmetic surgeon in Atlanta. The sea-colored eyes were veiled from time to time by melancholy light, and her smile had that same underlying worry. Her raucous laugh came as a welcome surprise; sometimes it seemed to surprise even Connie Zide.

"Well, Mr. Jaffe, what happens next?"

A question wild with meaning. I held her gaze as steadily as I dared. It wasn't possible, I decided, that she was reacting to me the way I was reacting to her. Such things didn't happen—not to me.

"You have to go down to the courthouse first thing tomorrow morning," I said. "File a complaint. Make a statement. Otherwise they can't hold this guy."

"He'll get sprung?"

"You watch cop shows?"

She laughed wickedly. "Good heavens, Mr. Prosecutor, everyone knows *sprung*."

"Here's how it works, Mrs. Zide. In most states, this kid would have to be indicted by a grand jury. In Florida, to speed things up, we do it differently. One of the people in my office will be there at the jail to hear what the cops have to say. They'll file a probable cause affidavit, and the assistant state attorney will file what's called an information. Unless the kid wants to hire his own lawyer, someone from the public defender will be there to represent him. The point is, nothing will happen from then on if you don't go down to the courthouse and make a sworn statement. I'll have to do it too. I was a witness."

She sighed. I had heard that kind of sigh before.

"I know," I said. "But if we let him get away with it, he'll be at another mall in a few days. Hit on some other woman. The cops found a switchblade knife in his pocket. You don't know what he might have done to you if I hadn't been here."

She thought that over and then asked, "Who do I make the statement to?"

"The assistant state attorney who gets the case."

"Won't that be you?"

"It'll be someone who works for me. I'm chief assistant state attorney." I shrugged, meaning: that's a big deal in my world, not yours.

"Would you be able to handle this personally?"

"Why?"

"Do I have to tell you?"

She looked at me calmly. She could have said: Because I feel comfortable with you. Or even: Because you were here. But she had said, *Do I have to tell you?* What was she telling me? I felt guilty already, and nothing had happened.

"I'm a witness," I said. "I'll have to bow out at a certain time. But until such time comes, yes, of course I'll handle it."

It will be difficult to justify that, I thought. And absurd. And I'll kill anyone who tries to stop me.

"Are you married?" she asked.

My heart pounded; her bluntness frightened and captured me.

"Happily married. With two kids."

"And one more dumb question. Are you Jewish?"

"Yes."

"I knew it. Something in your voice. Old World warmth. My goodness, you're blushing. A bashful Jewish prosecutor. There aren't many, are there?"

She didn't have a southern accent, and I asked where she was from. Scranton, Pennsylvania, she told me. I asked more questions; it seemed safer than answering them. She had done a little modeling after high school, she said, then gone out to L.A to become an actress. But there were too many actresses, and some of them—this was a shock to her—could really act. In five years a few bit parts were all she managed to land. Then she got married and was brought by her husband to Jacksonville.

"What name did you use on the screen?"

"Constance Clark. My real name."

"So you're not Jewish."

"I converted."

"Why?"

"Out of respect for my husband."

I liked that answer. It gave her a weight and depth that she hadn't had. It also implied that she was involved in her husband's life, cared for him, could fend off anything alien and potentially damaging. I had never met Solomon Zide, although you could not live in Jacksonville without knowing Zide Industries. Not just the conglomerate, that statewide octopus, but Solly's local projects. ZiDevco, the real estate development subsidiary, was changing the bulkhead line of Duval County, buying up mud flats and bay bottom and then, with the approval of the county commissioners, converting them to golf courses, yacht harbors, and home sites. FROM THE LOW 80S TO THE 200S, as the ZiDevco billboards proclaimed. Progress, Florida style—full speed ahead, and damn the ecologists.

"May I call you Edward?"

"Ted will do it."

"I know you're a prosecutor and a happily married man, which on both counts I find interesting, but what else?"

"What do you want to know?"

An intense, clear light seemed to pour through her eyes. Much later, looking at some wallpaper samples in a department store, I identified their color as Copenhagen Blue. The color illuminated my dreams for a long time.

She said calmly, "If I said 'everything,' would you feel I was rushing things?"

I felt a sensation in my spine and fingertips: that spiraling high again. But I couldn't help wondering: why me? She's rich, beautiful, intelligent, and she's courageous to boot. And what am I?

I believed then that I was a man of value, but other than in the courtroom, I had never seen myself as a star. A good lover, good thinker, good father: all that. But not great, and I did not aspire to greatness. That was too narrow and rocky a path. I aspired to harmony, to ease of conscience, to well-being for myself and those under my wing.

Now I saw myself capable of losing all that. A great chasm, what I would soon think of as the Grand Canyon of my life—that wide, that colorful, that glorious—had appeared directly in my path. And I was stumbling toward it.

I didn't answer Connie Zide's question, just moved my hand toward hers; she clasped it, squeezing it as hard as I reckoned she could. Her fingers were thin and cool. Her eyes were knowing.

Nothing more happened that evening. I backed off. I said good night to her and reminded her to call me at the office. "You have to file that complaint." I gave her my business card.

The next afternoon, at the courthouse, she wore a beige suit, a dark-blue silk blouse, matching high heels, pearls, and a sapphire ring. In the daytime, I soon realized, she always wore gray or neutral-colored suits, but the austerity only heightened her sensuality. Was there something so primitive about her that it had to be cloaked in straight lines and muted colors? I wondered about that. And I still do.

I gave her a little tour of the prosecutorial warrens, introducing her to some of the peons. Then I took her statement and had it filed. My office, on the fifth floor, faced the river, a parking lot, a construction crane, and the Prudential Building. I had always been satisfied with it until Connie Zide visited—then it seemed shabby. There was an organizational chart on the wall next to my diplomas and the Great Seal of the State of Florida; on the desk was a mug that said BOSS, some leather-framed photos of Toba and my kids on the beach, and a brass pendulum clock. There was nothing original about the decor; I felt she must view me as utterly prosaic.

When Connie had called, she'd said, "After we go through the business end of it, can we roll double or nothing? I mean"—chortling a little—"will you buy me another drink?"

"If you come here at four-thirty, Mrs. Zide, I'm sure I can manage that." I was in conference then with two assistant state attorneys.

We went to the Marriott. At a table under a palm tree on the terrace, we had that conversation where she told me it had been "all adrenaline." We chatted for an hour, and then I smiled in what I hoped was a gracious manner and said, "I'm afraid I have to go." I realized that I had made a mistake. She was as lovely and dazzling as before, but she seemed nervous, as if she didn't quite know how to extricate herself from what I may have perceived as a commitment. I felt like a fool.

Out in the hotel parking lot she led me to her pearl-gray Mercedes convertible. When she brushed up against me, I grew a little giddy. I stared at her face in the shadowy light, wanting to say goodbye with at least a trace of style.

She sprang the locks of the car with a crashing sound like the great brass gong being struck in an old J. Arthur Rank movie. With firm and lunatic intent, I strode around to the passenger's door, slid inside, and got all mixed up by the aroma of foreign leather and perfume. (Opium, she told me later; I didn't doubt it.)

"Connie . . ."

"Ted . . ."

"Look, I know this is crazy . . ."

"No, it's not crazy at all."

She reached out for me, and I kissed her. About ten seconds into

the kiss, Connie Zide began to moan. I had never known a woman
—or, when I was younger, a girl—who moaned that way when she
was merely kissed. I crushed her against me, bit at her lip, seized her
arms. There was a recklessness in all this that was beyond thrilling:
her breasts seemed to swell, her face grew hot, and my own body
throbbed with a sense of power that I hadn't felt in years. Connie
groaned urgently, then quivered . . . then suddenly relaxed.

We disengaged, breathing unevenly. "Jesus," she said.

"What is it?"

"You don't know what happened?"

I had thought so, but dismissed it as male fantasy.

"If you think I do this often, or even now and then," Connie said,
"you're wrong. This is major madness."

"I've *never* done it."

"I didn't think so."

"And I don't know what to do now."

"I do," she said.

I told Toba I had to go to Savannah to take depositions and meet
with government informers in an interstate drug case. I would drive
up on Sunday and spend the night, get an early start at the Effingham
County Courthouse on Monday morning. It might take a couple of
days.

Toba said, "I love Savannah. I could ask your mom to baby-sit."

"Probably have to fly up to Chattanooga too, and that wouldn't
be fun at all. Let's do it another time."

That was the worst part. I felt morally shriveled for a day or two
and considered backing out.

But didn't.

I will get this out of my system. I will feel sufficient shame never
to do it again.

Some of Connie's decorator friends had a cottage on Cumberland
Island, across the Georgia state line south of St. Simons Island and
Brunswick. On Sunday afternoon I put my car in an underground
garage close to the courthouse. Connie picked me up and we drove
along the coast in the gray Mercedes. I was behind the wheel; she
had handed me the keys in a calfskin wallet.

"What did you tell your husband?"

"That I needed a few days of R and R on my own."

"That was enough to say?"

"We've been married for twenty-two years."

She seemed to think that was sufficient answer. And I didn't press. There were certain things I didn't need to know.

I felt like a bumpkin, a cracker. I was thirty-six then. I asked myself, Did I really think that for the rest of my life I'd be with only Toba? Have no other women?

I had simply never thought about it.

When the ferry from the hamlet of St. Marys reached Cumberland Island, the sun was resting on the sawgrass marshes like a drop of blood on a leaf. A fitful rain had died away. The night insects gathered in a humming cloud. At the cottage, Connie drew me inside and shut the screen door quickly. It was a log cabin with a stone fireplace and colorful Miró prints in niches. She moved me toward the piney bedroom, where a many-colored patchwork quilt covered a king-size bed. She lit scented candles on the bedside tables.

She didn't seem the type for log cabins and patchwork quilts. This was no earth mother. I held her for a moment at arms' length, studying the expressions that flickered in her eyes, not letting her come closer.

"I don't think I'm cut out for infidelity," I said.

"How do you know? You haven't ever been unfaithful." She laughed good-humoredly; she wasn't angry at all. "What you can't handle is the *prospect* of infidelity. You get over that hump, honey, it'll be a different ball game."

"Honey" was what a whore would call you. But it aroused me. She slipped out of her clothes, and the smell of her, as well as the sight of her nipples jutting from her white breasts, turned me into a rutting primitive. I took her from behind. I rammed at her that first time with no foreplay and without finesse. The finesse could come later.

Connie kept screaming with pleasure.

We were on an island, the house had its own little inlet. Only the night birds and the marsh mosquitoes heard.

The affair lasted seven months, until two months before Solly was murdered. Connie went with me once to Tallahassee, took me again to Cumberland Island, often to local motels in the late afternoon, and once to her house, when Solly flew to New York. Weekends were difficult, but I did manage a few. A friend down in St. Augustine loaned Connie a guesthouse. Once Connie came to the courthouse in the early evening; I locked the door to my office and fucked her on my metal desk. Indictments, sworn witness statements, and JSO crime reports were flung about like candy wrappers in a high wind.

My sex life with Toba had not been better since we were kids at FSU. I was a bull, resurgent. *I can do it all.* I'm not in love with Connie, I concluded. That would be the end of everything. But like the beautiful lady in the poem, *la belle dame sans merci* had me in thrall.

With time, certain things about *la belle dame* became clear to me.

I was not the first. I was one of a continuum. Perhaps this time was better for her than the others—how could I know?—but still I was sure it was part of a pattern. She was too skilled at her arrangements. The ease with which she borrowed the weekend cottages was the giveaway.

She was on the board of two Jewish charities, and she asked me to join. I would have to do very little; it was the prestige of my name they needed. This amused me. I agreed, with reservations and caveats; it was usually: "Connie, I can come for an hour, no more. I've got a child rape case on the docket, and at three o'clock I'm giving a lecture in my trial advocacy course."

At one of these charity luncheons I met Solly Zide. In his mid fifties, he was a medium-size man with hard little brown eyes. He wasn't particularly friendly to me or anyone else, but he displayed brief sparks of wit. Connie said of him, "He gets his major thrill from making money. He sees himself as a descendant of Mellon and Flagler. He's not quite in that league, but if you tell him that, he freaks out." She had married him, she said, not so much for money as for the security that attended it, and to put an end to her whoring, which is what it had come down to in the last year she was alone in Los Angeles. That was not a word she used, but I picked up hints.

"Solly had two daughters by a former marriage. Nasty, spoiled brats. When he met me, he wanted a son and heir. I gave him one. After that, I considered that I'd done my duty." They had a minimal sex life now; what her husband did outside their bedroom was his business, assuming that he was reasonably discreet about it. "He likes to watch two women making love to each other. Little staged seductions, stuff like that. It's about the only thing turns him on anymore. I was never interested in joining in. He tried to get Neil into that scene too, I hear from my spies. Without success."

Neil was twenty-two when I met Connie. He had graduated Duke and was living at home, working on the big ZiDevco landfill project with his father. I asked how they got along.

"Like the proverbial cat and dog. Neil's a spiritual person. He can paint, he can write, he's got a natural talent in music. He could become a world-class photographer if he wanted. He's the light of my life," she said.

What she didn't say, but what I heard elsewhere, was that Neil was gay or at least bisexual. Her silence on the subject indicated to me that she accepted it, since she was too sophisticated a woman to be ignorant of such a fact. She wanted grandchildren; but gays married, made certain arrangements, had children. How Neil's father felt about all that was another matter, and not one that Connie ever brought up. I didn't care. I really wanted nothing to do with Connie's life outside of what we did together in bed, and on government-issue desks, and on carpeted floors by various fireplaces, and by the sides of swimming pools and on the decks of borrowed boats, and once on the furry blue toilet seat of a locked bathroom at a luncheon given in honor of the famous Rabbi Shimkin, up from Miami Beach to raise funds for Israel. I was in thrall, palely loitering. But for me, although not for the knight in the poem, birds sang. I was not wholly happy and yet I felt wholly alive. My guilt did not rise to the level of my desire and the resultant pleasure. I expected some thunderbolt to strike me from heaven, or the vengeful Mother Earth to open up and swallow me, or some terrible revelation that would put my marriage and career in peril. None of that happened, then.

6

DURING LUNCH BREAK on the first day of Darryl Morgan's trial in April 1979, I strolled along the south bank of the St. Johns River with Connie Zide. I still remember how the gray surface of the water barely moved in the April heat. To the east of Jacksonville, over the Atlantic, lightning flared.

"Ted, darling, I need to ask you a favor."

I let the endearment pass without comment. The hangover of love, if indeed that's what it had been.

Until that past December and the night of the murder, Connie had been a beautiful woman. Now a scar puckered her left cheek, and dark pouches sagged under bloodshot eyes. She had gained weight. But I felt close to her; I had allegiance to memory.

"Ask, Connie. . . ."

In the middle of the day, I had my shirt sleeves rolled up, my suit jacket flung carelessly over one shoulder. She placed her fingertips on my bare arm. Little beads of sweat started where our skins touched. She still had a power.

"I know there are no guarantees in life, Ted, much less in a murder trial. But I need to know what will happen."

Her husband, however little she had cared for him, had been murdered before her eyes. I thought I knew she was thinking: what if by some bizarre mischance Darryl Morgan walked out of the courtroom a free man? The justice system was not perfect, lawyers and judges less so. In former circumstances, when I was anything but on guard, I had told her enough horror stories to have planted that idea in her mind.

We stopped by the river, which was cloaked by a violet haze. Looking into her ruined face, I said, "The jury will find Morgan guilty."

"That's not what I meant. Ted, do you ever feel pity for a murderer?"

I hesitated, and she caught her breath.

"Oh, Connie, my love." The endearment was out before I knew it. I took her arm. "So many of these kids are dealt bad cards. That Morgan boy would probably put a rattlesnake in your pocketbook, then ask you for a light. But I pity him, yes, because something had to happen to make him that way. And he and William Smith didn't come to your house that night intending to kill Solly or cut you."

Her face was slightly averted, so that the scar was less visible, and it was not easy for me to read her reaction.

"Will you argue for the death penalty?"

I hesitated. "Do you want Morgan to die?"

"No," she said, revealing her purpose and surprising me.

"And neither do I. But you have to understand, after we get a guilty verdict I'll argue for death. I have to do that." I touched her arm again, felt its heat. "But perhaps not with sufficient vigor as to win."

A marauding spring shower slanted down. Sunlight glimmered through a pillar of rain that cannoned against the windows of the courthouse. Inside the courtroom, Gary Oliver had to raise his voice to be heard.

"The defense calls Darryl Morgan!"

It was not required: every defense attorney stressed this to his client, and prior to trial every judge stressed it to the jury. The basis of our system and our laws, ladies and gentlemen: innocent until proved guilty. And so you mustn't hold it against a defendant if he chooses not to testify.

In my experience, guilty men seldom took the stand in their own defense. They were frightened of cross-examination. A good prosecutor would carve them into bite-size pieces. Morgan was a self-confessed murderer; he had no business up there unless he believed that he could con his way to freedom. Was Oliver so incompetent as to permit it?

I was angry, but there was nothing I could do.

The defendant slouched to the witness box in just a few strides. He wore a long-sleeved blue denim shirt, khaki trousers, jail-issue black shoes. A youth of twenty, Morgan dwarfed everyone in sight, including the beefy deputy sheriffs on hand to guard him in case he went berserk. His white teeth stood out against berry-brown skin, and a hard jaw jutted forth under a powerful face. Despite his mass, he seemed unripe. I didn't know it then, but a tattoo on the inside of his wrist said FUCK YOU. In bright-blue ink on one deltoid muscle, PAULINE was immortalized, and BORN TO RAISE HELL was printed crudely across one rocklike biceps. They were prison tattoos; he had spent much of his life there. Gary Oliver had said to him, "Booger, whatever you do, don't roll those sleeves up in that courtroom, you hear?"

Morgan slumped awkwardly in the wooden chair. The oval whites of his eyes were rimmed with pink. The dark irises had tigerish flecks, glinting with suspicion as they stared out at the threatening world. In the air-conditioned courtroom, he sweated.

Oliver led Morgan through self-serving testimony for over an hour. Near the end, he said, "You're not denying that you tried to rob Mr. Zide's house?"

Morgan had a resonant baritone voice. "I done that," he proclaimed.

"But you didn't shoot and kill Mr. Zide?"

"No, sir."

"Tell this jury the God's truth, and may lightning strike you dead this minute if you lie! Did either you or William Smith slash Mrs. Constance Zide in the face and then leave that poor woman there for dead?"

Morgan said, "No, sir."

No conclusive white bolt came flying through the courthouse roof. The jurors were grateful, for they were only ten to twenty feet away. Under the fluorescent lights, Morgan's cheekbones gleamed a copper color as if daubed for some tribal ceremony. Not good for him: nine of the jurors were white. White people, I had come to realize, were frightened of young black men. If I had passed Darryl Morgan on the street at night, I would have given him all the elbow room he needed.

"Darryl, did you throw away a thirty-eight-caliber pistol that night? In the ocean?"

"No, sir."

"Anywhere?"

"No, sir, I didn't throw no thirty-eight away, 'cause I don't have no thirty-eight. William was carrying a thirty-two that night. He threw *that* away in the ocean before they arrest us."

"Pass the witness!" Oliver cried, casting a smile toward the jury box, as if his client's denials were triumphant.

Rage, not triumph, flowered on Darryl Morgan's face. He glared at his lawyer, then at me, then up at Judge Eglin. I almost felt I could read his mind. It was all there, and he didn't hide it.

Don't matter what the man do, these motherfuckers gone find you guilty. The hind wheels of hard time coming down on your head. They gone kill you or make you a trained animal for the rest of your life.

Then, unaccountably as far as I was concerned—for at the time I was not privy to his thoughts except in my imagination—he smiled.

His stepfather, A.J. Morgan, had always counseled him to "Walk light. And be cool. You smile at the man, he don't know dick about what you thinking. You yassah him, he always say, 'I've got this nigger where I want him.' "

Walk light, Darryl thought, because life got no weight. Walk on tiptoe, see what happen, boy. How much you can bear.

From my chair at the counsel table I looked up at the black youth: six and a half feet tall, two hundred fifty pounds of muscle and shining skin. I wondered why he wasn't in the backcourt with Earl Monroe or being touted by the NFL as the next Mean Joe Greene. Some young men could claw their way up out of any pit. Most could not, and this was one who had not. And the law decreed that he, not his genes and most certainly not society, was responsible for his acts.

The rain eased. Sunlight arrowed down on concrete and glass, probing for a way into the cool courtroom. I stood up to cross-examine, facing Darryl Morgan for the first time.

"Mr. Morgan, you don't deny breaking into the Zide estate with William Smith at two o'clock in the morning, do you?"

"I say I done that."

"You don't deny giving poisoned meat to Paco the Doberman on the beach side of the house, do you?"

"I done that too. But I didn't know it was poison. I thought he just go to sleep. William, he lie to me."

He seemed aggrieved by that lie, if indeed it had taken place.

"You were able to get close to Paco, weren't you, because he knew you? Trusted you and liked you? Isn't that a fact?"

"A fact," Morgan agreed, his face like dark stone.

"But you deny being surprised in the act of entry by Solomon Zide?"

"I never saw no one except her," Morgan muttered. He pointed toward Connie Zide.

"And you deny that William Smith ever slashed Mrs. Zide in the face with a knife?"

"William never do that."

"And on the morning of December 6 of last year"—looking directly into the violent yellow eyes, I raised my voice a notch—"you didn't shoot Solomon Zide twice in the chest?"

"I never do that."

"And on the evening of December 9, 1978, just a few nights later, in the Duval County Jail, you didn't confess that murder to Detective Floyd Nickerson?"

"Never do that, either."

"And on or about January 3 of this year, 1979, in that same Duval County Jail, you didn't say in front of one of your cellmates, Jerry Lee Elroy"—I glanced at my notes—" 'I'm in deep shit because I was robbing this house and shot some Jew . . . then his wife came running out and I had to shoot the bitch too.' "

"Never said that. Ain't so."

This young giant had gall; I had to give him credit.

"Your contention is that Constance Zide—who testified under oath that you were standing over the dead body of her husband with a pistol in your hand—is lying or mistaken?"

"Didn't do it. Don't know why she say what she say. She know it ain't so."

"And the eyewitness testimony of Neil Zide, the victim's son—that's also mistaken, or false?"

"Didn't do it," Morgan said.

"Your Honor, please ask the witness to be responsive."

Judge Bill Eglin looked down from the bench. "Darryl, just tell us if the eyewitness testimony of Neil Zide was mistaken or false. That's all Mr. Jaffe asked."

"Was one or the other."

"Officer Nickerson and Jerry Lee Elroy are also either lying or mistaken?"

"They ain't mistaken," Morgan said. His voice rose to a tenor. "They lying."

I let the jury savor that. The panel had been asked in voir dire if they would automatically take the word of a police officer. All those accepted as jurors had replied, in effect, "No, I would make my judgment based on his credibility." But the truth was, they would always believe a cop.

"Mr. Morgan, would you lie in order to save your life?"

I waited for an objection, but Gary Oliver chewed the end of a stubby yellow pencil.

"No lie here," Morgan growled.

"That's not what I asked you. I asked: Would you lie, if your life depended on it?"

"Can't rightly say."

I announced that I had no further questions.

"No redirect," Gary Oliver said. "And the defense rests."

But Morgan continued: "Man do a lot of things he don't think he can do, is what I'm saying. But I don't kill no one! You wrong about that, mister."

"That's enough!" Judge Eglin began to cough; he was suffering from a respiratory ailment, and his cough sounded like the bark of a dog. "Step down!"

After a brief recess, Gary Oliver rose from his chair and positioned himself a few feet from the jury box, instantly invading their precious space. They drew back an inch or two without realizing it. Oliver was unaware. He launched into his final argument.

"Look at him, folks. Just a simple colored boy from the ghetto! He might smoke some dope on Saturday night, he might steal from a man, but it's not in him to murder anyone! I think that Mr. Solomon Zide, a rich businessman, he had plenty of enemies. Plenty of people with motive enough to want him dead, and one or two of them were probably the ones who did it. Mrs. Zide says, 'It was him, it was Darryl Morgan did it.' Her son, Neil, says the same. But it's real dark that awful night, and this defendant, as you can see, is a dark-complected boy. So how can they know for sure it's him? Who knows who else came there that night? I believe this boy when he says he didn't do it. I don't believe his cellmate, that man Jerry Lee

Elroy, at all. A professional snitch, folks, is what I think he is. Scum! And the detective who says my client confessed to him . . . well, yessir, I admit that's a high one to jump over, but why should we take his word? . . ."

During this, I doodled exploding space-age rockets on the legal pad in front of me. I could have jumped to my feet and objected to Oliver's offering opinions as to which evidence should be believed and which shouldn't, and to the denigration of witnesses, but I kept silent.

When he finished, I stood. I counted to ten and then said, "If I am ever seated in that chair over there, facing the possibility of death by electrocution, I guarantee you one thing, folks: I will lie until my hair turns white and my teeth fall out on the courtroom floor."

A few jurors smiled. Most of them nodded, for they would lie too.

"Physical evidence has placed the defendant on the Zide estate at the hour of the crime. And he's admitted to being there. Mrs. Zide has identified him as the man who brutally murdered her husband. He was in her employment as an assistant groundskeeper. She's not just picking him out of a police lineup. She *knew* him. Comes Neil Zide, who witnessed the murder of his father—and he also identified the defendant here in court. Under the circumstances, that is sufficient to warrant a guilty verdict. And yet, beyond that, two men, one of them a veteran Jacksonville police detective, have stated unequivocally that the defendant confessed to the murder. Combined with the positive identification, ladies and gentlemen, that is powerful. That is conclusive *far* beyond reasonable doubt. But still Mr. Morgan says, 'I didn't do it.' "

I paused to let the next words gather some weight.

"Well, he has to say that, doesn't he?"

I sighed as if saddened by my prosecutorial duty and the defendant's plight, but that was not all acting. "The evidence is simply overwhelming. I beg you to do your duty. Find Darryl Morgan guilty."

From the corner of my eye, I saw Morgan smile at the jurors. That, I thought, was the smile of a madman.

It took the jury less than twenty minutes to return. The foreman delivered the expected verdict.

Judge Bill Eglin said, "Thank you, ladies and gentlemen. Y'all have found the defendant guilty of first-degree felony murder. Tomorrow morning, evidence and argument will be presented by both sides that will help you to recommend one of two punishments for the defendant. I'll list and explain nine statutorily defined aggravating circumstances, as well as seven mitigating circumstances, that you must weigh carefully in order to guide your decision. You'll recommend either death by electrocution or life imprisonment without the possibility of parole for twenty-five years. In our law here in Florida, there is no alternative. Your recommendation will not be binding on this court. The final decision is mine. Court is adjourned until nine A.M." He barked twice, then rapped his oak gavel.

7

ARRIVING HOME ON Longboat Key every evening, I tried to do fifty laps in the pool. Then, feeling righteous, I went straight to the wet bar in the living room to mix an Absolut martini.

Our house was brick and marble and glass, with an atrium foyer and tropical landscaping. A twenty-eight-foot sloop was tied up at the private boat dock, from where we had views of both Sarasota Bay and the Gulf of Mexico. We had moved here from a wooden A-frame on Siesta Key, a more jungly area. We had traded up, no doubt of it, to a showcase home befitting a partner in a prestigious law firm.

But that was not why we had moved.

One morning almost two years earlier, on Siesta Key, I had been squeezing orange juice and trying to read the national edition of the *New York Times,* when the telephone rang. Our son, Alan, was an eighteen-year-old high school senior—the early-morning caller was his guidance counselor, Mr. Variano. He asked Toba and me to come see him.

We dutifully and apprehensively appeared at the high school that same afternoon.

"Alan is a good-natured boy," Variano said. "Sensitive, friendly, interesting to talk to . . ."

Toba blushed as if she herself had been complimented. "We thought you'd brought us here to tell us he was in some sort of trouble."

"... when he's not stoned," Variano continued, "which isn't often."

Twice, he said, Alan had been caught smoking marijuana on school grounds. He often fell asleep in class. He cut classes regularly. "Didn't you know this?" Variano asked.

"Not really," I managed.

"He's been arrested, hasn't he?"

I nodded cautiously. "With Bobby Woolford on the beach last Fourth of July. They had a pipeful of grass they were sharing. They were let go at juvenile court with what's called a withhold. It amounts to a lecture. I'm sorry, but I can't consider that as really serious."

Variano looked at his notes. "We have reason to believe that Alan and his friends—the Becker twins, the Woolford boy, Susan Hoppy —have been heavily into dope-smoking since they were thirteen. And selling small amounts of it to the other kids for the last year or two. Are you aware of that, Mr. Jaffe?"

"Definitely not the selling. The other, not the way you put it. In a sense, perhaps, but ..." My stomach tightened into a ball of turbulence. "Mr. Variano, do you know our daughter Cathy?"

"I knew her, although she wasn't in my case load. Isn't she a freshman now at Cornell?"

What was I trying to say? *She's a terrific kid, an A student, she wants to save the planet. So don't be so damned hard on us.*

"Are you talking about hard drugs"—Toba's voice was chilly— "or just marijuana?"

"Marijuana, Mrs. Jaffe, although I'll bet my paycheck these kids have dabbled in other stuff. LSD, mushrooms, hashish, cocaine, Ecstasy, crack, speed—everything's available."

"Marijuana isn't going to kill them, is it?"

"In massive amounts, Mrs. Jaffe, yes, it might. We're talking cigar-size joints. Your son's brains are being fried."

The walls of Alan's room were covered with posters of rock stars, bodybuilders, Harley-Davidsons, and Bogart movies. Dumbbells and free weights were flung carelessly on the floor. Alan had inherited Toba's dark hair and my lean physique; he was determined to swell his biceps and pectorals to the size of a teenage Schwarzenegger's.

He cried when I talked to him that evening. He admitted that the boys smoked in the janitor's storeroom; they had stolen a key. He'd sold a few lids to friends.

"I didn't make any money on that. I was just doing these guys a favor."

"What about crack?"

"No way. That's bad karma, Dad."

"Cocaine?"

"Once or twice. Didn't do anything for me. And it costs a fortune."

"Cigar-size joints is what Mr. Variano said. Is that true?"

Alan bit his lip, but he nodded.

"Do you want to quit?"

"Yes. I know it's ruining my life."

I was pleased. These admissions had to be therapeutic.

"If you know that, Alan, and you want to quit, you can. And you will."

Briefly I remembered what Toba had said to me years before about leaving black Jacksonville in the search for a "decent, safe" school. I sighed.

In spring the school advised us that Alan would not be graduated with the rest of his class. He had failed required courses in American history and science.

That was when we decided to move to Longboat Key. Take the kid away from his dope-smoking pals, get him in a new environment for the makeup semester.

"And I want to put him in a drug program," I said. "I've done some investigating. There's a good one downtown."

Toba resisted my depiction of our son as an addict. "Ted, back in the sixties, at college, grass was a way of life. Did it fry *our* brains? We still take a few hits now and then at a party—you do, anyway. Alan's just . . . well, I don't know what he is."

"Then we'll find out," I said.

After we moved to Longboat Key in August, Alan began a twice-a-week evening program. Parents were advised to come for separate guidance sessions those same evenings. Toba dropped out—"You never learn anything new," she explained—but I drove there with Alan the evening after I met Jerry Lee Elroy at Sarasota County Jail.

Thirty adults gathered in an elementary school classroom in Newtown, a black area north of the city center. The walls were papered with children's drawings, and we sat at small wooden children's desks scarred with initials. Most of the parents were black or Hispanic.

A bowl was passed, and I slipped a check for fifty dollars under some crumpled tens and fives.

I made it. Why can't my son?

There was a fundamental parental dilemma. You loved your kid, so you got involved. A sailing trip down to the Keys, Beethoven or U2 together in the evening, a discussion of the book he was reading for his school assignment. But after a while whatever advice you gave or whatever example you set, an unwritten law declared that the kid would do virtually the opposite. Or hate you at some level for meddling.

"Don't lecture him so much," Toba told me. "You have a tendency to pontificate."

I hated that word, *pontificate*. Probably because it was accurate.

I tried to pay attention to what was going on in the hot schoolroom. A single mother was telling us about her twenty-year-old son who had come home, begging to be fed. "But I knew he'd steal whatever money he could find, make me real crazy. I say, 'Go away until you clean!' Two days later they call me from the hospital. They say, 'Elston's here, he's undernourished, he's sick, he say his mama kick him out.' I say, 'When he quit killing hisself with that rock cocaine, I come see him.' "

The group applauded her, while she wiped her eyes. But what would happen to Elston without his mother? Could I do what she did? Tough love, they called it. Coddle them, forgive them, and they assume the world will too.

That night, on the drive home to Longboat Key, I said to Alan, "How are you doing, son?"

"Fine, Dad. We sit in a big group, and everyone gets up and raps about the shitty things they did when they were on dope, and how they've been clean for ten days, or thirty days, and we all applaud. Then we hold hands and say the serenity prayer."

"Do you get up there and talk?"

"Not anymore. I'm clean."

"Do you want to leave?"

"I know what a terrible thing drugs are now. I could use the time for studying. I'm having a real tough time with physics."

FINAL ARGUMENT

We were home. Alan hit the button that opened the electronic security gate, and it whirred open.

"Let me think about it," I said. "I'll talk to your mother."

Stars glittered above Sarasota Bay. Standing in the driveway, I reached out to give Alan a hug, remembering that my own father had never done that to me. Leonard, who had died a few years earlier in St. Augustine from a heart attack, had been a handshaker, not a hugger or a kisser. Coming back from my licentious summer in Europe before law school, I'd greeted him with an embrace and a kiss on both cheeks. He had flushed, drawing back a bit to make sure our groins didn't touch.

Toba was upstairs, watching *thirtysomething*. With a snifter of Rémy Martin for company, I went out on the boat deck. Under gathering clouds the Gulf was a silvery gray, and from the other side of Longboat Key the waves splashed and receded gently.

Years ago, I thought, life had been simpler. In Jacksonville I could grab a cold piece of chicken and a Mexican beer and feel happy. Now we searched for three-star restaurants, and I wouldn't consider a Chardonnay for under twenty dollars. I used to drive my old Honda, Toba a tanklike Volvo wagon. We currently owned four cars: my Porsche, Toba's Jaguar, Alan's hand-painted, gas-guzzling '82 Pontiac, Cathy's Toyota hatchback up in Ithaca. I was kicking in for four insurance premiums and supporting the economies of four nations.

The oiled black arc of a porpoise appeared out on the water. Cathy had brought back a bumper sticker for me that said: MY DAUGHTER AND MY MONEY GO TO CORNELL, and I had laughed. But some days when I saw it on the rear of my car I felt more plundered than validated. She was already talking about graduate school. Not to become a lawyer, but to earn a degree that would allow her to get in line for a low-paying job in Washington where she would help give away part of my tax dollar to the poor in Ethiopia or Bangladesh. This fucking recession, I thought, came at the wrong time.

But when is there a right time?

I went back inside the house to the den, where I read for a while in a new le Carré novel. A clock was ticking softly in the kitchen. Gulls flew over the atrium, so close that I could hear the rushing choral beat of their wings. The pool filter stopped. A rich and gracious silence filled the night.

There was a rhythm to any life, I thought, a routine that both sustained and deadened. Countless moments became strung together in the guise of a whole, punctuated with flashes of pleasure, ache, doubt, and desire. *I want. I can't. I wish*. Those were the themes. I was forty-eight years old. It would be over all too quickly, and if I had the courage at the end, I would ask myself: What was it all about? What did you do that really mattered?

And what would I answer?

I thought of my seventy-two-year-old mother then, for I knew what she would answer. I visited her whenever I could in her Century Village condo in West Palm Beach, where she had moved after Dad's death. Set free from marriage, she had become a world traveler. She visited Israel, cruised the South Seas, flew up to New York with a friend for a fortnight of theater, and toured all the national parks in the West before arriving in La Jolla to baby-sit her California grand-children. My sister joined her once in Jerusalem for a few days of guided visits to West Bank settlements. Rhoda called me after she got back to La Jolla.

"They were a group," Rhoda said, "but I picked up on it right away—she was with this man named Sam Schatz. A retired Cadillac dealer from Cleveland."

"Did Mom admit it?"

"Teddy, I'm not a cross-examiner like you. I'm a shrink. In my world, intuition has more validity than proof. I *knew*."

My mother was fatter now, but her eyes had more radiance than I was used to seeing. She had had a tuck. She dyed her hair a light rust brown, had given up girdles, and wore pistachio-colored slacks, flowered Mexican blouses, white Italian shoes. She said "shit" and "screw," words I couldn't recall her using at home in Jacksonville, and watched A&E and *60 Minutes*.

To all my musings and soul-searchings, she once said, "Teddy, most of what happens isn't planned. Who knows what's going to be? So do your best. Be kind, enjoy, try not to worry."

I tried.

When I went up to bed at half past eleven, Toba didn't even stir. I loved her; she was my companion. But she snored. If I woke her she would be annoyed, deny it, soon snore again. In the dark I searched for the wax earplugs that I kept in the bedside table. When they were in place, I heard nothing except a faint neutral sound, as of distant surf.

FINAL ARGUMENT

The foam of perilous seas, in faery lands forlorn . . .

Once I had read Keats. Once I had dreamed of standing before the Supreme Court and arguing for a man's life.

My mother's advice was good only up to a point. In the silent darkness I thought of Jerry Lee Elroy, and then of Darryl Morgan, the man I had sent to death row. And I didn't even have to dream that recurrent horror. Now I saw it and heard it while I was still awake: the black head in the leather cap, the crash of the switch, the dimming of the lights—the burst of blue fire.

8

YOU TWIST, TURN, cast off the sheets, know you should be able to escape. And *must* escape. But you remain in the nightmare's sweaty grip.

Twelve years before, the second part of the Morgan trial in Jacksonville had gone quickly. But in memory it would always have the quality of drawn-out nightmare.

I had risen at first light that morning and gone running barefoot along the sand of Neptune Beach. Waves shattered against the dunes, and the last of the night wind chanted through the sawgrass. When I came puffing back, Toba appeared on the beach near the house, bearing a mug of fresh coffee. She shivered in the morning chill.

Sweat ran down my neck from my forehead. "Thanks, my love," I gasped, clutching the coffee.

Our street was quiet as she walked home with me.

"Sleep well, Ted?"

"Do I ever?"

I meant on the night before final argument in a murder case. Toba understood.

"Ah, but rejoice," she said. "This is the last one you'll ever have to do."

"Yes!" And I hugged her.

"Shall I come to court? I've got the time today. Would you like that?"

"Yes, come."

. . .

I rose from the counsel table. It was my duty to seek the end of the convicted murderer's life.

But Connie had said she didn't want him to die. And neither did I. How could I, in conscience, seek a man's death if I didn't hate him? And didn't see him as a threat to the survival of others?

"The State of Florida," I said calmly, "will present no new witnesses. The state rests its plea for the death penalty on the previous evidence."

With a perceptible scowl on his lips, Judge Bill Eglin looked down. He had been on the bench for three years; he was not new to this. But I had confused him.

Gary Oliver strode toward the jury again, a hearty man, arms spread as if to embrace the world.

He called Marguerite Little as his first witness. She fidgeted in the witness chair as if it might be the very chair her son was headed toward. With her wild iron-gray hair and Mother Hubbard dress, Morgan's mother had the look of a woman let out of a mental institution for the day.

"He always been a good boy."

That was the sum of her testimony, and I passed my right to cross-examine.

A.J. Morgan, the stepfather, in a black suit whose jacket seemed two sizes too small for him, took the stand. "I always told him he was gonna go too far. He never listen to me. He don't know what he about, that boy—"

"Sir!" Oliver shot forward, cutting him off. "Tell us this: in your home, was your stepson violent?"

"I don't permit that."

"Outside your home, that you know of?"

"That's what he here for, right?"

Oliver sank back toward the defense table, defeated by this friendly witness.

The time came for final argument in part two.

Rising, Gary Oliver faced the jury. "This is a young boy," he begged. "He shot this man without meaning to. He didn't go to that house to kill anyone, he went there to rob them."

From his seat at the defense table, Darryl Morgan rumbled, "I didn't shoot *no one!*"

The eyes of all the jurors swung toward him. Damn fool, I

79

thought. You've accused these people of error in the most serious judgment any of them has ever made.

The judge eschewed the use of a gavel. Calmly he tapped his ballpoint pen on the oak bench from where he dispensed justice.

Oliver stared at his client, then turned back to the jury. "Robbery's a crime, but not one you have to die for. The killing was bad, but 'twasn't meant to be. The one boy, his friend William Smith, is already shot dead by the police. One dead . . . don't you think that's enough? And you can't really blame *this* boy for what his friend did to that lady's face. Twenty years old! Be merciful! The Morgan boy will be forty-five years old when he comes up for parole, if you let him. Maybe they'll give it to him, maybe not. But he'll be a new man then. Give that new man a chance. Do the Christian thing! Give him the opportunity to repent!"

After Oliver sat, wiping his forehead with his ever-present white handkerchief, Judge Eglin waved his hand at me. The state, saddled with the burden of proof, was granted the right of the last word. A kind of coda: conclusive major chords, knells seeking doom.

Whatever I wished privately to happen, I had the obligation to set forth the opinion of the State of Florida. It had occurred to me that if I didn't offer rebuttal, some zealot such as Judge Eglin could move for my disbarment.

I stood and said: "Ladies and gentlemen, the defendant was surprised in the act of burglary by Solomon Zide, and indeed, thinking he was threatened, may have reacted quickly and irrationally. But our common sense tells us that he carried a loaded weapon he was prepared to use. We've also heard testimony that after Mr. Morgan shot Solomon Zide, Mr. Smith turned on Mrs. Zide, a defenseless woman. Smith slashed her twice, in the arm and the face. That does not strike me as merely an irrational act. It strikes me as brutal, and certainly deliberate. And I ask you: Did Mr. Morgan make any effort to stop Mr. Smith from doing what he did? Did he say, 'That's enough, William Smith! Let's go!'? You've heard Mrs. Zide testify to the contrary. The judge in his charge will tell you that our law requires that all participants in a criminal act be responsible for the actions of the other participants. Otherwise, imagine: in a bank robbery, one man would say, 'Oh, *I* didn't take any money, I was just standing there with a gun.' If William Smith were alive, he would be equally responsible with Mr. Morgan for the death of Solomon Zide. In the same way, Mr. Morgan is equally responsible for the attack on the person of Constance Zide. The brutality of this crime is an aggravating circumstance that may outweigh any mitigating circumstances such as the defendant's youth. Therefore the state moves for the application of the death penalty."

I had a seafood lunch with Toba at The Jury Room, with Connie and Neil Zide at a table on the far side of the restaurant. We went back to the courtroom and at a few minutes past 4:00 P.M. the jury announced that they had reached a decision. Filing in, they took their seats on the padded wooden chairs. The foreman rose; he was a retired electrical engineer with yellowing hair. He read from a slip of paper in his hand.

"The jury advises and recommends to the court that it impose a sentence of life imprisonment upon Darryl Morgan without possibility of parole for twenty-five years."

I met Connie Zide's eyes; she was nodding her head up and down in what I knew was relief. Toba nodded at me too, and smiled. I looked across the table at Darryl Morgan.

There was pure hatred in his gaze. I had tried to kill him, he seemed to be thinking. Tried and failed.

Judge Bill Eglin tapped the pen again. "I want to remind you," he declared—his voice penetrated and instantly stilled the light murmur that had swept through the courtroom—"that I have the right to uphold or override the jury's recommendation. This provision is a safeguard built into the law of our state, so that if a judge feels a jury has given too much weight to either aggravating or mitigating circumstances, that judge can rectify what he perceives as an error."

He leaned forward, a pockmarked man in his late forties, and turned toward the jurors. "I suspect y'all have cast your verdict on the basis of the defendant's youth, although I want you to realize that by the current laws of our nation he's considered old enough to vote. But in addition, I'm moved by Mr. Jaffe's final argument. Prosecutor for the state correctly points out that this defendant was responsible for the acts of his accomplice, now deceased. That accomplice, Smith, attacked and might have killed Mrs. Zide. Now I ask you, is the convicted man penitent? Does he apologize for the scarring of a beautiful woman? Does he show remorse for taking the life of a beloved husband and a benefactor of this community? Does he say those simple words we all want to hear: 'I'm sorry'? You heard his outbursts! *He does not!*"

The judge was grimly quiet for a few moments.

"I have to tell you, I find this a reprehensible crime. And I'm going to override the jury's recommendation of a life sentence. Darryl Morgan, I sentence you to death. I order that you be taken by the proper authorities to the Florida State Prison and there be kept in close confinement until the date your execution is set. That on such day you be put to death by electrical currents passed through your body in such amounts and frequency until you are rendered dead. And may God have mercy on your soul."

I couldn't believe what I had heard. Connie Zide, her face gone white, looked at me. There was nothing I could say, nothing I could do. Twelve years would pass before I would see her again.

I stared dully at Judge Bill Eglin, and then at the defendant, whose lips twisted in fury.

The judge tapped his pen. The two deputy sheriffs standing behind Darryl Morgan swiftly clicked handcuffs on his wrists. "All rise!" the bailiff cried.

The judge in his black robes swept from the courtroom.

9

MY COLLEGE FRIEND Kenny Buckram was a short, thick-chested man with the curly hair and friendly appearance of a teddy bear. In 1990 his third and most recent ex-wife had a bumper sticker made, which she glued to the rear of his Lincoln Town Car. It said: HONK IF YOU'VE BEEN MARRIED TO KENNY BUCKRAM.

Having taken a sabbatical now from marriage, Kenny told me that he had fewer affairs; instead, two or three times a year he flew to Rio or Bangkok, where he would hire a hotel suite for a long week-end and install a pair or even a trio of young hookers. "Simplifies my life," he explained, "and in the long run it saves me money. As well as vital bodily fluids."

Vital bodily fluids. Straight out of *Dr. Strangelove,* our favorite film back in the days when we thought we could save the world. Or even change it.

At forty-seven, Kenny Buckram was now the elected public de-fender for the Fourth Circuit of Florida. After Ruby had told me that Darryl Morgan was still alive and on death row, I asked her to put in a call to Kenny at his Jacksonville office.

"You can't stay in a hotel," Kenny said. "That's crazy, Ted. I haven't seen you in years! I've got a house out by the beach, with plenty of room. I'm between wives."

I flew to Jacksonville on Wednesday. At half past six that evening, carrying cold bottles of Pilsner Urquell, Kenny and I walked past the surf shop and Silver's Drugs and the Sun Dog, and onto Jacksonville

Beach. Seagulls screeched in the cool evening air. I finally got around to telling Kenny what I had learned from Jerry Lee Elroy in Sarasota.

"But you were a prosecutor," Kenny said. "You're not telling me you didn't know there were people out there who'd sell their souls to get out of jail. Hey, put me behind bars, I might be one of them. . . ."

We passed a sign: CITY OF ATLANTIC BEACH. *Please no picnicking, no littering, no alcoholic beverages, no glass containers, no motorized vehicles, no surfboards without tether lines, no dogs unless leashed and having Atlantic Beach City tags. All animal droppings must be disposed of. Strictly enforced. Thank you.*

"Lucky they still allow you to fucking breathe," Kenny muttered, taking a pull from the bottle of beer.

"Tell me what you know about Floyd Nickerson."

"I don't know anything. In Homicide they're whores, they'll sleep with anyone. You got some good ones, and some you have a hard time believing if they tell you, 'I had tuna on rye for lunch.' Nickerson's supposed to have got a confession out of Morgan? Okay, assume that's true. It's a big case for the detective who's on it. Years later they'll say, 'Floyd Nickerson? Oh, yeah! Dude who nailed down the Zide murder.' So he thinks: I'll hammer in an extra nail to make sure. No big deal to convince a scumbag like Elroy to lie. And it paid off, didn't it?"

"Why is it," I asked gloomily, "that I never smelled it?"

A blind young musician passed by, strumming a guitar. He was followed by a tall, good-looking blond woman in a bikini, wheeling a bicycle. Kenny and I both turned for a moment to look.

"Because," Kenny said, "you had your head up your ass in a plastic bag, trying to pretend you had a clean job. What I hear, Ted, a lot of things went on, you just said, 'No, that can't be, so I won't look.' And you marched merrily onward until it suited you to cop out for Sarasota."

"You heard *that*? Are you bullshitting me?"

"Listen, it's nothing new. Ambition is the fuel of the justice system, denial is the grease. Why should you be different?"

"You make it so personal," I said.

"So do you. You came up here looking for Nickerson's balls. All he did was what half the guys in his shoes do all the time. And you should have known. Talk about snitches, listen to this. We investigated a complaint a few years ago—you remember Bongiorno, our local organized crime boss? This Homicide detective was accused of planting a story in order to get Bongiorno on a murder one conspiracy rap. Detective goes to a professional snitch and says, 'What we heard is, So-and-so provided the murder weapon, and they made the drop over there.' And the snitch goes, 'Yeah, that's exactly what this dude admitted to me!' "

"What happened to that detective?"

"Bongiorno had political connections in Tallahassee and he put a lot of heat out. The snitch changed his mind. They needed a fall guy —come to think of it, it was a fall gal—so they suspended the detective from JSO, and eventually she got married and quit."

"Kenny, never mind that. I need to find out what happened. Who lied, and why. Do you know where Nickerson is?"

"Long gone, and the sheriff's office isn't that buddy-buddy with me these days. You'll have to go through Beldon. Are you still friends?"

"I send him a card for Christmas, he sends me one for Hanukkah. Sure we're friends. Why shouldn't we be?"

In the deepening twilight the tourists headed for their efficiency units. Somebody in the parking lot was yelling about sand in the new Hyundai and wet bathing suits on the upholstery. Kenny craned his neck in several directions, but the tall blonde in the bikini had vanished.

"With all this AIDS shit," he said, "I was thinking of giving up my trips to Rio and getting married again. That tall blonde would have been fine . . . if she was rich. I love tall women. But I love rich women too. I know this terrific rich widow down in St. Augustine. But she's only five feet tall."

"So marry her," I said, "and she can stand on her money."

Kenny threw an arm around me affectionately. "My practical friend. And how's your marriage?"

"Fine."

"I'm your oldest pal, you're supposed to confide in me."

"Do I sound like I'm lying?"

"I'm an experienced cross-examiner. You don't sound like a credible witness."

"I have a lot on my mind. All right . . . it's something I just say, but actually it *is* fine. It's not all that exciting anymore, but it's something to depend on. Does that answer your question?"

"Yeah, but it doesn't make me envy you. So what is it you have on your mind?"

"This business about Darryl Morgan. For Christ's sake, that's why I'm *here*."

"You're making too much of it. A snitch perjured himself. So what else is new?"

"But if Nickerson got Jerry Lee Elroy to lie, maybe Nickerson lied too. Did that ever occur to you? It does to me."

"But how are you gonna find out? Hunt him down and ask him? And even if he said, 'Yeah, I made it up, so fucking what?'—what would you do?"

I had no ready answer for that.

"I remember the case," Kenny said thoughtfully. "The Morgan kid admitted being there. The Zide widow and her son ID'd him. Even if Nickerson lied too—and it's a big if—it still comes out to be harmless error. Nasty, but still judicially harmless."

"If Nickerson was lying, then whether Morgan was guilty or not, the trial was not a fair trial."

"Gimme a break. What are we, back in law school?"

"You're the public defender!" I nearly shouted.

"And as the public defender, I have to be a realist. If I played 'Hearts and Flowers' on my violin all day long and worried whether every trial was fair, nothing would get done."

"Your office handled all the Morgan appeals, right?"

"Up to five years ago. Then the Florida legislature created a job called CCR—the Capital Collateral Representative. It's a political office in Tallahassee, and they take these cases at the review stage. Because it was a fucking traffic jam, all those hundreds of guys convicted and sitting there on death row."

"You mean they weren't frying them fast enough," I said.

Kenny nodded vigorously. "Probably half the work of the Florida Supreme Court was devoted to death penalty cases. Biggest waste of human legal resources known."

"Can I see your files?"

He nodded again. "We always try for ineffective assistance of counsel. We never get it. We lose, and the defendant always looks depressed and says, 'Where do we go from here?' The PD lawyer says, 'You go to prison. I go back to my office.' "

After dinner I walked alone on the beach to listen to the Atlantic crash against the shore. Tiny shining white animals washed up on the sand with each succeeding wave. Things Kenny had said nibbled at my mind . . . *trying to pretend you had a clean job.*

Was I like that? If, for example, I denied for so long that Alan was a druggie—and that was right before my eyes—wasn't it possible that I denied other things?

I tried to focus on Darryl Morgan. A man I didn't even know, somewhere far away in another darkness. In Raiford, on death row.

Why do I need to get involved in this now? What am I trying to achieve? What do I smell?

I looked down the beach and realized that if I followed its wide path far enough to the south, I would reach Connie Zide's house. I knew she still lived there. I hadn't asked, but over the years bits and pieces of information slipped through the ether and came my way. The lonely widow—become a little reclusive and, they said, a little odd. Took a young lover now and then, gave him expensive gifts, fended off the older fortune hunters, declined to remarry. Solly's estate had been divided into five equal portions: one part each to the two distant daughters, one of whom lived in Connecticut and the other in Santa Barbara; one part to Connie, one to Neil; and one part divided among a clutch of southern universities, each of which received either an endowed chair in the humanities or a varied scholarship fund. Most people were surprised at the wisdom of Solly's generosity.

Neil had stayed in the development business, also surprising most people by his efficiency and political smarts. The inherited millions he had parlayed into many more.

I walked back toward the cheerful lights of Kenny's house. See what you can find out tomorrow, I decided. A day is what you promised yourself. Perhaps—even for a day—recapture that feeling you used to have of being involved, of wanting to do something decent. Do what can be done, but don't tilt at windmills. You have responsibilities elsewhere: to your family, your firm, to other clients. A day, then go home.

At home that night Toba was watching TV upstairs in the master bedroom. There were nightly reruns of *M*A*S*H,* her favorite program. She had bathed and put on a bathrobe and old pink furry slippers that she wouldn't part with even though the quilted outer part looked raggedy enough for the Salvation Army.

She'd had a hard day and was feeling just a tad sorry for herself. Nobody was buying houses, and even if they were of a mind to do so, they made ridiculously low offers. Sellers were saying, "We'll wait until this bad period is over."

Toba had been concentrating on rentals. A tenant to whom she had rented a house on Longboat Key had called the office on the day he was scheduled to move in. "Ms. Jaffe, there are mouse droppings under the sink!" The family was moving into a motel until the mice had been exterminated. "And no poison, please! We have a toy poodle." Toba rushed to the hardware store on St. Armands Key and bought twenty Sure-Kill traps. She set the traps with Camembert cheese that she snatched from our refrigerator.

The next morning my intrepid wife carted away the little gray bodies with their bloody mouths. "God forbid the tenants should have seen," she said to me. "They're from Manhattan. They don't accept anything that crawls, except cockroaches."

It was a season of animal troubles. One midnight in December she'd been awakened by a call from a hysterical tenant in the woods of Siesta Key. The tenant was in bed, and a monstrous ten-inch-long, eight-legged hairy animal was perched on her chest. It was staring at her in an unfriendly manner.

"Mrs. Hart," Toba said cheerfully, "I think you've either been partying too much or you're having a nightmare."

Mrs. Hart called the police. When they arrived, they removed a rare, poisonous wolf spider.

At about the time that I boarded the flight to Jacksonville, Mrs. Hart, through her lawyer, informed Toba that she was suing her for negligence, malpractice, and slander.

While I was walking on the cool sands of Jacksonville Beach with Kenny Buckram, Toba cooked a meal of lamb chops and apple sauce and frozen french fries. Alan set the table with red linen napkins, took out his old Zippo and, with a flourish, lit a candle. Finishing her vodka tonic, Toba opened a bottle of cabernet sauvignon.

"Mom, the Becker kids are going sailing over the weekend down at Captiva Island. They've got an uncle who has a fifty-six-footer with standing headroom, sleeps seven or eight, must be fantastic. They invited me along. Can I go?"

"Of course you can. You're nineteen years old—you can do things like that without asking me."

"We'll probably check out the night life on Captiva, which I'm sure is nonexistent. But I don't like to be without any money, hang around like a damn parasite. I hate to ask, but—"

"Don't worry," Toba said.

"You're great, Mom."

"Just don't get too sunburned. The sun on the water is very powerful."

After dinner she heard Alan on the phone in the den, leaving a message for someone to call him back. He dropped into an easy chair to watch a video on the TV, and that was when Toba said good night and went upstairs to bathe. She could hear the sound of gunfire and screeching tires; it seemed to her that he always watched different versions of the same movie. She took the bottle of cabernet with her. After she had settled among the warm bubbles and lemon-scented oil of the bath, she drank another glass of wine. Later, in the bedroom, wrapped in her terry-cloth robe, she lay on the bed, supported by the special backrest with arms, while she watched *M*A*S*H*. From time to time she heard the little *ding* as the phone was hung up elsewhere in the house.

I miss Cathy, Toba thought. It's hard when a daughter leaves home.

In Ithaca, Cathy would be awake, studying. The question was: wait until eleven, when the rates go down, or call now?

Toba poured the last bit of the wine into her glass. She picked up the phone.

Alan's voice filled her ear.

". . . man, good and fucked! I'll get the money tomorrow for sure. It was hard tonight. She fucking drives me crazy. . . . "

Toba's cheeks heated up steadily. She couldn't put down the phone.

A young male voice on the other end of the line said, "One fanfuckingtastic blast. Fucking *wasted* is what we'll get."

"Fuckin' A!"

Far across the room, in the mirror above her dressing table, Toba could see the moronic look on her own face. Her mouth had fallen open.

Alan said, "Got 'ludes, quarter grains. . . . Bobby's holding the caps. . . . "

"Gotta hang up, dude."

Toba carefully replaced the receiver and slid out of bed, drawing the belt of her bathrobe tightly around her waist. Her knees felt like pudding. In the bathroom she washed her face in cold water in an effort to get the fire out of her skin. Barefoot, on shaky legs, she padded downstairs to the kitchen, to the wine rack on the wall next to the microwave. She removed another bottle of cabernet. With the bottle and the corkscrew, she climbed back upstairs to bed.

10

T HE NEXT DAY, in one of the public defender's dusty storage rooms on the third floor of the courthouse, I thumbed through what was left of the *Florida v. Morgan* file. A memo told me that on August 22, 1986, most of the original documents had been shipped over to CCR in Tallahassee. At the time, the assistant PD on the case had been someone named Brian Hoad.

I asked for him, and a legal intern looked up from a volume of Shepard's *Federal Citations*. "Try Courtroom Four."

I entered Courtroom Four, on the second floor, and took a seat in one of the pews. It wasn't hard to pick out Brian Hoad, a pale man wearing glasses and sitting next to the defendant, a skinny black man. A young police officer was testifying on direct examination. The prosecutor was a well-built Hispanic woman in her thirties, wearing a dark-blue suit. The judge on the bench looked bored.

The young cop admitted that having been fired at by the defendant at the scene of the robbery, he didn't want to give chase. "A man who's fired a shot will stop and shoot again, and we couldn't see him."

Hoad said, "Objection—"

"Overruled."

"Your Honor—"

"Don't argue with the court," the judge commanded.

"I haven't stated the basis—"

"Next question," the judge said, stifling a yawn.

At the recess I introduced myself and asked Hoad if we might talk in the snack bar. This was a thirty-five-year-old lawyer making barely forty thousand dollars a year; many of his clients, who filed affidavits of insolvency or hardship and thus received free legal services, would earn more than he did. He was probably in it because he enjoyed battling authority, didn't like billing clients, distrusted cops, and believed that the state should interfere as little as possible with people's lives except to redistribute the wealth.

I paid for coffee and crullers, and we sat down in two red plastic chairs. "Is that a strong case you've got up there?" I asked.

"About as strong as this coffee," Hoad said glumly.

"Then how come you're in trial?"

"I handle over three hundred felony cases a year. I try to plea-bargain all but the best. This is a hard-assed prosecutor. She wouldn't deal. I got screwed."

Not as much as your client, I thought.

"I wanted to talk to you about an old case," I said. "You handled the appeal. Darryl Morgan—first-degree murder. The trial was back in '79, so you may not remember it."

Hoad nodded a few times. "Visible case. Shot Solomon Zide."

"I was the trial prosecutor."

"Jesus." Hoad laughed. "You?"

I frowned and said, "I'm a defense attorney now, down in Sarasota." Hoad was still looking away from me and chuckling. "What the hell's so funny?" I asked.

"Well, it's not really funny. It's just surprising. When you introduced yourself in the courtroom it was just another name. But now I've got it. You're a kind of legend around here."

I remembered what Kenny Buckram had told me: *A lot of things went on, you just said, "No, that can't be, so I won't look."* I hadn't realized how much that had hurt me until now, when I found myself virtually praying that this young fellow didn't have the same opinion, even secondhand.

"Beldon Ruth asked me to prosecute Morgan," I said. "It was the last case I did before I packed it in."

"You mind if I tell you something?"

"I hope I'm not going to mind."

"I had that Morgan appeal in my caseload for a long time. I've read that trial transcript three or four times, looking for error. You did a fine job in the first stage. Hard to argue with any of it. But in the punishment part, you were lousy. You just gave up."

"I didn't want the Morgan kid to die."

"Well, that didn't help me at all. My chief point on appeal was incompetent defense counsel in the sentencing phase, and one of the judges up in Tallahassee commented, off the record, 'Mr. Hoad, just between us, it may have been the other way round.' Another one told me, 'We can see clearly why the trial judge didn't accept the jury recommendation of a life sentence. A specific argument in favor of the death penalty, detailing the aggravating circumstances as per Florida Statute 921.141, was not advanced by counsel for the state.' "

I sighed. "You had the appeal from the beginning?"

He nodded. "But I didn't get over to Tallahassee until '81. I had half an hour to persuade the seven dwarfs that Morgan shouldn't be strapped into an electric chair and jolted to death. Hopeless. Then we got turned down in the Eleventh Circuit. Didn't have anything to take to the feds in Atlanta, but I went anyway. It's a beautiful old court. Gives you a feeling that justice might be lurking. But it's an illusion." He peered at the dregs in his coffee cup. "One of the judges up there was sympathetic. He said, 'Counsel, if we rule your way, won't we also have to grant relief in a lot of other cases that present the same claim?' "

"You had an answer for that, I hope."

"I said, 'Yes, probably you would, Your Honor, and probably you should.' They kicked me out of there in under a hour. But that was already in '86. That's the name of the game. Keep your man alive."

"Did you argue against Eglin's override of the jury recommendation? That there was a rational basis for the jury sparing Morgan and that the trial judge abused his discretion?"

"Sure. It didn't work. In 1987 a man named Beauford White was executed after the jury gave a twelve-to-zero recommendation for life. And there was an override on a guy named Dobbert in 1984, where they'd voted ten to two for life."

I didn't know what to say. But he did.

"Florida, Indiana, and Alabama are the only three states that have the post-*Furman* override provision. There's been one override in Indiana, about six in Alabama, and more than ninety in Florida. This is the killer state."

I told him about Jerry Lee Elroy's 1979 deal in exchange for perjury.

"And the cop, Nickerson, he set that up?"

"If Elroy's telling the truth."

Hoad seemed excited. "Will your client testify to what he told you?"

"There'd have to be something in it for him. Elroy is not your basic altruist."

He looked at his watch. "Damn, I have to get back to court and help put the judge to sleep again."

Going up in the elevator, I said, "Why did you get so involved with this case?"

"Have you ever been to Raiford, Mr. Jaffe?"

"No."

"An execution is not something you quickly forget. You know, they're having one day after tomorrow. A local boy."

"Who are they burning?"

"Sweeting. Remember him? Killed a pair of coeds at Jacksonville University eight years ago. Chopped them up, buried them down by the river, dug one up again because he had these dreams that she might still be alive and *blaming* him. Well, he dies on Saturday. You should go and watch Eric Sweeting pay for his sins. Then you'll understand why I get involved."

The elevator stopped at the second floor. The woman prosecutor was waiting for us. She said to Hoad, "Can I talk to you for a minute?"

They talked, then Hoad returned, the prosecutor preceding him, heels clicking, moving briskly on strong legs into the courtroom. She carried her head high and didn't smile. She was a good-looking woman, I thought.

"Making any progress?" I asked.

"Suarez is backing off," Hoad said. "Looks like she'll cut a deal. Fifteen years for armed robbery and attempted murder, concurrent. That's not bad. I'm gonna tell my guy to go for it."

"That's Suarez? The woman you were talking to?" She was the assistant state attorney who had prosecuted Jerry Lee Elroy and let him go.

"Right."

"I'll hang out for a while," I said. "Maybe we can all have lunch together."

FINAL ARGUMENT

. . .

By noon the armed robbery case in Courtroom Four was history. The prosecutor, Muriel Suarez, and the public defender, Brian Hoad, shook hands, and both went off to lunch with me. I remembered the ritual. You laughed and didn't talk much about the case, but you gossiped a lot about other cases, other lawyers, judges. In the courtroom the lawyers had snarled and yelled at each other, because that was the protocol—the adversarial relationship was the basis of the system and the only way approximate justice was achieved. Justice was not the same as mathematics.

That was why no one ever wanted a truly innocent client. That was nightmare. That was something you couldn't joke about so easily.

In Worman's Deli near the federal courthouse, seated at a table in the back, Suarez munched on a pickle. She said to Hoad and me, "I heard a good one yesterday. These two lawyers—civil lawyers"— grinning, showing badly capped white teeth—"are walking along the beach, and they see this gorgeous woman in a thong. One lawyer says, 'Boy, I'd love to fuck her.' Second lawyer says, 'Yeah? Out of what?'"

In this country, it seemed to me, lawyers had taken the place of Poles as the butt of jokes. The only difference was that we may have deserved it.

We had corned beef sandwiches for lunch, and when we were finished Hoad stood and said, "Folks, I have to fly. I've got a woman over in the jail pled guilty to possession of crack cocaine. It turned out to be wax, but the state attorney won't let her rescind her plea. I have to get over there."

"Speedily, I'd imagine," I said. "I've got the check. I'll call you about the *Morgan* file."

When he had gone, Muriel Suarez said, "The name Morgan rings a bell."

I brought her up to date.

"I remember the case. Floyd Nickerson told me Elroy was a creep, but a reliable creep. Gap in his tooth, right? I remember him. And Carmen Tanagra."

The way she said that last name made me wait for something more. But there was nothing. Her eyes moved away, and she reached for her mug of Michelob.

"Carmen Tanagra was the other detective on the Zide case. She have anything to do with Elroy?" I asked.

"She was Nickerson's partner. I knew her. But it was Nickerson who came to me and proposed the deal."

"Tanagra still around?"

Muriel shook her head decisively. "Got more or less kicked out. She wasn't a really smart cop. I mean, she was a good woman, but they corrupted her."

Something clicked in my memory. "Was she by any chance involved in the Bongiorno episode? The cop who got the snitch to lie? And they found out in time?"

"Right. They nailed Carmen's ass to the wall. She didn't like it, so she quit."

"To do what?"

"We're not in touch," Muriel said, and there was still an edge in her voice, something I didn't understand.

Then she smiled and looked at me with more cheerful eyes. They were dark and Latin; they actually flashed, as in the old songs. Her parents were Cuban, she told me, and had brought her here as a baby. Once again I became aware of how attractive a woman she was.

"So, Mr. Jaffe, Mr. Civil Lawyer from Sarasota, what are you going to do about all this?"

"Morgan's still alive. Barely. They're going to execute him in April."

"You think you could get him a new trial?"

"I could try for a stay of execution. That's what I told Beldon."

"And what did my lord and master say?"

"You can't guess?"

" 'Morgan was guilty, he shot those people. Leave it be.' " She grinned. "You care if he lives or dies?"

"Yes, I damn well do," I said, with a vigor that surprised me. And so I repeated it. "I care. And I'm going to do something about it."

"You losing any sleep? That's my standard. You hit the pillow and pass out, you're okay."

"Do you always hit the pillow and pass out?"

"Not lately," Muriel said.

"What's happened lately?"

"One of my first cases as a felony prosecutor was Eric Sweeting. The name mean anything to you?"

"Brian mentioned it," I said. "They're burning him Saturday morning down at Raiford."

"Right. Unless the governor grants clemency."

"Why are you losing sleep? Sweeting was guilty."

"And the jury recommended death by a vote of nine to three." Muriel drank some more beer. "But I'm going to be there when they pull the switch. Witness it, by God."

"Why do you want to do *that*?"

"Because when I did the case eight years ago, the morning before I asked the jury to bring in a verdict of death, I looked in the mirror and said, 'Muriel, this is not a statistic you read in a book. This is a human being, with a mother and father and three sisters who love him, and you're arguing in favor of his being killed. You're not only trying to kill him, you're condemning those other people to grieve for maybe the rest of their lives. If you haven't got the guts to witness that execution and the moral fiber to face his family on the day it happens, you shouldn't argue in favor of it.' So I promised myself, if it ever happened, I'd go. Well, he's exhausted his appeals quicker than most, and now it's happening. The day after tomorrow. Only an hour away from where we sit. Unfortunately, I don't have any excuse."

I said nothing. Could I do that? No. That was one of the reasons I had quit the business of putting people in barred cells.

"If you recall," Muriel Suarez went on, "it was a particularly heinous murder. So the first time I met Sweeting, I expected a monster. I gritted my teeth, walked into the jail with the public defender to meet this beast who chopped up his teenage victims. Eric was nineteen years old, weighed about a hundred and fifteen pounds, about the size of a jockey. Red hair, freckles, braces on his teeth. A polite, dumb country boy—looked like a cross between Alfred E. Neuman and a pit bull."

"Retarded?"

"The defense tried to prove that. But it wasn't so."

"How do you account for his committing such a heinous murder?"

"I don't," Muriel said. "That was the scary part. But he did it. That was the true part. That's all I had to know and believe, and I did. Like you knew and believed Morgan did it. Why is not our province."

"It's brave of you to go down there," I said.

"I know," Muriel said.

. . .

That evening, on the porch of his house in the black neighborhood where he'd always lived, Beldon Ruth brought out a pitcher of iced tea and settled down in a rocking chair to talk to me.

"I want to tell you a story," he said. "When I was younger, I prosecuted a seventeen-year-old black kid. This kid rang a doorbell over on Blodgett, put a gun in some woman's face, and said, 'Gimme your money or I'll blow your head off.' She gave him the housekeeping money—so the kid came back a few weeks later and did it to her again. I was a brand-new assistant state attorney, and to me this kid was dangerous. Day before sentencing, the public defender in the case—your pal Kenny Buckram, fresh out of law school—gets the woman, the complainant, to sign a statement saying, 'I've just heard about how this boy's father sexually abused him and beat him with a wooden plank, and his mother was a drunk, and they wouldn't let him go to school even though he got good grades. I think what he did to me was terrible, but now I can sort of understand why he did it. And I'd like to see him get another chance.' "

Beldon poured the tea. Laurette, his wife, was inside the house, preparing dinner.

"Buckram gave this letter to Judge Fleming. You remember him? White-haired, crotchety good ole boy, rolled his own from those little sacks of Country Gentleman? Still around, although he's older'n dirt. And Fleming sat in his chambers from noon to three, we're all waiting, it's hot enough for a hen to lay a hard-boiled egg. Finally Fleming hobbles out and says to Kenny, 'If you're right about this boy and I put him in prison and he gets ruined in there, his blood is on my hands. If you're wrong, I'm gonna bring him back in my court and pound his knuckles to the floor with a sledgehammer, and he's gonna do every goddam day of the ten years I could have handed him.'

"He gave the kid probation. Some people were shocked, including me. I said, 'Judge, how can you do that? I mean, in conscience?' Fleming sizzles and said, 'Because, son, the people voted me into office, and I got the right to do it. Y'all don't have the right to question me or my conscience.' Stuck his finger right in my face like 'Fuck you, Mr. Ruth.'

"That was twenty years ago. The kid graduated from college. The judge, Kenny, and I got a wedding announcement. Fleming took him off probation after five years. The kid went into computers, moved his family up to Atlanta. If Fleming had sent him to prison he'd be out there now, perpetrating more robberies and doing more time and butt-fucking people. Or he'd be dead. Do you know that twenty-five percent of black men in this country have done time, are doing time now, or are on probation? In the case I'm talking about, the system wouldn't allow for the fact that a potentially good kid had done a violent crime. Fleming grasped it, and he was right."

Beldon sat back on his porch and sucked iced tea through a child's bent straw.

"You know what the point of that story is, Ted?"

"No, but I know if I sit here long enough on this porch, you're sure as hell going to tell me."

Beldon smiled. "In twenty-five years, that's the only time I've ever known anyone to be right when they gave someone a second chance. *All the rest were disasters.* That's a pretty piss-poor record, wouldn't you say? And that's why I still believe we're on the side of the angels. And you defense guys, you do your job, but you don't really help people. The PD's office has got the right idea. Churn 'em out, cut a deal. Hired lawyers waste time trying to show clients they're earning their fee."

"You're a disgusting old cynic."

"I'm a disgusting old realist."

"Why did you ever become a lawyer?"

"Fascination of aberrant behavior," Beldon said, and let that hang in the air while he went inside to refill the pitcher.

When he came back, I said, "Tell me about Muriel Suarez."

"Could be a division chief in a year or two, unless she goes for the bucks and becomes a partner in a fancy law firm. Like some others we know."

I hadn't come back to Jacksonville to be lectured, not even by Beldon. But my compulsion was more than theoretical. A man languished out there on death row—he wasn't an anonymous black thug, he was a human being I had once looked in the eye. In the last ten years I had helped many a businessman and entrepreneur become richer; in the process, I had become part of their club. That was one thing a lawyer did. The other thing he did, and what I had neglected to do for too long a time, was help people survive and live free with pride. A part of me, over the years, had been slowly and painfully eviscerated by my own greed, if I dared call it that. But that part wasn't dead. I could revive it if I wanted to, if I had the courage, and the stubbornness.

In time. I was here because I had new information that I was obliged to turn over to the state attorney, and I had done so. That was the first step.

I said to Beldon, "What are you going to do about it?"

"Not a goddam thing," he replied, "other than to add it to my long list of incidents that tend to prove that the human race at best is capable of anything under the sun, and at worst is deceitful, hypocritical, opportunistic, and generally no fucking good."

It wasn't exactly a complete vision. I ground my teeth, but didn't comment. "Where's Floyd Nickerson these days?"

"I somehow thought you'd ask that."

"Does that mean you know?"

"Didn't until yesterday, when you phoned. Then I dug a little. He left JSO nine years ago and went over to Gainesville. Chief of security in a big real estate and country club development. Place called Orange Meadow."

I wrote that down. "Must be on Orange Lake. We used to go down from school on weekends to water-ski. What's it all called? Orange Meadow Estates, something like that?"

"I guess so. Don't really remember."

"Is Nickerson still there?"

"Can't say. He ain't a pen pal."

"Who's the developer he works for? Do you know that?"

After just the barest hesitation, Beldon said, "ZiDevco."

11

I MADE UP my mind in the late afternoon, a couple of hours before I was due to drive to the airport. I called Muriel Suarez at her office in the courthouse.

"You want to *see* it?" she asked.

"I want to be there. Then I'll decide if I want to actually see it."

"You a death freak or something?"

But she called the superintendent at Raiford and requested that I be put on the list. Then she rang back.

"Done. They allow twelve witnesses other than the media goons. They've only got seven."

We arranged to meet at her place on Washington Street. I called home, and Alan answered on the first ring. "Bobby?"

"No, it's me. How're you doing, kid?"

"Fine, Dad."

"All well on the home front?"

"It's cool. I was just reading by the pool."

I liked hearing that. There was hope. "I've been thinking about our talk the other night. If you're ready to leave that drug program now, it's fine with me."

"I'm really ready to leave it."

"Then go for it. Where's Mom?"

"Taking a nap upstairs."

"I was supposed to come home this evening from Jacksonville, but I have to postpone. Tell her I'll be back tomorrow."

Alan said he'd write a note; he was leaving in another hour for a weekend of sailing at Captiva. I called Royal, Kelly and spoke to Ruby, who recited a list of death threats from my partners.

"I didn't hear any of that," I said.

That night Kenny Buckram had a date with his short rich widow in St. Augustine. "I probably won't be back here until morning," he said. "So you are the lord of the manor. You have plans?"

"A late date. Four A.M."

"Are you serious?"

"Yes."

"What're you going to do until then?"

"Hang out. Listen to some music. Get drunk, smoke some dope. Is that okay, Dad?"

"Your car or mine?" Muriel asked.

"Sounds like a proposition from high school days," I said. At four o'clock in the morning we stood in the cool darkness in front of her house on Washington Street. "I'm driving a rental. Let's give the wear and tear to Mr. Hertz."

Through silent streets we headed out of town on the Fuller Warren Bridge across the St. Johns on I-10. There was no traffic at that hour. Replacing it was a predawn sense of adventure.

"Twenty miles," Muriel said, "and then you bear south on 121 to Raiford."

"Can we stop for breakfast in Raiford?"

"It's a prison, there's no town. You want to eat, cut off south on 301 to Starke. Often called the Paris of Bradford County." She was silent a minute, working that over. "Probably because some good ole boys still piss on the sidewalks."

We drove through the darkness, past mobile homes and strings of darkened Baptist churches. Moonlight reflected off the mirrored silver skin of RVs and trailers that had come to rest along the road. Scrub palm grew thick in the sand hills, and night air brought the smell of wood smoke. This was not the Florida gold coast, where you tanned and partied, or the Keys, where you fished, or St. Pete with its shuffleboard courts, or Disney World, where you took the family to gawk and frolic. This was the Deep South. Black men, not too many years ago, had dangled from pine trees. People lived in clapboard houses with rusted washing machines and truck parts in the yards. After the sun rose, Florida crackers in faded overalls sprawled on wooden benches in front of general stores, drinking long-neck Buds and home brew.

Muriel and I reached the town of Starke at a quarter to five and had breakfast in a greasy spoon on Main Street. A note on the menu said, "We shur hope ya'll have a nice day." Sitting in a plastic booth, I ordered black coffee and poached eggs on toast. Muriel chewed thoughtfully on a toothpick. She was not a cheerful woman today.

After breakfast I followed the signs and turned west on the Raiford road. Some scruffy palm trees thrust themselves against a lemony dawn sky. Concertina wire stretched between electrified fences and machine gun towers.

Birds began to warble. In the growing light we noticed that a half-dozen RVs, some pickup trucks and a few station wagons were parked in front of the prison on the crabgrass. People had set up picnic tables with plastic cloths. The women were making coffee and flapjacks, the way they used to do during lynchings. The smell of maple syrup drifted through the early-morning air.

"Death penalty groupies," Muriel said. "Come from all over Florida, camp all night here. They can't get in to see anything, but the lights dim when the dude inside throws the switch. They stomp and cheer. One less bad guy to threaten the good life in the U.S. of A."

A man was selling doughnuts and T-shirts. I couldn't see the printing on the T-shirts, but I could imagine it.

In a gun tower a telephone sat in a niche. Muriel spoke into it, and a voice on a speaker told us to proceed to the first gate. Beyond it was a moat of stainless-steel barbed wire. I looked up, and in the pale light could make out the faces of men in the upper windows of a cell block, staring down. Like panthers, they had eyes that seemed to glow in the gloom.

We passed through a series of gates into an indoor reception area with peach-colored walls. The linoleum floors smelled of fresh wax. The air was chilly and musty. While we waited for our escort, I read items on the staff bulletin board. One of the guards offered a mobile home for sale: "3 BR 2 BA $3500 OBO, with 5 acres, $24,000." This was a long way from Longboat Key.

Identities were checked. Our hands were stamped with a glowing violet mark, as in a nightclub. We passed through a metal detector. We left our keys and Muriel left a Llama .32 Blackhawk that she brought forth from her handbag. She smiled a little, as if in apology. "You never know," she said.

Our escort was a clean-shaven, thin-lipped young FSP administrative assistant, who introduced himself as Fred Olsen. He wore a pale-gray suit, a pale-gray tie, and shiny black shoes.

"I'll be taking you through the procedure," he said quietly, "and if you have any questions, please don't hesitate to ask. Right now we're going to breakfast."

"Thank you, we've eaten," Muriel said.

"It's part of the procedure," Olsen explained.

He led us down a long waxed hall, through a door into a cafeteria with light-green walls. Two large flags dominated the room: the Stars and Stripes, and the red-and-white flag of Florida with the state motto, "In God We Trust." The other witnesses were there: half a dozen reporters, various state and FSP officials, the lawyer who had handled Sweeting's appeals, the father of one of Sweeting's victims, and an uncle of the other one. One representative of each victim's family was invited, and the condemned man was allowed one relative. Sweeting's mother sat with the appeal attorney. All of these people except Mrs. Sweeting were eating scrambled eggs, bacon, grits, and hash browns.

"Coffee?" Olsen asked. "There's no charge."

When Olsen left to get it, I asked Muriel if she knew the appeal attorney.

"Sure."

"What kind of a job did he do?"

"Thorough. But he didn't stand a chance."

"Do they ever?"

"Sometimes. Weird things happen."

"Like clemency?"

"That would certainly be weird. Well, if it's ever going to happen it might happen with Sweeting, because he's white."

Olsen came back with the coffee and his own plate of eggs and bacon. I noticed then that another young man in a gray suit sat at the table with the other witnesses, taking care of them in the same way that Olsen was taking care of me and Muriel.

"Would you like me to tell you the rest of the procedure?" Olsen asked. "It's what we recommend. It spares you any surprises."

I heard myself say, "All right."

"My colleague, Mr. Crocker, has already explained it to the other group. May I?"

Muriel finally nodded. There were dark smudges under her eyes today.

Olsen said, "For the last thirty days Mr. Sweeting has been in a program we call Death Watch. There are two phases. Phase One of Death Watch begins when the governor signs the death warrant. Mr. Sweeting was moved at that time to Q wing, which is a good deal closer to the place of execution—it's completely isolated from other inmates. He was permitted to read any religious books or tracts he chose, and he continued to receive any magazine or newspaper subscriptions he previously had. He was still fed three meals a day, and any dietary restrictions—that is to say, for medical reasons—were strictly observed."

"You want him in good health," I said.

Olsen nodded, glad that I understood. "He still can receive approved visits, but all contact visits terminate. That's in Phase One of Death Watch. In Phase Two, which began five days ago, Mr. Sweeting was permitted to retain only the following items." Olsen reached into the breast pocket of his jacket and consulted an index card. " 'One black-and-white TV, located outside the cell, one radio, one deck of cards, one Bible, one other book, periodical, or newspaper.' " Olsen put the card away. He waited.

Muriel and I both nodded our approval.

"During Phase Two, the condemned is under constant surveillance by a trained officer, who sits outside the cell and records in writing every fifteen minutes what the condemned is doing. Four days ago, Mr. Sweeting was asked to inventory his property and indicate its disposition, and asked to specify his funeral arrangements. Mr. Sweeting requested standard burial. He was therefore measured for a suit of clothing. Two days ago, he was allowed an interview with a media representative of his choice. He declined this interview. Yesterday, twenty-four hours before execution, our chef took Mr. Sweeting's order for his last meal. Would you like to know what he ordered?"

Muriel grunted softly, a word or two that I couldn't understand. I found that no words formed on my own lips, or even in my mind.

Olsen looked at another card. "Mr. Sweeting ordered a sirloin steak dinner, a pint of chocolate ice cream with hot fudge, a Coca-Cola, and a large-size buttered popcorn—all of which we were able to provide. This meal was served at approximately four-thirty A.M.

this morning, following the condemned's final visit with a clergyman of his choice. In this instance Mr. Sweeting met for one hour with the prison chaplain. . . . Do you have any questions thus far?"

Muriel and I shook our heads in the negative.

He was spooning up his hot fudge sundae, I calculated, when I was chewing my poached eggs in that Starke diner.

Olsen said, "The rest has to do with the execution procedure, which you'll witness shortly. Witnesses will be escorted at five forty-five A.M. to the witness room of the execution chamber in Q wing. At six A.M. an FSP administrative assistant, namely myself, three designated electricians, two FSP correctional officers, a physician, and a physician's assistant will be assembled in the death chamber. Mr. Crocker will establish telephone contact with the office of the governor, in case there should be any last-minute clemency."

"Will the governor be awake and in his office at six A.M.?" I asked.

"That's a good question," Olsen said, "and frankly I don't know the answer. Meanwhile the condemned will have his head and right calf shaved to better conduct the electrical charge. He will take a supervised shower, and he will be dressed in his new burial clothes, omitting the suit jacket and shoes. Conducting gel will be applied to his scalp and shaved leg. The prison superintendent, Mr. Tate, will read the death warrant one final time to the condemned. The condemned will be strapped into the chair. He will be permitted to make a last brief statement. A conducting sponge and cap will be placed on his head. I might mention," Olsen added, "that last night I and my colleague, Clive Crocker, who as I've said is over at the other table with those other folks, noticed that the sponge to be used this morning was, to say the least, dirty. So we went out and purchased a brand-new clean sponge to be used for this occasion. I don't think they *ever* had changed that other sponge, if you can believe such a thing."

Under the Formica table I dug my fingers into the muscles of my legs.

"Mr. Wright, the assistant superintendent of this facility, will then engage the circuit breaker. The chief electrician will activate the panel, Mr. Tate will signal the executioner to throw the switch, and the automatic cycle will begin. Once it's run its course, the physician will pronounce the condemned as dead. You will all exit the viewing chamber, to the rear."

"Who's the executioner?" Muriel asked quietly.

"An anonymous local private citizen dressed in a black hood and robe," Olsen said.

"Jesus, a volun*teer*?"

"Yes, except that he'll be paid one hundred and fifty dollars for his services."

"How many volts?" I asked.

"Two thousand four hundred."

"And it takes?"

"I beg your pardon, sir?"

"How long to kill him?"

"Oh, instantaneous. Perhaps a few seconds. You may see some movement in the condemned's body, but I assure you, consciousness ends instantly."

Fred Olsen excused himself to go to the bathroom.

I stared into Muriel's eyes. The pupils were dilated. She said, "I don't know if I can go through with this."

"Then let's skip it."

"No, I've got to do it. I took a vow on the Virgin. *Chinga la madre!* What was I thinking? This man Olsen is certifiably insane. Will you come with me? Can you do that for me?"

I shook my head. I had come this far, but it seemed far enough.

She gripped my wrist. She had thin fingers, and strong. "Please. Help me."

"All right," I said, my stubbornness melting before the heat of her plea.

A van took us in a group to Q wing. A rosy sun was inching above the pines to the east. During the ride, no one spoke. The appeal attorney nodded at Muriel Suarez; he knew who she was, even though they had never been in court together.

I whispered in Muriel's ear. "Can you see Mrs. Sweeting? Next to the appeal attorney?"

"Yes."

"She stumbled getting on the bus. She's brought her coffee along. Just poured something into it from a flask. How old a woman is she?"

"Sweeting's twenty-seven. She's probably in her fifties."

"She looks seventy, for Christ's sake."

"*Dios mío.* I hate this."

"Let's get the hell out when the van stops."

"I'll be all right. Just hang tight with me. I'll shut up, I swear I will."

Inside Q wing we were led by Clive Crocker to rows of white wooden chairs. The chairs faced a glass wall. On the other side of the glass, about fifteen feet away, stood a high-backed, solid oak chair with black straps—as large as a throne. Behind the chair an open panel contained coils and lights. Two domed light fixtures hung from the ceiling.

I shifted in my chair, pulled my suit jacket a little closer. The witness room was damp.

The condemned shuffled into the death chamber. He was manacled at his ankles, and his wrists were cuffed to a chain.

Sweeting looked like a freckled boy dressed for an adult party. He wore a red and blue striped tie that hung well below his waist, a white button-down dress shirt that was too big for him, baggy dark-blue suit trousers, black socks. He was about five feet four, thin and sinewy. His ears stood out at right angles to his head, like a mongrel dog. His knobby shaven skull glistened where it had been rubbed with gel.

His mother waved to him.

Our guide, Fred Olsen, was in the death chamber, as was a doctor in a white coat, the doctor's assistant, the prison superintendent, the assistant superintendent, three electricians, two bulky correctional officers of the Death Watch squad, and a small man dressed in a black gown and a hood with a slit for vision.

For some time I had been hearing a regular rhythmic sound, like a feebly ticking drumbeat. Now it grew louder. I looked to my left, two seats away, where Olsen's colleague, Clive Crocker, was seated. I raised my eyebrows by way of inquiry.

Crocker leaned over to whisper. "The men on death row know our schedule. They tap on the bars with plastic spoons. I think we can assume it's a form of saying goodbye."

The correctional officers unchained Sweeting. One of them said, "Sit down here, please." Through the glass, although a trifle blurred, the words were still audible.

The men helped Sweeting up into the chair. His stockinged feet dangled in the air. The men cinched the various leather straps around his waist, legs, and arms.

We heard Olsen ask him, "Would you like to say a few words now?"

"Yes, please," Sweeting said, and turned toward the visitors.

"You'd better speak up to be sure they hear you," Olsen cautioned.

Sweeting nodded. "Goodbye, all. Goodbye, Mama."

"'Bye, son," Mrs. Sweeting called. "Give my love to Jesus. Tell him to take good care of you."

"Merciful God," Muriel murmured.

I took her hand, gripped it as if we were husband and wife.

"Is that all?" Olsen asked Eric Sweeting.

"Well, I'm sorry for what happened," Sweeting said. "But I guess y'all know that. I have no hard feelings, and I want to thank everyone, what they done for me. So . . . I'm ready to begin my journey."

Muriel groaned. I clasped her other hand as well.

The superintendent read the death warrant a final time. The distant sound, the rhythmic beating of the plastic spoons against the bars, continued without pause. One of the correctional officers tilted Sweeting's head back and fastened a chin strap around his small jaw. The other correctional officer placed a black rubber hood on Sweeting's face. The new sponge was wedged inside the top of the hood. Electrodes led from the hood to the control box set in the wall. The first man parted Sweeting's right trouser leg; it had been slit up the side, almost to the knee. He fastened a second set of electrodes to Sweeting's slender and shaven milk-white calf.

He signaled to the hooded executioner. Thumbs up. The executioner pushed the button in the control box.

The automatic cycle began. Lights dimmed. Sweeting's body jerked, and he moaned softly as if in sleep.

Blue-and-yellow flames shot from Sweeting's head, firing radiantly upward and outward like the corona of the sun during a total eclipse. Sweeting screamed like a pig being slaughtered. The flames crackled, while his flesh sizzled audibly. We couldn't smell it, but we did hear it.

In the witness room with us, Clive Crocker, Fred Olsen's associate, jumped to his feet. In the death chamber, two of the electricians were tugging at the sleeves of the prison superintendent.

. . . *Perhaps a few seconds. You may see some movement in the condemned's body, but I assure you, consciousness ends instantly.*

Sweeting kept screaming. The flames continued to leap upward from his head. His toes stretched and tapped angrily on the concrete floor. The skin of his leg, as everyone could see, began to scorch and turn black. In the witness chamber, Mrs. Sweeting started to blub-ber.

The executioner released the switch.

"We seem to have a problem," Crocker said quietly to the rest of us in the witness room. "But I'm sure it will be remedied."

The electricians busily readjusted the straps and the electrodes. In a minute or so they seemed satisfied. They signaled to the execu-tioner. Thumbs up a second time. The executioner didn't see the signal. One of the electricians came over and whispered in the ear of his hood. Nodding, the executioner pushed the switch a second time.

The flames jumped forth from Sweeting's shaven skull and out on all sides through the rubber hood. A video record kept by the physi-cian's assistant later demonstrated that these flames varied between three inches and fifteen inches in length. Their color was mostly blue, although they were interfused with yellow streaks. Sweeting's piglike screams became the baying of a hurt dog. His little body twisted against the straps; at times he seemed to be dancing in place. A thick dark-brown fluid flowed out from under the rubber hood and down the front of his white shirt. Liquid, as well as bloodied white and yellow kernels of popcorn and bits of chewed, charred sirloin, landed in his lap, then spattered on the floor in a pool of undigested Coca-Cola, ice cream, and black fudge.

Through it all, the other men on death row beat with their spoons against the bars. Mrs. Sweeting buried her head in her arms and whimpered prayers to her Jesus.

The electricians shouted something again at the executioner, and again the executioner removed his finger from the button.

Sweeting shrieked, "My eyes are on fire! . . . I can't breathe! . . ."

"Stop this!" Muriel yelled. She jumped to her feet. *"In the name of God, stop it!"*

Clive Crocker rushed over. "Ms. Suarez, please don't interfere. Control yourself!"

She began to curse at him, and Crocker tried forcefully to jam her back down into her seat. I half rose from my own chair, felt power in my thighs, bunched my right hand into a fist, and drove it straight into Crocker's face.

On the third try, fourteen minutes after the first jolt of electricity had surged into his body, Sweeting was pronounced legally dead.

Olsen entered the witness room, wiping sweat from his neck. "The sentence of the State of Florida has been carried out. Please exit from the rear and proceed to the van."

In the hallway Muriel clung to my arm, shuddering. I looked in amazement at the raw-skinned knuckles of my hand, which was already beginning to swell.

Crocker's nose was broken. He passed me in the hallway. "You can't get away with that kind of behavior"—he pointed a shaky finger—"even if you're a lawyer. I'll sue you."

"Fuck you, asshole," I said.

I couldn't remember the last time I had spoken that way and struck a man in anger. Perhaps never.

The dirty sponge that had stood the test of so many executions was a natural sponge. The one that Crocker and Olsen had bought at the Circle K in Starke was made of nylon, and when two thousand four hundred volts of electricity rocketed through it, it had caught fire. Blue fire.

My nightmare.

A few days later, the official FSP report to the media included an affidavit that read in part:

"There was understandable human consternation, but there was no collapse. There was understandable human perplexity, but there was no panic. What was necessary was done. What was intended was accomplished. Under given circumstances that surfaced, the results were far less than aesthetically attractive. But with rare serene exceptions, after forty-odd years experience, it is held that most deaths are without aesthetic attractiveness, regardless of causation.

"Further affiant sayeth naught."

And it was signed by a medical director of Florida State Prison.

But long before I read that, I had moved from just being involved to a state of total commitment. I couldn't stand the thought that in some way I was responsible for Darryl Morgan's being sent to this place, where he would suffer, if not the same corrupt fate as Eric Sweeting, then a similar one. Whatever it took, I swore, I was going to save Darryl Morgan's life.

12

STILL WEARING HER nightgown under a terry-cloth bathrobe, Toba curled against silk pillows on one of the sofas in the living room. Slanting afternoon sunlight beat against the picture window facing west. A half-full bottle of chilled chablis stood on the coffee table. The phone plugs had been pulled out of the jacks.

The twenty-five-inch Sony console was turned on to CNN. Toba had been watching the news since early in the morning, she told me, but nothing of interest had happened in the world. In fact, it was practically the same news now at 4:00 P.M. as it had been at 9:00 A.M. "Isn't that ridiculous?" she said. "You would think that in six or seven hours something new would happen in the world. A new war, maybe, a revolution in some banana republic, a juicy sex scandal in D.C.—*something.* But it hasn't. I mean, I'm sure it *has,* it's pretty impossible to believe that it *hasn't,* but they're not telling us about it! Why is that?"

"I'm going to brew coffee," I said. "While I do that, you drink this glass of water. Alcohol dehydrates the brain."

"Sounds like something you read in a magazine on the plane," Toba said, chuckling.

"Matter of fact, that buzz you get from alcohol, you know what that is?"

"Brain cells being destroyed."

"How did you know that?"

"Because I was at the same dinner party you were at where that

112

pompous brain surgeon lectured us. But I figured out that there's probably a billion brain cells we never even *use,* so what's the difference?"

"I'll get the coffee. Then I'll cook some scrambled eggs and make whole wheat toast."

Toba sat up straighter and put down her glass. "Ted, you haven't asked me *why* I'm drunk."

I patted her shoulder. "I will, after I've fed you. I love you and I'm trying to be kind to you. Isn't that better than asking a lot of questions?"

She began to weep.

We sat by the edge of the pool in the early-evening light, while the sun began its meltdown into the green Gulf. A school of fish moved downshore. Pelicans circled, then plunged. Toba was drinking her third mug of decaf.

I clutched a vodka tonic. "I just can't get it through my head. You heard this telephone conversation on Thursday evening. You didn't say anything to him then, you didn't tell me, and on Friday afternoon you just let the kid go. You knew what was going to happen, and you *let* it happen! What the hell's the matter with you, Toba?"

"I couldn't handle it."

"You . . ."

I didn't view my wife as a weak woman, and this was something I had to understand. I thought back then to many years before, when a young assistant state attorney on my team in Jacksonville, assigned to a case of child battery, had come back to my office from the hospital with tears in his eyes. He said, "I want the mother and father who committed that act to be flayed alive. I can't try this case objectively. *I can't handle it.*"

I hadn't thought of him as weak, and I hadn't chastised him. A month later he went into private practice.

You can't handle it, Toba? All right, I accept that too. Mothers and good women shouldn't have to deal with such things, just as men shouldn't have to deal with kids getting tortured with lit cigarettes, and heads—their own heads or the heads of others—bursting into flame.

The gulls came back, flying so close to the dock and the pool that I could hear the beat of their wings. They hovered against the drift of evening breeze, black eyes scanning the water below.

"I could cheerfully kill him," Toba said, using an expression that she'd inherited from her mother the hotelkeeper. "If you had heard them—"

"I know how young men speak."

"He said something like, 'I couldn't squeeze the money out of her tonight because she drives me fucking crazy!' Is that fair, Ted? Is that his vision of his mother? Every other word was 'fucking.' It just wasn't *him* speaking."

"Who was it, a ventriloquist? It was him. That's the first thing we have to accept."

She let that work around in her for a while, then sighed tremulously. "So what is the way to deal with it now?"

"Maybe another drug program. Therapy, psychiatry—I don't know yet. I need to ask some questions and get some straight answers. And if he tells me again, 'Yes, Dad, I know I'm ruining my life,' I may just take off my belt, like my grandfather in the Bronx did to my father, and whip his ass."

I glanced down at the swollen knuckles of my right hand. Already today I'd hit one man in rage. And now I was threatening to do it to my own son. Where did such anger come from? Where did it usually hide? Was that how people were surprised into the act of murder?

Evening descended; the land that we could see across Sarasota Bay looked a picture blotted in with ink.

"You don't think they might have been boasting?" Toba asked. "He and the Becker boy? You know, being macho, psyching each other up, not really telling the truth . . ."

"Toba!"

She hung her head a moment. In the twilight I clasped her hand. The second time in one day that I had held a woman's hand to give comfort.

On Monday morning the partners of Royal, Kelly, Wellmet, Jaffe & Miller sat round the walnut table in the conference room for their weekly meeting. Don Kelly, our brilliant, two-hundred-ninety-pound tax expert, was negotiating a settlement for several local boatyards represented by the firm. Litigation, he explained, was possible but unlikely. Harvey Royal, the senior partner, a distinguished-looking, sword-thin, and somewhat humorless man in his sixties, was spearheading the defense of the S & L president. He told the rest of us that on Friday he and Marian Miller had met with the attorneys representing the depositors. "They're intractable at the moment. Marian feels they'll negotiate, but I fear the worst."

"And what's the worst?" I asked.

"For them, drawn-out civil litigation. Possible criminal charges. We will almost certainly have to go to Washington to meet with the resolution trust people. Ted, you and I will have to burn the midnight oil this week. Barry?"

Barry Wellmet, a plump and cheerful man who smiled his way to one settlement after another, had been dealing with the local real estate arm of ZiDevco. They were our client, and they were suing the general contractor. Barry detailed the state of negotiations. He also discussed the antitrust case where the government was charging Sarasota and Manatee county milk distributors with price-fixing. "Ted, let's you and me hike up to Bradenton this week and meet with counsel representing the Manatee guys. United we stand, divided we may take a milk bath. And I stopped drinking milk years ago."

Harvey turned to me. "Ted?"

I had found it difficult to concentrate. I moved swiftly through a discussion of several cases, and then the new representation of Jerry Lee Elroy.

"Was that why you went up to Jacksonville?" Harvey inquired. "I needed you on Friday."

"I went up for something else." I told my partners about the Morgan case twelve years ago and my discovery that one of the state's witnesses had been suborned into perjury. I told them what had happened in Jacksonville. I omitted the story of my visit to the death chamber.

Marian Miller, a handsome woman of about my age, and a graduate of Harvard Law, said, "Well, I'm not a criminal attorney, but it strikes me that you've done your duty by informing this Mr. Ruth."

"Agreed," Harvey Royal said. "Beyond that is pure conjecture."

Barry Wellmet nodded. "The toils of the law. And won't it all become moot, Ted, when they pull the switch and fry this poor guy? That's all she wrote, no?"

"Not quite," I said.

There was the possibility, I explained, that Detective Floyd Nickerson, who had suborned the perjury by Jerry Lee Elroy, might also have lied about Morgan confessing to him.

Harvey Royal cleared his throat and frowned.

"Wait," I said. "There's the fact of where this detective found employment after he left the Jacksonville sheriff's department. It's damned odd." I told my partners what I had learned of Nickerson's move to Orange Meadow, the ZiDevco development near Gainesville.

"Coincidence," Don Kelly said, looking at his wristwatch.

"Maybe," I said. "And maybe not. I'm not satisfied."

Harvey raised a pale eyebrow. "Ted, you sound a little aggrieved. As if you're taking it personally."

"I sent Morgan to Raiford. To Death Watch, and maybe to the electric chair. Yes! It *is* personal!"

Harvey Royal would have been calm in a typhoon. "I can grasp that part of it," he said soothingly, "but you were doing your job in a just manner twelve years ago, following the law and the canons of ethics."

"Harvey, you haven't been there. You don't know."

"True, and I'm grateful for that. In any event, we need you here. We don't need you in Jacksonville. You and I may have to fly to Washington next week, and we've got to shore up our position before we do so. And Barry made an excellent suggestion that you and he solicit some input from the Bradenton fellows in the antitrust suit. Before the milk curdles, as Barry might say. Table this other business, Ted. That's my strong suggestion. Anything else?" He glanced around the table, but no one spoke. "Meeting's adjourned, gentlemen and madam, and I thank you for your time."

I appeared at the Criminal Justice Building at 11:00 A.M. for a meeting with Buddy Capra, the hard-nosed Sarasota assistant state attorney handling the case against the man known to them as Elroy Lee. Capra informed me that the sheriff's department had checked Lee's fingerprints with the NCIC computer. He had four prior convictions in other parts of the state, under the various names Jerry Lee Elroy, Lee Jayson, J. V. Lee, and Elroy Lee. "Clearly a man of limited imagination," Capra said.

"Or of unlimited loyalty," I replied. "Buddy, this case may be a bonanza for you guys—if you can cut a deal."

He and I talked for nearly an hour with Charlie Waldorf, his boss, and then I met Elroy in a little bar on Main Street. I ordered steamed oysters and a draft German beer. Elroy said, "Hey, I just found out Pee-wee Herman was born here. That something?"

"How about that," I said.

I had learned the necessity for ritual with clients. You couldn't simply start off with "Let's cut the crap, you know you're guilty and so do I. If you plead out, I can get you five years pen time. Take it or leave it." They didn't feel they were getting their money's worth, and the ultimatum didn't include the proper catharsis.

So I said, "Did you find any witnesses to back up the story you're going to tell about the car with the Baggies in it?"

"A couple, yeah."

"Who are they?"

"Well, one's out of town right now. I spoke to him. When's he gotta be here to talk to whoever he's gotta talk to?"

"He has to talk to *me* first," I said, "and convince me he's a reliable witness. Where is he?"

"In Miami. He's in a little trouble . . . he can't get here right away."

"Forget him. Who's the other?"

"My sister."

"Where is she?"

"She lives in Orlando."

"Was she here in Sarasota those three days before the cops picked you up with that cocaine in your trunk?"

"If she says she was, who's to say she wasn't?"

"You're out of your mind, Elroy. Forget it."

The steamed oysters arrived. I let Elroy ramble for a while, offering theories of what might have accounted for the cocaine being in the trunk of the car, while I dipped the oysters and chunks of sourdough bread in hot melted butter and drank cold beer.

"That's it?"

"Yeah . . . Well, you're the lawyer. You tell me what to do."

"Depends on your love for adventure. You want to go to trial or cut a deal?"

"I tell you about my pulse bladder?"

"Yes, you did. Let me lay this out for you as simply as I can. You have no witnesses worth a fart in a hurricane. You gave the cops probable cause to search the car. If you go to trial, what can you say? You didn't know the cocaine was there? Before you do that, I have to tell you that a fingerprint expert will take the stand and swear that your prints were on that paper bag and at least two of those plastic Baggies. And when that happens, you can stick a fork in your ass, Elroy, because you're *done*. You and your pulse bladder are headed to Raiford for a twenty-year bit."

"Okay, okay . . . you made your point." Elroy began to pick nervously at the skin of one thumb. "So what's the deal you can get me?"

"I spoke to Charlie Waldorf, the state attorney for this district. He got on the horn to Robert Diaz, the state attorney in Miami. They know you over there. They know who you work for. Guys named Alfonso Ramos and Marty Palomino, right? I'll give you the bacon without the sizzle, Elroy. They want your friend Ramos really bad. You give them Ramos, you do a nickel. Give them Ramos and Palomino together, you walk away laughing."

"I can't do that," Elroy said quietly.

"Why not?"

"They'll inch me."

"I told you, there's a federal witness protection program. The state can tap into it."

Elroy mulled that over for a minute. "Where would I go?"

"Far away. California, Oregon, maybe North Dakota."

"Yeah, but Florida's where my friends are, my sister and her kids."

"Okay. If you turn Waldorf down and plead guilty, he'll go for fifteen years. You probably won't do more than three or four at Raiford. Plenty of time for your friends and your sister to visit."

"I'll die in there!" Elroy whined. "This thing I got could turn to cancer."

"Then take the deal. Save yourself. You've done it before."

Elroy nodded gloomily. He had hardly tasted his Bud. "I don't wanna go somewhere and freeze my ass off. California sounds okay, but fuck North Dakota."

"There's another part of the deal," I said, making up my mind how to deal with this lying bastard.

"What's that?"

"The business in Jacksonville twelve years ago, with that guy Darryl Morgan. You'll have to retract that testimony."

"Are you kidding?"

"Before the same court, whatever judge is presiding."

"I should go up there, face a perjury rap? No fucking way."

"The statute's run on your old testimony. They couldn't prosecute you if they wanted to."

Elroy considered this. "When?" he asked.

"Soon. First you provide an affidavit. Then you testify. Then you give them Ramos and Palomino. Then you go into the program. Then California," I said, "unless you'd prefer North Dakota."

"Let me think about it."

"Elroy, you have no choice. It's part of the deal."

It wasn't, of course. Neither Charlie Waldorf nor his counterpart in Miami would have stood still for that. I was lying to one client in order to save the life of another one—maybe. No matter how much I tried to justify it on that basis, I knew beyond any doubt that I had no right as a lawyer to do it.

And I didn't give a damn.

I knew a bit about things such as laserless holograms, DNA replication, Picasso's blue period, igloo construction, Van Allen belts, virtual reality, even gout. But I did not know how to talk to my own son.

On Sunday night when Alan returned home from Captiva, I faced him with what his mother had overheard.

"I don't yet know how to handle this," I said. "So let's both of us ponder it awhile. Then you come and talk to me. Cards on the table, no bullshit."

Monday was a holiday. Alan sulked by the pool, working his way through two packs of cigarettes, while I took Toba sailing in the sloop, aptly named *Dreamboat*. She slept three comfortably and was small enough to sail single-handed, even though she had no winches, radio, or radar. I hoisted sail and took the tiller; Toba, wearing only the bottom half of a bikini, spread an air mattress and stretched out on the bow.

The bay gleamed bluely in the sun. I headed north on a broad reach toward Whale Key, about an hour away, where I anchored about fifty yards off the lee shore. Few boats would pass by here. I lowered the sails, tied them loosely on the boom, then dropped a wooden ladder off the stern.

Toba knew exactly what I was doing.

The marital bed after a while can become boring; there seems a limited amount of things for the same two people to do there. Long ago I had studied the Kama Sutra and decided that most of it was silly. Could I really maneuver into those positions without a muscle spasm? Can I nibble on her earlobes and suck her toes and talk dirty and still keep a straight face? But I understood the need for variety, to make the manifestation of conjugal love and hormonal need a bit more memorable than merely the component sequential movements of a routine act. There had to be more to it than driving a golf ball properly off a tee so that it soared true for two hundred yards or more. (That also was an act composed of interlinked sequential movements.) And of course there *was* more to it. If you connected properly, as sometimes happened with the golf ball, the result was thrilling.

But with us now, that didn't happen often. In fact, lately it happened more often at the golf tee, which was why on certain weekends, weather permitting, I cast off the lines at the dock and sailed *Dreamboat* to Whale Key, or White Key, or the relatively empty waters off Bay Isles. I had learned a long time ago—and not only from my wife—how stimulating that change of venue could be.

Today a rare white heron stalked the shallows near the key. The sun beating down on Toba's bare breasts tended to make her feel lascivious. When she was lascivious, so I tended to be—and vice versa. That circle with no beginning that makes so many good things possible.

I dove in, and Toba followed. The coldness of the water stunned us a little. We were quickly back on board, reaching for towels.

But I wanted her, and the touch of her cold hand was exciting. I licked her nipples, erect and salty.

A ketch was beating up on the windward side, heading toward Cow Point on Tidy Island. In a few minutes it would pass close enough for anyone with binoculars to see us. "Let's go below," I said, resting on my elbows, with my wife's strong ankles up around the back of my neck. She went to exercise-and-stretch class three times a week.

"Let them look," Toba panted. "Maybe they'll throw money. . . ."

All the next day I kept thinking about what I had done. I had never lied to a client before. I could be disbarred. But images of blue fire were never far from my consciousness.

When I reached home at seven o'clock, sweaty and ready for a swim and a Bloody Mary, Toba was waiting by the side of the pool.

"Alan talked to me," she said. "He thinks you don't respect him. You're disappointed in him."

"He's right," I said.

"He's depressed. His father's a high-powered lawyer. His mother, in his cockeyed view, is a successful real estate agent. His sister's a whiz kid off at an Ivy League college. And he's a failure. Drugs are the only solace in his life, he says. Marijuana is his best friend."

I raised my eyes to heaven.

"And worst of all, I think," Toba said, "he's suicidal."

"You think he's suicidal?" I felt my shoulders sag, my heart seize up with despair.

"You're hearing what you want to hear. *He* says he's suicidal. He says he climbs into his car, drives across the causeway, and he gets this urge to shut his eyes. He does shut them sometimes, for a few seconds. But then he turns chicken. He says to himself, 'Dad'll be furious, and it'll ruin Mom's life.' "

"Did you tell him that was the understatement of the year?"

"No. I just cried."

That's what I wanted to do. This was my son's life. I would have given anything for none of this to be true. I was supposed to do whatever fathers did to protect their young, so that the species didn't die out. If spotted hyenas and Bengal tigers and birdbrained robins could do it, why couldn't I?

"Ted, what are we going to do?"

But I had no answer. I was heartsick. Unless I could intervene, my son, like Darryl Morgan, was on the road to death.

13

I FLEW ON a little feeder flight to Jacksonville, rented a car at the airport, and drove straight out I-10 and then down 121 through scrub woods and air heavy with pine resin. To Raiford again, and to death row.

Sneakers squeaked where black men played basketball on cracked concrete. Bodies glistened and iron clanged where others lifted weights. Angry voices drifted through sunlight.

At the main building of the prison, I was expected. My ID was checked, I passed through the metal detector, and I was led into the cool office of the assistant superintendent. A placard on the desk read: RAYMOND G. WRIGHT.

There were two telephones on the desk: a red instrument to communicate with the outside world, a black one to communicate within the perimeter of the prison. Raymond G. Wright wore a white button-down shirt and a striped tie. A creased brown suit jacket hung on a wooden clothes tree in the corner of the room. I remembered seeing Wright for a minute or two in the death chamber when they had electrocuted Sweeting. Fred Olsen had told me that the assistant superintendent engaged the circuit breakers before the switch was tripped by the executioner and the automatic cycle began. Everyone had a hand in the killing, literally.

"We don't get many prosecutors visiting here," Wright said.

"You may have misunderstood. I'm not a prosecutor now." From

122

the breast pocket of my suit jacket I extracted a card from Royal, Kelly, Wellmet, Jaffe & Miller. I slid it across the desk.

I had come prepared to face the consequences of having struck my fist into Clive Crocker's face on the day of Sweeting's execution. Prepared to apologize, offer some compensation if necessary. But my name seemed to mean nothing to Raymond G. Wright. Or perhaps, I thought, FSP administrative assistants were struck so often that no one took much notice.

"The man I want to visit is Darryl Morgan."

"You're Wizard's attorney?"

"Who is Wizard?"

"That's what the guards call Mr. Morgan."

"No, I'm not his attorney yet. But I will be. I've just come from Tallahassee, from CCR—they're handling his current appeal. The governor's already signed the death warrant. I believe Morgan's in what you call Phase One of Death Watch."

Wright said, "But you're not on Mr. Morgan's visiting list."

"I called and your secretary said there wouldn't be a problem. I prosecuted Morgan," I added.

The logic of this seemed to baffle the assistant superintendent. And that was understandable.

"If it will help," I said, "you can call Beldon Ruth, the state attorney up in Jacksonville. Or the public defender, Kenneth Buckram. Verify my credentials."

Wright cleared his throat and began moving some papers back and forth on the neat surface of his desk. From the expression in his eyes I finally realized that he found it difficult to deal with a situation for which no specific written guidelines existed. A telephone call wouldn't help.

Wright frowned. "How could you become his attorney if you prosecuted him? Wouldn't there be some sort of conflict of interest? You can't defend someone you once prosecuted."

"Are you an attorney-at-law?" I asked.

"No."

"Then I'd appreciate your not telling me what, as a lawyer, I can and can't do. I don't tell you how to run your prison, sir."

Wright said, "I wasn't telling you, sir, I was just asking." But he reached for the black telephone.

.   .   .

The attorneys' interview rooms were in the main building, a quarter of a mile away from Q wing. An underground tunnel connected the two. There were two folding metal chairs and a metal table. Through a glass wall a correctional officer could observe anyone in the interview room but couldn't hear.

In another room Darryl Morgan was strip-searched. His waist chain and handcuffs were removed. I stood up when he entered. I avoided his eyes, conscious only of a physically large, dark presence in prison denim.

Darryl Morgan was thirty-three years old now. If I hadn't known that, I would have guessed him to be forty. There was gray in the kinky black hair above the temples. The eyes were deep-set and dark, but they no longer smoldered with anger, as they had in the courtroom where I'd last seen him. They were wintry with resignation. They were old.

I realized that he didn't recognize me.

"You know who I am?"

"They tell me you're a lawyer."

"You don't know me?"

"You looks familiar."

"I was at your trial," I said. "I was the prosecutor."

Morgan slowly nodded his huge head up and down. He said nothing. I waited for a reaction, but there was none, or so it seemed.

"Ted Jaffe is my name. Do you remember me?"

Morgan nodded again. The eyes barely changed.

I fought against the instinct to lower my gaze. I could smell Morgan now, an alien bitter smell.

After a minute he said, "Why're you here?"

"To try to help you."

That was all I could think of after weeks of gnawing doubt that bordered on torture. Those five words.

"You help me best," Morgan said, "by getting the fuck out of here."

I had expected that and believed I could deal with it.

"I understand how you feel, Mr. Morgan."

"You do?"

Abruptly I felt drained. All that was left was my sense of foolishness. I was an intrusion here, my presence a terrible tampering with what remained of a condemned man's life. What I've got to remember, I thought, if I'm going to get through this and accomplish whatever is still worth accomplishing, is that this man did in fact murder an innocent person. Whatever he is now, he was that then. Some outermost punishment was required, or there is no proper equation in events. But by law, not by error or judicial whim.

"Darryl," I begged, "please listen to me. I have some new information about your case. I know that your cellmate back in Duval County Jail, Jerry Lee Elroy, lied about overhearing you confess on the telephone. If this comes to light, it could win a new appeal for you—maybe even a new trial. I don't promise anything. I definitely don't promise that the verdict will be different. But there's always a chance that we can get the death penalty decision reversed. I met with the CCR group in Tallahassee yesterday. They're willing to let me take over the case."

Morgan, through all this, kept shaking his head. Not in denial so much as amazement.

"You're crazy, man."

"I don't think so." I almost added: "Although quite a few others agree with you," but I clamped my teeth together in time.

"You put me here, man."

"Yes, I did. I was part of that process."

"Something's wrong," Morgan muttered.

"I need to ask you a lot of questions."

"Suck my dick."

"You have nothing to lose."

"You always got something to lose," he said.

"Not at my hands."

"Some kind of flimflam here. I told you, I ain't interested."

"Darryl, I don't work for them anymore. I can't harm you. I can only help you."

"Who you work for?"

"I'm with a law firm in Sarasota."

"You still think I kill that man. Think William Smith stuck a knife in that lady."

He was right, but I couldn't tell him that. "What I think doesn't matter," I said carefully.

"Better you split from here," Morgan said. "I kill you, what I got to lose?"

"Didn't you just say you always have something to lose?"

"Maybe you right and I wrong. Forty-four days, they gone kill me. What do I care if they kill me for doing you too? Who deserve it more than you and that snitch and that motherfucker cop? Maybe my life have a purpose then. Least then I done something for what they done to me. I strike a blow for brotherhood. You know what Malcolm X say?"

There was a light in his eyes now for the first time since I had entered the room.

"Take it easy," I said.

I had to dominate him. Every lawyer has to dominate his client. In this case, it was a little more necessary than usual. Morgan was a big, powerful man. I held my ground, and for the first time I locked eyes with him.

"I tell you how it is over on Q," Morgan said. "They take my cards and my magic stuff away from me when I get over there, and my cards and my magic was all I got. So I hook cockroaches together, sort of like they was a team of mules. They drag a matchbox around on the floor. That pass the time. Then a little frog come up through the shit jack. I kept that little frog a couple of weeks and I give him my roaches to feed him. But froggy hungry, he ain't gonna last, so I flush him back down the shit jack. See what I'm saying?"

"I'm trying to," I said.

"Cockroach, froggy, Jew lawyer—what the difference in the end? They hurting me over there, waiting on Big Wooden Mama. The real mean thing what they done in here is keep me waiting. You feel like, when you first get in, it ain't real. Got locked up for something I don't do, and I say, 'Hey, this can't be right, couple months I be out of this.' I get here, a dude tells me, 'Man, one night you gonna find yourself crying, there be tears in your eyes, and you gonna wonder why.' I said, 'Shit, I don't cry for *nothing*.' And three, four years slide by, I cry. I did, man, I swear. Twelve years gone by. You talking about another appeal? What do I need it for? Every day go round, it come in my mind, 'When all this be over with?' Feeding me to Mama, they ending my hurt. I get rid of you, dude who put me here, maybe they do me that much faster."

I watched him rise from his chair and glide toward me. I didn't have the power to move an inch. I just waited for him.

14

THE ROOM SLOWLY resolved into focus; it had a sharp smell of Merthiolate and disinfectant.

"Rest here for a while," a voice said. I didn't argue.

My fingers trembled when I held my hands out in front of me. I had been taken from the visiting cubicle to the prison hospital—I was conscious by then and, with a bit of help, could navigate. The doctor, a pale young man who was trying without much success to grow a goatee, said that nothing had been broken or damaged. My larynx was bruised, that was all. There would be some discomfort for a day or two; I would be better off talking only when necessary.

I asked the doctor, "Do you know what happened back there?"

"An inmate tried to strangle you."

"Jesus Christ," I gasped, "I know *that*. I mean, how did it end?"

"The guards came in and subdued him. There are always two guards outside. They got there just in time."

I lay on a hospital bed in a room with two white inmates; one had had his appendix removed, the other's leg was in a cast. They were swapping stories of other joints where they had done time. "Now, Terre Haute," the broken-legged one said, "that was a bad stop. I'm in the chow hall one day, there's one jelly doughnut left on the tray. Nigger at the head of the chow line starts to take it, then the nigger in back of him grabs it. So the nigger in front whips out a shank and shoves it into the other nigger's guts. And he goes over to a table and eats the jelly doughnut while the other nigger just lays on the tile right at his feet. No shit, I saw that happen."

This is a dangerous place to be, I thought. On my first visit, I hit a man. On my second, someone tried to kill me. Violence might be infectious. Or perhaps, as the philosopher Hobbes had suggested a few centuries ago, it was the natural state of man outside the constricts of society.

Be kind, enjoy, try not to worry. Okay, Mom.

I signed the necessary release papers and left the prison. I didn't stop off at the administrative office to see Raymond Wright; he hadn't come to visit *me*.

In Jacksonville I checked into the Marina Hotel again, showered, then called Ruby at the office. "What's new, sweetness?"

"Jerry Lee Elroy's getting paranoid. Wants to know what he's supposed to do."

"If he calls again, remind him not to leave town. And be cool until I get in touch."

"I have difficulty hearing you, Ted. Do you have laryngitis?"

"Something like that. Who else called?"

"Charlie Waldorf. Says, 'Do we have a deal? Miami needs to know.'"

"If he calls again, tell him yes, be cool, I believe we do."

"Barry buzzes you twice a day, and also your other partners. In varying states of apoplexy."

"Same message. Be cool. I'll be back on Monday."

"Are you sure you're not in the Caribbean with a bimbo?"

"Goodbye, Ruby."

I called home. "How is Alan?"

Toba's voice, like the weather at the end of summer, had a chilly edge. "He's all right. Today he's at the beach with Sue Hoppy."

"Could this be romance?"

"The dope fiend and the anorexic. Made for each other."

"I'll try to be back by the weekend."

"Were you out carousing last night?"

"Yes, at the CCR law library in Tallahassee. I have a sore throat. I love you."

She didn't say it back to me, as she usually did.

I put in a call to Brian Hoad at the public defender's office. He had gone but had left a message: a name, address, and telephone number.

On the second ring a woman answered. "Yes?"

"Carmen Tanagra?"

"Yes."

"Ms. Tanagra, excuse me, but this is Ted Jaffe. I was chief assistant state attorney here a long time ago."

"I don't want to go through this again."

"I'm not out to hassle you. I'm in private practice now. I'd like to talk to you about something."

"I'm not interested," she said, and hung up.

I called Muriel Suarez at her office. "You knew Tanagra. Can you help me with her?"

"It was too long ago. I can't get involved."

I clenched a fist in frustration that bordered on anger; she couldn't see that. But perhaps she could sense it.

"I'm not being unfriendly," Muriel said. "There's a reason. What are you doing tonight?"

"I plan to shove a fist through the cardboard wall of my hotel room and go to bed early."

"I'll cook you dinner."

"And you'll also tell me the reason you won't help me with Carmen Tanagra?"

"That's not on the menu. Do you eat meat?"

"Yes. And potatoes. And cheese, and butter, and chocolate mousse. The life expectancy of lawyers is not quite as good as that of NFL defensive tackles. Eat, drink, and be merry, for tomorrow you go to trial."

"A lot of people don't eat meat nowadays. In the short run it'll make you aggressive, in the long run it'll kill you. Nevertheless," Muriel said, "tonight I have the urge. So to hell with my arteries, I'm roasting a leg of lamb in fatty gravy. Eight o'clock. And since you're about to ask . . . yes, a very good bottle of red wine."

The slim forms of the Bordeaux bottles were patterned by the candlelight in wavering black shadows upon the walls. Muriel wore a scooped-neck blue silk blouse and floppy white harem trousers. With her golden skin and moody dark eyes, she captured my attention not only as a lawyer.

129

I told her in detail the story of what had happened that morning at Raiford. I was glad to be alive, despite the traps that seemed to lie ahead. Maybe the wine had given me a fit of optimism.

Muriel brought coffee. "You liked the lamb? Really?"

"Loved it. I ate too much, but I'll sleep well."

"You're lucky you're not sleeping the big sleep tonight, hombre. I guess you see now that you'll have to turn this case over to someone else."

Coffee in hand, I moved over to the couch and replied, with the air of a perfectly sane man, "Just because the client tried to strangle me?"

"Do they have to draw blood to make you lose interest?"

My smile flickered briefly.

She said, "All right, then. How about on general principles?"

"Such as?"

"Since you can't defend a man you once prosecuted, it stands to reason that you can't file an appeal for him, either."

I shook my head firmly. "Why does everyone think I can't defend this guy? There's no law says I can't, just a guideline from the Florida Bar. You can do it if you get permission from the appropriate government agency. Which in this instance would be the Office of the State Attorney, Fourth Circuit."

"Would Beldon agree?"

"He's no killjoy."

"Don't be naive. If Beldon wants to, he'll find a reason. Inappropriate, tainted, unseemly, against the canons—there are plenty of words for it."

"But there are no laws or rules."

"Has it ever been done before?"

I had done my homework in the Tallahassee law library. "Not in Florida," I conceded. "But yes, once, about nine years ago, in California. A capital murder case: *State v. Owens*. A new witness popped up who confirmed the defendant's alibi."

"There's no alibi. Darryl Morgan admitted he was there."

"He didn't have a fair trial," I said. "For all I know, he may have been not guilty."

"Then who *is* guilty? Who did it?"

I'd been thinking about that. "Could have been someone else who looked just like Darryl."

"Didn't Darryl work for the Zides?"

"Yes, but how much attention do you think Connie Zide really paid to the help?"

"You told me he was six foot six. You'd pay attention to *that*."

"Yes, you would," I said, and then remembered something out of the long-ago past, some words that I hadn't thought of for a dozen years. The hairs rose on my forearms. I remembered Neil Zide's description of the men who had shot his father: *Young, black, wearing sneakers, jeans, and I seem to remember a dark T-shirt.*

Was I remembering it wrong? If not, why hadn't I, as the prosecutor, understood its significance then? Why hadn't Gary Oliver?

Muriel was still waiting.

"For the moment," I said, putting my vision in a place where I could recall it when I needed it, "there's no contrary evidence. I've got to hang the case for a retrial on fundamental error."

She shook her head so that the dark curls flew. "Listen, I respect Beldon. But you know as well as I do he thinks a balanced jury means six in the front row and six in the back. Prosecutorial misconduct is when the state loses a felony case. And fundamental error was what happened in the Garden of Eden."

"He's still a friend, Muriel."

"In which case, also, he might want to stop you before you get murdered by the client."

I left her house just after eleven o'clock. At the door she raised her head without shutting her eyes, and I kissed her lightly on the lips. It was a little more than a brotherly kiss, but it was far short of a kiss from a would-be lover. And that seemed, for the moment, absolutely right.

Duval County and the city of Jacksonville were by decree synonymous, making Jacksonville physically the largest city in the United States. It called itself "the insurance capital of the South," and its avowed ambition was to be the home of an NFL franchise, but until that day it had to make do with college football, minor league baseball, and greyhound racing.

I left the Marina Hotel at seven-fifteen the next morning. A lot of concrete had been poured here since I was a boy; gone were the old savannas, the wild marsh along the river. Now I drove from strip mall to strip mall, to intersection after intersection with a Publix, Winn-Dixie, Food Lion and Albertson's facing each other on opposite corners.

131

Muriel had told me that Neil Zide's latest project was to build a two-story art deco shopping mall, in conjunction with a water park, all of it to be located a few blocks from the ocean.

"A water park?" I asked. "Next to the *ocean*?"

"You think that's redundant? You against progress?"

I crossed the Main Street Bridge, and fifteen minutes later stood in front of Carmen Tanagra's front door. The small wooden house on Alabama Avenue was set back from the sidewalk. A plaque by the side of the door gave the following information:

GLORIA WILLOUGHBY—CARMEN TANAGRA
Crystal Balancing   Nutritional Therapy
Iridology   Herbalism   Kinesiology
Colonic Irrigation

I clucked my tongue a few times, preparing myself for various possibilities. Then I rang the bell. A tall, stern-looking woman of about forty opened it. She glared at me.

"I'm sorry to bother you this early, ma'am. Is Ms. Tanagra in?"

"Are you a patient?"

"Not yet. But who knows what may happen?" I handed her a business card.

Carmen Tanagra came to the door. I recognized her from her days as a detective; she looked older, but she also looked healthier. Plenty of high colonics, I imagined, not to mention crystal balancing. She also looked more butch. That was something I hadn't grasped until now. It threw an oblique light on other matters.

"Ms. Tanagra, I'm not here to talk about the Bongiorno case or your private life. May I come in?"

In the living room five minutes later, I drank chicory coffee and ate a croissant. From the swinging door to the kitchen, Gloria Willoughby still glared at me. I wasn't a patient. I was a man who had rung the doorbell at a quarter to eight in the morning. I decided I'd better move things along.

"You don't have any connections still with the sheriff's department?"

Carmen Tanagra shook her head firmly. "And I don't want any. They shitcan the good cops. Only the vanilla people make it to the top. Then they become officious pricks."

Her feelings didn't lack for definition.

"You don't miss it at all?"

"What's to miss? Carrying a gun? I have a better life now, here with Gloria, believe me."

"I do believe it," I said. "Which one of you does what?"

"Huh?"

I felt my face begin to turn pink. "The colonic irrigation, the crystal balancing . . . I saw your sign. Are you both iridologists? Do you both do everything?" But I was aware that I kept growing redder.

"We both do it all," Tanagra said icily. "But Gloria taught me just about everything. Look, Mr. Jaffe, what is it that you want?"

"Do you remember the Solomon Zide murder?"

Carmen Tanagra gazed at me waspishly for a few seconds. From her throat blared a harsh sound that might have been interpreted as a laugh. But I knew it wasn't.

"The black kid in the truck," she said. "The one who got killed in the parking lot of that Lil' Champ. The one supposed to have cut that woman's face. William Smith was his name."

"Didn't Floyd Nickerson shoot him when he was escaping?"

In response, Carmen Tanagra made that harsh sound again.

"Isn't that what your police report said?"

"That's what it said."

So there was that too. I was getting in even deeper. I told her what I had learned from Jerry Lee Elroy.

Tanagra said, "Uh-huh."

"You're not surprised," I said. "So Nickerson must have told you himself that it was bullshit."

"I don't recall what he told me."

"You're still friendly with him?"

"Are you kidding?"

"You know where he is now?"

"He got a good job as a rent-a-cop."

"Do you know for who?"

"Is this some kind of cross-examination?"

"Sounds like one, doesn't it?" I smiled. "You want me to get off your tail? Am I walking too close?"

"Close only counts in horseshoes and dancing," Carmen Tanagra said, but without an answering smile.

I wasn't sure what I had done or said to lose what little of the high ground I'd occupied.

"Morgan is still on death row. They're supposed to pull the switch next month. But there was one witness at his trial who lied."

Tanagra said, "And you want to know if there was a second one."

I hadn't had to prompt her. She had said it. My heartbeat quickened, and I put a clamp on my tongue.

"If I told you there was," she said, "what would you want out of me?"

I leaned forward in my chair. "I'd want you to make a statement under oath. Back it up at an appeal hearing."

"Mr. Jaffe, let me tell you a story. A while ago these barges with fake ballast tanks off-loaded a hundred tons of marijuana at Fort George Inlet. JSO got tipped. They made a big bust, including the Cuban guys who were meant to pick up the stuff. Those Cubans are at the dock in two Mercedes. Amazingly—figure this one out—the two Mercedes wind up in the garages of two high-ranking police officers. But one day a file clerk down at the courthouse got pissed off and snitched on them. The cops had to give back the two Mercedes. Were they prosecuted? No, sir. You hear of any resignation? No, sir. The file clerk, though, *he* has to resign. Now he's a cook in a short-order joint downtown. . . . You see what I'm saying?"

She had told me what I wanted to know.

"If I snitch on Floyd Nickerson," Tanagra offered, "it won't matter how long ago he was a cop."

"They busted *you* in the Bongiorno case," I said, "and you were a cop."

"To be in the brotherhood you need a dick. That time in the Gambrel murder, the snitch I had was for real. But Bongiorno had real good friends in Tallahassee. Money and political clout is what it came down to. The snitch changed his story, and I got shitcanned. And if I do what you'd like me to do . . ." She drew a finger across her throat. "I don't have a medical degree or a license to practice. I could wind up with that clerk, taking orders for grits and eggs."

"I don't want that to happen to you, either, but—"

"Then don't threaten me," Tanagra said.

"William Smith is dead. You remembered that. There's another man on death row waiting to be executed. Don't you think one dead is enough? You want to remember *him* too?"

"I can't help you," she said, putting down her coffee cup with a gesture of finality. Her friend Gloria still listened to us from the kitchen door.

"I could put you under subpoena," I said. "You'd have to tell the truth."

Carmen Tanagra got up from her chair and walked across the room. She opened the front door and then banged open the screen door against the wooden front of the house. She said, "Why don't you go cry in one hand and piss in the other to see which one gets full first? But do it outside. And don't bother coming back to tell me how it worked out."

15

THE REST OF THE MORNING I spent in the library at the public defender's office. In the early afternoon I went to the courthouse to visit a judge I knew. I asked him a favor he had the power to grant, and at three o'clock I climbed into the rental car and headed west again on I-10.

Twenty-five minutes later I took the now familiar turnoff south onto State 121. I recognized landmarks: the Country Variety Store, the sagging white clapboard Raiford Road Church. A dry winter sun burned into the meat of my left arm resting on the car door. Tuning the radio to a country-music FM station, I snapped my fingers to the beat.

The whine and wail of violins filled the car, then swirled into the leafy green afternoon that rushed past the open window. *Call me on the telee-phone . . . Daaaarrrrlin' I am always home . . . If you ev-errrrr change yore mind . . .*

Back in Sarasota were my wife and son and law firm: problems closer to the bone. This was as good a way as any—a kind of chemotherapy of the soul—to keep all that in remission. And to recapture whatever it was I had lost in the last decades that now seemed so dear, and necessary, in the time remaining.

I remembered how once I had wanted to be of service, how my deepest ambition had been to argue a case before the Supreme Court and save an innocent man's life. In the quest for creature comfort and security, somehow that had faded from my consciousness. Just

136

a short while ago I'd thought that I had almost everything I wanted. All that blocked my path to the happiest of endings, I'd decided, was the economic recession and the torment of my son.

How shallow I had become in these years. Do we do the right thing, I wondered, by giving up our youthful fantasies?

But I might not have to now, for I'd found what I wanted in those old dusty files at the courthouse. Now I knew that Neil Zide, on that bloody December night at the beach a dozen years earlier, had not described Darryl Morgan as tall.

The same creased brown suit jacket hung from the wooden clothes tree in the corner of the office. At his desk, FSP Assistant Superintendent Raymond G. Wright wore a white button-down shirt but a different-color striped tie. Blue and green yesterday, red and brown today.

Wright made a humming sound in his throat. "Yesterday, Mr. Jaffe, you made a point that I wasn't qualified to tell you what you could or couldn't do as a lawyer. No more, you said, than you could tell me what I could or couldn't do as a prison administrator. After yesterday's unfortunate incident of violence, the decision concerning your request to visit Darryl Morgan falls into the category of how to run the prison. I have a right to deny it. I have to consider your safety."

"If you deny my right to visit," I replied, "I'll have a court order from Judge Krawitz in Jacksonville on your desk by ten o'clock tomorrow morning. Do you really want to force me to go to all that trouble?"

He does, I thought. He truly does. But he's got to suspect the judge will bust his chops. And if the judge does that, Raymond G. Wright's boss may do the same thing. The motto of any prison system, carved in the hardest stone of its walls, is: *Keep out of the public eye and judicial disfavor.* If they don't know we're here, then we're doing the job right. And we'll retire on full pay.

Wright's hands rested on the desk, motionless, like empty gloves. He said, "In the light of what happened, the physical circumstances of your visit would have to be different this time. We can't take responsibility for your safety unless we can protect you."

That wasn't unreasonable. "Good. I like the idea of protection."

"We'll ask you to sign a release."

"I'll do that."

137

"There'll be glass between you and Morgan, and you'll have to talk on a telephone."

"Not acceptable," I said flatly.

"Then we'll need two correctional officers in the visitor's cubicle with you both."

"No. Our conversation falls under attorney-client privilege. I can't have anyone listening, or I abrogate that privilege."

"The alternative is to cuff and chain and shackle your client."

"Fine," I said. Let them put him in a straitjacket if they wanted to. I feared Morgan now. You can't feel a man's hands try to throttle the life-giving air out of you and be easy with him after that.

"We can't do that in a visitor's cubicle," Wright said. "There's only a table and chairs. Nothing fixed. No ring bolts in the walls."

"So what do you suggest, Mr. Wright?"

"You can talk to him on the row. In his cell."

I hesitated a moment. "Death row?"

"That's where his cell is."

I looked into the assistant superintendent's narrowed, unblinking pale eyes.

"All right," I said.

Wright smiled smugly. "What we need, then, is for Wizard to agree to the visit. If he doesn't, all this is beside the point. Not even a judge can force an inmate to talk to a lawyer."

"You're absolutely right. Will you ask him?"

"Not until later this evening. If he agrees, you can be here at eight o'clock tomorrow morning."

"Tell him," I said, "that I think he may be innocent. And I intend to save his life."

In the morning the guards led me into Q block through a series of double gates that were operated from behind a bulletproof-glass control center. We entered the block. When the gates shut, they clanged for ten seconds, humming a symphony of discordant sound. The hot air smelled stale. The reek of cloistered bodies attacked my nostrils. A wail of voices struck at my eardrums.

Three tiers with catwalks rose above me. My escorts and I climbed the concrete stairs to the second tier, then marched down the catwalk. Hard leather heels echoed off the concrete. Men shouted at each other through the bars in their cells. Faces peered out of the shadows at the three of us marching by.

I didn't see James Cagney anywhere. I didn't see George Raft, either. I saw a few thin white faces, but mostly in those shadows I saw the haggard red eyes of caged black men blazing out like the eyes of maniac animals. In my youth I had seen such dementia behind bars at the zoo, where brainsick creatures, torn from all that was natural and dear, stared, or paced, or lay in urine and torpor. I had smelled that same stench, and I had turned away. I had never taken my children to zoos.

Here, quarantined from daylight, men lived in order to die. They lived like subhumans, shut in Q block until the last appeal had been exhausted by the last weary lawyer, and they were granted what amounted to the mercy of Big Wooden Mama.

There is a great deal about Darryl Morgan that I learned, then and later, but I'm going to tell it now.

Darryl's first beef was larceny, after he had broken two school windows and been placed on probation. The larceny charge came after he had boosted a tape deck from a Chrysler New Yorker and been caught trying to pawn it. Looking down from the bench, the judge said, "I want to help you, son. And I think the kind of help you need is jail therapy, because it'll make you think about the consequences of your acts. Understand what I'm saying? Let's try six months to a year at ACI."

Apalachia Correctional Institute, or ACI, was in Liberty County, west of Tallahassee in the Apalachicola National Forest. Darryl entered ACI a week before his sixteenth birthday. He was housed in Dorm 5, a ramshackle single-story white wooden building that over the years had acquired the hue and wrinkled texture of a sheet that hadn't been changed for months. The smell of sweat oozed not only from the residents' bodies but from the walls and the creaking wooden floors.

Darryl's supper that first evening was baked beans with chunks of pork fat, a glass of milk, a cookie with a few raisins in it. Later in Dorm 5, Darryl's new neighbors, seventeen-year-old boys named Hubert and William, got into a religious debate. William's last name was Smith, and he was destined to die outside the Lil' Champ food store four years later in Jacksonville. "In this life, brother," William said, "ain't no such thing as no motherfucking salvation. This just one mean motherfucker from the time you born to the motherfucking end when you go."

"Amen," Hubert said.

Darryl had been assigned an upper bunk next to the showers. The mattress was thin, the springs sagged. By midnight his back ached. So did his knees, from growing pains.

He had never been away from home before. Not too bad. Sure don't miss no one.

He woke at three o'clock in the morning. Hot water dripped in the shower room, steam billowed into the dorm: well over one hundred degrees in there. With the crawling mist, rising steam, the steady drip of the water as from branches, the dorm was like a tropical rain forest.

None of the other boys seemed to mind. I be as tough as they be, Darryl decided. So I don't mind neither.

Soon he learned a new language. Your house was your bed, your slice of territory. The hole was solitary confinement. A shank was a homemade knife made from the guts of an iron cot. A one-year sentence was a bullet, two was a deuce, three a trey, five a nickel, ten a dime, twenty-five a quarter.

Darryl's new friend, William Smith, said, "I had bad luck. I go before a dime-store judge. All this motherfucker knows is five, ten, 'n' a quarter. First time out of the box, motherfucker slips me a nickel. Open my mouth, I say, 'It ain't right, Judge, it's too much . . . ,' and he laughs. He says, 'Keep the change, boy.' "

Hubert and an older boy called Suitcase approached Darryl on a Saturday night. "How about us have a little fun together, dude?" Darryl knew from the look in their eyes just what they meant. He growled, "Fuck you, faggot. Touch me, I'm a kick yo' natural ass." He flexed his muscles.

Sunday afternoon Hubert and Suitcase and a couple of other dudes threw a blanket over Darryl's head and stuffed a towel in his mouth. They carried him kicking and grunting to Suitcase's cot, and fucked him in his natural ass. Four other boys, including William, were playing cards on the porch. One of the most uncool things you could do in the joint was interfere with another dude's serious intentions, especially if those intentions were unlawful.

William talked to Darryl that evening, trying to explain the way things were. "A dude tell you, 'I wanna fuck you,' you say 'no,' he feel insulted. Hubert and Suitcase don't wanna hurt you. Hubert, he gentle as a lamb. They just need some place to stick they meat."

. . .

After seven months Darryl returned to Jacksonville. For a while he had a job at a car wash. He found a girlfriend named Pauline. When Pauline got pregnant he needed money to pay for an abortion. A friend said, "Be cool. We go down to the beach tonight. Find us some fun-loving dudes with cash in their jeans."

Using two-by-fours to threaten, they jackrolled drunks and white teenagers successfully for two weeks, and on the third weekend were caught by a black undercover cop posing as a drunk. The juvenile court judge sentenced Darryl to a year at the Arthur C. Dozier School for Boys.

The Arthur C. Dozier School for Boys was in the Florida Panhandle, only twenty miles from the Georgia state line. In the official state literature it was called a "treatment center for delinquents." The residents chopped sorghum and harvested sugarcane and sometimes went to school.

The boys lived in bunks with armed guards outside. When it grew dark there was nothing to do except talk and play cards and jerk off and cornhole and suck dick. Darryl made friends with two boys named Hog and Isaac. They agreed they would have sex together when they got horny but would stand united against anyone who tried to rape any of them.

Isaac had two decks of playing cards under his pillow. He said to Darryl, "You got big hands. I teach you to shuffle the cards good, do some tricks. We do some neat things." At lunch breaks he showed Darryl how to shuffle so the cards didn't change places, how to make a one-hand cut, how to deal off the bottom of the deck.

Darryl's house in the bunk was five feet by eight feet, bounded on the sides by four-foot-high sheets of stiff cardboard supported by the backs of his neighbors' upright lockers. Between Darryl's lockers a thin plank of plywood rested on two hinges to form a wobbly desk area. On it, Darryl placed a photograph of Pauline. One day while the boys were at work, a group of hacks and the superintendent ripped apart the cubicles in the bunks. All the flimsy plywood desks and the personal decorations were removed and destroyed. The photograph of Pauline was gone.

Hog said quietly, "I never had nothing on my locker or under my bed. I don't keep nothing personal, 'cause I know them pigs tear it off sooner or later, and I catch them doing it I bust some hack's motherfucking head and get sent to the hole. And I don't need that shit. So I got nothing. They can't take *that* away from me."

141

. . .

Back on the street after eight months, Darryl discovered that Pauline had gone to Miami. He decided to go down there and claim her and his possible child. But he had no money. He was seventeen. He could work as a laborer, a dishwasher, a waiter, janitor, porter, maybe a mechanic or a carpenter if he learned how. Pump gas. Couldn't be a cabdriver or a barber now, because he had a record.

Don't know how to do this, don't know how to do that. What I know? Know how to jackroll drunks, bust windows, set fires, crack warehouses, grab money from cash registers, stick a dude up, break into cars with slimjims and slaphammers, and swipe a tape deck. Know who dealing in weed, coke, dust, black tar, hash, speed, uppers, downers, smack, meth, acid, spikes, and hypos. Got me some connections now from the joint—I find you a Saturday Night Special, a sawed-off, a blade, gravity knife, butterfly knife, a bayonet. Man, I find you a fucking Uzi you want one bad enough. Want a cooncan game, I know where they playing. A color TV? I knows the truck one just fell off of.

Just need something to do. Goof around . . . you know, have some fun. What I learn in the joint is, people got to prove things to people. Watch people's faces when they see you—they scared, or they don't care? One or the other, nothing between. Like if I had a .357 magnum right now, you'd do whatever I want you to do, right? I be Jesse James, John Wayne, that dude Shaft from Harlem. And you couldn't do nothing about it. All my life, people been doing that to me. Now I like to get that feeling where they do what I want them to do.

So he snatched fifty dollars from a Burger King cash register in a town called Middleburg, but was picked up by the cops that evening in Jacksonville; he was too recognizable. He did four months in Clay County Jail. He said to his cellmate there, "I can do this kinda time standing on my head."

A few months later he was caught with goods from an auto parts warehouse burglary. He was eighteen, an adult, and he drew seven years.

The joint was called Branville, and a sign painted on the wall of the chow hall read: IF YOU WOULD HAVE A MAN STAY AS HE IS, THEN TREAT HIM AS HE IS. IF YOU WOULD HAVE A MAN CHANGE, THEN TREAT HIM AS THE PERSON YOU WOULD WANT HIM TO BECOME.

By some dude named Goethe. Darryl looked at that sign and thought: one thing sure, this Goethe dude never did no time.

FINAL ARGUMENT

Isaac was there at Branville, and so was Darryl's old friend from ACI, William Smith. Old home week. Best part of the joint, keep meeting old friends. Stick around long enough, you never lonely.

At Branville there was a factory that made furniture. They made desks for prosecutors. They made swivel chairs for judges. Men working there earned eleven cents an hour. But Darryl was put in food service, washing dishes, earning nothing. He lived in a dormitory with seventy howling maniacs. They played sports at Branville. Darryl was six feet four by then, over two hundred pounds. They gave him a baseball glove and put him in right field. He was a poor fielder, but with brute power he could hit; when he connected with the bat, the softball soared and struck high up on the concrete walls.

The team played games against teams in the local North Florida Factory League. The factory teams were almost all young white men. In the first game that Darryl played in, Branville lost by the score of 33 to 5. Darryl got two hits, made one leaping catch of a line drive, and let one ball scoot between his legs for an inside-the-park home run. After the game he said to William, "How come we not good enough to beat these dudes? We all brothers 'cept for the white motherfucker at second base and Rivera on third. Brothers up in the majors, the NBA, they beat the shit out of the white boys. What wrong with us? Don't we wanna win?"

Isaac was in the same cell block, happy with his decks of cards. He ran a little poker game, won a few cartons of cigarettes a week. Booze was made at Branville—yeast from the bakery, sugar, raisins, and apples from the chow hall, alcohol from the medical department. Darryl won some cartons of Marlboros playing poker. He bought a pint of home brew. He felt sick, threw up, was found by a hack in the shower room with what was left of the pint and sent to the hole for a month.

The door of his cell was steel, with just a tiny slit for a food tray and mail. Darryl never got any mail, he never received a visit in any joint he had ever been in. It was winter in northern Florida, and heat came from a pipe that extended from ceiling to floor. He threw water on the pipe and it sizzled.

In the morning he looked through the iron bars of the window. He could see a pewter sky, half of an unused pitted concrete tennis court, a gun tower, and some men in gray sweatsuits jogging through the fog like ghosts.

There was a dude across the way called Crazy. Crazy told Darryl that he'd been in the hole for eight months.

"What you do?" Darryl asked.

"Don't remember," Crazy said. "Musta been something pretty good, though."

With a long wire, Crazy passed Darryl an old crumpled Camel pack with three Marlboros and a Viceroy in it, and a book of damp matches. Now Darryl was in Crazy's debt and couldn't tell him to shut the fuck up when Crazy shouted at the top of his lungs all evening long until after midnight to a brother called Teabag, who was on the tier above. It sounded to Darryl like they were yelling in Swahili.

Twice a week each man was allowed a shower and an hour's exercise in a walled yard. During Darryl's month in the hole there was a murder in the shower room. Teabag went berserk, killed one dude he didn't like, and cut two others—he'd been carrying a shank under a towel. Darryl asked another brother why Teabag had shanked the two other dudes. The brother said the hack had asked Teabag that same question, and Teabag had looked puzzled and said, "Well, they was standing right there."

When Darryl got out of the hole, there was a movie in the Branville auditorium that Sunday afternoon. The movie was *Hotel*. One of the characters, a professional thief, was played by Karl Malden. The men yelled for him whenever he was on-screen. At the end, led away in handcuffs by the police, Karl still managed to steal an ashtray. The men cheered wildly.

Coming out of the movie into the suddenly bright sunlight, Darryl felt a moment or two of dislocation. In the yard he could see a couple of palm trees, a few men in T-shirts and denims tossing a football back and forth. A jogger moved by, face slick with sweat, sneakers scraping on concrete. Darryl heard the iron of the weights clank in the distance as dudes did bench presses and curls.

Stupid, Darryl thought. Got to be something better. But what? Nineteen, and this all I know.

On parole after twenty months in residence at Branville, he returned home to bunk down on the wooden boards of the back porch of his mother's house.

". . . Mama there, drinking herself into the dirt. Sister selling pussy and sleeping on the job. A.J. live up at the Palmetto Club, cut the white man's grass. He say to us, 'Anytime you happen to pass by my place, I'd sure appreciate it.'

"I borrow a Colt forty-five from a dude I knew. I hike down to St. Augustine on a Saddy night and score off some faggots in a nightclub parking lot. Rule of the street is, live good while the bread's there. You ever hear what that TV brother Redd Foxx say to the white dude? 'Want to know what's it like to be a nigger? Friday, take out all you got in the bank. Spend it by Sunday.' Say that, peoples laugh. But it true. You do what you do not because you stupid but 'cause you know what's coming. You got a sense of the future—there ain't none, man.

"One dude say to me and a couple of friends, 'Run up and down Main or Union, niggers, take what you want! Take their lives if you got to, but get what you need! We must make our own world, and we can't do this unless the white man is dead! Kill him, my man— gather the fruit of the sun!'

" 'I ain't ready for that shit,' I say."

He hadn't read Malcolm X then, he said. *Racial justice* were words mouthed by other men; they passed him by like fast foreign cars. In music he liked soul: Aretha Franklin, Curtis Mayfield, the Motown sound, Isaac Hayes and the *Shaft* theme, which set his fingers snapping. But they were only background rhythms to the pointless flow of his life on the street. When he passed the Mount Calvary Baptist Church on Front Street he heard the passionate cries of big-bosomed gospel singers but never went inside.

He worked for a while pumping gas in a Mobil station, sold some weed on the side in the playground of the white kids' high school. A dude called Shorty Bigshoes ran the policy racket in black Jacksonville. Darryl went to Shorty Bigshoes for a job.

"You ain't got the class for the numbers," Shorty Bigshoes told him.

"I can learn," Darryl said.

"Man, you been arrested for every petty crime in the book. You never did settle down to no one kind of hustle. You been locked up too much, doing life on the installment plan. The cops know you too good. I'm giving you the best idea you ever had—put the life down, get you a lunch pail."

A lunch pail was a legitimate job.

Shorty Bigshoes' words carried weight. Darryl went to his so-called stepfather at the golf club. He asked for help.

A.J. said to him, "I'm gonna speak to you of the good, the bad, and the ugly, while standing between questions and answers, knowing and not knowing. You listen real careful. Such uglinesses are now living on our planet and we pretends not to know why. But I can tell you—because the bad has changed places with the good! Godliness and respect for elders changed places with macho man and worship for the angry side of life is why! Pollution's the theme of this part of the century, outer and inner, and we hiding our heads in the muck of it so's not to see how high the tide's rising. Am I connecting? Touching what's left of your soul? You've always possessed a special tenderness for the aged and infant. You've always cared about animals—you remember your cat, Snuffy, got run over by a red GMC pickup? How you cried? Where all that gone to?"

"What you been smoking?" Darryl asked.

"The pipe of amazing truth, boy!"

"You a sick man, A.J. Was you run over Snuffy in the pickup, was a black Ford, and you was drunk. You whupped my ass every chance you got. You fucked my sister in the back of that pickup when she was ten years old, and after that you did it to her every chance you got, and that's why she is what she is, a sleepy hoo-er. You never in your life give me the kinda help I need."

To Darryl's surprise, a few days later A.J. came round to Marguerite's clapboard house and told him that a friend named James was head gardener at a fancy beach estate. James did the hiring of all groundskeeping staff. They needed a handyman.

"Handy at what?"

"Don't matter. James teach you. Just go where it says on this here piece of paper. You see James. Tell him you willing to learn."

James, a sinewy, bald old man, asked Darryl if he believed in Lord Jesus and the Christian work ethic. As if he were talking to a white man, Darryl said, "Yes, sah! I sure does!"

That was August '78. The following April, twenty minutes after sentencing by Judge Bill Eglin, shackled at the ankles and cuffed to a waist chain, Darryl found himself in a DOC van headed for Raiford and death row.

The day he arrived, three of the hacks took him into a room and showed him the chair. "That's it, nigger. Gonna sit your black ass in Big Wooden Mama's lap and pull the switch. Ever see an egg in a real hot pan?"

"You can appeal, boy," another told him. "Got a whole system of appeals now. The last guy appealed, he lost every time, except right at the end his lawyer come running down here and goes, 'Rastus! Good news at last! I couldn't get 'em to reduce your sentence . . . but I got 'em to reduce the voltage!' "

The hacks cracked up laughing. Darryl said quietly, "Fuck you, motherfucker"—figured he had nothing to lose, but he was wrong. On the way to his cell—he was handcuffed behind his back—they pushed him down a staircase. By the time he had bounced to the bottom his nose was broken, his forehead and one ear flowed with blood, an ankle had been sprained. The official report: "Inmate tripped and fell."

He often wondered why they didn't just kill you when you got there. Make you kneel by a ditch, put a bullet in the back of your head, boot you in. He'd seen that in a movie about a Nazi death camp. It had seemed pretty awful then, but not anymore.

Lights came on at 4:30 A.M. Feeding time was an hour later. You never left your cell except twice a week to shower and get an hour's exercise on the covered roof. You had your own black-and-white Emerson TV, your own radio. The power stayed on all night. There was no work to do. Now and then, if you knew how to read, you could get hold of a book, usually tattered Erle Stanley Gardner murder mysteries or appeals for Christianity. You slept and ate and pissed and crapped in your cell. You never saw the men in the other cells except when they passed by or during exercise hour, but you could talk to them—shout through the bars, play long-distance chess or checkers, make bets on ball games. Darryl knew the batting averages of nearly every player in the major leagues.

He had known some bad dudes but never been around such sorry motherfuckers in his life. He heard two men arguing over who had raped and killed the oldest woman.

"Hey, mine was seventy-two!"

"Well, you win, man, mine was only sixty-five. . . ."

Visitors were allowed once a week. Darryl put his family's names down on the list. No one came.

Three years later his old buddy Isaac, from Apalachia, made the trip to Q block and Big Wooden Mama. Isaac had robbed a liquor store of $240 in cash a few weeks after he got out of Branville back in '77. Two police cars had chased him. Isaac squeezed off a few shots from his Colt Detective Special, and one of them struck a young patrolman between the eyes. Cop killers moved more rapidly than others through the appeal hierarchy. Came time for Isaac to bequeath his worldly goods, he gave all his clothes and cigarettes to the boys he'd jailed with earlier in C block, and said, "None of these threads gonna fit Darryl, so he can have these here mementos of a wasted life." He left Darryl two packs of playing cards, a box of number 6 rubber bands, some plastic glasses and coins, as well as a couple of dog-eared, cellotaped paperback books on magic tricks. Darryl taught himself to be a magician.

16

A SEMICIRCLE OF thick black iron protruded from the wall next to the toilet. The shackles and chains wrapped around Darryl's ankles and waist were looped through the ring bolt. The handcuffs were shackled to the steel waist chain. This system of restraint had been invented three decades earlier by a U.S. Army general. Later the general was convicted for embezzlement of government funds. On the way to a federal prison camp in Pennsylvania, he was shackled and chained with his own invention. He was seen to smile.

Darryl, similarly trussed, sat on the concrete floor of his cell, back braced against the wall, long legs splayed out like a pair of scissors ready to close. He didn't smile.

One of the guards entered the cell with me. He blocked my path with a rigid arm and said, "If you move from this area of the room, sir, we have orders to immediately terminate this visit."

The guards seated themselves on the green-painted catwalk in opposite directions, each one on a metal folding chair about fifteen feet away from the foot of the bed. They were beyond earshot, but I was in both their lines of vision.

I sat at the foot of Darryl's bed. My pigskin briefcase, which the guards had searched, lay on the khaki blanket. In my lap I had a Sony tape recorder and a yellow legal pad.

I said to Darryl, "I can help you."

"Why you come back?" he asked, his eyes unblinking.

"I like your company."

149

"Sound like crap to me. You a free man."

"I made a choice. Coming back is part of it."

"Last choice I made, I say to the hack, 'Gimme channel seven.' "

"You made one when you tried to strangle me," I reminded him.

"You a smart dude. I keep forgetting."

"So why did you agree to see me? You said it was some kind of flimflam, you weren't interested."

"Man, you don't know shit from wild honey."

"Then maybe you can enlighten me."

"Something to do, man. Pass the time."

"Why do they call you Wizard?"

"I had a deck of cards or some rubber bands, motherfucker, I'd show you."

I wiped some oily sweat from my forehead. If this was winter, what was it like here in August?

"Where did you learn magic and sleight of hand?"

"Here on the row, man. Taught myself."

He told me then about his dead friend Isaac and his time at Branville. "And from books. One called *The Secrets of Alkazar*. No dude ever named Alkazar. This magician dude named Kronzek make that up. But what he show you, that is definitely real."

"What can you do?"

For the first time, Darryl chuckled. His sleeves were rolled up; I saw his tattoos clearly. "Sweet deception," he said, "is the name of the game. I can cut rope, put it back together. Can do things with cards, make you think I's a real magician. You don't gonna believe what I can do."

"Why did they take away all your magic stuff?"

"This is Q block. They take all you got. What you want from me?"

"I want you to tell me what happened that night."

"What night?"

"The night you went to rob the Zides' house at Jacksonville Beach."

"You not gonna believe it. You never did believe it."

"Try me. Enlighten me."

"Okay," he said, smiling at last. "I enlighten you."

He didn't like the job at the Zides' because the chief gardener, James, got on his case all the time. Cutting the grass too short, boy.

See that bit of brown turf? No good. Now you're cutting it too long, boy. Have to do it all over again in a day or two.

He was given the job of hunting all over the estate for dogshit. The lady had three dogs already: Paco, the eight-year-old Doberman and guard dog; two amiable and witless cocker spaniels named Myra and Mickey; and now she'd just bought a pair of three-month-old puppies, some kind of Chinese name Darryl couldn't pronounce, and turned them loose on the lawns. They crapped six or seven times a day each.

"You look for their doodoo," James said. "You find it, first you dump a lot of earth on it. Pick all that up in a shovel, get it into this barrow. Put it in one of those plastic sacks."

"Make good fertilizer," Darryl said.

"You don't know nothing, boy."

"You don't teach me. How'm I gonna learn?"

Old James turned away, said nothing.

But Darryl, no matter how hard he tracked, never could find all the soft smelly heaps. The lawns and flower beds were huge, and the Chinese puppies ran everywhere.

James confronted him. "The lady says she nearly step in doggy poo yesterday. Right by the front door. And she says they getting flies in the house. You too far away from the ground to look real good at it? You want binoculars? You need to crawl round on your knees to find all that stinky-poo?"

"My daddy say you teach me about gardening."

"When you're ready."

"How many tons of dogshit I have to pick up 'fore you think I'm ready?"

James ignored him.

Darryl rapped now and then with Terence, the chief security guard, and Terence smoked a cigarette with him one evening and told him that James never taught anything to his assistants. He was sixty-three years old and fearful that one of these years he would be put out to pasture in favor of someone who knew more than he did.

"That sure won't be me," Darryl said. He had a better view now of his own abilities and future. But he liked working outdoors. He could be a gardener, if he could ever get past mowing lawns and shoveling dogshit.

Paco, the guard dog, had to be taken for a two-mile run every afternoon. That became one of Darryl's chores. He and Paco bounded up the beach until Darryl's soles were swollen and his lungs felt on fire. But he liked it when they stopped to rest, liked the tangy salt air and the cold bite of surf on his big bare feet. Day by day the run became easier. He breathed rhythmically.

I could be a sailor on the ocean. Except no one never taught me to swim. Ship go down, be one dead nigger go with it.

He saw freighters on the horizon, sometimes even inshore. They moved placidly on the blue skin of the Atlantic. He liked the way they coasted along: serene, dogged, yet quiet. Must be pretty out there.

Work on boats. Build boats. Do something with these hands. . . . He spread his fingers, gazing down at the wide palms, the thick veined wrists. Where am I gonna learn to do that? Go down to Lauderdale where they got boatyards. Find Pauline somewhere. I could be a daddy for all I know. And I be a good one—don't slap my kid around, don't laugh at him all the time, call him "useless moron" and "retard." Teach him what I know, soon's I can learn it myself.

He told his friend William only part of what was on his mind. He didn't want William to laugh at him. William was working from eight to five as a porter at the Greyhound terminal. "Hey, I go to Lauderdale with you," William said.

"With what, man? You got no money."

"Neither have you. We do a little night work, man."

Darryl scuffed his shoes on the pavement where they stood outside a Kentucky Fried Chicken. "Shorty Bigshoes told me the cops know me too good."

"Coupla scores down by the beach, we outa here. We on our way to Lauderdale."

"I don't want to hurt no one, man."

William shook his head energetically. "Main thing is, take what you want, get away. You in bad luck with a dude who say, 'I ain't giving up nothing,' but you can change his tune easy. Ain't got to kill him, just smack him with the gun or shoot him in the foot. He give it right up. I know this other dude done his score one time, then broke this bottle and stabbed this other dude's eyes out. One thing for sure, he say, that dude don't be looking at no photographs or no lineup down at no poh-lice station."

Darryl said in disgust, "William, you talking like all them dudes over at Raiford who be doing quarters back-to-back. I don't want to smack no one in the head, and I don't want to shoot no one in the foot, and sure as God made chicken I ain't fixing to stab no dude's eyes out."

"What you want to do in Lauderdale after you find this fox Pauline?"

"Get a job. Learn something. Don't know what yet." He knew it would be uncool to say he thought of becoming a ship's carpenter.

"This place where you picking up all that dogshit . . . they wealthy folks, right?"

"Wealthy don't cut it, man." He described the grounds and what he had glimpsed of the interior of the Zide house. "They *rich*."

"You know where things at?"

"What things?"

"Whatever they got we can sell, man."

Darryl mulled that over. He wanted to leave Jacksonville. "I been away. You know a dude buys TVs, paintings, and shit?"

"Course I know a dude, and I got wheels, and I know where we can pick us up a couple nice guns. Use 'em one day, give 'em back the next, cost twenty bucks apiece rent money. You know how to get in there at night? That fancy house?"

Darryl said, "I look around. I think about it, figure it out."

He figured it out. But he didn't want to hurt Paco, he told William. He liked old Paco; they were buddies. Paco had been trained not to take food from anyone he didn't know, but he knew Darryl. William promised to get some pills that would put Paco to sleep for six or seven hours. He'd wake up good as new.

Rich folks were having a fancy party in a few days, Darryl said, and pretty sure they'd do some drinking. Be over by midnight, they'd be happy to hit the pillows, sleep good.

"What they like?" William asked.

"Who?"

"White folks you work for."

"I don't hardly know 'em. She a foxy old bitch—got a boyfriend come over one afternoon when her old man out of town. She feeling him up by the side of the pool. Next thing you know, they jump in the pool together and start fooling around. Pool so big you could get lost in it."

"Shee-eet," William said, puckering his lips, shaking his narrow head.

153

"She come out on the lawn once and ast me how I like my job. I say, 'Jus' fine, ma'am.' She give me this big smile, like she done her good deed that day. Don't see much of her old man, and when he there, they always fights."

"Only them two?"

"I told you, the son live there too. Got his own part of the house. His daddy always yelling at him, and he yell back. He got this squeaky voice. He be a girl at the joint, they rent him out good."

"What these other dogs do? They bark?"

"Myra and Mickey so dumb they lick the hand of the devil."

"You tell me the other day there's a guard?"

"Terence too far away, down by the road."

"We home free, man."

At four o'clock on the day of the musicale, the groundskeeping staff was given two bottles of chilled Moët & Chandon and two trays of smoked salmon and chopped chicken liver canapés. Under a yellow-and-white-striped awning, Darryl drank two glasses of the champagne—a new experience—and left the Zide estate just as the twenty-person catering crew was finishing their setup for the concert and buffet. Usually at 6:00 P.M., or whenever the day's load of dogshit was disposed of, he took the northbound bus on A1A and then transferred to the westbound on Beach Boulevard. But today William was waiting for him outside the gates in his rattly blue Ford pickup.

They drove south through the scrub forest, past the Methodist church and the Florida National Bank. "Where we headed?" Darryl asked.

"Got eight hours to kill, man."

They went to a bar for a while, drank Michelob on tap, became bored. "Better sober up, man," Darryl said. They drove west to a mall with a triple movie theater, took a cold six-pack of Bud in with them and saw *The Buddy Holly Story* and then a revival of *The Guns of Navarone*. That excited them. Each in his secret thoughts pictured himself as Gregory Peck and David Niven going in to destroy the giant German guns. But it was still only midnight. Still time to kill. William bought two more six-packs in a Lil' Champ down in Ponte Vedra, and they pulled the truck into a parking lot at the public beach and sat there in the darkness, popping the cans. An owl hooted in the forest. Darryl climbed out to take a leak against a sign that said: *Warning, no dumping or littering, St. Johns County. Misdemeanor, punishable by fine $500 and/or 60 days in jail or both.* At least two dozen crushed beer cans and six-pack cartons were scattered in the sand at the base of the sign.

With a powerful stream of urine Darryl sank nine or ten of the cans. They were the German battleships and submarines; he was a strafing dive-bomber. He went back to the truck to pop another Bud.

Close to 2:00 A.M., William said, "Hey, man, we gotta go. We late."

They reached the area of the Zide estate, passed the black gates. "Where we gonna park?" William asked.

"Got to be a public beach nearby."

"You don't know where the beach is?"

"Sure I know. You doing fine, you heading right."

But Darryl didn't know where the public beach was. They parked half a mile away, in a clump of sawgrass off the road. The moon had already set, but the night was thick with stars. Darryl stuffed a pair of wire cutters into his belt and a flashlight into the back pocket of his Levi's. William had only been able to find one pistol, a Colt Python. He carried it, and a plastic supermarket bag with some beef liver in it. The liver had already begun to smell, and the plastic was leaking blood. They shouldered their way through the brush, to the dunes, and then onto the beach.

After fifteen minutes of slogging in the darkness through soft sand, they reached the edge of the Zide estate. A disturbed seagull gave a raucous cry.

William said, "What kinda TVs you say they got there?"

"Got a big screen Advent, got a RCA console, and shit, must have two, three more nineteen-inch babies upstairs somewhere."

"Man, how we gonna carry them mothers back to my pickup? I thought we park right nearby."

Darryl laughed wickedly, deep in the center of his chest, and said, "Won't be easy."

"You didn't plan this good."

"Was your idea, man."

"But you the one on the inside."

"We just take the paintings," Darryl said. "Can't weigh too much, and they worth big bucks."

A fog rolled off the ocean as they reached the beach gates, and out of the gloom they could hear Paco growling.

William halted. "He don't bark?"

"He bark, you don't have to worry. He growl, he getting ready to grab your throat and eat you up. You ready with that meat? You got the pills in it?"

Darryl approached the gate. "Hey, old Paco, it's me. . . . Be cool, boy."

The dog lay in the sand near a clump of sawgrass.

William cut through the barbed wire with the clippers. They made their way up through more dunes and then along a boardwalk, past sea grape and a line of palm trees, ebony fronds against a suddenly cloudy sky. Off to the right, through the fog, the swimming pool and the tennis courts began to show their shapes.

"Don't shine that light," Darryl whispered.

"Why I need to," William grumbled, "when this place lit up like it Christmas?"

Orange insect lamps glowed on the lawn and by the pool. Lights burned on all three floors of the house, which was as big as a monastery. Wings and covered walks arrowed out in different directions. Look like a haunted house, Darryl thought. With William following, he moved across the soft springy lawn, along a line of hibiscus, onto the terrace. They cut across the ultraviolet beam of a security lamp. It blazed swirling yellow light across their path.

They heard voices. Both youths crouched against a fluted marble column. Darryl rested his hand on it and felt the chill of the stone right up to his wrist. William started to hiss at him, and Darryl growled, "Shut up, fool. . . . "

The voices rose in pitch. Downstairs in the house, people were arguing.

A man's voice snarled in rage. A light snapped on upstairs. Then the Lhasa apso puppies sprinted down the terrace toward Darryl and William, yipping and baying like baby wolves from hell.

They knew Darryl and liked him, and they had smelled him. Tails wagging furiously, they skidded to a stop on the tiles. They rose on their hind legs, clawing at his jeans.

Wearing a billowing white bathrobe, Connie Zide stepped suddenly out of the house through French doors. She was about thirty feet away from Darryl when he saw her. She looked pale enough to be an apparition from an old black-and-white horror movie. She stopped and stared at him.

Instantly Darryl jumped from his crouch, bellowed like an elephant whose young were threatened, and ran. William followed, crouched low and weaving, emulating the fighting men they had seen in the movie.

The puppies believed it to be a fine game, and they pursued. William kicked a puppy out of his path. He had killed a dog; what did a puppy matter? The puppy, striking against a marble column, screamed.

Darryl pounded across the grass toward the beach gate, tripping another light beam; it blazed in his eyes. He heard a crash behind him, as of pottery smashing, but when he flung his head around to look, he saw through the swirling mist only William's long-jawed face bobbing up and down in stride, the lips, bathed by the harsh light of the tennis court security lamp, drawn back over white teeth in a rictus of terror.

I raised a palm, meaning "Stop right there." Darryl nodded, adjusted himself against the cool wall of the cell. He moved the waist chain, flexed his wrists.

"I have a few questions," I said.

This story of Darryl's hadn't come out at trial. Bits and pieces had been alluded to during Gary Oliver's direct examination of his client, but never in a narrative. For the most part, in that testimony long ago, Darryl's lawyer had allowed him only to deny what the state's witnesses had sworn to. In that, if only in that, I thought, Oliver had been wise.

If Darryl had told this tale then, I would have ripped it apart. Because who were you going to believe—the wife and son of the murdered man, or the hulking black youth who had admitted being there on the terrace and confessed the murder to a homicide detective and later in the presence of a cellmate? If someone else had shot Solomon Zide that night, how could Connie and Neil have made such a firm identification of Darryl Morgan? Darryl was not someone you forgot, not someone you easily mistook for another man.

The two guards appeared at the door to the cell. "Sir?"

I turned.

"It's time for this prisoner to exercise."

I asked if it wasn't possible for him to do that later, when I had gone.

"No, sir. It's supervised, and we have a schedule. This is his time."

I turned to Darryl, slumped against the wall of the cell. "Can you skip your exercise today?"

"We get up on that roof twice a week," Darryl said. "For one hour, man. I skip it today, I got to wait three days. It rains three days from now, they tell you, 'Bad luck.' Which you think I rather do—rap with you or breathe fresh air and stretch my bones? You don't believe me, nohow. You think I kill that old Jew. You was a scumbag then and you a scumbag now. Day you say to me, 'Maybe I'm wrong, maybe you telling the truth,' then we talk. If I don't be dead by then. That happen, I talk to you from the grave, motherfucker." He chuckled. "Yeah. I haunt you. See how you like it."

17

WE HAD JUST finished our weekly partners' meeting, and Harvey Royal asked to see me alone. He slid an antacid pill into his mouth, leaned back in the leather chair and said, "Ted, just what the hell are you doing up in Jacksonville?"

"I explained it last week, Harvey."

His bony head with its thin mat of gray hair bobbed up and down. "There's an entire organization in Tallahassee devoted to these appeals, isn't that so?"

"Yes, it's called CCR."

"An organization far more suited to do this important work than our little provincial firm here in Sarasota, wouldn't you say?"

"Not necessarily. Darryl Morgan's run out his string. He's been on death row for twelve years. He's due to be executed four weeks from today."

Harvey knew, of course, that the winning of the case hinged on the testimony of the firm's new client, Jerry Lee Elroy. But what I didn't dare tell him, or anyone, was that all hope of Elroy's testifying would go down the drain if I turned the case over to CCR. The CCR lawyers wouldn't lie to Elroy and pretend that his recantation was part of the deal to get out of the drug charge. And if they didn't lie, Elroy would never testify. If he didn't testify, Darryl Morgan died.

Harvey peered at me over his reading glasses. "I am not unsympathetic to what you're feeling," he said. "But at the meeting today we discussed several cases in which you're involved. Barry and Marian have filled in while you were up north trying to play the role of good samaritan. I have to ask you, Ted—are you ready to pull your load once again with this law firm?"

"I've got to put out the biggest fire," I said. "And I don't need to apologize for that. If this firm won't accept my doing that, then I don't want to be a lawyer here. I'm flying up north again in a few days. I'm going to take over the defense of Darryl Morgan."

The phone beeped in the conference room. Harvey picked it up and told his secretary to hold all his calls. He turned back to me.

"Let me be cruel, Ted. From everything I've learned, you stand no chance of winning. You'll be drawing out this man Morgan's agony for an undetermined period of time before he receives the coup de grace. Can you justify that?"

Darryl Morgan had said, *Every day go round, it come in my mind, "When all this be over with?" Feeding me to Mama, they ending my hurt. . . .*

"There's an old saw," Harvey said, relentless now, "that applies to all capital cases: the better the lawyer, the longer it takes."

"I know." He was too smart for me to pretend to optimism. "I'm trying to convince the system that it made a mistake. And that's like trying to piss up a rope."

"Those aren't the words I'd have chosen, but they may be apt. Ted, we need your billing and your visibility here, not in Jacksonville."

"Then we have a conflict."

"How do you propose to resolve it?"

"By doing what I have to do," I said.

And I kept working. I drove up to Bradenton with Barry Wellmet for a meeting with the firm's cocounsel on the milk price-fixing case. I met with local ZiDevco executives to discuss the witness list for the real estate lawsuit. The next day I interviewed five subcontractors whom we were considering as witnesses and began to prepare a detailed report on what they might say under both direct and cross-examination at trial. I edited Barry Wellmet's brief in the S & L case, then met with Harvey Royal and worked on another revision. *Work.* The word sounded so clean, so meaty. So righteous.

So fucking absurd too, because all I was doing was battling and scheming so that people could wring money out of other people or keep others from wringing it out of them, while at the same time piling up my hourly fee. What did that have to do with something so rare as justice?

I hurried downtown one afternoon to meet Elroy at Buddy Capra's office on the fourth floor of the Criminal Justice Building. While Charlie Waldorf sat on the couch in the corner of the room, filing his fingernails with an emery board that looked as if he'd used it since he got out of law school, Capra laid out the state's deal. It hinged on Elroy testifying against his suppliers, Alfonso Ramos and Marty Palomino.

Elroy asked where this would take place.

"The grand jury is sitting now in Miami. They'd like to indict this spring. Your presence is requested," Capra said, making a graceful gesture with his hand. "After you testify, we'll drop the cocaine possession charge here. You'll walk away, Mr. Elroy, under the federal witness protection program."

"To where?"

"I'm told your preference is California."

"But not up in the mountains," Elroy snarled, "with a fucking grizzly bear for company."

"California has held a lottery," Capra said, "and you've been won by the city of San Diego. They're thrilled that you're coming."

"What do I live on?"

Finished with his nails, Charlie Waldorf said gruffly, "The government will provide you with a new identity and pay six months rent on an apartment. We give you walking-around money for ninety days. After that, Mr. Elroy, you're on your own."

We rode down in the elevator, which piped a Vivaldi flute concerto to its passengers. You got to listen to it on the telephone too, when you were put on hold. That was Charlie Waldorf's style; he was a Sarasotan.

Elroy and I walked west on Main Street in the afternoon heat. "You couldn't have made a better deal," I said. "And there's the other part of it, which I hope you didn't forget."

"What was that exactly, Counselor?"

"Jacksonville. Testifying about that fake confession in the Morgan case. You recall?"

Elroy scratched the stubble on his chin. "Capra and the other guy didn't mention that."

I said firmly, "They didn't mention it because they didn't need to. But you have to do it. We start with a sworn affidavit. Now. Up at my office."

"Can we get it done by seven? I got some nice pussy waiting at the motel." He smiled, showing the gap in his teeth. I didn't know whether he believed me completely; but he wasn't about to test me, not with San Diego in the offing instead of Raiford.

When I surfaced from the pool that evening, Toba frowned and said, "I have to tell you, trivial as it may seem to you, a man came to the door today and served me with a notice of deposition."

I shook water out of my ears. "For what?"

"That crazy woman who called me in the middle of the night from her bed with the *thing* sitting on her tits. The wolf spider."

"Some lawyer actually wants to take your deposition about a bug?"

"Yes!"

I broke into laughter, then saw the look on my wife's face and said, "Well, words fail me. And that's probably for the best."

After dinner I asked Alan into the den. I sat in an easy chair, wearing a black sweatshirt, old jeans, running shoes without socks —my I'm-mature-but-still-young look. Alan sprawled on one of the sofas, allowing himself room to twist his legs, stretch his muscular arms, and generally keep in constant wriggly motion. A thatch of black hair curled out of the throat of his sport shirt. Adjusting my horn-rimmed glasses, I felt old.

"I won't smoke, Dad, I know it annoys you and I know all about the smell in the air-conditioning ducts. But can I keep an unlit cigarette in my hand?"

I leaned across from the easy chair and placed a hand on his shoulder. I was trying to communicate my concern, which was deep. "Alan, you talked to your mother about suicide. I have to take that seriously, and it frightens me. I'm sure it's hard to elaborate, but can you tell me what depresses you? I need to know."

"I just feel useless. You said it—I'm a fuck-up. A failure."

I'd never called him a failure, and the worst I might have said on other occasions was: "I think you're fucking up your life." But I didn't contradict. This wasn't court.

"I'd like you to go into therapy. Do you have anything against that idea?"

"No," Alan said.

There was more, and I had to get through it; I remembered El-ston's mother in Newtown. "You can stay in the drug program or not," I said to Alan. "That's up to you. But I won't house a practic-ing addict. If I find out that you're doing any drugs at all, it'll be like a fucking hurricane around here without a hurricane warning. You can get down on your knees and beg and weep—I'll still kick your druggie ass right out of here."

Toba hunted down a recommended therapist in the high school system who took patients on a private basis for sixty-five dollars an hour. Her name was Dorothy Buford.

We went one evening to see her in her office at home; it was full of porcelain and ivory knickknacks and reminded me of my grand-mother's house. Dorothy Buford was in her early thirties. "I don't really want to talk to you two," she said. "I'd rather not have pre-conceived ideas. Have your son call me."

"We'd like to tell you what the problem is," I said.

"What you'll tell me, Mr. Jaffe, will be what *your* problem is. Tell that to your own therapist. Have your son call me. He'll tell me what *his* problem is."

In the car on the way home, I laughed. "You know, she's abso-lutely right. I like her."

"I don't," Toba said. "I thought that was smartass."

Sitting on the edge of the bed, unhooking her bra under her blouse and not looking at me, she said, "Ted, I wish you weren't going on Monday."

"I'll try to be back for the weekend."

"Have you got a girlfriend up there in Jacksonville?"

"For God's sake, no." Nevertheless, a picture of Muriel Suarez flashed into my mind unbidden. Well, what the hell. You can't be indicted for your fantasies, which is why they're so much fun.

"If you do," Toba said, "I'll break your knees with a sledgeham-mer and cut off an inch of your cock while you're asleep in bed."

"You and the Mafia could do business," I said.

"Just how long are you going to keep this up? This running off to Jacksonville?"

"As long as I need to, Toba."

"Our son told us he was suicidal. What if *he* dies," she said, "while you're off trying to save some murderer's lousy life?"

I didn't know how to answer that. There was no answer. She walked across the room, and I realized she had brought up a bottle of Chablis, which now stood on her makeup table. She poured some of the wine into a bell-shaped glass.

"It helps me to sleep."

"Let's fool around," I said brightly. "That used to do the job pretty well."

"After I've had some wine. Don't worry, I'll brush my teeth."

"You've had enough this evening to knock out a moose."

She glared at me. "Up yours, Ted. You do what you want to do. I'll do the same, thank you very much."

Sheets of rain swept down on Longboat Key. On such nights Toba and I—often without knowing it—took comfort from the boats that bobbed at anchor in the bay, blinking friendly signal lights into our bedroom, our sanctuary. Tonight the waves crashed on the beach with force enough so that the land seemed to shudder.

We didn't fool around. A few minutes after turning out her light, Toba began to snore lightly. Funny, I thought. At the beginning of a marriage, if you were told your wife was going to become a serious snorer, you might think twice about taking the marriage vows. But once it became a fait accompli, it was endearing. It was proof of her vulnerability. It was *her*. You almost loved her for it—not in spite of it but for it. And of course it gave you the freedom to practice your own antisocial habits, which in turn were *you*.

Soon I drifted toward sleep.

That time in the Gambrel murder, the snitch I had was for real. . . .

I sat up in bed in the semidarkness. Thunder growled from far away in the night, like a vicious dog giving fair warning. I was awake, focused on a name, hearing it in the reedy voice of Carmen Tanagra.

I remembered that name from twelve years ago. And the man himself: Victor Gambrel. In his early forties, reminding everyone of Basil Rathbone playing Sherlock Holmes. A former Jacksonville cop, and at that time chief of security for Zide Industries. Nickerson's police report had quoted Gambrel as stating that following Neil Zide's telephone call, he'd arrived at the estate a scant few minutes before the Homicide team. Gambrel had seen nothing. I had interviewed him at the state attorney's office then but decided not to use him as a witness.

FINAL ARGUMENT

Five years ago, according to the casual recounting by Kenny Buckram and Carmen Tanagra, Gambrel had been murdered. But why? And by whom? Organized crime, they thought. And what else had Tanagra said? I hunted in the debris of memory and found it:

. . . Bongiorno had real good friends in Tallahassee. Money and political clout is what it came down to. The snitch changed his story, and I got shitcanned. . . .

Even a blind dog finds a bone once in a while. I had a new vision, one that staggered me. I slipped out of bed and padded swiftly down the stairs to the living room. The sky crackled with lightning. From my briefcase I fished out a legal pad and a ballpoint pen.

Hours later, when I slept again, I dreamed of a woman who resembled Connie Zide. She held a knife to the throat of Darryl Morgan.

18

CONNIE ZIDE ONCE said to me, "Solly can't stand me. He thinks I'm deceitful, neurotic, self-centered, lazy, vain, demanding, greedy—if you wonder why I have that list down pat, like the Boy Scout oath in reverse, it's because I hear it all the time when he's around. If he can't control someone who's close to him, he has to destroy them. Lately he's mixing alcohol with cocaine, so he gets really nasty. A couple of weeks ago, when we were arguing about Neil, he hit me."

We were having a drink that evening at Ruffino's, which was halfway between the courthouse and home. Connie would call, tell me she was in the neighborhood. Just a drink, she would say. She just wanted to hold my hand, look into my eyes. And usually she meant it.

My fists clenched in anger—how *dare* the son of a bitch hit her? —and I knew I had to be careful. Her life with Solly and Neil wasn't my business. But it's someone you care for, another of my voices said. You can't pick and choose what will move you.

"You remember when I didn't see you for a whole week? That was because I had a big bruise here." Connie touched her cheek. I saw a faint blue tinge that I'd noticed before but ignored out of politeness; you didn't comment on the changes in the face of a woman of forty-seven.

"Neil saw it next morning," she went on. "I told him the truth, and he went straight to the office. Apparently he called Solly a few names that even Solly had never heard."

If it was true, it was the best thing I'd ever heard about the light of her life.

"Since Neil turned thirteen," Connie said, "and started writing poetry and taking photographs of flowers, Solly's let him know that he thinks he's a sissy. And when Neil began to realize how his father abused me, he began to despise him."

"They work together, don't they?"

"Neil's a glorified gofer on starvation wages. Why do you think he lives at home?"

That made no sense to me. There was a missing element to the equation.

"Why don't you stake Neil to a place of his own?"

"He won't take anything from me. He thinks I should leave Solly, and if I did, he says, I'd need every penny I've managed to save. I signed a prenuptial agreement—Solly was way ahead of his time when it came to protecting his financial ass. I can live well, but only if I'm in residence."

"You said that Neil was a good photographer."

"He's brilliant. But he lacks the confidence. It will come—with time."

I concluded that Connie had less than a realistic view of her son. I had met Neil at one of the charity luncheons. The young man had Connie's full-mouthed sensuality, but there was a cold, appraising look in his eyes that may have been a paternal legacy. He was soft around the jawline, nervous, and arrogant. He knew what I did for a living, and at one point in our conversation said, "Well, what good luck to meet you. If I ever get caught speeding or holding a bag of coke, I'll give you a ring."

"There better be a five-carat diamond in it," I said, "or you'll get short shrift."

"Oh? Are you bribable? What a revelation! My mother always talks of you as the essence of probity."

"Piss off, Neil," I said quietly.

Neil was wearing Gucci shoes and an Ermenegildo Zegna black silk sport jacket draped over his shoulders like a bullfighter's cape. When he left, he kissed his mother hard on the lips, then waved to a few people and cried out, "Ciao!" He drove off in a Lamborghini with silver wheels.

. . .

During the seven months of what I came to think of as my period of primal madness, I took care not to fall in love with Connie Zide. Like an immune system that battles against infection, my defenses battled against emotional involvement. I knew it could lead to the destruction of my marriage, my family, maybe even my career. And I didn't want that.

Struck by the thunderbolt, I'd veered off course, sailed into treacherous waters. The harmony of my life was close to foundering on the reefs of sexual infatuation. You could see them sticking up from the frothy surf.

But the winds pushed you there, anyway.

A while later, in that summer of my ongoing derangement, for part of a weekend Connie and I managed a second time to get to the cabin on Cumberland Island. On Friday afternoon we were sailing a borrowed cutter offshore in the Atlantic chop, when Connie turned to me in the cockpit and said, "Neil knows about us."

She saw the expression of dismay on my face.

"It's all right. He approves. Thinks you're the strong, silent type. 'A Jewish Gary Cooper on the short side' is how he put it."

I checked the luff of the mainsail, then looked at her darkly. "How did he find out?"

"We have no secrets."

"Connie, you told him? That was dumb."

I could imagine all kinds of scenarios. Neil—if he despised his father as much as Connie told me he did—in a fit of pique, or out of revenge, laying it out at the dining room table for the paterfamilias. Then Solly, in a rage, confronting me in the state attorney's office in the Duval County Courthouse. Or at home in front of a wide-eyed Toba.

I needed this like a hole in the head. Get Toba angry, and the hole might be more truth than cliché.

Connie sat cross-legged on the teak deck, clasping her hands around her ankles. She seemed oblivious to these possibilities. "Neil said to me the other day, 'Con, is it possible that about nine months before I was born, you might have been messing around in California? With Gregory Peck, for example? Even Chuck Heston? If you say yes, even if it's Right-Wing Chuckie, I'm going to jump for joy.' I almost hated to disappoint him. I had to tell him again that in those years I was young and hopeful and faithful."

I brought the cutter through the wind, hauling in the sheets and turning the bow into the Atlantic chop. My thoughts may have shown on my face. Connie rose in one motion and moved midships to deal with the jib. She was sure-handed with all the lines that had to be bent around cleats. She glistened from head to toe in the afternoon sun, and a freshening breeze brought the scent of coconut oil straight to my nostrils. The job done, she came aft, stalking toward me across the deck. A lovely predator. She never lacked a plan and the confidence to implement it.

In the cockpit she untied the top of her bikini. The nipples stiffened in the breeze. Her African nipples, she called them, because of the way they protruded. She stroked them with her fingertips, which always roused me. Sometimes in motel rooms she insisted that I watch her masturbate; she would start with her nipples and work her way down. She had narrow hands and long fingers, and on occasion she used a vibrator. In St. Augustine Beach one rainy Monday, just before my birthday, she hired a call girl named Sue Ann. In the late afternoon, the heartbreakingly pretty nineteen-year-old knocked on the door of our motel room. Sue Ann was from Cairo, Georgia; she had just graduated high school. At first I couldn't believe what was going on.

"A birthday present," Connie said.

"I don't want it," I replied, which was an outright lie.

"I do," she said.

After a while I began to laugh, and I joined them. Thus she purposefully gave to me the gift that she had always denied her husband.

As she settled to her knees now on a cushion in the cockpit of the cutter, her sea-green eyes were weighted with purpose. She worked my bathing trunks down to my ankles while I leaned on the tiller to keep us on a close reach toward open ocean. The sails fluttered a little, like my heartbeat. Leaning forward over me, Connie clasped her hands together in the pose of an eager child.

"Pretend it's Sue Ann," she whispered.

As intended, at least for the moment, her indiscretion with Neil seemed beside the point.

That evening in the pine cabin by the inlet, she sautéed chicken fillets in a mushroom sauce with Spanish sherry—a dish she claimed had no name or recipe, like everything she cooked. She cooked quickly, singing Broadway show tunes while she worked. The endive salad and a vinaigrette dressing seemed to appear in a matter of a few minutes. I poured the wine. This domesticity, as opposed to the domesticity of my home, had a forbidden flavor to it: a spice. As if she read my mind, she said to me, "Ted, when I met you, you told me you were a happily married man."

"Yes, I remember saying that."

"You lied to me, darling."

"No, I didn't."

"How about trying 'maybe'?"

"I didn't lie."

"All right, you lied to yourself. Is that better?"

We began to eat but had little to say. I praised the sauce and the salad, then cleared the table and brewed coffee.

Connie said, "Ted, tomorrow will be six months since that Cuban kid mugged me in the parking lot."

"I know."

"Ted, I love you."

Those three words had not been used between us before.

"I told Neil that I loved you," she said. "If I could, I would tell the world."

"Connie . . ." I tried to speak her name with unalloyed tenderness, but something else clawed its way into my tone. My eyes may also have betrayed me; I sensed that a spark of warning flickered in them for half a second. She saw it. But she was a stubborn woman—much that she had achieved in life had been against the prevailing winds.

She said, "Let's go for a walk on the beach."

The ocean gleamed a silvery gray, and fish left faint trails of phosphorescence. The water was warm enough for us to swim in starlight. A wild turkey gobbled in the bush, and we could hear distant music over the speaker at the pavilion near the mainland town of St. Marys. When I stood naked in the shallows, the slow waves slapped my thighs. I looked up at the stars. The universe was indifferent—even to lovers—but nonetheless conveyed majesty.

Connie floated toward me and then stood by my side, gazing up. We were silent.

In bed later that night, she whispered, "Let's just sleep. Cuddle me."

She liked me to hold her from behind. One hand cupping the weight of a breast, I bent my knees into the crook of her knees. The globes of her buttocks pressed in rare innocence against my thighs.

We both drifted toward sleep, like seaweed swept out by a tide. It was when I did this that I felt most unfaithful to my wife.

At dawn we made love. The act lasted long enough for the sky to change from a flawed black to a pale blue that had the clarity of glass.

I had told her that I wanted to be back in Jacksonville by nightfall so that I could spend Sunday with my children. There was a boat to catch to St. Marys. In the early light, over coffee, Connie said, "If you were happily married, what exists between us wouldn't be possible. There are things you're not facing, Ted."

I wasn't sure what those things were. They ran deep in the blood. I'd never claimed to be perfect. I didn't *want* to be perfect.

"I would leave Solly to be with you."

"Connie, even if—" But I bit that off short. We had never gone in this direction before. It was a collision course.

I set myself to be honest. "Connie, I don't want you to leave Solly for me. I will not leave Toba and my children for you. Maybe you and I have come to the end of our good luck. Maybe it's time to quit."

"How cruel you are," she said softly. "If you were honest, you'd give in to your wanting me."

Why was she doing this to herself? Each word pushed me farther away from her.

"Connie, my wife and family are engraved in my life."

Her hair was matted with the sweat of the morning. Her eyes flared. "And you want to end this now? You're telling me it's over with us? You can't truly love her!" she burst out. "Not if you make love to me the way you do! My darling, don't you see that? Ted, you're lying!"

She equated passion with love. But I didn't.

"I don't want to hurt you," I said.

"You're so goddamned cold!"

I was miserable. I hated what was happening. But I knew what I felt and what I had to do.

She let out a wail that made me shudder. "Is it because I'm older than you?"

"Connie, you're not hearing me!"

"There isn't anything I won't do for you! I swear I'll make you happy!"

This wasn't the woman who'd called me "honey" when we first

met. I got out of bed quickly. With my back to her, I stood at the window, looking at the blurred ocean, where a pair of ibis were in flight. She came up behind me on the planked floor and put her arms around me. Her hands were flat on my heart. For a moment I had the terrible vision that with her knifelike nails she wanted to tear it from my chest, rip it out as if I were some captive sacrifice to an Aztec god.

But that was not to be. I was not the one to be sacrificed.

A few mornings later, at dawn, I made love to Toba. Before the event began I closed my eyes and fantasized that there was another woman in the bed with us. She was Sue Ann, and she nestled behind my wife's pale buttocks, stroking the suntanned muscles that flanked her spine. A milky light—dawn gliding across the curve of the Atlantic to awaken the southeastern shore of the United States—crept into the bedroom. Motes of dust danced in the air. Sue Ann's hazel eyes smiled at me through the skein of Toba's black hair. Toba twisted her body around so that I could take Sue Ann's place and enter her from behind and grip her breasts. "Squeeze them," she said. This happened in fact. In fantasy I imagined that my cock slid between the oiled copper globes of our guest, who became Connie. A form of adultery, I thought, but with consent. Therefore without pain or risk. Without guilt too? On the edges of old maps were legends that read: Beyond here are dragons. I now believed that I had journeyed in my life to the edge of the map. Not in fantasy. In reality.

Toba's lips were flushed. "Fuck her, darling. I won't be angry."

Hearing those words in my imagination, I soared to orgasm in a sequence of turbulent spasms. The force of it startled Toba, and her body arched to join me. The veins of her neck swelled with blood. She cried, "*Ted!*" and we clutched each other as if we were on a jet plane plunging toward jagged peaks.

Connie telephoned and told me that Solly had gone to Hong Kong on business. He would be away a week. "Please come over."

"That would be unwise," I said. I couldn't believe those words had formed in my mind and left my lips.

"Ted, for Christ's sake, haven't we gone beyond that?"

I didn't *want* to go beyond that. But I suddenly sensed that if I didn't agree, I would be postponing the inevitable. And the inevitable had to be faced. If not, the dragons would eat me alive.

FINAL ARGUMENT

At five-thirty, when I had cleared my desk at the office and told
Toba that I'd be in conference at the federal courthouse until late
that evening, I drove south and then east past the Mayo Clinic of
Jacksonville until I arrived at the iron gates of the Zide estate. I had
been there only once before. The gray-uniformed security guards
were just changing shifts. The older of the two men—his brass name-
plate said Terence O'Rourke—leaned out from the guardhouse. I
realized he was a former cop; they had that special way of looking
through your eyes and beyond, making you feel they glimpsed every
mistake you'd made and had a sense for ones you were capable of
making in your corrupt future.

He looked up from his clipboard. "May I please see some ID, sir?"

Stupid of me. If I'd thought about it, I could have instructed Connie in advance, as I'd done the last time: "I don't want him to know
my name, so just tell him it'll be a man driving a gray '75 Honda."

From my pigskin wallet I extracted my driver's license, cupping
my hand over the wallet shield that identified me as an assistant state
attorney. Terence scanned the license. "Thank you, Mr. Jaffe."

The electronic gate rolled open.

I parked near the front door, with its etched-glass panes and flank-
ing stone lions. Two Lhasa apso puppies were playing on the gravel.
Connie was waiting for me by a hedge of scarlet hibiscus. She wore
white from neck to toe. With the puppies following, she led me on a
paved walk and under some awnings to the swimming pool. "Let's
jump in and make love," she said, running a hand up and down the
front of my suit trousers.

"Connie . . ." I indicated a large black workman half hidden by a
grove of banana trees. He headed toward the lawn, pushing a wheel-
barrow.

"I pay their salaries," Connie said.

"Which means they won't gossip?"

"Ted, you worry so much."

"Yes, lately I do."

There was something portentous in my tone, and it quieted her.
Infidelity was a cruel sport.

We began to stroll around the pool.

Hollow-hearted, stomach fluttering, the words tasting sour even
before they left my mouth, I told Connie it was over. I was no longer
at ease in the affair. I feared for my marriage. I told Connie that I
would always cherish her as someone who had given me something

of inestimable value. I suppose men the world over have made that speech for centuries, and plenty of women too. It has that hollow ring of truth. My voice seemed to come from an inner distance.

Connie, even in white, looked a little pale under the buffeting.

"There's an alternative," she said. "You could leave your wife."

"I've been trying to tell you, that was never in the cards."

"You've always told me your wife was a sensible woman—"

"That's how I see her."

"—and of course your wife has your best interests at heart."

"I'm sure she does."

"Then if there was someone else in your life, why would your wife want to hang on to you? Isn't that demeaning to your wife?"

The repetitions of the words "your wife" were like darts inserted to pierce the skin. Make the beast *feel*. Make it stand its ground and fight rather than run away.

It's a cruel sport.

"Connie, *this* is demeaning. Let's cut it out."

Shadows slanted across the pool from the banana grove and the royal palms. In her broad garden hat and sundress with its scooped neck and flaring skirt, Connie looked like a haughty and angry princess. I must have looked like a tired man in a wrinkled business suit who'd been sitting in crowded courtrooms since eight o'clock that morning.

"I have to go," I said.

"Your wife is expecting you?"

I had seen Connie as a beautiful older woman having an exciting affair, and not her first. I had seen myself as a man in thrall. Then, from what seemed one moment to the next, the net had lifted. The roles had reversed.

I couldn't tell her that. She wanted to hear words of love and regret deeper than the earth. But I didn't have such feelings. I felt sad —and I felt on the edge of an extraordinary freedom. I will soar. Then maybe crash. But survive.

"Goodbye, Connie."

She clutched at me, and a harsh sound rose from her throat. She let go of me, turned, and toppled into the pool.

A white parachute floated on the disturbed surface of the water. There were bubbles, circles of foam. The parachute slowly sank. A woman's body was attached to it. I heard sucking sounds, like soapy water swirling down an emptying bathtub drain. The bottoms of my trousers were drenched.

Rescue was definitely required, and I jumped in after her, the soles of my shoes striking soundlessly on the bottom of the pool. I was in about four feet of chlorinated water. I heard many dogs barking in excitement.

Connie was heaved out of the pool by her erstwhile hero—water-logged, breathing like a half-drowned cat, but alive. A uniformed brown-skinned Latino maid about four and a half feet tall emerged from the house and waddled over, smiling cautiously. The expression on her face said: The Señora sure is a fun-lovin' lady.

I explained that Mrs. Zide had fainted and fallen in the pool. The maid looked disbelieving, but she stayed calm.

"What is your name?" I asked.

"Martina." Later, during the murder investigation, I learned that she was from the city of León on the high central plateau of Mexico.

Martina and I hauled Connie through the French doors into the living room and onto a twelve-foot-long sofa next to a marble back-gammon table. The white Berber carpet and the sofa were quickly soaked.

Looking up, Connie said quietly, "I'm all right."

Martina asked me if she should call a doctor.

"No. Take Mrs. Zide up to her bedroom. Bring bath towels and dry clothes. Is there other help around?"

"I will call the security guard," Martina said.

"Yes. Do that. Goodbye, Connie."

She coughed and spat water on the carpet. Then I backed out of the room, the house, and her life.

When I got home twenty minutes later, Toba stared and asked, "What the hell happened to you?"

"If I told you, you wouldn't believe me."

"Try me—you never know."

"I had to go to someone's house to talk to a witness in an extortion case. The woman fell backward into her pool. I jumped in and fished her out."

"That sounds like something that could happen," Toba said. "Why shouldn't I believe it? Any man who would eat a whole banana would jump into a pool to save a woman who fell in backward."

At the University of Florida, about the time we began the affair that would lead to marriage, I had discovered that Toba liked to eat parts of fruits and rarely the whole. In her fridge I often found half an apple, or a pear with a slice missing. When I reminded her of that, she always looked annoyed. Finally, one evening in my bachelor apartment, she said to me, "Can I have a third of one of your bananas?"

I rolled my eyes and looked at her as if she were demented.

"Stop that," Toba said. "Do I make fun of you when you eat a whole one?"

Then I knew that I loved her and could make a life with her. She wasn't simply being cute or lovable; in the season of my youthful ardor she was exhibiting to me a sophisticated sense of justice, promising balance and good cheer. Ten years later, in the kitchen of our home, holding her in my arms against my wet and wrinkled suit, free from whatever spell Connie Zide had woven around my heart, I vowed in my heart to be truly good to her.

I called Connie the next day to ask if she was all right. She thanked me for rescuing her from the pool. "I must have had too much sun."

There was an awkward pause.

"Well, goodbye again," I said.

"Yes. Goodbye again."

I couldn't believe it was that simple.

A week later, one morning when I was in court, Solly Zide called and left a message with my secretary. I returned the call later that afternoon. I imagined only the worst.

Zide said, "I was going to ask you to lunch to discuss this, but now I'm tied up for the rest of this week and the next. Anyway, it's not me you need to talk to." He told me about the opening at Royal, Kelly, Green & Wellmet in Sarasota.

"If I were in your shoes," he said flatly, "I would take advantage of the opportunity. Nothing better will ever happen to you."

Was that a threat? Did he mean that *worse* things could happen? Did he mean leave Jacksonville or else? I wondered but never asked. Would never have the chance to ask, either. The next time I saw Solly Zide was two months later at the benefit black-tie musicale. The host, in his white dinner jacket, was surrounded by guests. We spoke a few words as we passed each other by the side of the pool, just a few feet from the spot where Connie had toppled in. Zide was crisp in his manner but not unfriendly. He had a lot on his mind, I assumed. There was no way of knowing what that was, although one day I was destined to find out. Seven hours later he was dead.

19

BELDON SHUFFLED ACROSS his office to dump some wilting red roses into the only wastebasket that had space. Then he turned on me and said, "You've got some fucking nerve, Jaffe."

He had never called me by my last name before. There was a warning there.

Next to his diplomas and police department citations for bravery hung the motto of the Justice Department, proclaiming that the government wins its point whenever justice is done. I waved at it and said, "If you believe that, you won't stand in the way of my representing Darryl Morgan."

"You can't defend someone you once prosecuted!" Beldon snarled. "You *know* that!"

"No, I don't. The State of Florida is an entity. How can it claim confidentiality and privilege?"

"Cops told you everything they knew. Prosecution witnesses talked freely to you. You can't switch sides, damn it!"

"Elroy didn't tell me then that he was lying. He told me twelve years later."

"He's your client now, isn't he?"

"But now he's agreed to testify that he lied about hearing Morgan confess." I didn't dare admit that I'd conned him into it by calling it part of the deal offered down in Sarasota. "Beldon, I told you the last time we discussed this—it was not a fair trial."

"And I disagreed. And what have you told me to make me change my mind? Shit!"

"I think Floyd Nickerson perjured himself too."

"Since when does 'think' count in a court of law?"

"I may have a witness."

"Who?"

"I can't tell you."

"Oh? Now we're being cute? Is this all a bluff? You bored down there in Sarasota?"

"Let me ask you a question," I said. "Why are you scared of this thing being retried?"

"Wait a minute!" Beldon yelped. "Who's talking about a *retrial* here? We're talking about a motion, that's all. Justice might—just *might*—require a hearing before the judge, if only to save this dude from the electric chair and put him in Raiford for life. But if it ever comes to a whole new trial, there is no way that justice requires your presence. CCR can do it. Two or three people over at Kenny's office are capable of doing it. You are emphatically not the right man to do it. This is for a guy who likes to get off by himself and sniff dust and stick his nose in books."

"Will you let me handle a motion and an appeal hearing?"

"You think I'm gonna say yes because we're friends?"

"The bayou dog who gave me my first job took me to lunch at The Jury Room and said, 'You're not supposed to win any friends at this kind of job.' "

"So what will you do if I say no? Pout and cry?"

I locked eyes with him. "I'll fight you all the way. I'll yell 'cover-up.' The Florida Bar will probably bring charges and try to kick me out. I'll fight them too. There'll be a big fuss in the newspapers and on TV. In the end I probably won't be able to do the case, but someone else will, and you'll look like an Uncle Tom who wanted to fry a black kid who shot a rich white entrepreneur. You'll look like shit. Come next election, you may lose."

Beldon guffawed. "You think I care if I look like shit and lose an election?"

"Probably not."

"Well, you're wrong," he said. He pointed a finger at me, and somehow his mood had changed. "See, you don't know everything, do you?"

He was silent for a few moments, thinking things over. "Okay," he said, "I'll tell you. Horace Fleming's finally retiring next January, when he's eighty, and the governor wants to give me Horace's court. Still be three and a half years left on the term."

"Judge Ruth?"

"How about that? You know, I never knew I wanted it until Horace hinted and Tallahassee made me the offer. I guess I'm tired of working a ten-hour day, and I'm tired of the phone ringing on Sundays and just about every time I sit down to dinner with Laurette. I asked Horace, 'What do you do on weekends?' He said, 'Fish, go squirrel hunting, sleep a lot, mess with my great-grandkids.' Sure sounded good to me."

"And who wants a judge starting out with shit on his face?" I asked.

"Right. So I'll make a deal with you. You handle your motion for Morgan, assuming you're rich enough and crazy enough to waste all that time. The state attorney's office won't object. If you win— meaning if Horace grants a new trial for Morgan—you step down. Let another lawyer do it. Get the hell back to Sarasota where you belong. For your sake, believe me, not mine. Is that a deal?"

One step at a time. I shook the offered hand and said, "Toba and my law partners will certainly be grateful to you, Judge."

But at the door, Beldon put his other hand on my arm. I felt a slight trembling in the fingers.

"You're not telling me everything," he said.

"About what?" He couldn't mean my con job on Elroy; he had no way of even guessing at that.

"Your private life's your own business, asshole. I'm talking about this case. Something else is happening here. Else why would you be so anxious to do it?"

I didn't answer.

"It's not evidence," Beldon said. "You'd tell me if you had more evidence, wouldn't you?"

"No, it's not evidence," I said.

"But it's a little more than a hunch."

"A little more."

"You gonna keep me guessing like a fool?"

"I have to, Beldon. We're not partners in this one." That was as diplomatic a way as I could phrase it.

I was smiling woodenly and trying to get out, but he still touched my arm. There was a message in the touch, and it held me.

"I know something too," he said. He let the words hang there, like drifting tendrils of smoke.

Wary, I said, "About the case?"

"It's not exculpatory. I wouldn't fuck with you like that."

I believed him.

He said, "It's just something that makes me feel you shouldn't be involved, not even at this level. So what I'm saying is, be judicious. Do what you think you have to do, but don't go too far."

"What is it you know?"

Beldon's eyes were quiet with warning. "You can figure it out."

He knew about Connie. It had to be that.

"Think about it," he said. "Don't be stubborn and get yourself hurt." He lifted his fingers from my arm. It was as if a weight had been withdrawn.

Beldon had said, " . . . if Horace grants a new trial." That was because Judge Bill Eglin had retired from the bench and gone into politics. He was a state senator now, bringing all his enlightenment to bear on moral and legal issues in Tallahassee. Horace Fleming had inherited all his cases. The mandatory age for a Florida judge to retire was seventy. Horace Fleming was the only one I knew who had fought against that and won.

I asked Kenny Buckram if his presence on the bench was good or bad for me.

"It would have been good five years ago," Kenny said. "Maybe even two or three. But Horace is an old man. He forgets things, he makes mistakes. It's a weird courtroom. I'll tell you one thing, though—it's always interesting."

The next day I drove the four hours to Tallahassee and spoke to the people at CCR. They were happy to have me take the case; they were always hunting for pro bono volunteers. I worked most of that evening in my room at the Ramada Inn and the next morning returned to Jacksonville.

Kenny made available to me the facilities of the public defender's office, including its law library, newspaper files, and computerized case histories.

"I need a desk and a telephone extension."

181

"We'll also provide a chair and a sharp pencil. You can use our Xerox machine. Fifteen cents a page to everyone else. For rich lawyers like you, a dollar."

That evening I took Muriel Suarez to dinner at my favorite seafood joint at the beach. Muriel dropped into a red plastic booth and said, "I'm bushed, so would you do me a favor? I'd like a vodka gibson with a twist straight up—that's to revive me—and maybe some wine with dinner, but otherwise, you do the ordering. I eat everything that swims except jellyfish."

After the drinks came, I ordered fresh conch and mesquite-grilled snapper. "What else do you do besides try cases?" I asked. "Is there a man in your life? You're too good-looking and intelligent a woman not to be involved. That's not a pass—just a question and a statement of fact by an interested party."

"I didn't take it as a pass," Muriel said. "No, hell, there's no man in my life. No woman, either. Who has time?"

I'd given her a chance and she'd jumped at it, but told me in a way that I could either grasp or evade. My choice. It also explained the catch in her voice that time she'd talked about Carmen Tanagra.

She raised her glass to me. "And what's happening with you these days, Mr. Hotshot Civil Lawyer from Sarasota?"

I had told her about the deal with Beldon, so I began to talk about my family. I quickly realized that this monologue was going to depress me even more than the gabble about the appeal. I had left home at a bad time. I should be there for Alan, and I hadn't wanted to face what was happening with Toba's drinking.

"Your son's grown," Muriel said. "He has to solve his problems by himself."

"Wait until you have children of your own."

I laughed at my words, remembering how often my mother had said them to me.

"I have a kid brother, David, who's an addict," Muriel said. "Did a lot of cocaine in his time."

"And what happened to him?"

"My father, before he died, persuaded David to go into a drug program. At first they didn't want to take him. They said you can't be persuaded by anybody to quit. You have to admit you're an addict, grovel, ask to be helped. But they finally let him in."

"And?"

"He stayed there seventeen months. It was in New York State, up in the Catskill Mountains. He told us it was like a prison. He knew, because he'd been in one. He managed to call me once—he said, 'Muriel, I'll die if I stay here.' He'd been there about five months then. I said, 'No, you won't.' That was a night, believe me, I didn't sleep. But when he got out a year later, he was cured."

"He wasn't an addict anymore?"

"You're always an addict. No, David's attitude was: 'I spent seventeen fucking months in that god-awful miserable freezing hole in the back of beyond, and if I go back to drugs now, then it was a total waste of time. That I won't accept.' He's a stubborn kid."

"What does he do now?"

"He's a cab dispatcher in West Palm Beach. They don't turn you into lawyers and doctors. They just teach you to survive."

We went back to Muriel's house after dinner. I hadn't planned anything, and I don't think she had, either. Since that calm kiss at the door when she'd fed me the lamb, nothing had happened between us, and I hadn't even fantasized about anything happening. But women have a way of letting you know what they want. It's in a look, an arch of the shoulders.

She took my hand at the door and drew me inside. And we kissed. She smelled of salt and charcoal and red snapper.

"I thought you liked women."

"Well, that's true," she murmured. "But I don't dislike men, except guys like Jaime Ortiz, who made me jerk him off in the front seat of his Mustang back in high school."

"I don't know," I said honestly. "I'd hate like hell to convert you."

"Not much chance," she admitted.

"If it's a challenge, I'd rather stay friends."

It was as simple as that. We had a drink together, and then I went home. And in time I was more grateful than I could have predicted.

The Zide Building was out in the suburbs, behind the Regency Plaza Mall.

Neil Zide ran the empire now and was the principal stockholder. He let more competent specialists and Ivy League M.B.A.'s handle the various arms of the Zide Industries octopuslike conglomerate. But ZiDevco was his. At that enlightened time in the seventies when county commissioners all over Florida set what was called the bulkhead line, theoretically protecting the wetlands and the coastal inlets, they also reserved unto themselves the right to change that line. Not long after his father's murder, Neil Zide on behalf of ZiDevco bought options on half the mud flats in seven coastal counties. He petitioned the county commissioners for a change in the bulkhead lines, and at the same time requested permission to buy the bay bottom from the State Internal Improvement Fund.

In North Florida the county commissioners met to consider the propositions. Cash changed hands in manila envelopes, shoe boxes, suitcases. Stock options were courier-delivered to corporations in Liechtenstein, Grand Cayman, Mexico. Permissions were granted. Neil Zide, who had been rich, became very rich. He let his hair grow down to his shoulders in unruly brown waves, shaved only when the whim took him, went to work in Levi's and Italian silk shirts with flowing d'Artagnan sleeves, and wore only scuffed basketball shoes with the laces loose and dragging on the parquet floor of his office. He looked like a young Hollywood producer. He was thirty-four years old now. He no longer needed to live in a wing of his mother's house but had built his own white Moorish fantasy down at Ponte Vedra and bought a flat on the Île de la Cité in Paris, an office-apartment on Central Park South in Manhattan, and a vacation home on Red Mountain in Aspen. Photographs of all these places, signed on the mats by Neil, lined the black walls of his office.

"You ski?" he asked me.

"Used to. Now I don't have the time."

"I often hear that excuse. I've got two guest cottages on that Red Mountain property. You're certainly welcome to come out. Great skiing, greater partying, and the greatest air. Now that they've got the gondola, you get to the top of Ajax in fifteen minutes."

"Sounds like progress of a sort. How's your mother?"

"Very well indeed. Thank you for asking. I'm pleased it's not a subject that has to be avoided."

I leaned back in my chair and decided to do just that: avoid it. Neil was not the right person to discuss it with, if there was such a thing as a right person.

Neil was quick. He could hear what was being said by silence. Sitting behind his glass desk, he glanced at his watch to make sure I realized his time was valuable and limited. He looked up. In the past twelve years the eyes had gained no warmth.

"You're here in your capacity as an attorney, I take it. How can I help you?"

Beyond his desk, through a half-open doorway, I could see a bed with a golden bedspread, gold-colored sheets, and a gold headboard.

"I'm representing Darryl Morgan," I said, "to see if I can win a new trial for him."

The flesh was still slack around Neil Zide's jawline. It seemed to go even slacker.

"Did I hear you correctly?"

"I think so."

He studied me carefully, waiting. He was a bright man despite his foppishness. He knew when to shut up.

So I fired from the hip. "There are a few questions I'd like to ask you about Floyd Nickerson and Victor Gambrel."

Neil exhaled quietly, then inhaled deeply. But the blue eyes told me nothing. He said nothing. I waited, and so did he.

He ended the uncomfortable silence. "Go ahead."

"I'll refresh your memory. Nickerson was with Homicide. He investigated your father's death."

"I remember that."

"And until some five or six years ago Victor Gambrel was head of security for Zide Industries, the main Jacksonville office. Right?"

"That's correct."

"Nickerson took a confession from Darryl Morgan—do you recall?"

"Yes, I do."

"And Nickerson also dug up a cellmate who heard Darryl Morgan confess. Does that ring a bell?"

"I remember that too," Neil said. He shook his head as if to free it from a web; the long brown locks waved and settled back into place.

"Jerry Lee Elroy."

"I beg your pardon?"

"That was the name of the cellmate."

"If you say so."

"I'm not cross-examining you, Neil." But in fact that's exactly what I'd been doing.

"You still haven't told me how I can help you."

"You can satisfy my curiosity about a few things. I'd like to find out what happened to Floyd Nickerson. If you know."

"I'm not sure." Neil scratched his nose, then his unshaven cheeks, and blinked a few times.

"Well, I didn't mean I didn't know where he was," I said easily. "He's over at Orange Meadow Estates in Gainesville. What I meant to say was, I wondered how he got there."

Neil shrugged.

"He's chief of security there," I said.

"Oh?"

"It's a ZiDevco project."

"That's correct."

"Do you recall how Nickerson got that job?"

"I'd have to ask someone to check the personnel records," Neil said, starting to work on his stubble again. "Would you like me to do that?"

"You don't recall giving him the job?"

"Ted"—smiling now, trying to appear friendly, worldly—"that's a long time ago. How could I remember that? One forgets a great many things. In fact, prefers to forget them."

"And there's no way that your mother could have given him the job? Or recommended him?"

"Of course not. Con had nothing to do with the business. Didn't then, doesn't now."

"Then I *would* like to see those personnel records. That would be kind of you. If you could arrange to have a copy sent down to me, care of Kenny Buckram at the public defender's office here in Jacksonville?"

"I'll try." Neil scratched a note on a desk calendar. "If they still exist, that is. We may not keep records like that for as long as nine years."

I was silent for a moment. "And Gambrel. What do you remember about Victor Gambrel?"

"Victor . . . well, I remember him, of course. He came to an unfortunate end."

"He was shot and killed in his car at the parking lot of the Regency Square Mall in July of 1985. Yes, you could definitely call that an unfortunate end."

"A real whodunit," Neil said. "Might turn up one of these days on that TV show—what is it? *Unsolved Mysteries.*"

"Maybe," I said. "I heard recently, and this is between you and me, that the Bongiorno people were behind it. But I'm still not sure why Gambrel would be a target for organized crime. Doesn't make sense. Does it to you?"

Neil seemed to consider that for a few beats. "Are you implying that the investigation is ongoing?"

"I wasn't implying anything at all. I didn't know Gambrel. You did, though. You knew him well."

"I wouldn't say that."

"The night that Darryl Morgan broke into your house and you panicked him so that he shot your father, you called the police and then you called Gambrel. That's what you told me, and that's what you told the court. Didn't you testify to that when I had you as my witness on the stand?"

Neil cleared his throat. "Ted, the truth is, I don't remember what I said on the witness stand about Victor Gambrel. That was an exceedingly traumatic time for me—not that I was in mourning for my father, as you well know, but simply that I was deeply concerned about my mother. She had no one else to lean on but me. I called Victor that ghastly night because he was chief of security at what was then my father's company, and it seemed appropriate to do so."

"What's your theory as to why he was murdered?"

"What I heard was . . . gambling debts. Large sums. To the wrong people."

"Such as Bongiorno?"

"Might well have been. May I ask you a question now?"

"Fire away, Neil."

"Why are you getting involved again, and on the other side? Why are you handling Morgan's case?"

"Everyone asks me that," I said, shaking my head sorrowfully. "My wife, my law partners, my friends, the state attorney . . . and I don't seem to be able to give a very satisfactory answer. I was never happy with what Judge Eglin did—that's one reason. So I suppose it's because I don't think Darryl Morgan received a fair trial and therefore doesn't deserve to die. I've learned something that's fact-specific along those lines. Nothing earth-shaking, but it's of some significance."

"Which is?"

I sighed and said, "It's confidential. Something a client told me. Sorry."

Neil looked at me steadily. "Is that all?"

"Yes, that's all—and thanks, Neil. My best regards to Connie, and I appreciate your taking all this time."

We shook hands; then, at the door, I turned. The night before, I'd watched a few minutes of *Columbo,* with Peter Falk. I said, "Oh, by the way, there's just one more thing I wanted to ask you . . . may I? It's okay?"

"Yes, it's okay," Neil said.

"I asked you how Floyd Nickerson got that job over at Orange Meadow, and you said you didn't know. Isn't that right?"

"Yes, that's right."

"*You* didn't give him the job."

"That's correct."

"Because you had no reason to."

"Correct. I had no reason."

"And a few minutes ago when I asked you for the personnel records, which you very kindly said you'd provide, you said you didn't know if your office kept those kinds of records for as long as nine years. You did say that, didn't you?"

"I believe I did."

"Well . . . I don't believe I told you when it was that Floyd Nickerson quit JSO and went to work for ZiDevco. So how did you know it was nine years ago?"

Neil stared at me calmly. But he was upset. I could see that. You can't control certain bodily functions, and the body never lies.

"I was guessing," he said.

"You just picked a number, like out of a hat?"

"Yes."

"And hit it right on the button. That's remarkable. Can I ask you one more question?"

"If you must."

I opened my mouth, then shut it. "I can't believe this. I forgot what I was going to say. It's just *gone.* Does that ever happen to you?"

"Sometimes," Neil said quietly.

"If I remember," I said, "I'll be in touch."

I went to see a judge again and secured a court order. Then I bought two decks of playing cards and put them in my briefcase. The next day I drove down to Raiford. After I'd presented the court order to Raymond Wright, I waited an hour and a half on a bench in a hallway until I was escorted to the cell on death row. Today Darryl wore a Mickey Mouse T-shirt and bluejeans. He was shackled and chained, and the two correctional officers sat outside again, at the proper distance.

"I'm going to file a petition for a retrial," I told him. "There may be a hearing. Will you cooperate with me?"

Darryl asked, "Where there gonna be a hearing?"

"Jacksonville. With a different judge than before."

"Do I get to go?"

"You have to go."

"What do I have to do?"

"Just keep quiet, listen to what goes on, don't try to strangle anybody. If it's overnight, you stay in the Duval County Jail."

"You say *may* be this hearing. You don't say going to be."

"That's right. No promises."

"You promise, I don't believe you nohow. What you want me to do for you?"

"I want you first of all to agree that I represent you. That I'm your lawyer, your attorney, your counselor."

"Lot of weird things happen in my life," Darryl said. "This got to be near the top of the list."

I gave him the two decks of playing cards.

Just after 5:00 P.M., from the deep shadow of the gun tower at the main gate, I stepped forward onto the gravel. Two men were waiting for me. I noticed how their boots shone in the slanting sunlight. They wore the pale blue-gray uniforms of Bradford County deputy sheriffs.

"Edward M. Jaffe, sir?"

"That's my name."

"We have a warrant for your arrest for aggravated battery."

"You have *what*?"

But I had heard him clearly, and he really didn't have to repeat it.

"Look"—I tried to smile and be nonchalant—"I'm a lawyer, and I'm here to see a prisoner, a client. My home is down in Sarasota. I'm a former chief assistant state attorney from Jacksonville. I'll be glad to show you all the ID I've got and give you some numbers to call."

They read me my *Miranda* rights and asked me to place my hands behind my back in order to be handcuffed.

It would be tempting, but inaccurate, to say that I didn't believe this was happening to me. I understood the process all too well—I had been part of it many times. But I'd never played this role. I may have been in shock.

One of the deputies took my briefcase from me. Cold steel cuffs clicked into place on my wrists. I was stuffed into the caged back seat of a patrol car.

It didn't take me long to figure it out. Clive Crocker had filed a complaining affidavit that I had hit him and broken his nose. He had sworn that he hadn't provoked me, and undoubtedly he produced witnesses who filed other affidavits, including a doctor's statement.

But I recalled that the law stated that unless the injury was permanent or disfiguring, it was simple battery, a mere first-degree misdemeanor. Normally I would have been asked to stop off at the sheriff's office and tell my side of it. That would not have been a custodial interrogation.

"It's simple battery, not aggravated battery," I explained to the deputy sheriffs who were driving me to jail. "I'm a lawyer. I know what I'm talking about."

"You can explain it to Judge Burchell."

We reached the sheriff's office in the courthouse on the main street of Starke. A red ribbon stretched across the courthouse door, proclaiming that WE ARE NEIGHBORS DRUG-FREE AND PROUD. But we didn't stop there for me to see the judge; we stopped so that one of the deputies could pick up his coffee thermos, which he'd left on a chair. From the courthouse we drove to the Bradford County Jail, a two-story red-brick building on a side street.

"I can't get out of this car," I said.

"Why not?"

"My knees are stuck."

"Try," the deputy with the thermos said.

It was important to stay calm. I asked if I could make a telephone call to a lawyer.

"After you've been booked," the deputy said.

Was that how the law worked? That didn't seem fair. There was a great deal, I realized, that lawyers didn't know.

In a small room downstairs I was booked, fingerprinted, and photographed. I was stripped of my belt, wristwatch, shoelaces, wallet, and keys. A deputy placed me in a green-walled cell upstairs with a single frosted window that opened on a hallway. The deputy left. I heard the downstairs door clang. I heard a car engine start.

FINAL ARGUMENT

I had seen no one in the other cells. They weren't doing a very good business here. Starke, understandably, wasn't the crime capital of North Florida.

My cell had a toilet with no seat, two double-decker metal bunks, a fire extinguisher, and a black telephone on the wall. But when I picked up the telephone and put the receiver to my ear, there was no dial tone.

"This phone doesn't work!" I yelled.

But there was nobody there to hear me.

"Goddammit!" I yelled. "What's going on? Who's here? Isn't there *anybody* here?"

It began to grow dark. I shook the bars, hoping to rattle them. But they were solid. They made no sound.

20

AT SIX-THIRTY in the evening another prisoner arrived, to be placed in the cell with me. With him came spaghetti and meatballs and two slices of white bread on a yellow plastic tray, as well as a deputy I'd not seen before.

"This phone's broken," I said, as calmly as I could. "I haven't made a phone call yet to a lawyer. Can I do that from another cell?"

"Phone doesn't work after five o'clock," the deputy said.

"None of them?"

"You want Coke or Sprite?"

"None of these telephones work after five o'clock in the afternoon? Is that what you're telling me? I don't believe it! How is that possible?"

"Mister," he said, "you don't look like a kid. You should know that anything is possible."

I knew it. Had always known it. And there was no sense whatever in my asking him why.

"When do they start working again?"

"Seven o'clock in the A.M."

"And when does the judge start work? When does he hold bail hearings at the courthouse?"

"Nine, ten o'clock. Depends."

I didn't dare ask on what.

The deputy escaped, and I sank down on the cot like a man who's been told he has a fatal disease. My fellow prisoner—a drunken white man in his thirties, unshaven and red-eyed—lit a cigarette from a new pack of Kents. He saw me staring at him.

"You want one?" he asked.

"Yes. Please."

By eleven o'clock the following morning, when I went before Judge Burchell, I had smoked five of my cellmate's Kents plus two Marlboro Lights that I'd managed to bum from the morning deputy. The mattress I'd been given was two inches thick and positioned above a steel slab. I slept in my underwear and socks, and at one point, in the blackest part of the night, had to piss. But my sodden cellmate had been there before me, on unsteady feet, and had missed the bowl, so that after a moment or two I realized the uncomfortable feeling in my feet combined with the rising odor indicated that I stood in a pool of his stale urine. My cotton socks were quickly wet through. I had to yank them off, toss them in a far corner, and sleep without them. The cold reached up from the steel bed into my ankles and the bones of my feet and the joints of my toes, chilling them as if they rested on the polar icecap. I slept a total of two hours.

At a few minutes past seven I called collect to Kenny Buckram's office. He wasn't in his office yet, and the machine couldn't accept the charges. Then I called his home at Neptune Beach. Same problem. Kenny was probably out fucking. How dare a lawyer do that when his client needs him? By ten o'clock, when I'd been brought to the Bradford County Courthouse—unshaven, gritty-eyed, smelly, sockless, without having brushed my teeth—I was still alone.

"Your Honor," I said, looking up, as I had looked up many times before on behalf of other men (and, in the dark past, on behalf of the State of Florida), "I probably don't look it, but I'm an attorney, a former chief assistant state attorney in the Fourth Circuit. It hadn't been my plan to do this, but now I'm here representing myself. And so I'd like to begin by asking the court, why is this an aggravated battery charge? It's my understanding that unless the injury is permanent or disfiguring, it's simple battery. A misdemeanor, not a felony. I believe that Mr. Crocker has accused me of striking him and breaking his nose. For the sake of argument, even if that's true . . ."

I tailed off, because Judge Burchell, the county court judge, a cherubic southern man of perhaps sixty, no doubt as dangerous as a coral snake, was shaking his head at me as if I were a backward child.

"Mr. Jaffe," he said, "I think you've got a fool for a client. You're accused of striking a correctional officer at the prison. He's the equivalent of a police officer. That's *always* a felony. I can see by the look on your face that you've forgotten that. But do you remember now?"

"You're absolutely right, Judge. I forgot about that little detail."

Judge Burchell surprised me. Or took pity on me as a man in a rumpled suit who didn't quite know his trade—a has-been, or maybe a never-was. The bond for a second-degree felony was $2,500. I had a hundred and twenty dollars in my wallet, no checkbook, and I was well aware that the State of Florida didn't accept American Express or even Visa.

But the judge said he'd be willing to let me go ROR—released on my own recognizance—and the young assistant state attorney, who had to live with Judge Burchell in this courtroom five days a week, announced that he had no objection. The judge set a court date for the future.

"You'll show up, Mr. Jaffe?"

"Your Honor, I wouldn't miss it for the world."

"Goodbye, sir."

"Goodbye, Judge."

I took a taxi back to the prison parking lot to pick up my rental car. My hands were trembling, and the inside of my mouth felt as if I'd eaten glue. I knew that if I weren't a lawyer, and if I hadn't been wearing a suit, and if I had been black, I'd be back on that steel cot in the Bradford County Jail.

On the way to Jacksonville I stopped at a gas station and bought a pack of Benson & Hedges Lights.

The next morning I stared into the bathroom mirror of my hotel room. Whatever suntan I had was gone. My eyelids were red, and my eyes itched from the smoke that curled from the ashtray.

Just one after each meal, I told myself, to make life a little easier, to calm these rapidly aging nerves. Then just one after each cup of coffee during the day, or each vodka tonic in the evening. Maybe half a pack. And soon an extra one with coffee in the morning, because those were the best ones of the day, before your tongue turned numb and your throat to dry fire. And then the hell with it, I'll smoke whenever I goddam *want* to smoke!

I understand you better than before, Alan. I'm an addict too.

· · ·

Behind his desk at the public defender's office, Brian Hoad said to me, "There are procedural land mines, so watch out. Your main issue is the false testimony on the confession, but you've got to include every other possible argument you can think of. Because if Judge Fleming denies relief and you go up the ladder to the Florida Supreme Court, or file a writ of habeas with the feds in the Eleventh Circuit, you can't introduce any new issues."

"But what if something new comes up?"

"Tough titty. The bastards want to be able to read it all in the record—that way, they can say no before you even get to Tallahassee."

Without thinking, I reached for the pack of cigarettes in my shirt pocket and lit one with a plastic throwaway lighter. I scanned the desk for an ashtray, but there was none.

Hoad was looking at me curiously, rather as if I had produced a turd from my pocket. "I don't remember you smoking."

"My life's changing," I said.

I didn't go down to Raiford again on that trip. Darryl had nothing to do with this. He was the man meant to die, not the advocate for his survival.

I tried to communicate with Toba now and then. How goes it? How's Alan? They were fine, she told me, with unremitting hostility. At the offices of Royal, Kelly, Wellmet, Jaffe & Miller I felt the same coolness. I was working on my cases but not putting in a lot of billing time. Harvey Royal wanted me in Washington. Barry Wellmet wanted me in Bradenton—the chief client among the milk distributors was counting on my experience. I told Barry, "The case will settle out."

"But they want you there, and they'll pay for it."

"Buy them lollipops," I said.

I was not a man who dreamed much—or rather, not a man who easily remembered his dreams. But at night now the dreams were thick with fear and often breathless with flight from unknown pursuers. Or I was being led somewhere by uniformed men who meant to do me harm. Worse, I felt I was always on the edge of the dream where a human head flamed heavenward, but in sleep I managed to keep that at bay. I was warding off evil. The head that threatened to burn was not Darryl Morgan's or even Eric Sweeting's. Some part of me feared that the head was my son's.

. . .

I submitted my motion to Judge Horace Fleming on the last day of March. Morgan's execution at Raiford was scheduled for Thursday, April 11.

On Monday, April 8, at noon, Fleming called me into chambers at the Duval County Courthouse. A little one-on-one game without the adversary lawyer on the scene—ex parte, it's called, and it's definitely not done by ninety-nine percent of decent judges. But old hands in the game never play by the rules we learned in law school, and sometimes not even by the canons.

The judge slouched in his chair, silver hair brushed back, glasses perched on the edge of his red, veined nose. He spoke slowly, and he looked as if he should have been in a rocking chair on a country porch, sipping a mint julep. In chambers he had taken off his robes and suit jacket and sat there with thumbs hooked in leather suspenders. Potted plants stood in all corners of the room, and greenery climbed all over the judge's diplomas. On the walls and on his desk were photographs of his grandchildren and great-grandchildren and various hunting dogs. There were some of the judge, younger, kneeling on various docks and pridefully inspecting large game fish. Also on the desk, surrounded by other piles of papers, were my petitions for a stay of execution and relief in *Florida v. Morgan*. The pages of the petitions, removed from their black spring binder, had been fanned out in the center of the desk like a giant deck of cards.

"I read it," Judge Fleming said.

"Good, Your Honor. I'm glad."

"Well?"

I waited a moment. "What do you mean, Judge?"

"This is all you got to say?" Judge Fleming asked. He ran a gnarled arthritic finger along the spread-out pile of papers, as if he were saying: Pick a card.

"Yes," I said, agonizing, wondering what I had left out.

"You were the prosecutor in this case, am I right about that, Mr. Jaffe?"

"Yes, Judge."

"I talked to Mr. Ruth about this. Now, I have an opinion about Mr. Ruth that I don't mind communicating to anybody. If Mr. Ruth says a squirrel can pull a freight train from here to Tallahassee, you can hitch up that rodent and clear the tracks. You understand what I'm saying?"

"Yes, Judge, and I agree. You can trust Mr. Ruth."

"And he says you're a good lawyer. But that can't influence my decision. You realize that?"

"Yes, I do, Judge."

"You want some coffee?"

"That would be welcome."

"Over there in the corner. Bring some for me too. My mug is the one with my political philosophy written on it. You'll find it. You like it strong?"

"Political philosophy?"

The judge smiled. "No, Mr. Jaffe. Coffee."

"Strong will do just fine, sir."

"I brew it so you can use it to stop leaks in your radiator. How's your radiator?"

I found the judge's mug. On its side was inscribed: THE GREAT ADVANTAGE OF A DEMOCRACY IS THAT ONLY ONE OF THESE PEOPLE CAN GET ELECTED.

While I was pouring the coffee, Judge Fleming said, "I'm going to say yes to your petition. Grant you a ninety-day stay. Least I can do if they're getting ready to fry a man. You bring your witness in here, and Mr. Morgan, and anyone else you want, on June 24—that's a Monday, according to my calendar—nine o'clock in the morning. I'll be there too, if nothing breaks or comes untwisted. Suit you?"

"Yes, Judge," I said, my heart pounding with joy.

"I take it with cream and sugar."

"How much sugar?"

"Half of one of those blue packets says Equal."

I brought the two mugs of coffee over to the desk. "Judge, forgive me for reminding you," I said carefully, "but they're due to pull the switch on Mr. Morgan in three days. You'll have to file an order at the state attorney's office, in writing, that you've granted a stay of execution. And probably the same thing in Tallahassee at the attorney general's office."

"Mr. Jaffe, this is Monday, isn't it?" Judge Fleming asked.

"Yes, sir, it is."

"I did all that on Friday afternoon, my boy," the judge said, sounding a little annoyed.

21

TOBA AND I WAITED for the summer rains. The Gulf skies were swollen with heat, the air was gummy and breathless. Despite the sprinkler system, the crabgrass lawn grew brown at the tips. In the evenings I smelled swamplike odors wafting up from the Everglades. Orchids flowered on the trunk of the jacaranda tree outside our bedroom window, but at midday the waters of Sarasota Bay looked warm enough to boil.

In the artificial coolness of my office, I gazed out the tinted window. Afternoon thunderheads massed on the horizon and the sun hung overhead like a ball of smoldering sulfur. It was difficult to face what I knew, what I believed, what I suspected. One step at a time was what I kept telling myself—first the hearing before Fleming, for the important thing was to make sure that Darryl lived.

I picked up the telephone and buzzed through to the firm's senior partner.

"Harvey, I've gone over our proposed submission in the S and L case. Do you and Marian have a few minutes?"

In his office, I set forth my objections. The FDIC had amended their complaint against the defendant, a man named Novak. He was now due to reply. Harvey and Marian had drafted that reply.

"The government's allegations are inaccurate," I said. "Things sinister are being made out of nothing, and we should say so. The Reagan administration encouraged S and Ls to expand into commercial loans. Novak exercised due diligence—there was no private jet, no political graft. He became richer, but so did most of Reagan's business pals. How dare these federal sons of bitches accuse him of chicanery?"

"Calm down, Ted," Harvey said.

With that remark, Harvey only annoyed me further. "Our client," I said, "is being slandered by employees of his government, and his taxes pay their salaries. We're kissing ass when we should be kicking ass."

If I want to stay in this law firm, I realized, I'd have to be more tactful. But it wouldn't come easily.

A crust of gray ice seemed to spread across Harvey's face. "I take it you intend to rewrite this denial."

"No, that's Marian's job. I'll argue the case in court if it comes to that, but if the job's done properly, it shouldn't. I have to fly to Miami day after tomorrow, pick up Jerry Lee Elroy, my witness in *Morgan,* then haul him up to Jacksonville. I may have to chain him to the bed in the hotel. But on Monday we have our day in court."

Thursday morning I began making telephone calls. I was informed that Darryl would be brought by bus to the Duval County Jail early Monday morning and then escorted to Judge Fleming's courtroom at 8:30 A.M. He would be held in the jury room, where I could meet with him.

I asked who was working this case for the state and the clerk gave me the name of an assistant state attorney I didn't know. The clerk also told me that an assistant attorney general would be in attendance, dispatched from Tallahassee.

That was the way the game was played. One of the thrills of being a criminal defense attorney was that you stood alone on a hilltop, battling the full awesome power of the state. You were a heroic figure, a David against Goliath. But Goliath's power was daunting; it could easily trample you. Or your client.

On Saturday evening I flew to Miami. Below, as the little plane gained altitude, were the blue dots of lighted pools and the yellow chains of headlights strung back and forth on arrow-straight highways. Forty minutes later, from the black void of the Everglades, Miami sprang like an immense treasure chest of neon jewels, pulsing to every horizon. I found this urban sprawl remarkably beautiful. A pity you couldn't circle forever, believing such beauty to be the evidence of intelligent human life.

199

I took a taxi to the address I had in Hialeah. Behind the reception desk of the Man O' War Motel hung old black-and-white photographs of famous thoroughbreds. A man looked up from a lounge chair near the cigarette machine: a man in his thirties, with a mustache and a Hawaiian flowered shirt under a seersucker jacket. He was drinking a Coke and reading a paperback crime novel. He might as well have had COP branded on his forehead.

The room I was given was clean and odorless, yet it reeked of lost bets and accepted sorrows. A parade of human beings had trudged in and out for twenty years. It seemed to me that their ghosts were still there.

Elroy had given me his room number, so I dumped my single piece of luggage and walked upstairs, following the outdoor walkway with its green AstroTurf carpeting. I heard footsteps scraping behind me. I turned to face the man in the Hawaiian shirt. He had a leather wallet in his palm, and I caught a flash of a gold shield.

I told him I was Elroy's lawyer from Sarasota and offered my business card and driver's license.

"Okay, Mr. Jaffe. Just checking."

When I knocked and called out his name, Elroy flung open the door to his room. He wore new decor: a silver cross on a chain around his neck, baggy mod trousers, a white golf shirt. In his hand he clutched the usual can of Bud. Above the blare of the TV, he cried, "Hey, Counselor, just lemme catch the end of this show." He was watching an episode of *Star Trek: The Next Generation*. He flopped back down on the bed.

"I love that future shit," he said, when it was over. "How about we eat?"

"Do they let you come and go as you please?"

"They watch, they follow. They're getting paid, what do they care? There's this place down the block, not too bad."

Even in the night air I felt the pavement heating the soles of my shoes. Hialeah Park was nearby, and Lacy's, the restaurant Elroy had chosen, catered to retirees and horse players. It offered bargain dinners, and I ordered meat loaf that was promoted as "the way your mother's tasted." (My mother's meat loaf was usually dry, which is why she drowned it in turkey gravy.) I glanced around at the senior citizens in plaid shirts and bright-colored trousers, with their iron-gray hair and bulging spectacles. One couple at the next table had their arms intertwined in the last gasps of togetherness. He had a sporty gray goatee, she red shriveled lips. They studied the menu as if it were a treasure map. After they ordered food, they studied the racing form with the same devotion.

Elroy said, "The track, that's action, man. That's what I really love."

I looked at Elroy and didn't smile. A chain begins somewhere in the mountains of Colombia. It passes through Alfonso Ramos and Marty Palomino and their ilk in Miami. Then through Elroy and maybe a few others under him; then to the addicts, the assorted hip city folk, the legions of kids. One of those chains had ended with my son dangling on the end of it. And somewhere in San Diego, I thought, there's a kid like Alan who'll soon buy his stash from this piece of human garbage sitting across the dinner table from me.

The waitress passed by. "Hey, sweetie pie, we have a little more gravy here?" Elroy turned back to me, grinning. "We got an unforeseen problem, Counselor."

"How do you mean?"

"Guys downtown at the state attorney's office, they don't want me to leave Miami. Worried something could happen."

"Like what?"

"Palomino, Ramos, they're out on bail. Wouldn't they love to find me." Elroy drew a finger across his throat.

I put down my knife and fork. "I spoke to you in the middle of the week. You said no problem."

"There's this guy Baxter, see? I told him, 'Look, I want to see my sister in Jax. A day or two, family stuff, gimme a break.' Guy says, 'Hey, Jerry Lee, we'll give you a break, we'll keep your ass alive.' So I go, 'I thought it was part of the deal.' He says no, there's no deal for you to testify in Jax."

I had never told Charlie Waldorf in Sarasota or Robert Diaz, the Miami state attorney, that I needed Elroy as a witness in Jacksonville. If there had been a timing problem, I would have spoken up, but Elroy wasn't due to testify in the Miami trial until August. What they didn't know wouldn't hurt them. And I definitely didn't want them to know how I'd lied to Elroy.

"See, they got these plainclothes guys watching me. You met one of them at the motel. Another one's here in Lacy's right now—I just spotted him." Elroy's eyes flicked to the left. I looked, and saw the man sitting by himself about five tables away: about forty, prematurely gray with a crew cut, wearing a pale-blue silk sport jacket. He was eating meat loaf and drinking a 7-Up.

"It ain't gonna work, Counselor," Elroy said.

"It has to work," I said flatly. "That hearing is Monday morning. You don't show up, they'll execute this man."

"Hey, I'm sorry, I really am. But they said I don't have to. Maybe you misled me."

That was what I had feared. I had that same awful feeling in my chest that I'd had when those deputy sheriffs in Bradford County had said to me, "You have the right to remain silent . . . "

"If you had some pussy waiting up in Jacksonville," I said, "you wouldn't give a flying fuck what Baxter or Diaz or anyone told you. Jesus could rise from the dead and beg you, 'Stay,' and you'd still go to Jacksonville."

"Yeah, but that's different, ain't it?"

I gathered up all the cold hard anger that usually stayed trapped beneath the surface of my life as a lawyer, and I drummed my fingertips on the plastic surface of the table. "Elroy, if you don't go up with me tomorrow, Marty Palomino gets your address and room number delivered by Federal Express to his home on Key Biscayne. I'll remind him, when he comes to visit you, to bring his machete. And his ruler."

Elroy laughed nervously.

"Keep laughing, pal." I glared at him.

"I'm your client," Elroy said.

"And I'll be sorry to lose you. I'm making so much money out of you I could retire."

I could put him under subpoena. I had thought of that before. But the Miami state attorney's office might interfere. And even if they didn't, there was no guarantee that Elroy would tell the truth on the witness stand. I would have no leverage.

The table vibrated as the heel of his foot thumped up and down. This cretin believed I'd do it.

"If I leave this town tomorrow without you," I said, "you're a dead man."

"Hey, hey, hey . . . " Elroy's eyes darted left, right, then up.

"Your fate's in your own hands. Not many men can say that."

"Just take it easy, Counselor. Calm down."

Everyone was telling me that lately, I realized. Maybe there was something to it. And maybe not. And even if there was, who gave a shit.

Elroy sighed. "So I do it, what's in it for me?"

That was progress. A whore's a whore; now all we had to do was haggle price.

"I told you I'd pay all your expenses."

"Big deal." He thought about it for a few moments. "Jax, they race in the summer at the Kennel Club, right? McDuff Avenue, off I-10?"

"Greyhounds?"

"The crazy doggies, yeah. You don't need me up there at night, do you?"

I had taken a thousand dollars in crumpled cash from Elroy as a down payment on his legal fee. "When we get up there," I said, "I'll give you back the thousand. That way there's no fee on the drug case. So if you're asked on the witness stand if you were paid to testify, you can say no."

Elroy grinned; he was a natural scammer. "How're we gonna get rid of these guys at the motel?"

I considered that problem for a few minutes while I asked the waitress for the check. When I focused on him again, Elroy was still grinning. But now craft had blended with triumph.

"Got any ideas?" I said.

"You don't want to be involved in this operation, right?"

"I *am* involved."

Elroy explained it to me. He would leave at noon for Hialeah Park. Two cops always tagged along and stayed by his side, but when he went up to the pari-mutuel windows or to take a leak, only one of them came along. The track was a crowded place. "Leave it to me," Elroy said. "Just tell me where you want to meet."

I suggested the main entrance to the track.

"You're not thinking, Counselor. They spot you out there, they put two and two together. The airport's only ten minutes away. Let me stay for five, six races. I can get out by three-thirty. Which airline we flying?"

Back at the motel, I called and booked two seats on USAir.

"Flight 133 takes off at four-thirty. Meet me at the check-in counter at a quarter to four sharp."

"You got it."

203

. . .

Waiting for Elroy the following afternoon in the jabbering chaos of Miami International Airport, I sweated. At ten minutes to four I began to pace. The son of a bitch might stay at the track for just one more race. I walked a few steps, put on my glasses, and checked the departure board again. Another flight left for Jacksonville at 6:00 P.M., another at eight-thirty—if Elroy showed up at all. I cursed and scowled. A woman standing nearby looked at me and took a step backward toward the protection of her husband.

At three minutes past four I felt a tap on my shoulder. When I turned, Elroy stood there in his baggy trousers and white golf shirt and Florida seagull cap. He was still grinning.

"Worried, huh?"

"Who, me?"

"Next race, I had this twelve-to-one shot I *knew* was gonna be in the money. No fucking *way* that horse can go off at twelve to one. You probably don't give a shit, but you want to know how I know? . . . Hey, what's the matter?"

Behind Elroy, from the revolving door, emerged the gray-haired cop who had been sitting near us at Lacy's for dinner the night before. Or at least someone who resembled him. This one wore a brown cardigan and carried a small airline bag. "Don't turn around," I said.

He merged into a group that included a Latin-looking team of laughing athletes wearing purple striped shorts, a pair of pale young priests, and a woman with two crying children. The gray-haired man vanished.

"So what is it?" Elroy asked.

"I thought I saw one of your shadows."

"No way." Elroy searched for a while, then shook his head emphatically. "One of those deputies followed me from the track, he ain't gonna stand around and jack off while we jump on board no airplane. He's gonna come right up to my face and go, 'What you up to, amigo?' "

"I'm worried."

"Believe it, they don't know dick what happened. I'm at the five-dollar betting window, see? I don't even bet. I just walk back to where the cop is waiting. I go, 'Oh, shit, I forgot to tell you, man, I got a tip from a trainer. Twelve to one, number six horse.' The cop can't resist—he runs up to put his five bucks down. And I'm *gone*, man! Faster than a speeding bullet. How about that?"

"Let's go through security," I said, still sweating.

The plane was full. I walked twice through the aisle to the toilet aft to see if anyone looked at all familiar. Elroy was drinking his second double Dewar's on the rocks when we began the descent into Jacksonville International.

"Where we staying, Counselor? Ponte Vedra? Plantation Club? Nice suite for us at the Omni?"

I had planned to make those arrangements the evening before from the Man O' War Motel, then catch a Sunday morning flight, spend part of the day prepping my witness and the rest of it arranging the papers for the hearing and going over my summation. But the need to spirit Elroy out of Miami had changed all that.

From the Avis counter I called the Omni downtown. With its upper-middle-class solidity, it seemed safer than the Marina or a suburban motel.

In the rental car, Elroy cleared his throat. "We were talking about what you might call a rebate? That thousand? You got it handy?"

"Not tonight."

"How about a down payment? I wish I'd been born rich instead of so good-looking, but that ain't the case. I'm down to my last chip."

"I can give you a hundred. What do you need it for?"

"Hey, I told you the doggies race in June. I ast if you need me at night. You said no. Right?"

"You want to go out to the Kennel Club tonight?"

"Man wins the jackpot. He figured it out."

"Elroy, you were just at the horses this afternoon. The same night, you want to go to another track to see the greyhounds?"

"That's a kick, man!" he exclaimed hotly. "Can't do that unless you go straight from Hialeah, fly Miami-Jax, get your ass out to the Kennel Club by eight o'clock! So here's this golden opportunity! Something I can tell my grandchildren, I ever have any."

"Let's get up to the hotel room," I said, "and then we'll see." That's what I would have said to Alan and Cathy years ago. Dad was back again.

Elroy sulked. I took two rooms, hoping that he would settle down on his bed in front of his own TV. I called room service for a club sandwich and coffee. But it was useless. Within a minute, Elroy knocked on my door. "Counselor! You comfortable? Everything cool? I been thinking . . . just give me whatever cash you got, keep a few bucks for yourself. You do your thing, I'll do mine. That okay?"

"Stay here," I said, hoping to sound sage. "It's safer."

"I told you, if that guy at the airport was a cop, we wouldn't be here now."

I thumbed through my wallet. I had two hundred fifty in cash.

"The last race is over by eleven. Few beers, I'll be back by midnight."

He could go anywhere. I'd have to wait up for him, biting my nails. This one night could be longer than a wet week. We wouldn't finish the hearing tomorrow, which meant I could work on the summation tomorrow evening.

"I'll go with you," I said.

"You really want to do that?"

"No, but I'm doing it anyway. And when the last race is over, we're coming back here. Want to eat first?"

"Get a hot dog out there," Elroy said. "Come on, let's move. We already missed the first race."

I had been to the dog track once, with my parents and sister when I was a boy. But on the drive out, I let Elroy explain everything. I let him pay the fifty cents admission for both of us and lead me to the seats in the glassed-in, air-conditioned mezzanine. I let him buy a tip sheet, choose the dogs to bet on, and place the bets.

"You got something on your mind, Counselor?"

"The hearing tomorrow."

"Yeah, but it's not a trial, is it? Nothing serious like that."

"It's serious, all right. That's why you're going to tell your story under oath. We're trying to save Darryl Morgan's life."

"Three minutes to post time . . . "

Held by the track handlers, the dogs in their blankets paraded around the track in front of us. The palm trees swayed in the night breeze. There were twenty minutes between races. Elroy kept checking the odds as they changed on the monitor. His pale eyes were never still. Finally he jumped up from his seat. "I'm putting twenty bucks across the board on the number two dog. This fleabag is always in the money. How much you in for, Counselor?"

I handed him a five-dollar bill and he marched off buoyantly toward the betting desk. A few minutes later the lights dimmed and the mechanical rabbit was released. The dogs flew wildly around the oval.

I stood to stretch and glimpsed through a gap in the crowd the hard, attentive face of a gray-haired, crew-cut man in a brown cardigan. He was twenty feet away and watching me. He was the man who had been in the restaurant the previous night, matching us bite for bite with the meat loaf, and at Miami Airport earlier that evening, crowded in among the soccer players.

He wasn't a cop, I realized.

But he had been following Elroy. Following from the motel to the track and from the track to the airport. Missing USAir 133 out of prudence or because he needed backup. Probably catching the next flight at six o'clock. Checking the rental car companies at Jacksonville International: "I believe my business associates came through here?" *As a matter of fact, sir, one of the gentlemen used our telephone . . . I heard him mention the Omni, sir. . . .*

Easy enough to wait outside the Omni, or in the parking garage where the car was.

But why is he watching *me*, not Elroy? Because, a quiet voice whispered, someone else is with Elroy now.

I stood unmoving except for my heart jackhammering against my ribs. The gray-haired man blocked the aisle I would normally take to get to where Elroy had gone.

Other aisles also led to the betting desk and the payoff windows. I moved toward one of them. I felt as if I were underwater, breast-stroking against a stiff current.

By the time I reached the betting desk a crowd had gathered, and the police were already linking arms and holding people at bay. Jerry Lee Elroy sat upright on the carpet against one of the cashiers' cages. His eyes were sightless. Blood leaked from his side, staining his white golf shirt. A thin blade had been slid between the ribs and into the left ventricle of his heart. A thick black object choked his mouth. It took me a minute or two to figure out what it was. Someone wearing gloves had taken the time to reach around Elroy's dead body, wrench open his jaws, and thrust a sea urchin into his mouth, so that its spines bit deep into the offending tongue.

Talking about how to leave Miami unobserved, Elroy had said to me, *You don't want to be involved in this operation.* And I had replied, *I am involved.* Involved but not committed. You have ham and eggs for breakfast, the chicken that supplies the eggs is involved; the pig that supplies the ham is committed. In this trip to Jacksonville, Elroy had been the pig.

Sirens screamed in the night. I had been careless, and Elroy had lost his life. And I had lost the witness who might save Darryl Morgan.

One of the JSO officers was staring at me.

"I'm that man's lawyer," I said quietly.

The cop shrugged. "Bad luck. What do you want to do?"

Make a miracle. Wake up and find out I'm dreaming.

I followed the patrol cars downtown to the Police Memorial Building, which housed the Jacksonville Sheriff's Office. Once I'd admitted my relationship with the deceased, the Homicide cops had no intention of letting me go. Most of the murders they dealt with were barroom shootings and Saturday night mom-and-pop stabbings. The slaying of Jerry Lee Elroy—"a fucking sea urchin in the guy's mouth!"—was stimulating. You could see that they liked it.

One of the detectives put in a call to Robert Diaz's office in Miami. Then he turned back to me. "You said you took the deceased out of Miami with you?"

"We left together, yes."

"You encouraged him, Mr. Jaffe—is that what you're saying?"

"You're putting words into my mouth. I have to be in court at nine A.M. on a murder hearing. Can I go?"

They wanted me to stop first at the morgue and make a positive ID of my client's body.

Elroy lay on a metal gurney. The sea urchin had been removed from his jaws. His eyes were closed and he looked at peace. Well, why not? When you went that quickly you were literally gone before you knew it.

In the corridor leading from the courtroom to his chambers, Judge Fleming swayed a few feet to his left in order to write some notes, resting his paper on the surface of a file cabinet. The gang of lawyers, the court clerk, and the court reporter shifted with him, like tick parasites following a water buffalo. A few feet away, Darryl Morgan's bulk took up most of the space on a heavy wooden bench; and he was manacled to the armrest. Superman might have picked up the bench and made his escape, but if Darryl had such visions, two gray-uniformed deputy sheriffs with holstered .45s sat on metal folding chairs by the water cooler at the end of the corridor. Outside the court's holding cell stood three other defense attorneys, all jostling for position to talk through the bars to their clients, who were awaiting the eventual attention of the judge.

Judge Fleming surveyed this scene. "Dance floor's getting crowded," he said to me and the representatives of the state. "Care to join me in chambers?"

Once in there, I slumped in a chair. I had managed about two hours of restless sleep.

The clock on the wall in chambers said 9:20. The other lawyers found chairs, and the young assistant attorney general from Tallahassee hoisted himself up on one of the file cabinets. The slender, bespectacled assistant state attorney from Beldon's staff was named John Whatley, and next to him sat Muriel Suarez.

She smiled cordially at me. I went straight over to her and asked what she was doing there.

Whatley had just come out of FSU law school, she explained, so she was there to make sure he didn't make any mistakes.

"But you and I have discussed this case," I said. "I can't remember offhand what I've told you, but whatever it was, it was in confidence."

"Beldon seems to think that's irrelevant."

"He assigned you?"

"What do you think, I volunteered?"

I understood. Tit for tat. I had been privy to the state's thinking twelve years ago. Muriel Suarez had been privy to my thinking just days ago. How could I complain? Beldon, you sly dog.

Judge Fleming unknotted his tie, turned to me, and said, "I think we can save a bunch of time by discussing this informally right here in chambers. Mr. Elroy, your witness, former cellmate of the condemned, is not present in this court. From what I gather, he doesn't have the pulse of a pitchfork. He's a lightning bug in the lemonade bowl. That's what you were trying to tell me outside?"

"Yes, he's shaken hands with eternity," I said. I heard my voice as from a distance, enunciating carefully.

"When exactly did this happen?" the judge asked.

"Last night, at about ten o'clock. Stabbed to death at the Jacksonville Kennel Club."

"As ye sow." The judge turned to Whatley and Muriel Suarez. "What sayeth the State of Florida besides 'amen'?"

Whatley said, "Your Honor, the entire thrust of the petitioner's position is the proposed testimony of Mr. Elroy as to alleged perjury concerning Mr. Morgan's confession in Duval County Jail in 1979. Nothing else in the appellant's petition is new: this court and other courts have heard all the other arguments before. Much as the state regrets Mr. Elroy's passing, our contention is that the deceased witness's affidavit is not sufficient to establish perjury. The state has no way of cross-examining an affidavit in order to test veracity and credibility."

"I understood him," Judge Fleming said, looking at me. "How about you?"

"There are precedents for accepting the sworn affidavit of a dead man," I said. "Considering when this thing happened, I haven't got case law ready yet. But if you give me time, Your Honor, I'll produce it."

That was pure bluff. I had no idea if any existed, although it seemed likely.

"There is far more precedent for rejecting an affidavit without a live and responsive body attached to it," Whatley said.

Judge Fleming nodded. "You're right, Mr. Assistant State Attorney. And you're right too, Mr. Defense Counsel. But you"—he pointed a gnarled and trembling finger at Whatley—"are righter than you are, sir." And he pointed the same frail digit at me.

"Your Honor—" I began.

"No, no, no," the judge said. "I don't want to hear argument. I know the issues. There's a man on death row. Man wants to live, state wants to kill him. Man's lawyer wants to string things out just as long as he can and keep his client sucking air. Judge wants to get on with the business of his court. Can't make everybody happy. You got any other live witnesses, Mr. Jaffe?"

"Not today, Judge. But I hope to find some."

"You pulling my leg?"

"No, sir."

The judge thought for a while.

"I'm going to allow this affidavit, but I'm going to find that this recantation would not have affected the outcome of the trial. What I'm saying is, Mr. Jaffe, you lose. I'm going to deny your petition for relief. I'm not going to hear argument over a witness who can't do more than pass gas and talk to us from the great beyond. Bad luck is what it is. But that's what a lot of things are."

"Judge—"

"Mr. Jaffe"—the judge leaned forward in his chair, his pale eyes watering—"it was nice to meet you again. Give my regards to Caroline."

"Caroline?"

"Isn't she still your wife?"

"No, sir. Never was."

"Must have you mixed up with someone else."

I left Fleming's chambers and walked out into the corridor to tell Darryl Morgan that the state still wanted him to die.

22

My NECK ACHED. My stomach complained, and my joints were sore. I thought I might have eaten a poisoned cheeseburger at the bar on Main Street where I often grabbed a quick lunch. The family doctor diagnosed the symptoms as a new strain of flu, but none of the prescribed medications helped. A blood test showed no evidence of a known ailment.

My fingers grew sluggish when I tried to write briefs or even letters. Ruby came to me one day, distressed, and said, "It's happened, Ted. I can't read your handwriting."

I sweated in air-conditioned rooms and had to keep extra shirts in a closet at the office. My hands shook, and coffee splattered on two new ties and my pin-striped gray suit. I gave up coffee, thinking that it might be the cause of my continuing upset stomach; it was certainly ruining my wardrobe. I cut myself almost every time I shaved. The final indignity was a cyst that appeared on my scrotum. I went to a urologist, who said, "It's not dangerous, and it shouldn't grow bigger. Lead a normal life."

The soles of my feet began to itch. During one Monday morning partners' meeting I had to take off my shoes and socks in order to rip away with my fingernails at the tender flesh. The pink soles turned red and began to bleed.

My partners stared at me. I didn't blame them. This was the time that both they and Toba believed I was going crazy.

I had taken my chief witness to the dog track and allowed him to be murdered by a Miami drug lord. As a result, Darryl Morgan had received another death warrant from the governor of Florida. Unless some other court granted a stay, he would be led from Q block and electrocuted in the death chamber at Raiford on August 2, 1991, at seven o'clock in the morning.

Desperate, I filed papers (including the affidavit of a dead witness) with the state Supreme Court in Tallahassee. I had no hope that the court would grant a retrial, but they might providentially grant the stay pending their decision. Indeed, a week later, the court granted another stay for a period of sixty days. I was invited to appear before them on August 27 for oral argument.

"Go for it, Ted!" I yelled, encouraging myself.

I was in the office. Ruby looked in at me. I shrugged, and she withdrew her head without saying a word.

I called Brian Hoad at the public defender's office in Jacksonville and told him the good news. I was curious as to why the court had scheduled oral argument so early. "I thought they delayed for months, sometimes years. What's the big rush?"

"They usually do delay," Hoad explained, "if we or CCR file the petition. But if there's a private lawyer, that tends to speed things up. They figure your time is valuable, and they know you're doing it pro bono. They don't want to keep you waiting."

"The guy on death row—*he* might want to wait."

"That guy, Ted, is a convicted killer. It costs the state money to feed him powdered eggs and keep his TV operating."

"Would you like to take this case back, Brian?"

"No." But then Hoad hesitated. "Does that mean you want to give it up?"

"If I did, from what you tell me, Darryl Morgan might live longer."

"You didn't answer my question."

"No, I don't want to give it up," I said. "And I will *not* give it up." Until he's free, I thought, or dead.

I instructed Ruby to cancel all my appointments for the next day, flew up to Jacksonville, hired another car, and in the August heat drove down to Raiford to tell Darryl that the Florida Supreme Court was willing to consider sparing his life. I wanted to look in his eyes and strike some spark other than disdain and hatred.

Darryl refused to see me.

Wright had the day off, and I was dealing with another functionary. He said, "There's nothing I can do about it."

"What did Morgan say?"

"That he's busy."

Jerking off or doing card tricks, I thought. Turning up the volume on the country-music station until my temples throbbed, I drove back to Jacksonville. I was the Don Quixote of North Florida. One of my clients had been murdered by the drug cartel because of my carelessness; I had another who was about to be murdered by the state and was too busy to see me. I kept on tilting at appeals courts, believing them to be instruments of justice when actually they were legal windmills.

On the jet back to Sarasota my feet began to itch. While scratching them, I felt a discomforting sensation in my testicles. I went to the toilet. The cyst on my scrotum had increased to the size of a small pea and now had the color of a strawberry. It itched almost as much as the soles of my feet.

Was there a God? Who else could be testing me this way? I considered going to synagogue next Saturday morning. I needed help from another source.

In Sarasota I was called one morning to Charlie Waldorf's office at the Criminal Justice Building. Buddy Capra ushered me into an office layered with cloudlike wreaths of smoke. Waldorf's potted rubber plant had butts stubbed into its gray soil.

From behind his desk, without any preliminaries, Waldorf said, "Robert Diaz in Miami is talking to me about indicting you for tampering with a witness."

"Diaz is full of shit." I dropped into an armchair; then I jumped up and began to pace the room while I talked. "Jerry Lee Elroy wasn't absent from an official proceeding. I didn't hinder him from doing anything legal, and I certainly didn't induce him to withhold testimony. All I did was ask him to testify in another case. And he agreed."

Capra said, "You took him out of Miami, where he was under the protection of the state authority."

"Took him? Fuck, no. He went willingly."

"But secretly. He gave the slip to two deputy sheriffs at the track, didn't he?"

"If he did, and I wouldn't know, that was his idea. I wasn't at the track. I said, 'Elroy, if you'd care to, oblige me by meeting me at Miami International.' Lo and behold, he showed up."

Charlie Waldorf leaned across his desk, like an attack dog ready to spring. I couldn't see the back of his neck, but I'm sure the hackles were up. "It boils down to this, Jaffe. Did Elroy tell you that pursuant to your request he'd asked one of the assistant state attorneys, a man named Baxter, for permission to leave Miami? And did Elroy tell you permission was refused? And after being told that, did you knowingly aid and abet him to leave? Care to answer?"

Before I tear your throat apart, he wanted to add.

I said, "Only two people know the answers to those questions, Charles. One of them ain't talking, and the other one can't. I didn't obstruct justice. I tried to *do* justice. And if Diaz wanted to keep Elroy in Miami, he was tampering with justice." I decided to lower the tension and, hopefully, the stakes, which happened to be my freedom and my license to practice law. "Listen, I'm truly sorry it happened—believe me, sorrier than you are. But it's blood under the bridge. So let's all relax, okay?"

Waldorf said, "You got some fucking nerve."

Beldon Ruth's exact words. People were telling me harsh things these days, and I was refusing to listen. I suppose that was the key to survival.

In the elevator I broke into a sudden sweat. The whole time in Waldorf's office I had wanted to tear off my shoes and socks and rip into the soles of my feet with my nails or a block of sandpaper. Could they indict me? Ridiculous. But yes, they could. State attorneys were lords of a fiefdom. If they woke up grouchy on a given day, they could tack on a hundred years of pen time to the lives of ten different human beings. That our criminal justice system should depend on such people was a mistake. That it depended on people at all made it irreparably flawed.

I was no longer baffled by the source of my maladies. I had to save Darryl Morgan's life and my health as well. A week later I flew again to Jacksonville, where I took Gary Oliver to dinner at a seafood restaurant on the river.

He was older and grayer now, more sure of himself, and with more of a sparkle in his eye. We had always been formal with each other, but I put an end to that. I'd never quite treated Gary as an equal, partly because he had a drinking problem and partly because twelve years ago I hadn't thought he was much of a lawyer. Since I'd started smoking again, I no longer had quite the same lofty attitude toward people who might fall into the category of addicts. And I'd come to realize that, in his own way, Gary had done his best for Darryl Morgan. No one could have done better. I sensed that he had what my mother called *sitzfleisch*—a certain earthy tenacity. I had to learn to look more deeply into people and see what was of value.

At the end of the shrimp cocktail, I said, "Gary, we're on the same side now. I came up here because I need your help."

Oliver nodded warily. The last time we talked, he'd been selling. Now he was buying.

"Back in trial, in April '79, you believed Morgan was guilty, isn't that so?"

"Sure, but the kid kept telling me he didn't do it."

"That didn't sway you to believe him?"

"Can you raise corn on concrete?" Oliver said.

"Then why'd you put him on the witness stand?"

"I told him, 'Darryl, don't get up there.' He insisted."

"He, not you?"

"You think I'm that dumb? He was gonna have his say if it hare-lipped every mule in Georgia."

"But when he was on the stand, he never really told his version of what he and William Smith did that night."

"That's right. I knew it'd hurt him. Jury'd find him guilty, which they were going to do anyhow, but then they'd give him death for making up such a ridiculous lie. I kept him away from that story of his. I just let him say, 'No, I didn't kill no one.' I figured that's all he really wanted to do."

"Gary, I want to run a few facts and theories by you, if you don't mind. Just consider that you're singing for your supper."

"If I can help that kid, I'll do it."

I told him just about everything that had troubled me since I had become involved in *Florida v. Morgan* the second time around. He already knew about Jerry Lee Elroy, and I told him about my hunch that Floyd Nickerson had also lied about Darryl's confession, and how Carmen Tanagra had all but confirmed it. And about the odd coincidence that had sent Nickerson from JSO to a plush job at a ZiDevco country club village near Gainesville, and about Neil Zide's slip when at first he'd denied any knowledge of how Nickerson got the job but somehow knew the date of the detective's departure for Orange Meadow. About the violent death of Victor Gambrel, security chief for Zide Industries—the man who had arrived at the Zide estate only a few minutes before the Jacksonville Beach patrol car.

"So what's your theory?" Oliver asked.

"Let's assume for the sake of argument that your old client and my new client is telling the truth. He was there at the Zides'—he admits that. But he didn't pull the trigger on the gun that never turned up."

Oliver looked at me carefully. "Well, Zide didn't turn that gun on himself, that's for sure. And Mrs. Zide didn't cut her own face that badly. *Someone* did it."

"Someone who looks like Darryl?"

"Not many fit that bill."

"Someone who *doesn't* look like Darryl?"

"Only other people around were Mrs. Zide and her son."

"Yes," I said.

"Could be. Unlikely, but could be."

"Why unlikely?"

"She got cut bad, Ted."

"But not necessarily by a burglar."

He mulled that over for a while, as I had done on other occasions. "Husband might have cut her. And then she shot him."

"It's possible."

"You don't sound convinced."

I asked Oliver how often he'd heard of a middle-aged multimillionaire cutting his wife in the face with a knife. While he was formulating an answer, I added, "In the presence of his adult son."

Oliver finally said, "Not a good bet. But that doesn't mean it couldn't happen."

"Set that aside for a while. Suppose Darryl and William Smith came there to rob the estate, which is what Darryl says happened. And they arrive in the midst of an argument, and get scared by someone, and run off. Darryl says he saw Connie Zide outside on the terrace, in a bathrobe. So she might well have seen *him*. Then the family argument resumes, and Zide cuts his wife. She shoots him. Kills him. Maybe she didn't mean to do it, but there he is, dead on the patio floor. She freaks out. It's justifiable homicide, maybe, by reason of self-defense, or maybe it's manslaughter. Or maybe it's murder. She doesn't really know. She's not thinking clearly. So she says, 'Hey, I'll blame it on Darryl Morgan. Just a big ignorant nigger. And he was *here*. That's a fact.' "

Oliver shook his head slowly. "That would make her out to be a mighty mean woman. She didn't strike me that way."

"No, she's not mean," I said. "But you never know, do you?"

He was silent awhile, but I could tell that the taste of the thought intrigued him. "You think that's what happened?"

"Not really." The truth is, I couldn't imagine the woman I had made love to, the woman who had wept in my arms on Cumberland Island, deliberately pointing the finger of guilt at a young man she knew to be innocent; proclaiming, "He did it." She would have realized that her word—and Neil's, if she convinced him to go along with her story—would be enough to put Darryl away for life or send him to the electric chair. But she hadn't wanted Darryl to die; I remembered that. She had felt for him as a human being.

But maybe she didn't want him to die because she knew that he was innocent.

Oliver stroked his jowls and said, "How does Floyd Nickerson getting that job tie in with the rest of it?"

"It's pretty blatant, but it could have been a payoff."

"And Gambrel's murder?"

"Maybe that doesn't tie in at all. You know how it is when you're trying to shape a theory of defense. You clutch at everything and anything." Finishing my coffee, I called for the check. "You were an investigator before you took up lawyering, and Beldon told me you were pretty good at it. Why don't you sniff around? You could talk to potential witnesses. I never sat down with the security guard back then—he may have seen something that he didn't report to the police. The deal is, if I win the appeal over in Tallahassee, and there's a hearing or a retrial, I'll ask you to sit second chair with me. For whatever's your standard fee."

"How much money are you making out of this?" he asked.

"Diddly."

"Well, I'll take a fair half of your diddly."

I had watched Oliver drinking. He seemed to be taking it easy, in control. I gave him a Xerox copy of my notes.

Changing the subject, I said, "Gary, when I was down at Raiford I assaulted a prison official. I broke his nose."

Oliver's eyes widened. "No shit."

"When the moon is full, I lose control. Turns out it's a second-degree felony. Will you represent me in Bradford County? Not for diddly, but for whatever your normal fee is. And we won't argue about that."

"Hell, you got werewolf tendencies and you broke a prison official's nose. Who's gonna argue with you?"

In a week's time he called me in Sarasota. He had gone down to Bradford County and poked around. Clive Crocker was willing to drop civil charges in return for payment of his medical bills, plus five thousand dollars as compensation for his physical suffering and the emotional humiliation in front of his colleagues. He would sign a waiver of prosecution, meaning he would agree not to testify. Then it was up to the state attorney's office in the county; they could still go forward if they felt they could win the case through other means, with other witnesses.

"Why would they do a shitty thing like that?" I asked.

"Hey, you were a prosecutor," Gary Oliver said. "You tell *me* why they'd do it."

"To be shitty."

"And that happens, as we both know. You got to risk it." He chuckled in my ear. "You know, if they nolle-pros the case, Ted, they're gonna want you to sign a waiver of liability against the sheriff's office."

"Anything else?" I asked. "Would they like me to bend over in front of the courthouse and take it up the *culo* at five bucks a man for the sheriff's annual picnic?"

But when I got home I closed a tax-free mutual fund, and the next day I had Ruby mail a certified check. I thought of signing it *Fuck you*. Who reads signatures? But I scrawled my name instead.

In Sarasota County, Toba finished her deposition. She was told by the wolf spider woman's lawyer that a settlement of $75,000 would be acceptable at this early stage of the proceeding. If not, Mrs. Hart was going to court to sue for half a million.

My fork paused in midair over the pasta salad. I looked at Toba across the dinner table. "This is God's revenge on me for being a lawyer."

"What do you want to do?" Toba asked.

"I want to import some Durango scorpions for Mrs. Hart's laundry hamper and some Brazilian piranha fish for her toilet bowl."

After dinner I began packing. I told Toba that I had to make oral argument before the Supreme Court in Tallahassee in six days. She looked bewildered. "I thought you'd lost that death penalty case last spring."

"I lost it *then*—I want to try and win it *now*."

"So you're flying up nearly a week ahead of time?"

"There are things I need to do. People I want to talk to. Judges I have to bribe."

"Lawyers should marry other lawyers," Toba said gloomily. "That's what they deserve."

The next day I bumped into Harvey Royal in the men's room at Royal, Kelly and told him that I was leaving for the north again.

"Ted, this case has become an obsession."

"Yes," I said, "and you should try it, Harvey. Aside from a few aches and itches in unmentionable places, obsession brings out the best in a man."

In the Florida Supreme Court, a lawyer is allotted half an hour to persuade the state's seven justices that a human being shouldn't be strapped into the electric chair and burned to death.

The judges looked at me with great interest. I thought: Yes, there's hope. I can do it. They will *see*.

To my left on the podium was a row of small lights. During my given half hour the lights would change from green to white, to warn me when my time was nearly up. When the lights flashed red, that was the end. You had to finish your sentence and step down.

I opened oral argument by pointing out that throughout the trial twelve years ago Judge Bill Eglin had called Darryl Morgan by his first name, had even called him "boy," and in doing so had demeaned the defendant and poisoned the minds of the jury. Defense counsel at the time had not objected.

One of the younger judges raised her hand and said, "Mr. Jaffe, which tree are you barking up? If you're arguing that the trial judge was wrong in what he did, you're estopped by procedural default, because, as you pointed out, there was no objection made by defense counsel. So we won't listen to that. If you're arguing ineffective assistance of counsel, I have to remind you that we've been down this road before in *Morgan*. Has anything changed?"

"I pray that what's changed," I said, "is the court's willingness to be swayed by the interests of justice and mercy." Looking into the judge's ice-blue eyes, I quickly added, "In addition, there's the new factor of perjured testimony by a state witness back in 1979. You have copies of his affidavit in front of you, Your Honors. I alluded to it in my opening statement."

The chief judge adjusted his bifocals and glanced at the papers in front of him. "Counselor, I have a problem here. I'm looking at the trial record, where the state prosecutor is listed as Edward M. Jaffe. Now I'm looking at your supporting affidavit—the appeal attorney is Edward M. Jaffe. Are there two Edward M. Jaffes practicing law in the state of Florida?"

"Not that I know of, Your Honor."

"Then you were the prosecutor at the original trial?"

"Yes, I was."

"That's already sufficiently irregular for me to wonder what exactly is going on and why it's been permitted. But added to that, Mr. Jaffe, is the fact that the witness you now claim was perjuring himself at the trial . . . why, he was *your* witness!"

"Yes, that's a fact."

The judge's eyes narrowed. He spoke into his microphone in a stage whisper. "Did you suborn perjury, Mr. Jaffe?"

He knows I didn't, I realized, but he's decided to have a little fun and games at an appeal hearing. Why not? Nothing at stake except a few decades of a dumbass nigger's life.

I explained the circumstances of my meeting Jerry Lee Elroy in Sarasota, and Elroy's admission to me. While I was doing that, the light bulbs turned from green to white.

"Five minutes, Counselor," one of the junior judges said cordially.

I made my final plea. The judges retired.

In ten minutes they were back in their seats at the horseshoe-shaped bench.

The chief judge said, "We don't intend to draw this matter out and leave the appellant in suspense. This court, more than most others, understands the gravity of a death sentence. This court also understands the desperate wish to take a second bite at the apple, and stresses that it will not tolerate collateral proceedings whose only purpose is to vex, harass, or delay. We believe it is unseemly for a prosecutor to wear one hat at one trial and, even with more than twelve years having passed, don another hat for an appeal hearing.

We suspect that the Florida Bar Association shares this opinion. It is our view that Mr. Morgan's trial was not perfect—few are—but neither was it fundamentally unfair. No relief is warranted."

The judge tapped his gavel on the table. The light bulbs turned red.

My deepest ambition, to argue before a supreme court and save an innocent man's life, had danced before me and slipped away. The state wanted Darryl Morgan to die.

"You've made a serious mistake," I said.

That was completely out of line. The chief judge said, "What did you say?"

"I said, Judge—because I know more about this case than you do—that you've made a serious mistake."

"Mr. Jaffe, we could hold you in contempt for that remark."

"You could indeed," I said. And I left the courtroom.

23

I HAD FAILED to save Darryl Morgan's life, and that plunged me into a pit of gloom that threatened to have no bottom. But life goes on. Though I was still focused on Darryl, there were other things I had to deal with.

Toba was having a hard time too. "The country's depressed," she said, "and so am I." Her office telephone rarely rang; she wasn't making money.

She set herself some new goals. To learn Spanish. To put in some serious time working for the pro-choice movement. To gain three or four pounds so that her face wouldn't look so drawn but so the weight wouldn't go to her thighs.

Cathy had a summer job as a cocktail waitress at a seafood restaurant on the Quay. Alan was working at a garage on St. Armands Key. He went camping one weekend down on the Caloosahatchee River with some friends. When he got back he told Toba that they'd never been able to set up the tent properly and, when a heavy rain began to fall, he and another kid found a station wagon with the back gate open. They went to sleep in it. Two cops woke them at 6:00 A.M. and took them in handcuffs to the Lee County courthouse in Fort Myers, where they were arrested for trespassing.

"Like criminals? That's absurd!" Toba cried.

He would handle it himself, Alan said.

Toba told me about it that evening. "If he pleads guilty, what sort of fine will they give him?"

"Couple of hundred bucks, maybe. Don't worry—the court will let him do community service. Picking up garbage in parks, scrubbing graffiti off school walls."

In order to make it easier for Alan to pay the fine for trespassing, Toba decided to pay his bill with Dorothy Buford. She called to make the arrangements.

The therapist said, "Alan's not been my patient for the last three weeks."

"Oh? May I ask why you let him go?"

"*He* left. It was his decision that he didn't need more therapy."

Toba sat on this knowledge for a full week. One evening, staring at the September sunset with a vodka tonic in her hand, she took an uncertain step in the wrong direction and fell into the pool. She came up for air, gasping, with the highball glass and the wedge of lime and the ice cubes floating on the surface of the water. She went upstairs and changed out of her wet clothes into dry sweats.

Then she called Dorothy Buford. "Do you have an opening? May I sort of take my son's place? I have some problems, but I can't put my finger on them. I've been drinking too much. This evening I fell into our swimming pool, fully dressed."

When I came home from the office, she told me what had happened. I began to pace the room, cracking my knuckles. "You're not making this up?" I said.

"Why are you so upset? I didn't get hurt."

"Years ago, do you remember I told you about a woman, a witness in a case up in Jacksonville, who fell into her pool fully dressed?"

"Vaguely."

"I pulled her out."

"So?"

"It just seemed strange for it to happen again."

"You didn't pull *me* out," Toba said, puzzled. "And I'm not a witness. I'm your wife. I was shitfaced. That's why I fell in."

She told me then what she had learned about Alan.

I left him a note: "Kiddo, I'll be waking you before I go to the office. I want to talk to you about your leaving therapy."

When I came downstairs at six-thirty in the morning, Alan was already pouring milk into his granola. He said sadly, "Well, I fucked up again."

"That's a way of putting it." I put a kettle of water on to boil. Tea promised to be more calming than coffee.

"This is what happened," Alan said. He wasn't getting anywhere with Dorothy Buford, and so for the last three weeks he'd taken the money that I'd contributed toward the therapy fee and spent it on marijuana.

"And the story I told you about what happened down on the Caloosahatchee, that's bullshit. We were in a car parked by the river. The cops rousted us about one o'clock in the morning because they were suspicious. They got us on possession. Two ounces, minus what we'd already smoked."

"How'd you like jail?"

"Not much."

And one more thing, he said. He'd told us he'd passed the courses in physics and American history, but that wasn't true. No diploma was coming in the mail.

"Dad, I was thinking of going to San Francisco. My friend Bobby Woolford is out there now. He's got his own apartment, and a job, and I can stay with him. Don't worry, he's off drugs. Frisco's a place I always wanted to go to."

"If you go there," I said, "be sure you don't call it Frisco. San Franciscans will throw stones at you." Into the teapot I measured out what I considered to be the proper mixture of Irish Breakfast and Earl Grey. I poured boiling water into the pot, and the fragrant heat of another continent rose to my nostrils. I wished I were there, sitting on a straw mat, absorbing enlightenment.

I gathered my family together that evening in the living room and told them that I had a proposition to make to Alan. I wanted their input as well as his.

I turned to him and said, "I want to thank you for your honesty. I understand now why you're depressed, and even why you've contemplated suicide. You'd have to have balls of iron and a heart of steel not to be depressed by your life. Because anyone who keeps making the same mistake over and over again has to know he's on a treadmill like a laboratory rat."

Alan lowered his head.

"I made some calls today," I said. "I wound up talking to a woman lawyer in Jacksonville whose kid brother was a coke addict.

He went into a state-sponsored residential drug program in upstate New York. I spoke to the head of the program, and he said he'd make an opening for you now. He'd want you to come to Manhattan within a week for an interview, and I'd have to go with you."

"Dad, I told you I wanted to go to San Francisco."

"Yes, you did, and so I also spoke to the assistant state attorney down in Fort Myers. They know about the other bust, on Siesta Beach—they could hit you with thirty days jail therapy now. If you go to San Francisco before all that's settled, it makes you a fugitive. But if you go into the New York drug program, the State of Florida will drop the charge."

We argued for more than an hour. Finally I called a halt. "Alan, I need to know by the end of the week. And the last time we talked, I made something clear to you—I'm not backing down on it. You can't stay in this house any longer. Go into the program or get out of here."

On Thursday morning, unshaven, Alan was waiting for me again at the breakfast table.

"All right," he said quietly.

When you've won, when the other party's agreed to your terms, don't gloat or encourage more debate. Walk away. I made the necessary telephone calls. On Friday we flew to New York.

We stayed in a hotel facing Central Park. Glass-and-steel office buildings soared into the sky, and homeless men sprawled in their shadows. On Fifth Avenue black men sold fake Rolex watches. Other men clutched at our arms and begged. Beautiful women, white and black, hurried by, heels clicking.

"You like New York, Dad?"

"Yes, but I doubt that I could explain why."

"It's a scary city."

The planet is scary, I wanted to tell him.

In the morning a warm September rain fell. Our cabdriver, a West African, spoke what to me was nearly incomprehensible English. Nevertheless, he got us to our destination on West 104th Street. In this neighborhood *bodegas* and *lavendarías automáticas* had replaced all the delicatessens and candy stores.

The drug program, occupying a ravaged brownstone east of Broadway, consisted of a reception room, a few offices, and basement dormitories. It was early in the day but already hot. No air-conditioning here. A young Puerto Rican woman with red plastic curlers in her hair sat behind a metal reception desk. I spotted a cockroach scuttling away from the water cooler.

Alan and I waited on a wooden bench. Three other young men—two black, one Hispanic—joined us. They were gaunt and worried-looking. Alan had brought a small suitcase, which he clutched between his knees. I was trying to see the place through my son's eyes. He was on the fringe of a foreign world that he didn't want to get involved in. To observe it was okay, to plunge into it was wholly unacceptable. I smiled with all the encouragement I could muster. But it wasn't much.

Our appointment was with Germaine Price, a frail, sharp-jawed woman in her late thirties, who led Alan into a small windowless office and asked me to wait outside.

Ten minutes later Alan came out and said, "Dad, can I talk to you privately?"

We went into a bare room that contained an old school desk. Alan said, in a strangled voice, "This program is for crackheads, real ghetto kids. The place they send you to, what they call the therapeutic community, is a hundred and twenty miles north of here, in the mountains near a town called Oakwood. You have to stay sixty days without even making a telephone call. You can't have anyone visit you for ninety days. You can't leave the grounds. It's like a prison. I don't need that."

"What do you need, Alan?"

"I think I could take care of that misdemeanor business in Fort Myers. Go to court, explain things to the judge. Then I'd go to San Francisco, get a job. Get rid of my drug problem."

"Alan, you're full of shit. I want to talk to Ms. Price. Stay here, all right?"

I went into her windowless office, wondering if Alan would be waiting when I came out. I saw myself arriving at Sarasota-Bradenton, saying to Toba, "Sorry, I lost our son at a Hundred and Fourth Street and Broadway."

I sat down with Germaine Price and said, "Does this kid need your program, or is it overkill?"

"Mr. Jaffe, I'm telling you, if he doesn't do this or something like it, he'll die."

I felt a worse chill than in the county jail at Starke. I reached for a cigarette, the first one I'd smoked that day. "I have to assume you're exaggerating," I said.

"No. Before their time, that's really what I'm saying. From AIDS, general deterioration, poverty, overdosing, shit that happens in prison. They can be bright, and they're usually good-natured, like your son seems to be. They lie a lot. They break your heart."

"What's your background, Ms. Price?"

"Drug addiction and a master's degree in social psychology."

I stepped back into the room where I'd left Alan; he was sitting on the desk, tapping his fingers on the scarred wood. His eyes were a little damp. But he hadn't fled.

I said, "I don't have the answer for you, son. I have my own choice to make, and I've made it. If you don't go into this program, I wash my hands of you." I made a sharp gesture with my hands, while I felt my heart cracking.

Alan's face twitched, and he shambled from the room.

Germaine Price came back to me half an hour later to tell me that he had gone downstairs to what they called Receiving. He had signed up. She shrugged; she'd seen this happen before. It wasn't a triumph, it was just a beginning.

He came up the stairs from the basement with two black youths who wore leather windbreakers and torn jeans. One of them was tall and looked like a younger, slimmer Darryl Morgan.

"Who are they?" I asked Alan, after they had vanished into an office.

"Two guys in the family. They've been residents for a while— they're what's called expediters. Bucky and Jack. They're down here on a pass. We'll go up to Oakwood together in the van."

He had the jargon already. Already he was Bucky and Jack's little white brother.

"Which one is the tall one?" I asked.

"Jack. Why?"

"He reminded me of someone."

I took Alan with me to the front door and out on the stoop, while the rain drummed on concrete. In all those years I had been a prosecutor, I wondered, how many fathers and mothers had said goodbye to sons this same way? I looked into Alan's face and saw that he was close to tears. But he was brave; he was going. I hugged him and whispered, "Good luck, my boy."

FINAL ARGUMENT

Withdrawing from the embrace, I twisted my mouth into a smile and walked off into the rain toward Broadway. I had no umbrella, but I didn't care. A few beats later I turned around for one last look. I started to wave, but the stoop was empty.

One of the reasons we'd been prompted to leave Jacksonville had been Toba's feeling that it was too black. "Black means more violence," she'd said. "More drugs." I smiled, a little bitterly, for to cure that possible mistake on our part, I had wound up entrusting Alan's recovery to that same black community.

I went straight from Broadway and 104th Street to La Guardia Airport. Now it was Darryl Morgan's time, and there wasn't much left of it. But I had a plan. I didn't fly back to Sarasota. I flew to Orlando and changed planes for Gainesville.

24

HE SAW ME first in daylight, sitting behind the wheel of a rented car and staring at him as he came out of a supermarket wheeling a cart full of groceries bagged in plastic.

He wore the usual floppy pastel-colored cotton slacks and oversize white golf shirt that middle-aged Florida men wear in order to hide their paunches. I had been in the supermarket with him, trailing at a distance, watching him pluck from the shelves two six-packs of Löwenbräu Dark Special, a quart of fresh-squeezed orange juice, a pair of tenderloin steaks, a pound of peeled Gulf shrimp, Ben & Jerry Chocolate Fudge Brownie ice cream. Eclectic tastes and little regard for price; he was divorced now and did his own shopping.

I bought some potato chips and exited via the express checkout lane. Then I waited in the car.

There was a melodic tweet-tweet-tweet as Floyd Nickerson hit the beeper that disarmed the Viper alarm on his Buick. He looked up, and his eyes locked with mine from a distance of about twenty yards. There was nothing unusual in a man sitting in a car smoking a cigarette, so he probably thought little of it, although I stared pointedly and didn't drop my gaze for even a fraction of a second. He looked away.

He had noticed me; that was what mattered.

His house was diagonally across the street from the fifth hole of the Orange Meadow golf course—designed by Robert Trent Jones, the brochure proclaimed. That evening he ate at home. A woman arrived at a few minutes past seven o'clock. She was blond and strong-looking, a Viking in her early forties. I sat across the street by the fairway in the rental car, waiting for her to leave, but at midnight I gave up and drove back to the motel on the edge of the campus in Gainesville.

I prayed I wasn't playing the fool, but I knew it was possible. I had to have patience. Even more than patience, I had to have luck.

At seven-thirty the next morning I parked there again, across from the two-story pink house with its trellises of roses and climbing violet bougainvillea. At a few minutes past eight the electronic garage door rolled up smoothly and the big blond woman backed out behind the wheel of her Jeep Cherokee. Nickerson, a wet bath towel draped around thick shoulders, took a few steps from the interior of the garage to wave as she drove off.

He saw me again.

Under my breath I counted slowly to five. We aren't that far removed in time from our primitive animal reactions; five seconds is a long time for an adult male to be stared at directly by another adult male, whom he doesn't know and who doesn't drop his eyes, doesn't smile, and doesn't speak. It's about as long as a man can stand to be stared at without needing to demand why. I had read that in a Tallahassee motel room in a book on police surveillance and interrogation.

I started the engine and cruised past the sand trap and out the eucalyptus-lined roads of Orange Meadow Estates. This was Floyd Nickerson's bailiwick, and he could easily have called security. He was still chief of it here.

I followed the woman's car north on 441 to a real estate office on University Boulevard in Gainesville. It was one of those modern glass-fronted offices where you could look in from the street and see the salespeople at their desks, exuding an air of important things getting done. Her desk was close to the window on the street. I didn't stop or park there; I just slowed down, had a good look, then kept driving.

The rest of that day I was more careful. I knew he'd be expecting the pattern to continue. If I'd had all the time in the world I would have taken a few days off, flown back to Sarasota, given him time to stew.

I didn't have the time.

I called him in the early evening from a public telephone in a service station. He answered with a gruff "Yes?"

I hung up.

The following morning I went to Avis and then drove out 441 again and cruised past the house. Parked fifty yards down the street in a cul-de-sac by the sand trap was an Orange Meadow Estates Security patrol car with two men in the front seat. They wore gunmetal-gray uniforms with red piping on the epaulets. They were looking for the white Chevy I'd driven the morning before. But I had traded it in for a maroon Toyota.

Wherever he went now, he'd be looking for me. He might even see me if I wasn't there.

Just games. The kind that grown men seldom play unless they're desperate.

A plaque on her desk said: SUZANNE BYERS. I walked in from the heat of University Boulevard, wiped my forehead with a sigh of gratitude for the cool indoor air, sat down at her desk, and said, "Ms. Byers, my name is Ted Klauber. I'm a psychologist from Jacksonville. I'm about to relocate here in the Gainesville area, and I'm looking for a house to buy. I hoped you could help me."

"You've come to the right place, Mr. Klauber," she said cheerfully.

A few minutes later she got around to asking me why I'd come to this office and why I'd selected her.

"Impulse," I said. "I saw you from the street, from my car, and I said to myself, why not Suzanne? She needs the business as well as anyone else who was recommended to me. And here I am."

It was false enough to put her on her guard and make her doubt me just a little, which is what I wanted. But of course she had to treat me like a potential customer. I showed enthusiasm, my shoes were shined, and I had an air of affluence. The recession had created a soft market in real estate.

Before we reached the first house I had told her the story of my life, some of it based on truth and—despite my mother's admonition that if you don't lie you never have to remember what you've said—some of it whatever popped into my mind. She also told a version of her life story: born in Michigan, secretarial school, marriage, later became a computer programmer, divorced and moved south to Florida ten years ago.

"No children?"

"Two. They're grown. Both graduated FSU."

"That's hard to believe. What's your secret, Suzanne?"

She smiled with satisfaction.

"Ah! There's a man in your life," I said.

"Yes, as a matter of fact, there is."

"Let me see if I can guess. He's in his early fifties. He's virile, naturally. Independent. Not rich but reasonably well off. Divorced, no children."

"That's very *good!*" she exclaimed.

"Thank you."

"Have you been spying on me?"

"Tell me about him," I said.

"Well, Ted, I'm not sure I want to. Or ought to."

It occurred to me then that she thought I was making a covert pass at her.

"There's a woman in my life too," I said. "She does colonic irrigation and iridology in Jacksonville. She's an ex-cop."

"An ex-cop? Really? That's funny."

"Why? Is your boyfriend an ex-cop too?"

"Yes. And also from Jacksonville. He was in the Homicide Division."

"How about that? So was my girlfriend. Maybe your friend knows her."

"He was there a long time ago."

"What's his name?"

"Floyd," she said, and she glanced quickly at me—she was behind the wheel of her Cherokee and trying to find a house number—to see my expression.

"That's his first name or last name?"

"Floyd is his last name."

Good. I was bothering her. "What's he do now?" I asked.

"I don't really think I should tell you."

"Cops usually go into private security work," I said.

"Do they?"

"Yes, they do. If they get lucky."

We visited two more houses, and I told Suzanne Byers they weren't quite right. One was too large, the other too small. "I'll call you in a few days. Maybe between now and then you'll dig up what I'm looking for."

"Where are you staying, Ted?"

"I haven't decided yet."

"You'll be here awhile?"

"A few more days. I'll call you."

I was at the University Motel on University Boulevard, under my own name. Not hard to find, if you were a well-connected ex-cop and had a good reason to hunt. Suzanne would give him one. And a description of me.

He was well connected, and he was quick.

That evening I left my motel room and drove to a steak house on the edge of town, where I ate a filet mignon and a baked potato with sour cream. After dinner I drove past the condo where Suzanne Byers lived. That hadn't been difficult to locate; she was in the telephone book. When I came opposite her unit I slowed as if I were scanning the windows for signs of occupancy. I had no idea whether she was there or not, and I didn't care.

I headed south on 441 to Orange Meadow Estates.

That night at Orange Meadow there was no security patrol car parked in front of Floyd Nickerson's home. But there was a Volvo curving through the streets behind me at a varying distance. I'd thought so when I left the motel, but I wasn't sure until now.

The Volvo speeded up, passed me, then swerved to cut me off. I touched the brakes.

Nickerson was out from behind the wheel quickly, and so was another man, who'd been in the passenger seat. Tonight he was in sports clothes rather than gun-metal gray with epaulets. He stayed by the passenger door of the Volvo, unlike Nickerson, who in a few strides was wrenching at the door handle of my Toyota. It wasn't locked.

"Come out of there, Jaffe."

He didn't seem to be armed, which gave me more courage than was reasonable under the circumstances. He was a cop, a man practiced in violence, burly and thick through the chest. And he had a backup.

"What the hell do you want? What are you butting into my life for?"

He wore khakis, his usual golf shirt, and, because the night was cool, a poplin windbreaker. There wasn't much light in that part of the street, so I couldn't see the expression on his face. But I expected he was more livid than red-faced. He kept clenching and unclenching his fists. He wanted to harm me. I believe he was frightened.

He obviously hated my silence.

"You follow me to the supermarket," he said shrilly. "You harass my friends. You're looking for big trouble, friend."

"Let's talk, Nick."

"There's nothing to talk about."

"How about the good old days? Before you were on the take."

"Fuck you," he murmured.

I heard his rapid breathing. No, he didn't want to harm me. He wanted to kill me.

I had thought for a while that I might try to move him by appealing to his humanity. He had to have some humanity. He was a man who had done terrible things, and maybe they kept him awake sometimes at night. Maybe in some part of him he wanted to be decent and make amends.

Yet I doubted it.

"I have an affidavit," I said, "from Jerry Lee Elroy. You remember him?"

"No," he said, and that was probably the truth.

"Darryl Morgan's cellmate in Duval County Jail twelve years ago. You got a battery charge dismissed for him. He was the guy you set up to lie on the witness stand that he heard Morgan confess to killing Solly Zide."

He took a step backward.

"He'll testify to that, Nick. And you'll go to prison."

He didn't know that Elroy had been stabbed to death at the dog track. He turned toward the Volvo and said, "Patrick, this gentleman and I are going for a little walk on the course. Stay here and keep your eye on his car, okay?"

Patrick's voice came out of the darkness. "Yes, sir."

Before Nickerson finally made up his mind what to do about me, he wanted to know what I knew. And he didn't want to be overheard.

With hard fingers he grasped my arm. "You play golf? This is a championship course. The fifth hole is right opposite where I live. . . ." He guided me past an oak tree, up a slope, onto the rolling fairway. In the gloom I could see a dogleg to the left, and two broad sand traps, and a pond.

235

A humid night breeze blew from the pond. An owl hooted. When we got to the edge of the first trap, about ten yards from the green, Nickerson halted. He placed his hands on his hips, probably to keep them from strangling me.

"I remember Elroy," he said. "But your story, that's all bullshit."

"You lied in court too, Nick. You testified that Morgan confessed to you. *That* was bullshit."

He snickered, but he didn't say any more.

"Carmen Tanagra will testify to that," I said.

"If she did, she'd be lying."

"A judge will decide. And not Bill Eglin."

"All crap."

From behind the clouds a thin crescent of moon appeared, and I breathed deeply.

"Nick, I'm trying to give you a break. You've got a new life, a new girlfriend. You want it all to go up in smoke? Your bank accounts at the Barnett Bank can be subpoenaed. You flew to the Bahamas in March of 1980 with your wife for a little holiday. The cash that Neil Zide gave you went with you, and later it paid off your mortgage in Jacksonville. You got a sweetheart contract here at Orange Meadow. You want to tell me it was a reward for catching Morgan and shooting William Smith? No, Nick, it was a payoff from Neil Zide."

In the past three weeks Gary Oliver had done some good sleuthing.

Nickerson was silent for a few moments. Then he said, "The big black kid shot and killed Solly Zide, and that's a fact."

"No, it isn't, Nick."

"If he didn't kill him," Nickerson asked, "who did?"

He was trying to sound sincere, but I knew too much to believe in it.

"Maybe you did," I said.

He laughed heartily.

"Right," I said. "It's funny. I know you didn't do it."

"Good," he said, still chuckling.

"All you did was destroy evidence. Keep other witnesses from testifying. I don't think they'll give you more than ten years in Raiford for that."

He stopped laughing. I saw his hands begin to clench and unclench again.

"Of course if you killed Gambrel, and they can prove it, then you'll swap places with Morgan. Where'd you put the payoff money, Nick? Bank of Nova Scotia in Nassau? Fidelity Magellan and Dreyfus? How about a junk bond fund with Vanguard—a nice little offshore annuity. The IRS know about that? You ever pay any bills —like your MasterCard and American Express—with that Vanguard checkbook?"

I'm not even sure what he did. I heard him grunt and I smelled his sour breath and felt a combination of pain and nausea all at the same time. He was big and quick. I think he did a karate step to the side and struck me in the groin with the toe of his shoe. And it was not a canvas Adidas or a leather Reebok; it was a real shoe, a brogan with a steel toe plate.

Dirt filled my mouth. I don't know if I fell into the sand trap or was borne there under the weight of his body. But I still smelled his meaty breath, because he was leaning over me and pressing his fingers into my temples.

Darryl had nearly choked me to death. I'd spent a night in a county jail with piss-soaked feet. And now Floyd Nickerson was doing something horrible to my nerve endings. This was the part of the legal profession they hadn't told me about in law school.

He was so enraged he could hardly speak. He didn't let up on my temples, so that his voice seemed to rasp at me from a watery distance, as if a killer whale had found a tongue. I couldn't understand most of what he said.

". . . to lose, so fuck with me, I'll *kill* you. Fuck with my bank accounts, talk to the IRS, anything happens to me, you're *dead*."

He raised his hand then and brought the edge of it down on the bridge of my nose. I heard the crack and immediately tasted salty blood. I'm sure he would have beaten me to death right then and there, but some worry must have nagged at him as to whether I'd come to Gainesville alone or told anyone where I was going and who I'd be seeing. Nothing else would have stopped him.

I think he called for help, because Patrick came up out of the darkness over the fairway. They dragged me down the hill to my car, and I felt myself shoved into the passenger seat. I was bleeding, my head hurt, my ribs hurt, and I wanted to puke. Patrick drove me out of Orange Meadow Estates and perhaps five minutes later—I was dizzy, and I couldn't see my watch—pulled over into the parking area behind a gas station on the highway. He never said a word; neither did I. Patrick got out of the car, and I never saw him again.

Nickerson had broken my nose and somehow bruised my ribs. Had he kicked me? I didn't remember that. I never did puke: mind conquered matter.

I checked myself into the emergency unit at County General Hospital. They asked me to undress, because my shirt was wet with blood. A nurse pointed to the wire taped to my chest. "What's that?" she asked, frowning.

"A wire," I said.

"You a narc?"

"No, a lawyer."

It seemed logical at the time, although I could see by the flicker in her eyes that the nurse didn't quite believe me.

I didn't listen to the tape until I was back in my room at the University Motel. And the next time I played it, forty-eight hours later, was for Judge Horace Fleming, in his chambers at the Jacksonville courthouse.

Muriel Suarez was present this time. It was too important a moment for an ex parte conversation, and it was I who had invited the state attorney's office to join us. She didn't argue much as to the legitimacy of the conversation; I'll give her that. The law was clear that both parties did not have to consent to a tape recording; otherwise wiretaps and narcotics informants would quickly be out of business, and no witness in a court proceeding would be allowed to testify as to what he or she had overheard without consent of the speaker.

Muriel frowned and said, "There is a certain sense of entrapment here, Your Honor. May I suggest that if Mr. Jaffe hadn't goaded him, and very nearly put the words in his mouth, Mr. Nickerson might not have said even what he seems to have said?"

"You may certainly suggest that," the judge replied.

"And it seems clear that Mr. Nickerson was enraged beyond reason," Muriel said.

"He sure sounds mad enough to kick the cat," said the judge.

"If you listen carefully to this tape, as I've done, Your Honor, you realize that Mr. Nickerson failed to confirm a single one of Mr. Jaffe's wild accusations. He threatened Mr. Jaffe, that's clear. He may well have attacked Mr. Jaffe physically, but we only have Mr.

Jaffe's word for that, and while I have nothing but respect for opposing counsel, it's my obligation to point out that he *is* opposing counsel. And so you might say he's a little prejudiced."

The judge looked me over. It was obvious that under my bandage I had a swollen nose, and I walked like a man who'd lost an argument with a truck. The judge smiled and nodded. "So you might say, Ms. Suarez. And I'd agree."

"Mr. Nickerson told Mr. Jaffe candidly that his accusations of suborning perjury and outright perjury were baloney."

"No, ma'am. I heard what he said. He told Mr. Jaffe they were bullshit."

"Your Honor, you're absolutely right."

"I'm going to think on this matter," Judge Fleming said, "and play this conversation on my stereo at home. Get my grandson to fiddle with all those knobs so it's real clear. I'll get back to you both in a day or so."

I remembered how he'd rebuked me the last time I reminded him that Darryl was close to the date of execution, and so this time I said nothing. But it wasn't easy.

Three afternoons later, Judge Fleming called us into his chambers.

"You're a persistent fella," he said to me.

"Yes, Judge."

"What is it you want?" he asked.

I cleared my throat. "That's in the motion I filed, Your Honor. Are you asking me to rephrase, or repeat?"

"Don't snap your garters. Just tell me, Mr. Jaffe, in your own simple words, if you can, what you really want."

"One way or another," I said, "I want my client to have his day in court."

"You want a hearing?"

"At least that, Your Honor."

He raised a shaggy white eyebrow. "With witnesses?"

"That would be a good idea," I said. I could barely tell if he was serious.

He turned to Muriel Suarez. "And ma'am, what is it *you* want?"

"Your Honor, I can tell you what I *don't* want. I don't want the state to have to go to the trouble, plus the considerable expense, of a full-scale hearing when there's already been an eight-day jury trial where Darryl Morgan was convicted of first-degree murder." She raised her voice a notch. "There is no new evidence."

"Well, there's this tape," Judge Fleming said.

"That's not evidence," Muriel shot back. She wasn't afraid of him at all.

"It's a lot of shouting and threatening, that's what it is," Judge Fleming said, nodding. "But if you listen real good, and you use your common sense, you get to thinking. Wouldn't you agree with that, ma'am?"

There wasn't much Muriel could do except shrug and reluctantly say, "I might agree with that. But it's still not—"

"Evidence," the judge said. "Maybe not." He turned back to me. "If I give you a day in court, who would you put on?"

"You mean which witnesses?"

He nodded, and I decided to roll the dice double or nothing. Which was an optimistic metaphor, because so far I hadn't won a damn thing except some septuagenarian indulgence.

"Judge," I said, "have you ever read the full transcript of *Florida v. Morgan*?"

He looked just a shade flustered, and I believed I had him. Well, you never knew with this man.

"Judge, I'm sure you've at least skimmed that transcript last April, and I'm just as sure that you got a good feeling about the case back then. And so you know that the transcript is interesting, but it's not the word of the Lord. Now, if you grant my motion, you'll of course want to hear from the moving party, which is Morgan. We will have one or two other witnesses. But I believe you'll benefit by hearing and seeing the state witnesses too."

Muriel jumped forward. "Judge, watch out: he's just about asking for a new trial!"

"No, ma'am," I said. "A hearing with no more than the principal witnesses. Mr. Nickerson is one of them. If you don't put him on, I will. And I don't think we can understand what Mr. Nickerson says unless we hear from Mr. Neil Zide. And if we're going to hear from Neil Zide, why not hear from his mother?"

"Judge—"

"Hang on there, both of you," Fleming said, and he turned to me. "Mr. Jaffe, if you're telling me you want to hear the state's principal witnesses, you've got more nerve than a toothache. *Is* that what you're saying?"

"I'm saying *you* should hear them, Your Honor, if only for the sake of enlightenment. It would certainly be quicker and simpler than reading that long and tedious trial transcript. We're talking maybe three thousand pages, Judge."

Fleming stroked his jaw and looked straight into my eyes without blinking. "You sure have got billy goat in your blood. You wouldn't mind doing a little cross-examination of those folks, would you?"

"Sir, I'm not going to retry the case, but yes, there's something to what you say. I wouldn't mind a little cross."

"Ms. Suarez?"

"Judge"—she was angry and didn't hide it—"he *will* retry the case if you allow him to cross our principal witnesses!"

The judge smiled mischievously. "Well, Ms. Suarez, I'll ask you again: what do you want? Not what you don't want, but what you *do* want."

Muriel rose to the occasion. "I want justice, Your Honor, leavened with common sense."

"Good for you," Judge Fleming said. "So do I, most of the time. But most of all, I want to be enlightened. You follow me?"

"Not quite," Muriel said.

"Ma'am, I want to know why this Nickerson fella was so het up by Mr. Jaffe's accusations. And since the principal witnesses are alive and kicking, why shouldn't we hear them? Think of it this way." He jerked a thumb in my direction. "By the time it's over we'll have this fella off our backs. That would make life a lot easier for the state attorney's office and this court, wouldn't it?"

"Your Honor—"

"Just a little hearing," Judge Fleming said, "for the purposes of judicial enlightenment and—what did you call it, ma'am?—justice leavened with common sense? I like that. But not until January, because I've got a full calendar right up until New Year's Day, and on Monday, January 13, I turn over this courtroom to Mr. Ruth. So make it Monday, January 6. I'll grant another stay. Come January, I'll give you three days, tops. I need Thursday and Friday before the weekend to pack up and get out. That gives you both plenty of time between now and then to think things over and refresh anyone's memory needs refreshing. Or maybe even cut a deal. Is that all right, Ms. Suarez? Does early January suit you? And by the way, do you like fruit?"

She took a deep, shaky breath. "Yes, Your Honor, I do."

"I always have fruit in my courtroom. Which is your favorite fruit?"

"A freshly picked Washington State Delicious apple," she said, once again rising to the occasion.

The judge turned to me. "And you, sir?"

"Honeydew melon," I said.

"No." He frowned. "I meant does early January suit you?"

"Yes, Judge." I was ready to let out a war whoop, but I controlled myself. "Suits me just fine."

25

CERTAIN CASUAL REMARKS echo with far more weight than the speaker intended. Some years ago the veteran Pittsburgh Steelers, a class act in football, met the upstart Los Angeles Rams in the Super Bowl. This was the first Super Bowl appearance for the Rams. The Steelers trampled them, and I remember the TV commentator explaining: "The Rams came here to play, but the Steelers came here to win. The outcome was never in doubt."

The keenness of that observation stayed with me, waiting just below the surface of memory until I needed it. I had felt triumphant, even vindicated, when Judge Fleming granted a hearing in *Florida v. Morgan*. It would have been acceptably human to prepare for the hearing, go to court, and do the best I could, for better or for worse, win or lose. That would be playing the game.

But unlike the Rams, I wasn't showing up in court merely for the glory of playing. Like the Steelers, I was going there in order to win. I *had* to win. I had to do considerably more than the best I could. And I had to make some sacrifices.

How large they would be, how they would reshape my formerly ordered life, I could only speculate; and then I had to say to hell with it and lower my head to plunge forward through the thickets of deceit and the swamp of denial that my life had become over the past dozen years. Somewhere in Camus, one of the characters mourns, "I see too deep and too much." Those words had always touched me, even if they struck me as hyperbolic. But now I lived

243

them, for I knew that Darryl Morgan was innocent of the crime for which he had been accused, convicted, and condemned to die. And I believed I knew who had murdered Solomon Zide. What I didn't know was how to prove it and how to escape with my marriage and my career intact.

In October, finally, I heard from the Florida Bar Association in the state capital. I never found out who lodged the complaint, but I suspect it was done at the behest of the chief judge of the Supreme Court, he whom I had accused of making "a serious mistake." I had been a wiseass; there was a price to pay. There's almost always a price for quixotic derring-do, and it's almost always not worth paying. This instance may have been the exception.

The Professional Ethics Committee of the Bar wanted to know how I could justify representing a man whom I had formerly prosecuted. They also asked me to respond to a complaint by the state attorney's office in the Seventeenth District—Robert Diaz in Miami —that I'd "knowingly and willingly" misrepresented to my former client Jerry Lee Elroy the terms of a plea-bargaining agreement between Elroy and the state attorney.

What was I meant to do? Since humankind emerged from the cave, we've lived by an evolving rule of law that allows us to face the sunset without dread. But there were times when the rule of law didn't keep its promise. There were even times when chaos was better than law if law proved barbaric.

Who defined "better"? The representatives of the law did, of course. At best, this was a tautology. At worst, it was a vicious circle.

I wrote a letter to the Ethics Committee. I said that I was representing Darryl Morgan because it was in the interest of justice for me to do so. He had asked me to represent him. And I intended to keep on representing him as long as he wanted me.

As regards Jerry Lee Elroy, I wrote, I didn't know what in hell they were talking about. They were mistaken.

Then Beldon Ruth called me from Jacksonville.

"How are you, lad?" He was already assuming a lofty judicial air, and I sensed that it boded me no good.

"I'm well, Beldon. And you?"

"Couldn't be better. And the family?"

"Great. And yours?"

That nonsense over, he got down to business. Our deal last summer, he said, hadn't been open-ended. It had applied to my motion based on Jerry Lee Elroy's affidavit. I had lost. It was a new ball game now. The state attorney's office for the Fourth District was still the "appropriate government agency" that supposedly had to grant permission for me to represent Darryl in court, Beldon was still the state attorney, and he'd thought it over and decided that it was tainted, unseemly, against the canons—"and," he said, "from what I hear, you've got your tail in a crack with the Bar Association. Time to back off, Ted my boy."

"Horace Fleming granted my motion," I said.

"For a hearing. That doesn't mean you can be the lawyer to conduct that hearing."

"Beldon, if nothing unravels, come January I'll be there. I'll have backup counsel, so you go ahead and file your protests and do whatever you feel you have to do. I think it's shitty of you, but I suppose you've got your reasons."

"You know them," he said.

"And they're not good enough."

He thought that over. "If you go out and break both your legs, don't come running to me."

A week later the Ethics Committee sent me a letter by Federal Express overnight mail. This time they didn't mention the accusation of my having lied to Jerry Lee Elroy; they had no proof, and the whole concept of plea-bargaining was best kept out of the public eye: it looked so tacky. But as regards the Florida Code of Professional Responsibility and its Rule 4–1.11, concerning successive government and private employment, the Bar Association felt I was guilty of "the appearance of impropriety." In other words, it didn't matter that Darryl Morgan wanted me as his lawyer. It didn't look right.

I wrote back politely and said that was unfortunate, but nevertheless I was going forward with the case.

Harvey Royal asked me into his office. As a matter of form and courtesy, the Bar Association had sent copies of all this correspondence to Royal, Kelly, Wellmet, Jaffe & Miller in Sarasota. The Bar Association, in other words, was snitching on me. They were in a fight they wanted to win.

Harvey sighed. "Ted, this is bad business. This is a little more serious than a broken nose. You could be censured. Even disbarred."

"But I won't be." I tried to put a great deal of confidence into my voice and body language.

"Why are you so certain?"

"Because I'll win the case in Jacksonville. If they disbar me, they'll look bad. And we know that what they care about most is how they look."

He tapped his fingers on the desk and said, "What about this other matter? That you lied to your client, this man Elroy. That's a terrible accusation. I'm positive it has no basis in reality."

I still don't know why I did what I did. I suppose because I was tired of being everyone's target. "Elroy is dead, Harvey. With a sea urchin shoved in his mouth. He can't talk."

Lines of age appeared to grow downward from Harvey's narrow nose. He coughed a few times. "What are you saying?"

"That it's my word against a dead man's."

The lines deepened. "Ted, I worry that you don't grasp the significance of this. The state attorney in Miami seems to believe you told your client that part of the plea bargain was a requirement that he testify in the *Morgan* appeal. If you told him that, and you knew it wasn't so, you acted unethically. Surely—surely you *see* that."

I got up from where I sat, on the edge of his desk, and moved toward the door. "It would have worked," I grumbled, "if some thug hadn't slipped an ice pick between this asshole's ribs when we were at the dog track. That was something no one could foresee."

Harvey's skin began to turn dapple gray, and his jaw was sagging. "You're not implying that it's *true*?"

I winked at him. To deny what he'd seen, he quickly closed his eyes, but I think it was too late; it also gave me time to slide out the door.

Fall moved slowly toward winter. I was nervous; I knew the upcoming hearing was the last chance to save Darryl Morgan's life.

Toba and I were finally allowed to call Alan up at Oakwood in New York. He explained that the telephone was in a hallway and there was a strict five-minute limit.

"What are you doing with your time?"

"There are a lot of family meetings. And I read a lot."

Family. Well, why not? I was doing what I could for Darryl, and Darryl's brothers were doing it for my kid.

"Do you run? Can you work out?"

"There's no place to run. And there's nothing to work out *with*."

"But you're not depressed?"

"I'm doing it one day at a time," Alan said gravely.

Prison inmates said that.

Toba was working only part time in her real estate office now and spending the rest of the time canvassing for the local pro-choice group. She seemed to have cut out all alcohol except for one large glass of red wine with meals, and she rarely discussed the therapy she was doing with Dorothy Buford. But one December evening after dinner, the day before I was due to fly up to Jacksonville, she flung her napkin angrily on the table. "What a bitch! I never grasped that until now. So *negative* about everything! At college if she called and I said, 'Hello,' right away she'd say, 'What's wrong?' I'm still never superficial enough or cheerful enough for her."

She didn't have to tell me who she was talking about.

"Or attractive enough," Toba said, going into high gear. "The last time I stayed with her, she barged into the bathroom—I was naked in the tub. She frowned and went, '*Hmmm.*' I said, 'What's the matter, Mom?' 'Did I say anything was the matter?' 'Well, you gave me a funny look and you went *hmmm*. Am I misshapen, or anything like that?' 'Tell me, Toba,' she said, 'does he still like to *touch* you?' "

"Tell her I do," I said. "In fact, how about after we stack the dishwasher?"

On the way upstairs, I asked if her mother knew what was happening now with her grandson.

"Of course. But she told my aunt Hermine that he's at a weight-lifting camp in the Catskills."

I flew to Jacksonville the next morning. The Friday before the hearing was scheduled to begin, when I was sitting by the pool at the Marina Hotel eating a late breakfast and swilling a gallon of coffee that I hoped would get me through the day, Gary Oliver called.

"I've got some people here in my office," he said. "I talked to them last night, but it was kind of late to contact you. I want to bring them over now."

"Who are they? I hate surprises."

"You might like this one," he said, chortling, and there was nothing I could do about it.

I was going over the Nickerson tape and getting some notes together before I drove down to Raiford that morning to see Darryl. I told Gary where I'd be. "If you don't see me, look underwater at the deep end."

Half an hour later he showed up at poolside with an attractive but fidgety black woman who appeared to be about thirty years of age. She was wearing brand-new bluejeans and a well-filled pink sweater, but her hair needed brushing. With her were three children, two girls and a boy. One girl was about ten years old, the other was probably seven or eight; they held hands, giggled, and whispered together while they stared at the pool and the rising sweep of the hotel. The boy was tall, lean, and good-looking, a bit surly in manner, maybe sixteen years old. He wore an old sweatshirt with a picture of Magic Johnson, and his jeans had the requisite holes in the knees. He looked like a young Darryl. For a few moments, as they all approached from the lobby, I thought that some cousins of Gary's might have hit town from the boondocks, and he didn't know what else to do with them other than drag them over to my hotel. This didn't please me. Then it occurred to me that the boy who looked like a young Darryl looked *a lot* like a young Darryl.

"This is Pauline Powers," Gary said, and the mother of the kids bobbed her head a few times and reached out to shake my hand. "And this is Polly and Priscilla"—the girls giggled even harder— "and this is Tahaun. His birth name was Peter, but he changed it himself just recently. Says it's everyone's right to choose his own name, and he thought Peter Powers sounded silly. That cute stuff's okay for girls, but not for boys. You get the picture? Tahaun's an African name, he tells me. He's Darryl's son."

We drove down to Raiford together in Gary's Cadillac. The men were in front, with Tahaun squeezed between us, and the women in back—that's how Gary set it up.

By the time we turned off the interstate I knew that Tahaun rooted for the Lakers and the Dolphins and the Braves, and wanted to be a basketball star but was worried because he was only six feet two. His favorite music was rap, but he surprised me by saying he liked the Beatles and Elvis too. He was still a bit surly, but I sensed you could beat through it if he believed you liked him. He was a high school sophomore down in Boca Raton, where Pauline was the assistant manager in a Kentucky Fried Chicken.

She was only fifteen when Peter/Tahaun was born, and a few years later she married. Her second child died of crib death. Then came

Polly and Priscilla, and then a while back her husband, Powers, an auto mechanic in Boca Raton, was killed by a hit-and-run driver. Recently she saw on TV that Darryl was getting a new hearing for a murder he'd committed thirteen years ago. She hadn't known about the murder or that the father of her son was on death row. She'd lost all touch with Darryl since he was a resident at the Arthur C. Dozier School for Boys. She had a car, and a week's vacation coming.

"My children never see where I was born," she said to me.

I could look at her face in the rearview mirror. I caught her eye for a moment, and she looked away. Then she shrugged.

"My husband, he was a short man. Tahaun wanted to know how come *he* get to be so tall. It ain't me, I tell him. After that, he asked about his natural daddy all the time. Drive me up the wall. Not much I remember about him, and that's a fact, except how big the man was."

"You want to meet him?" I asked Tahaun.

"Yeah."

"We'll try."

In a strange way, Assistant Superintendent Ray Wright and I had become friendly. I don't know how that had come to pass, except perhaps that we saw each other so often it was a bit absurd to go on sniping at each other. I suppose each of us suspected somewhere under the other's skin was a human being, if you dug deep enough with a pointed instrument.

I suggested to Gary that he take the girls into Starke for something to eat and to see the sights, and I would ask Wright if Pauline and Tahaun could join me in the visit. Darryl and I had met the last couple of times in the attorney's visiting room, the same room where he'd once tried to strangle me. There was an assumption now that my life wasn't at risk. I hoped it was correct.

When I explained to Wright who I had with me, he thought it over for a few moments. "How old is the boy?"

"Eighteen."

He peered out into the anteroom, where Pauline and Tahaun sat stiffly on two plastic chairs.

"He doesn't look eighteen. Are you sure?"

"Yes."

He sighed heavily. "You've got a lot of nerve, Jaffe. Anyone ever tell you that?"

"I've been told," I admitted.

"They can see him if you're with them."

So Darryl met his son and the woman whose photograph as a fourteen-year-old girl he'd had on the plank of plywood at Dozier. He was shy with her, and she with him. They were strangers, of course.

When I introduced him to Tahaun, Darryl blew out his breath in amazement. "God *damn*," he muttered. "I knew it."

They shook hands, then drew back and measured each other for a while. They looked more like brothers than father and son. Darryl, even though he had gray in his bushy hair, was a man of only thirty-three. To me that was young. He was huge and powerful, and even if Tahaun didn't grow that tall, he would look like his father one day.

"You play any ball in here?" Tahaun asked.

"Hell, no."

"What do you do?"

Darryl thought for a while. There was a great deal, I realized, that he could have said. He could have told this boy stories that would raise the hair on the back of his sixteen-year-old neck. He could have mesmerized him with tales of brutality and death and absurdity and hustle in the joint and on the row. He could have told him how in the chill early mornings they rattled the spoons against the bars until the lights dimmed and they lost another brother to Big Wooden Mama.

"I'll show you what I do," he said. Leaning forward a bit, in one smooth motion from his back pocket he slipped out a deck of worn playing cards—one of the decks I'd given him—and a few skinny rubber bands that looked as if they were ready to fray and snap.

He entertained Pauline and his son and me for half an hour. His bony brown fingers seemed swifter than rips of lightning; I never saw what they did. The moons of his fingernails flashed under the fluorescence that beamed down from the ceiling. Pauline squealed with pleasure. Tahaun just stared.

With Darryl there were no jerky motions, no hand wagging. His misdirection and timing were as elegant as I'd seen. The hand, of course, isn't really quicker than the eye, but it's more clever. And the tongue is the hand's partner. Darryl didn't say, "Pick a card." He looked at Tahaun and gravely intoned, "You're my son, so we got an affinity. I can read your mind, just like your mama can. I can see in your naked eye that you doubts me, so I'm going to prove it to you." And then, without touching the deck, Darryl ordered Tahaun to bury a chosen card and fan out the pack. "I wants you to keep your eye on my hands and this deck of cards, and don't let your mind wander. Concentrate! Think of that card! Think *hard,* boy!" And he guided Pauline's finger until it quivered over what turned out to be the king of hearts.

"That's it," Darryl cried, seemingly flabbergasted. "Pauline knows!"

"That *is* it," Tahaun said, and he *was* flabbergasted.

"Do it again," he told his father.

"Can't. I got to rest. The strain on my old brain is too much."

A few minutes later the boy and his mother left; Gary Oliver was returning to pick them up. Darryl and I went to work on what we wanted to happen in Judge Fleming's courtroom.

When I was gathering up my papers and about to go, he said, "What you think of my boy?"

"Good kid. Determined. What do *you* think?"

"Don't know what to think." He seemed mystified, as Tahaun had been at the sleight of hand. "He say to me, he don't like people to laugh at other people. Seem like a nice boy. But I tell you something you not going to believe. I knowed from jump street I'd run into him one day. Used to know that, I mean. Once I got locked up and they got fixing to kill me, seemed like I'd never see him—sure didn't think I'd run into him *here.* But I did. Fuck, man, I *did.*" He thought for a long time, brows knitted together, and then put his hard hand on my shoulder. That was the hand that had nearly strangled me to death last spring before the guards had stopped him. His fingers squeezed into my trapezius muscle.

"They come see me again?" he asked.

"You want that?"

"Sure I wants it."

"I'll try to arrange it."

26

I N THE YELLOW glare of the overhead bank of lights, Judge Horace Fleming's bald skull shone like a nearly full moon reflected in flesh-colored mud. His huge courtroom had a twenty-foot-high ceiling; it reminded me of the courtrooms you see in documentaries of Nazi Germany. The pale walls weren't particularly clean. The witness stand was a boxy desk far from the lawyer's lectern. The judge's oak bench swept in a magisterial arc halfway across the room. Such a courtroom was designed to invoke the terrifying potency of the law: to remind us, as if we needed to be reminded, that the law can change lives, that the law has the power of life and death.

This was the same courtroom where Darryl Morgan's trial had taken place and where Judge Bill Eglin had overridden the jury and pronounced his sentence.

Here now—half-glasses perched on the end of his bulbous nose, the whites of his dark eyes threaded with bloody little veins—Horace Fleming reigned, in his fashion. He drank cup after cup of strong coffee and sometimes during the examination of a witness would beckon to his court clerk to bring him the fruit bowl that she kept on her desk. In it was a cornucopia of fruits, which always included a couple of gleaming Washington State Red Delicious apples for Muriel Suarez. (There was no honeydew melon for me, but I didn't take that as a slur.) The judge himself, no doubt in deference to the state of his dentistry, ate only soft pears and bananas.

A moment came during our hearing when he halted a cross-examination, turned to the crowded courtroom, and dangled a banana peel at arm's length. "Ladies and gentlemen, behold—the perfect fruit!" He then waggled a finger at the court reporter and said, "I want that on the record. I want the world to know."

Then he indicated to the lawyer and the witness that they could proceed.

The judge was almost always cordial, and if you argued or contradicted him he didn't chop off your head or banish you from the realm. He simply ignored you. He went on his merry way, customary procedures be damned. It was all personal, all dictated by mood. The rules of evidence? You could throw them out the door. As Kenny Buckram had said, it was always interesting. Certainly challenging. But it was, also, often dangerous. Because when you got through chuckling, you realized there was a man in that courtroom whose life was on the line.

There was no jury. This wasn't a trial, merely a hearing to determine whether or not there should be any change in Darryl Morgan's status. The judge, after hearing the evidence, could dismiss or grant my motion for a new trial; he could commute the death sentence to life; and in extraordinary circumstances he could even send Darryl home, if such a place existed.

It was an open court, and the press had learned what was going on. A former prosecutor under threat of sanction by the Bar Association was attempting to plead on behalf of a black man he'd sent to death row. It was Horace Fleming's last case before Beldon took over his judicial appointment. Zide was a name to be reckoned with in Florida; the murder was remembered. It was rumored that the widow as well as the heir were going to perform on behalf of the state and do their best to enlighten Judge Fleming as to what had happened out at the beach on that terrible night in 1978.

The *Star* and the *National Enquirer* decided to give the hearing full coverage. The recession and the famine in Africa and the demise of the Soviet Union weren't hot news anymore. A black man on trial was hardly a rarity, but for precisely that reason this case suddenly captured people's attention. Then the *New York Times* and even the *Wall Street Journal* sent reporters down.

On Monday morning the courtroom was full.

Muriel Suarez and John Whatley—the young assistant state attorney who'd been there when Fleming ruled against us in the matter of the affidavit from a dead witness—carried the banner for the State

253

of Florida, but you could feel Beldon's presence as the *éminence grise*. In fact, on opening day in early January, in his navy blazer with nautical gold buttons, he was outside the courthouse to talk to the reporters and the TV cameras.

"Do you feel it's appropriate," *Time*'s stringer asked him, "for your former chief assistant state attorney to be representing the man he sent to the electric chair?"

"We're about to make our feelings known on that matter," Beldon said cordially, sucking his unlit pipe and looking like a college professor about to become emeritus. "And then it'll be up to the judge to decide."

As soon as Fleming rapped his gavel and asked if the state was ready, and then if the defense was ready, and I replied, "Yes, Your Honor," young John Whatley sprang to his feet. "If it please the court, the State of Florida moves to disqualify Edward Jaffe as counsel for the defense in the matter of *Florida v. Morgan*."

"Why?" Fleming demanded.

Whatley gave all the reasons, and it was clear to me he'd been coached by the master. He was no longer the long-winded boy who had argued the previous April against the inclusion of Elroy's affidavit. He was personable and deeply confident, a young man being groomed for higher things. His gray suit was perfect for the role: it didn't hang too well on the neck, and the dark-blue tie over the white shirt had a skinny knot that was slightly askew. Juries would love him. A great many judges would give him leeway.

Fleming peered at me over his tortoiseshell glasses. "Mr. Jaffe, what say you?"

I said, "Your Honor, I could answer in kind, and quote cases and precedents and high-minded concepts like impropriety and alleged confidentiality, but I think this argument boils down to answering just two questions. The first question is: Shouldn't a defendant in a case as serious as this—in any case, for that matter—have the right to be represented by the lawyer of his choice? And the second one is: In the interests of truth, shouldn't that lawyer be permitted to bring to bear all the facts at his disposal, provided he didn't come by those facts illegally? What is the state afraid of? That I know things I shouldn't know? Is that possible in a court of law? Is there *anything* that shouldn't be known? Doesn't full knowledge lead to an approximation of justice?"

I might have gone on, but the judge was frowning and waving

his hand back and forth at me in an admonitory gesture; so I shut up.

"You're wasting your breath, Mr. Jaffe," he said.

Now it was my turn to frown.

Judge Fleming said, "I don't mind people thinking I'm senile and stupid, but I don't want to give them any proof. If any of you lawyers think we've come this far just to turn tail and go fishing, you're in the wrong courtroom. State of Florida, call your first witness."

Whatley started to open his mouth again, but Muriel Suarez yanked him by the sleeve of his jacket and stood up at the counsel table in the well of the courtroom. In contrast to her colleague, who was dressed in what might well have been a mail order suit, she wore a black wool nipped-at-the-waist Italian-looking creation and filigreed gold eyeglasses. Other than lipstick she used no makeup today, so that she looked like a scholarly courtesan. Even Fleming couldn't keep his eyes off her. A couple of television reporters were in the courtroom, and their cameramen jostled to position themselves and their minicams on the other side of the glass-paneled courtroom door.

"Permission to approach the bench, Your Honor," Muriel said.

"Come right up." The judge crooked a gnarled finger to beckon. He couldn't refuse. And a closer look at Muriel probably didn't seem like a bad idea.

Up there we could only whisper. I leaned across the oak bench, with Gary Oliver at my side and chewing on the end of a pencil just as he had done thirteen years before. Muriel leaned from another angle, backed up by an eager John Whatley. The judge bent forward with an audible creak, turning up his hearing aid.

This was all off the record. Here at the bench, sometimes, trials were won or lost. And here, now, Muriel Suarez on behalf of the State of Florida played her hole card. It had been there all along to be played whenever she felt she needed it. Of course it had been provided to her by Beldon Ruth, who in turn had had it provided to him by the govorner of Florida, who needed Beldon's support in the always restless black community of Jacksonville.

"Your Honor," Muriel said, "we hope you won't take this the wrong way and think we were playing games. We weren't. And we aren't." She spoke softly and almost seductively. "The state is now willing to join the defense in a motion to commute the sentence of Darryl Morgan from death by electrocution to life imprisonment."

"Well!" said the judge.

He seemed surprised and not at all annoyed. Close to death, he probably didn't fear it, but he knew that at seventy-nine he had a somewhat different point of view than a man of thirty-three. He turned to me, beaming. "What say you, Mr. Jaffe?"

I was surprised too. I was more than surprised. I cleared my throat and told him that I'd have to consult with my client.

"How long will that take?" the judge asked, a little puzzled by what he took to be my coolness.

"I don't know, Your Honor. Maybe half an hour. Maybe a lot longer."

"But no longer than that?"

I wasn't quite sure what he meant, but I said, "No, sir."

"Mr. Jaffe, this isn't what I'd call a complicated decision. You get my point? But we'll recess until ten o'clock tomorrow morning. That should give your client plenty of time for making up his mind whether he wants to live or die." And for me to pack a lunch in the cooler and go fishing, his eyes said.

I hurried back to the counsel table. "Don't talk to anyone," I instructed Darryl. Two burly deputy sheriffs cuffed him and began to shove him toward the back door of the courtroom. "I'll be at the jail in ten minutes."

I had to elbow my way past the gang of reporters; they knew what the state had done. They could smell it, or they had been tipped by the court reporter who had been up there at the bench with us. "No comment!" I yelled, rushing past the wildly swinging boom mikes. Then I thundered down the staircase and out a side door that led to the Duval County Jail.

The press followed me into the street. High heels clicked and Reeboks scuffed on hot pavement.

"Did you tell Darryl? Will he accept?"

"Do you view this as a victory?"

"Why do you think the state caved in, Ted?"

"No comment," I said. You always feel a bit of an ass when you say that. But you have to. It's part of the game.

The jail was only a block from the courthouse, and I was there in less than the promised ten minutes. I turned to the media gang, all of us sweating in the midday heat. "Give me a break, guys. It's Morgan's decision, not mine."

And Darryl knew all about it by the time I reached him in the air-conditioned room given over to visits by lawyers. The deputy sheriffs couldn't resist; they had told all. Darryl kept clenching and un-clenching his fists, and now and then he beat with them against his massive thighs.

"You can live," I said. "That's what it comes down to."

He looked at me with hard eyes. "How much time I got to do that way?"

"Another twelve years before you're eligible for parole. There's no guarantee you'll get parole. Most convicted murderers don't, I have to tell you that. But you'll *live*."

"I ain't afraid of death," he said.

"I know that."

"But I don't want to die like Sweeting done."

"I understand. Listen, Darryl, if you take this deal, if they give you life, you get off the row. That's what you have to focus on. They put you into population. You work at a job, you walk around the yard, you talk to people. You have visitors and you do things. You take your cards and your magic with you. You can do those tricks for the other men. You hear what I'm saying?"

"I don't know where to look," Darryl said.

I didn't understand what he meant, but I didn't say anything.

"I take life," Darryl said, "this hearing, it's over, right?"

"That's right. I'll make a motion for a retrial, but I probably won't get it."

"How we doing?"

"In court so far? We haven't done anything yet. And we're a little short of time now."

"How it turn out if we keep going?"

"I don't know," I admitted.

"You ain't smart enough to figure that out?"

"No."

"You want me to take the deal, right?"

"If I tell you to turn it down, and we lose this appeal, and they electrocute you, I can't live with that, Darryl."

He put his hand on my shoulder again. "You got to think about what *I* can live with, Mr. Lawyer. What you can live with don't matter, 'cause you out there, a free man. Hear what I'm saying?"

I didn't know Darryl or understand his mind. He might have come from Mars or New Guinea for all that I was able to get into his thought processes and heart. He had always been one-dimensional for me, as I probably had been for him. I saw that now, and it made me ashamed. So I just nodded.

He began to pace the little room. Then he stopped and said, "Tahaun, he came back again with Pauline. You know that?"

"I heard."

Gary Oliver had told me about it. They had all driven down to Raiford the day before the hearing began. Once again Gary had taken Pauline's daughters for a strawberry milk shake in the town of Starke.

"I talk to that kid alone for a time," Darryl said. "I ask Pauline to step outside. She a real good woman. She do it for me."

"How did the visit go?" I asked.

"Real good." Darryl sounded surprised. "You know, he's my son." He said that to me as if I hadn't known, and almost as if he too had only recently figured it out.

"I know that."

"Nice boy. But he got problems."

"I have a son too. They all have problems."

"Black boy got different ones. We talk some shit for a while, then I say, 'How *are* you, dude?' And he turn away, he don't want me to see him cry. And I say to him, 'Dude, I know how you feel. You know how I got to be on this earth? My mama and some dude get it off in a one-night stand. Dude just split for she don't know where. She was drunk that night, she don't even remember his name for sure. And I always think, I ever meet that dude, I *kill* him.' I say to Tahaun, 'Maybe you think that about me too. And here I is, right in front of you, your daddy who never done nothing for you. How 'bout that? You want to kill me, boy?' He smile a little and say, 'No. Not anymore.' So we keep talking, and I see this boy don't know where he can go. Talks about playing basketball, but he tells me maybe he ain't really good enough. He ain't even a star on his high school team, so it must be true. I tells him, 'Stick with it, but don't dream about it no more. Dream about something else.' Then I figures it out, 'cause I remembers what it's like to be sixteen, and big, and black, and dumb. I figures out he's angry. Angry 'cause he know if he ain't good enough to play no ball he probably ain't smart enough to do nothing else. You dig? And he got to get past the anger so's he can see who he is and who he want to be. I tell him that."

"I hope he paid attention," I said. "It was good advice."

Darryl nodded, but he wasn't really concerned with my reaction; he was listening to himself. "You got to fight, I tells him. I ain't good at this, but what I'm trying to 'splain to you is this—if you like me, you think you're too big, too black, too loud, too clumsy, too ugly. I sees that in him, 'cause that's the kind of kid I was too. You don't like who you be, and that make you scared. You don't know where to look. I don't read good, I couldn't get it out of no books. Couldn't get it out of no job, 'cause what kind of job I ever get? Got it out of what I did, and you know what that was. You know how much pen time I done in my life? Shit, I'd have to add it up, and I can't hardly count that high."

He was silent.

Then he said, "I take the deal, where I got to go now? What kind of life that be at Raiford? Do my magic in the yard for cons and hacks? Listen to me, man, 'cause I don't believe you hear what I'm saying." His dark eyes glowed furiously. He had changed gears. I had seen his anger; I knew what he could do. But this anger was of a different quality.

"Where that boy gonna go?" he demanded of me. "He a lot smarter than me, but still he do some drugs, shit like that. I asked him, and he told me." Darryl leaned forward to me, so that once again I could smell him. But I was used to his smell now, the way I hoped he was used to mine.

"I didn't kill that Jew, you know that. You get me outa here, you get me free, I can take care of that boy. That boy want to be with me, want to see me. I knows that. Don't matter what we do, long as he with me. I can do it," he repeated doggedly.

I said carefully, "What about Pauline?"

"She a good woman. Shit, I don't talk about taking that boy away from her. I get a job, I stay with Pauline, if she have me. Says she got two other kids. Girls. You see them?"

"Yes."

"What they like?"

"Nice kids."

"So I have a family. I ain't against that."

"If you can convince her."

"Can't do that from no cell in Raiford," Darryl said.

"You're telling me," I said slowly, "that you don't want to take the deal the state's offered you."

259

"And you're hearing me," he said.

I felt my heartbeat quicken. "You're throwing the dice for your life, Darryl."

"No, *you* throwing the dice. I just putting up the stakes. You roll a seven, I live. You crap out, I go where that Sweeting boy went. I ain't completely crazy, so you got to tell me we got some chance to win. You say that to me, we go back in there and tell that skinny young dude and that sexy spic lady they can go fuck theyselves."

And Darryl smiled at the thought, showing white teeth and frightened eyes.

He wasn't letting me play the great white father; he was taking responsibility for his life, just as he had done thirteen years before with Gary Oliver. I had respect for this man.

"We have a chance," I said.

"Then go to the whip, dude," Darryl said.

27

On Tuesday morning, for the first time, Judge Fleming showed me an emotion midway between vexation and anger. His eyes were bleak, and his lips grew thinner. He said to me the same words I had said to Gary Oliver so long ago in my office. "Counselor, it's my duty to remind you that your first responsibility is to keep your client alive."

"My client knows what's going on, Your Honor. We'll gratefully accept the state's joining our motion to commute the death penalty, but we want a new trial on the guilt-or-innocence issue. Otherwise . . . no deal."

The judge beckoned, and I leaned forward across the bench. Muriel did too, but he waved her back. He broke the first canon of judicial ethics by whispering in my ear, so that opposing counsel couldn't hear.

"Mr. Jaffe, if your client's guilty, you'd do better trying to put socks on a rooster than looking for a new trial in *my* court."

I leaned farther up and whispered back into his white, hairy ear: "He's not guilty."

The judge told us all to step back a pace or two. Then he called shrilly, "Mr. Morgan, kindly step up here."

Darryl looked at me for approval. He wasn't fond of judges. I nodded, and he got to his feet and lumbered to the bench. He was a physically imposing sight.

Fleming wagged a finger back and forth at the court reporter, meaning: stop transcribing, you fool. The courtroom was full again. The judge knew that a defendant wouldn't invade his space, so he had to lean forward himself, his white whiskers almost touching Darryl's flat, broad nose. I could just barely hear him.

"Your lawyer," Fleming said softly, "claims you're turning down the state's offer of a life sentence. You aware of that?"

"Yes, sir."

"You agree with your lawyer?"

"Usually," Darryl said.

"How about now?"

"Yes, sir. I agrees."

"You think I'm a pussycat?" the judge whispered.

Darryl cocked his head. "What you say?"

"I say, you think I'm a pussycat? Think I care if you live or die?"

"No, sir," Darryl said. "I don't think you give a sick rat's ass."

"You can sit down," the judge said.

He raised his head then, sniffed the air, and said to the waiting courtroom, "Let's get on with this hearing." Then he turned toward Muriel. "You ready? Get it done."

Muriel understood that in order to make the judge happy she didn't have to bring on the Jacksonville Beach deputy sheriffs who had first reached the house and viewed the body of Solomon Zide, or the county medical examiner who had conducted the autopsy, or even the JSO ballistics expert. But she did have to offer up some background so that the court knew where we were and who had died.

Accordingly, the state called ex-JSO Sergeant Carmen Tanagra—under subpoena—as its first witness.

Muriel could as easily have called Floyd Nickerson, but she didn't want me cross-examining him. If he was to testify, it was I who would have to subpoena him as a witness for the defense—then Muriel, or John Whatley, would have the precious right to cross-examine.

That was the way the game was played. Muriel was no advocate of the death penalty, but her oath of service required that she battle to keep Darryl Morgan on his path to Big Wooden Mama.

And there was always the matter of ego. Nobody likes to lose.

Carmen Tanagra was sworn in by the court clerk. John Whatley rose from the counsel table to question her.

In clipped, unemotional prose, the former JSO Homicide sergeant set the scene for us: the luxurious beach estate, the tropical night, the hard glare of the floodlights.

She and Sergeant Nickerson pulled up in the driveway. The Jacksonville Beach patrolmen took them straight to the body on the terrace, which was identified by Neil Zide as his father, Solomon Zide, who appeared to have been shot at least twice. She checked for a carotid pulse. "There was none," she testified. "He was dead."

The crime scene, as far as she knew, had been preserved. She herself, after making sure that Mrs. Zide's bleeding had been stanched and that she was resting comfortably on a sofa in the care of a housemaid, who had been awakened by the commotion, talked briefly to Neil Zide and then left him with Sergeant Nickerson. She walked about the grounds and discovered the dead Doberman by the dunes near the beach cabanas. In the wet sand closer to the ocean she found the imprint of the sneakers of two running men. She determined that one of the fleeing murderers wore size fourteen or fifteen shoes.

I could have objected to her assumptions, but I kept still.

When she got back to the house, red lights were flashing. An ambulance had arrived, and paramedics were bundling Mrs. Zide into it. Her partner, Sergeant Nickerson, was questioning Neil Zide. The tech squad had arrived too; someone was taking photographs. Armed with Neil Zide's description of the two young black men who had apparently bungled a burglary, then shot and killed his father, she and Nickerson set out together into the dark night to see if they could find the perpetrators.

Tersely she described the encounter at the Lil' Champ, the death of William Smith, the arrest of Darryl Morgan.

"Pass the witness," Whatley said.

I rose slightly in my chair. My tone was as casual as it could be without putting everyone to sleep.

"Ms. Tanagra," I asked, "when you and Sergeant Nickerson arrived at the Zide estate in your car, how did you get in?"

"Through a gate down at the road," she said.

"The gate was open?"

"I don't really remember. Maybe open, maybe shut. There was a security guard there. Maybe he opened it. This was thirteen years ago—it's hard to say."

"I appreciate that. So the security guard may have unlocked the gate and let you in?"

"He may have."

"Did you speak to him?"

"I don't really remember."

"Can you describe him?"

"Not after this long a time," she said.

"Do you remember if he was young or old?"

"Old, I'd say."

"Over forty?"

"Definitely. Well, probably."

"By any chance, do you recall his name?"

"No. It's too long ago."

"Could it have been Terence O'Rourke?"

"That sounds familiar. But I don't really remember."

"Did you wonder, considering that several shots had been fired, why he was there at the gate and not up at the house?"

Carmen Tanagra thought that over for a while. "I seem to recall that someone had given him an order to stay there because the police were coming."

"He told you that?"

"I think so. I'm not sure."

"Did he say who gave him that order?"

"If he did, I don't remember."

"How far was it from the gate to the house?"

"Hard to say."

"If you don't mind, I'll try to refresh your memory." I signaled to Gary Oliver, who stepped into the hallway leading to the judge's chambers and returned with an easel and a large sheet of white cardboard. On it in bold black lines was drawn a plan of the Zide estate. It had been drafted with the aid of the original architect and landscape designer. Gary had been on their backs all fall for them to get it done, and they had signed an affidavit as to the plan's accuracy.

Muriel inspected the affidavit. All right, she was willing to stipulate that the plan was accurate. "However, Your Honor," she said, "I don't see the relevance. I'd like to remind the court that basically we're here to listen to fresh evidence promised by the defense. This is not fresh evidence."

"The purpose of this line of questioning," I said, "is clarity. And enlightenment."

That was the magic word. The judge said, "If you're objecting, ma'am, I'm overruling." He turned to me. "Just hurry it along, Mr. Jaffe."

Muriel smiled graciously and sat down.

I pointed out to Carmen Tanagra that according to the landscape designer's drawings it was approximately one quarter of a mile from the front gate, where she and Nickerson had entered, to the main rooms of the Zide house.

"That seems about right," she said.

"Ms. Tanagra, if a shot had been fired in the house while you were passing through that gate, would you have heard it?"

"Of course," Carmen said.

"But no shots were fired while you were there?"

"No." She seemed puzzled. That was fine. I meant her to be puzzled.

"When you reached the house, what other vehicles were parked on the driveway in front of the house?"

"Two black-and-whites from Jacksonville Beach. And one civilian car."

"Belonging to?"

"A man named Victor Gambrel."

Gambrel was in the main living room, she explained, when she and Nickerson entered the house. He identified himself immediately as director of security for Zide Industries. He was with Mrs. Zide, taking care of her. He had been there for only a couple of minutes, he told them, after a telephone call he received from Neil Zide.

"Were you able in any way to corroborate that last statement of Mr. Gambrel's? That he'd been in the house 'only a couple of minutes'?"

"I believe the security guard corroborated it."

"Oh? The one down by the gate?"

"There was only one, I believe. So yes."

"When did you talk to him?"

"Sergeant Nickerson questioned him the next day. Down at the sheriff's office."

"You weren't present at that questioning?"

"I was doing some other work. I don't remember exactly what."

"And did either of you question Mr. Gambrel?"

"Sergeant Nickerson did, then and later. He and Gambrel knew each other. As soon as we walked in, Gambrel looked up and said, 'Hello, Nick,' and Nickerson said, 'Hello, Victor.'"

"Like they were old friends?"

"Not quite. Like they knew each other professionally, I'd say. I think Gambrel had been a JSO officer before he went into private work."

Gary Oliver was scribbling notes as fast as his black Flair pen could fly across or over the lines of his legal pad. His handwriting was a large scrawl, so that every minute or so he would flip the page loudly to uncover a fresh one. For a moment I glanced at Muriel Suarez. Her eye for that split second was on Gary as he wrote; she was frowning. In this courtroom today the lawyers didn't have to hide their emotions. There was no jury to observe, to wonder.

I looked at my own notes. "Ms. Tanagra, you said in direct examination that, as far as you knew, the crime scene had been preserved. I'm curious—what did you mean by 'as far as I knew'?"

"Well . . . it didn't seem to have been disturbed."

"How did you make that judgment?"

Her nostrils flared; she was angry. She wasn't a cop anymore, but she still wanted to be thought of as having been a *good* cop. "I don't recall," she said.

"By 'the crime scene,' I take it you mean the immediate area around the body of the murdered man."

"Yes, more or less."

"Did you ask Mrs. Zide and Mr. Neil Zide if they'd touched anything in that area? And if they'd moved the body at all?"

"Yes, I did ask. They said no."

"And you believed them?"

"They were in a state of shock," Tanagra said.

"That's not what I asked you. I asked if you believed them when they said they hadn't touched anything or moved the body."

"Up to a point. I mean, this was a hysterical woman. She was bleeding all over the place. She might have moved the body, might have tried to cradle her husband. Sure, that could have happened. A lot of things happen that aren't meant to happen. But the medical examiner—"

"Was the son hysterical?" I persisted. "Neil Zide?"

"A little. Yes, he was."

"Was Mr. Gambrel hysterical?"

"I don't recall that at all. He'd just arrived."

"He was calm?"

"I believe he was calm, yes."

"You talked to him?"

"No, Nick—Sergeant Nickerson talked to him. I went off to find the dog."

I'd been fishing. The hook was wiggling a little in the murky depths, and I wasn't at all sure what was on it. But I felt that slight pressure.

Slowly I said, "Ms. Tanagra, you went off to find the dog at the beach cabanas, is that right?"

"Yes."

"And the dog, the Doberman, when you found him, was dead. Poisoned, as I recall, by Smith and Morgan." Darryl, at my side, shifted his weight and grunted. "By Smith," I corrected myself.

"Right."

"When you went off toward the beach, Ms. Tanagra, did you know the dog was dead?"

"No, of course not."

"Did you know there was a dog there at all?"

Her brow knitted; she was trying to recall. But it was thirteen years ago. That's nearly five thousand days and nights crammed with incident. She shrugged a bit helplessly.

"Let me see if I can refresh your memory again," I said, "and please stop me if I'm wrong. You left the living room, where all these people were gathered . . . you went outside onto the terrace." She was nodding, so I kept going. "You could have gone in any direction, but you didn't. You turned left"—I knew that house and lawn and terrace, of course; I had partied there, I had even fucked there—"and you crossed the lawn toward the beach. Why did you do that?"

"To see if the dog was all right," she said.

"Why did you want to see if the dog was all right?"

She spoke almost dreamily. "Because someone had said, 'I wonder why the dog didn't bark.' Or maybe, 'I wonder if the dog's all right. Why isn't he barking?' Something like that. I remember that now. And I went out there to find out. I went down to the beach. The son said that, I think. Said the dog was down by the beach and pointed in that direction. Yes, I'm fairly sure it was the son."

"Neil Zide?"

"Yes."

"Did you go down to the beach alone?"

"No, I took one of the Jacksonville Beach cops with me. Nick said, 'Don't go alone, Carmen. You never know who's out there.' So this cop went with me."

"And you left Neil Zide and Mrs. Zide and Victor Gambrel and Sergeant Nickerson and one other Beach patrolman in the house."

"No, there were two other Beach cops. Three of them came in two patrol cars. One went with me to the cabanas—I remember he had this huge, powerful flashlight that he could hang on his belt. Two stayed behind."

I took a chance. "When you and the third Beach cop got back from the cabanas to tell them about the dead dog, were the two other Beach cops still in the living room with the Zides and Victor Gambrel and Sergeant Nickerson?"

"I don't think so," Carmen Tanagra said. "I think the ambulance was coming up the drive and those two guys were out there to flag it down. Yes, I'm positive of that."

"Positive . . . after thirteen years?"

"Yes."

"Why?"

"I don't know," she said, but I could see by the fresh lines etched into her forehead that she was troubled by some memory or vision just beyond her grasp. Or maybe just within it, so that her mental fingertips touched it but couldn't haul it in.

"I have no more questions," I said, "for now."

28

In THE AFTERNOON, after lunch, Whatley said calmly, "The State of Florida calls Constance Zide."

Heads turned, and necks craned. A uniformed bailiff escorted Connie into the courtroom, down the aisle past the bar and through the well to the witness stand. Even as the door hissed shut you could hear the clicking of Nikons and the soft roll of the rubber wheels on the big TV cameras. I turned too, and saw that Connie's black leather purse was raised in front of her face in the direction of the cameras.

When she passed in front of me on her way to the stand, I understood why she was doing that. I hadn't seen Connie since the day Darryl Morgan had been given his death sentence by Judge Eglin. She was nearly sixty years old now. I had assumed that with her bone structure and her pale clear skin she would always remain a beautiful woman, that if you were young you would look at her and wish you'd known her in her prime.

That had not happened.

Her hair was the same color, dyed now to mask the gray, and it had lost some of its sheen. But her hair was almost the only recognizable feature.

Connie's cheeks were doughy, and a roll of flesh moved down from the chin to the thick throat. The scar was of course gone; cosmetic surgery had taken care of that. She wore a black suit as if she were still in mourning, but I remembered that she had once said,

"Darling, black's not my color, it's too dramatic, although it does make one look thinner. The day you see me in black, you'll know I'm an over-the-hill bag."

When she walked she swayed with uncertainty, as if it took a certain effort to move her hips down the aisle, and she seemed grateful to finally sit down in the witness box. Diamonds and emeralds and heavyweight gold bangles bedecked her as though she were a film star, and I sensed that today they weren't fake. I was about twenty-five feet away from her, and when she gazed across the courtroom there was hardly any expression in her eyes: a minimal greeting by way of rapid blinking, a bit of anesthetized pain, perhaps, but that was all. The blue-green eyes were flecked at the corners with a tracery of pink. Surrounded by heavy pancake makeup and set above thin vermilion lips, they seemed moribund.

Oh, Connie . . . my old dear Connie, what happened to you?

I wanted to reach out, touch her and comfort her. But I could hardly do that.

On the bench, Judge Fleming coughed, and when I looked quickly up I realized that for the first time he was wondering if it was so important to be enlightened. But it is, Judge—it is. I promise you.

John Whatley treated Connie gently.

He took her back thirteen years to the night of December 5, to the Mozart horn concerto and smoked Nova flown down from Zabar's on the West Side of Manhattan. And in a slightly hoarse but warm voice, which had hardly changed over time, she told the story of that night.

I had heard it before. She had been my mistress and my witness. I had read her testimony later in the trial transcript. And I had thought about it now for nearly a year.

Telling that tale now took only fifteen minutes. She had heard shots, she recalled, and rushed outside to the terrace, where her husband lay dead. Two black men had been standing there, one with a pistol in his hand. Someone had slashed her in the face. That's all she remembered.

Whatley moved a deferential step backward, like a courtier withdrawing before a queen, and gave her a gracious smile as accolade.

"No further questions. Thank you, Mrs. Zide. We're sorry to have troubled you this way." He turned to me and said curtly, "Pass the witness."

"I have no questions," I said.

And Connie's eyes shone at me with a gratitude beyond deserving. I added, "But I would like to have Mrs. Zide stay in the court-room, or nearby on call."

In most trials, witnesses are prohibited from hearing the testimony of the other witnesses. But that prohibition must be invoked by one side or the other—literally, the defense attorney or the prosecutor rises at the outset of trial and says, "Your Honor, we invoke the rule."

Neither Muriel nor I had done so in this hearing. I had my reasons, and I assumed that she did too. So Connie stayed in the courtroom to listen to her son testify. Neil had listened to her as well, and to Carmen Tanagra.

Neil's hair was still long and unruly, but he had shaved for this occasion, and wore a three-piece suit and pin-dot cranberry-colored tie instead of Levi's and silk cowboy shirt. The suit was black; Neil was slim and unafraid of drama.

His testimony about the failed burglary and the shooting echoed what his mother had said. He too had been my witness thirteen years before, so there were no surprises.

When Whatley said, "Pass the witness," I rose from my seat at the counsel table.

"Mr. Zide, you and I have known each other socially for about fourteen years, isn't that correct?"

"Yes, it is." He was already wary. I suppose he had thought I would let him go the way I had done with his mother.

"So you won't mind if I call you Neil?"

"No, of course not . . . Ted."

"I didn't want the court to think that I was taking liberties," I explained, and smiled up at Judge Fleming.

Then I turned back to Neil. "You've been in the courtroom, and you heard the testimony of Ms. Carmen Tanagra today, didn't you?"

"Yes, I was here," Neil said.

"So you heard her testify about going to find the Doberman in the dunes near the beach? And the dog was dead, she told us. Poisoned."

"Yes."

I consulted Gary Oliver's notes. "Sergeant Tanagra remembered that the reason she went down to the beach was because someone had said, 'I wonder if the dog's all right. Why isn't he barking?' And she thought that someone was you. Do you remember that, Neil?"

He laughed good-naturedly. "Ted, we're talking about thirteen years ago. I like to think I've got a good memory, but that's pushing it right against the edge of the envelope."

"You mean you don't remember?"

"That's absolutely correct."

"You didn't tell Sergeant Tanagra that the dog was down by the beach?"

"Look, I'm saying I may have. Or I may *not* have. I don't want to guess or speculate. I'm under oath, Ted."

"So you are." He was a wonderful witness: arrogant, well-spoken, almost cheerful.

I picked up a slim manila folder from the counsel table, asked the judge's permission to approach the witness, and handed the folder to Neil in the witness box.

"Would you open that folder, please, and look at its contents?"

Neil treated the folder as if it might have been a letter bomb. But he opened it carefully and flipped through the pages inside it. Then he looked up at me calmly. He shrugged. *What's the big deal?*

"Neil, would you tell the court what you've just looked at?"

"They seem to be copies of a statement I made to the police thirteen years ago—"

"That's all?"

"You didn't let me finish. And a couple of pages of my testimony at the subsequent trial."

"What's the gist of it all?"

"It's my description of the two men who tried to rob the house and then shot my father. And my description of what happened that night."

"Your memory was fresh then, wasn't it?"

"Yes, of course."

"You told the truth, didn't you?"

"Yes, I certainly did."

"Thirteen years have passed. Do you have any reason to change your mind about what you saw and what you believe happened on that tragic night?"

He looked at me for a moment, not sure if there was irony in my tone. There wasn't.

"Certainly not."

"You'll stand by what you said to Sergeant Nickerson on the morning of December 6, 1978, and under oath to the trial jury?"

"Of course."

I took the folder from his hand and read aloud to the judge: " 'They were young, black, wearing sneakers, jeans, and I seem to remember a dark T-shirt. There were two of them. I didn't get a decent look at the other one, who cut my mother. They were obviously clumsy, they didn't expect anyone to be awake at that hour . . . my father surprised them, and they panicked. . . . No, I don't know how they got onto the property.' "

I looked up at the bench. "That's from the JSO offense report, Your Honor. Mr. Zide signed each page in the margin, including the one I read from. And now, Your Honor, I'll read from the trial transcript. This was on direct examination. I was the prosecutor. I asked the questions, and Mr. Zide answered them."

I took a drink of water, then read:

"Q [*by Mr. Jaffe*]: Did you see them clearly?

"A [*by Mr. Zide*]: Oh, yes.

"Q: They weren't in shadow?

"A: No, I could see them quite well. One was a very tall young black man. The other one I don't remember as well.

"Q: Describe the lighting, if you don't mind.

"A: The lamps in the living room were on, and they were shining out onto the terrace. And in addition, as I recall, the spotlights on the lawn had finally been triggered, I assume by these two men, so there was a lot of light out there coming from several directions.

"Q: About how far away from you would you say the two men were standing?

"A: Oh . . . fifteen or twenty feet, perhaps. Hard to say exactly.

"Q: How is your eyesight, Mr. Zide?

"A: Excellent.

"Q: You don't wear any eyeglasses or contact lenses?

"A: I have twenty-twenty vision. All right, to answer your question, I don't wear glasses or contact lenses.

"Q: And for how long did the two men remain there on the terrace before they ran away? That is to say, from the time you first saw them to the time they turned their backs.

"A: It's hard to say. A few seconds. But it was long enough for me to see their faces.

"Q: And did you watch them run away?

"A: Yes, for—I don't know—a few moments.

"Q: Did either of them look back over his shoulder?

273

"A: Yes, the one who shot my father. The big tall one. Just for a second or two.

"Q: Did you see his face then?

"A: Yes.

"Q: Is either of those two men in the courtroom here?

"A: One of them.

"Q: Would you point to him and identify him?

"A: The man who shot my father is sitting at the table there, wearing a blue denim shirt and khaki pants. [*The Witness pointed to Mr. Morgan.*]"

I laid the papers on the table. "That's accurate, isn't it, Neil? I read it the way it's written and the way you testified, didn't I?"

"Yes, I assume so."

"Would you like to check?"

"No. I believe you read it accurately."

"Neil, Mr. Morgan's in the courtroom today too, isn't he?"

Next to me, Darryl stirred slightly in his chair. Neil scowled. He felt I was treating him like a child or an idiot, and he didn't like it.

"Yes, he's here," he said.

"Sitting next to me, right?"

"Yes."

"Mr. Morgan, would you please stand up?"

Darryl rose slowly to his full six feet six inches.

"Neil, what's the most outstanding characteristic of Mr. Morgan? What's the thing you notice first?"

"Objection as to relevance," Whatley interrupted.

"That will become clear," I said.

"Overruled," Judge Fleming said. "You can answer, Mr. Zide."

"Well," Neil said, "he's black and he's tall."

"Normally tall?"

"What do you mean?"

"Well, there's tall and there's very tall, wouldn't you say?"

"Yes, I see what you mean."

"How would you describe Mr. Morgan?"

"Very tall, I suppose."

"That's how you described him under oath at the trial thirteen years ago, isn't it?"

"Yes, exactly."

"How tall does he look to you?"

"I'm not an expert," Neil said uncomfortably. "I'm not a carnival weight-guesser."

"I'm not asking you to guess his weight, I'm asking you to estimate his height. That's not difficult. How tall do you think I am?"

"Objection," Whatley said.

"Overruled. You can answer. But move it along, Mr. Jaffe," the judge said.

"Probably about five ten," Neil said.

"That's it." I smiled. "Now indulge me, if you will, about Mr. Morgan. How tall is *he*?"

"Six four or six five," Neil said.

"Would it surprise you if I told you he's six foot six?"

"Not particularly. I told you I wasn't an expert."

"But six foot six is very tall, isn't it? Not as tall as Michael Jordan or Magic Johnson, but still very tall, wouldn't you say?"

"Yes, I would."

"Thirteen years ago, if you remember, was Mr. Morgan any shorter than he is now?"

"I doubt it."

"Is that a yes or a no?"

"It's a no. He wasn't shorter then."

"Thirteen years ago, on the night your father was shot and killed, when Sergeant Nickerson asked you for a description of Mr. Morgan, how did you describe Mr. Morgan?"

"That same way. Black. Tall. Young, I think. He was younger then, obviously."

Now came the litany. He had to be led and hypnotized. It would be excruciatingly boring if the end result didn't promise—barring accident—to be so pleasurable.

"Neil, I read the police offense report aloud, right here in this courtroom, didn't I?"

"Yes."

"And you heard me read it, didn't you?"

"Yes, of course."

"Heard me quote your words as spoken to Sergeant Nickerson?"

"Yes."

"When you spoke those words to Sergeant Nickerson, you were telling the truth, weren't you?"

"Of course."

"Your memory was fresh, wasn't it?"

275

"Yes."

"You had seen Mr. Morgan and Mr. Smith within the previous hour, isn't that so?"

"Yes."

"And you authenticated that report today, didn't you?"

"Yes."

"That night, you described Mr. Morgan as black, isn't that so?"

"Yes."

"And you did say he and Mr. Smith were young, didn't you?"

"Yes."

"And you described what you believed he and Mr. Smith were wearing, isn't that so?"

"Yes."

"And did you also describe Mr. Morgan as *very* tall?"

Neil was silent.

"Did you describe him," I said, "as merely tall?"

Again Neil didn't answer.

"Did you mention his height or size *at all*?"

Neil sighed.

I extended my hand with the manila folder. "Show us in this report, if you will, where you mentioned—on the night of the murder, less than an hour after it happened—that the man whom you saw shoot your father and run away toward the beach was very tall or even tall."

Neil didn't reach out for the folder.

"Isn't it a fact, Neil, that less than an hour after your father's murder, you didn't describe Darryl Morgan—the man who allegedly shot your father—as tall?"

"I remembered it, but—"

"*No*," I interrupted sharply. "I didn't ask you what you remembered. I asked you how you *described* him. Yes or no, please—isn't it a fact that an hour after your father's death, when you were asked to describe the man who shot him, you neglected to say he was tall? Yes or no!"

Neil looked to Judge Fleming for help, but none was forthcoming.

"If the police report is accurate," Neil said, "it would seem that I omitted that fact."

I let that go.

"And yet," I said, "three months later, in the courtroom at the trial, you described him to me as '*very* tall'—isn't that so?"

"Because by then I remembered."

I waited, but Neil said nothing more. There was no jury to impress. There was only Judge Fleming. "Quit while you're still ahead" was the best maxim for any cross-examiner—and the hardest one to follow.

So I started to turn away, but then stopped, scratched my head, looked indecisive. Sighed, as if I were tired of the whole business.

" . . . There's just one more little thing," I said. "I nearly forgot it." I shuffled through the papers in the folder I still held.

I came up with one page more of Neil's thirteen-year-old testimony in this same courtroom. I handed it to him and asked him to read it silently.

Neil did so. He looked up, a little puzzled.

"What you swore to thirteen years ago," I said, "is exactly what you swore to today, isn't it, Neil?"

"Yes, of course," he replied.

"You heard a noise, something like an urn breaking—is that right?"

"Yes."

"And your father got up from the backgammon table and went out to the terrace."

"That's right."

"Your mother followed him."

"Yes."

"You heard three shots."

"Yes."

"Not two shots, or four shots, or five shots?"

"No, three . . . as best I recall."

"Do you have any doubt as to the number?"

"Not really."

"How long did it take, Neil, between the time you heard the shots and the time you reached the terrace and saw your father lying there on the floor?"

"Probably ten seconds."

"You reached there just in time to see a black man, who we later learned was William Smith, make some movement with his hand toward your mother's face?"

"Yes."

"No more shots were fired?"

"No."

"And were any shots fired before that, while you and your mother and father were playing backgammon?"

"No."

"You're positive?"

"Of course I'm positive. My father wouldn't have gone outside if a gun had been fired."

"No more questions," I said.

Whatley asked for redirect. The last line of questioning had seemed like a fishing expedition, but he badly needed to rehabilitate his witness on the matter of Neil's first description of Darryl Morgan.

Whatley said, "Mr. Zide, that night thirteen years ago, you had just seen your father shot to death, isn't that so?"

"Yes." Neil nodded. "And it was horrible."

"Is it fair to say that you were shocked and stunned by what you saw?"

I objected; he was leading the witness. The judge sustained my objection.

Whatley asked, "What was your state of mind after your father's murder?"

"I was in a state of shock."

"When you talked to Sergeant Nickerson and described these two young men retreating across the lawn, were you at all concerned whether they were fat or thin, tall or short?"

"Not at all. I was only thinking about my father and mother and what had happened to them a few minutes earlier."

"Pass the witness," Whatley said.

"No more questions," I said.

"Is Mr. Zide released or on call?" the judge inquired.

"If it please the court, on call."

Whatley ended his presentation by reminding the court that the state had no burden of proof and therefore no more witnesses. Muriel must have felt they had met their obligation of enlightenment and of saving Judge Fleming the onerous task of reading through the three-thousand-page transcript.

Now it was my turn.

I hadn't known it until recently, but I had waited thirteen years for this moment.

So had Darryl.

It was also time for the lunch break, and I welcomed it. I needed to talk to Gary Oliver. But when I made my way to the back of the crowded courtroom and started carving a path between the reporters and the TV cameras, I saw what at first seemed to be a familiar face.

Then suddenly, startlingly, there stood my wife. She wore what I called her traveling outfit: a pair of floppy khaki trousers, a camel's-hair blazer, and leather boots. I shoved through the mob to Toba's side, and she fell into my arms.

29

I T WAS ALAN, of course. He had called at seven o'clock that morning from the pay phone at Oakwood. He didn't hesitate or waffle. He said, "Mom, I can't stand it here anymore. I'm going. I just thought I owed it to you and Dad to let you know."

Toba had wanted to ask, "Alan . . . are you cured?" But the key word seemed too raw.

"Will they let you go?"

"They can't stop me. There's this woman, Germaine, keeps yelling at me, tells me I'm a quitter and I'll go back on drugs. And the guys have stopped talking to me. But it's like a prison here. Germaine wants me to stay another three months. And when that's over, I know she'll say, 'Three months more.' "

"He took his GED test," Toba told me. "He's sure he passed, so he'll have the equivalent of a high school diploma. But he doesn't get the results until this afternoon. He said he'd wait for that, and then he's off tomorrow."

"And what are *you* doing?" I asked, for we were in the coffee shop at the courthouse, and her feet were propped up on her traveling bag. Her sheepskin winter coat was tossed over the back of her chair.

"I have a plane ticket that gets me into Newark Airport at six P.M. I can rent a car and be at Monticello certainly before midnight, and I'll find this Oakwood joint by nine o'clock tomorrow morning. If he still insists on going, at least I can make sure he doesn't go out on the road like a pauper."

"The road to where?"

"San Francisco, he said. He was going to hitchhike. Can you imagine? In the middle of January?"

"And why did you stop off here, Toba?"

"I had to talk to you first. I couldn't get through to you in the courtroom. So I thought: fuck it, why not." Toba glanced at her watch. "I have to be at the airport in two hours to make my connection."

I shook my head in despair. "We've been over this ground. It's a mistake for Alan to quit. Germaine Price is the woman who told me he would die if he didn't go through the program."

"Which I always considered a major hunk of melodrama."

"You always *hoped* it was a major hunk of melodrama."

Toba hunched her shoulders. I thought I saw new lines fanning out from the corners of her eyes. Or maybe she was tired, or hadn't put on her makeup with her usual fastidiousness. No, they were new crow's-feet. A gift from her son. From life.

She straightened up. "Well, Ted, you've done all you can. You can't leave in the middle of a trial, or hearing, or whatever it is. So I'll bite the bullet. I'll go up and deal with it."

She had once said to me, when Alan had told us he considered driving his car off the causeway, "What if *he* dies while you're off trying to save some lousy murderer's life?"

Wrong. Darryl wasn't a murderer. But neither was Alan. If I was battling to save Darryl, didn't I owe the same allegiance and effort to my son?

Judge Fleming had given me until 5:00 P.M. tomorrow to finish the hearing. He had to pack up and vacate his court; he couldn't change his schedule. It didn't seem that I could go up to Oakwood with Toba and get back in time.

But I had to, and there was only one way.

If it didn't work, Darryl could die. And maybe Alan too, if Germaine Price hadn't been serving up major melodrama to the peanut gallery. I felt a cold clamp of fear in the middle of my chest.

I threw coins down on the table for the coffee that was growing cold. "Let's go find Gary Oliver."

Toba and I flew to Newark together, grabbed a Hertz car, and by six-thirty had struggled through the maze of highways and late rush-hour traffic onto the Jersey Turnpike and then Route 17 into New

York State. The night was dark and the temperature well below freezing. Rags of snow lay on the edge of the road; it made me shiver just to look out there. I still wore the clothing I had worn in the air-conditioned Jacksonville courthouse.

The highway skirted the Palisades, and then we rose gradually through the foothills of the Shawangunks into the Catskills, past Tuxedo Park and Middletown and the Holiday Mountain Ski Area. Here, in another life, my grandparents had spent summer vacations, and not too far to the north, at Grossinger's, my mother and father had first met and courted. Now the snow was thick upon moonlit pastureland; the cold wind ripped past the car. This was famed speed-trap country so Toba was at the wheel—I didn't trust myself to keep within the 55-mile-an-hour limit. The heat in the car was stifling, but whenever I opened the window even a crack, needles of cold penetrated my trousers and chilled my flesh. I smoked a few cigarettes, until Toba said, "For God's sake, Ted, kill yourself if you insist, but give *me* a break. . . . "

We had telephoned from the airport. When we bumped down the icy dirt road outside Oakwood and spotted the ramshackle buildings of the therapeutic community, a flashlight beam shone out of the darkness. Toba slowed to a crawl. I opened a window.

"Dad? Mom?" It was Alan, bundled in a thick winter parka, waiting for us.

Inside the main building the heat pressed into my face like a hot towel. Alan looked grave, a little confused. He had lost a few pounds; he seemed leaner but healthy-looking, and certainly looked older. He embraced us. Behind him, sprawled in easy chairs, three T-shirted young black men and one young white woman watched us silently. Alan gestured at them with one hand.

"These are my friends, but they won't talk to me because I'm splitting. I mean, they're not *allowed* to talk to me. Bucky, and Richard, and Veronica, and Anthony. My parents."

They waved cheerfully. So did we. I remembered Bucky from my visit to the center at 104th Street and Broadway. "Where's your pal Jack?"

"Graduated." Bucky grinned. "You got a good memory, Mr. Jaffe."

Toba gazed at these boys as if they were behind bars at a zoo for aliens. Germaine Price, still frail and pale, bustled in from another room. "I have a few things to do," she said, "and I'm sure you want to talk to Alan alone. So I'll join you in ten minutes."

I had told her on the telephone that I was in the midst of trial, that I couldn't come any other time. She was breaking a number of the local rules by letting us visit at this hour of the night.

Alan led us upstairs into an office furnished with a sagging sofa, a bookcase filled with texts, a desk, and a single easy chair with, I soon found out, a broken spring. He finally smiled. "I passed my GED."

"That's great." I shook his hand heartily.

"Well, this is what's happening," he said, easing himself onto the surface of the desk, legs swinging, hands folded across his chest. "This was the wrong program for me, but I knew I needed help, and I got it. Sticking it out here was the hardest thing I ever had to do. The thing is, I've run out of problems. And patience. So it's time to go."

"And they don't want you to," I said.

"They tell me I'll die. They scream at me. Not just the counselors, but the kids. They tell me I'm not ready. But I am."

And we couldn't stop him either, he said. He had fifty dollars he'd saved from his last job and deposited in the office safe when he'd first arrived here. He wanted to borrow a few hundred more from us. But if we wouldn't lend it to him, he was going anyway. He'd hitchhike out west, work along the way, survive. That was it.

"And what about your addiction?" I asked.

"I'll always miss smoking dope," he said. "And I don't promise I won't ever smoke again. But not for a long time, and never like I did before."

"What will you do when you get to San Francisco?" I asked.

"Study and work."

"What will you study?"

"Art, or maybe journalism."

"Have you been doing any drawing while you're here?"

"Not really."

"Is that a yes or a no?" In the end, there was something to be said for the heartlessness of cross-examination.

"It's a no," he muttered.

"And have you written anything?"

"No, but I'd like to."

I said nothing.

Germaine Price slid into the room. "What has he told you?"

Toba repeated most of what Alan had said, and finished with: "I'm impressed. I trust him. I think we have to trust him."

Germaine dropped into the one empty chair and gave a thin laugh. "Why? He's a lying junkie motherfucker."

I glanced at Alan, who smiled nervously. Toba's lips quivered; her cheeks brightened as if she'd been struck. "That was unnecessary," she said.

"A little rough," Germaine said, "but no less true." She took out a pack of Marlboros and offered them around. We all shook our heads.

"What do you mean?" Toba demanded.

"Mrs. Jaffe." Germaine lit her cigarette, then took a deep drag. "He wanted you to come up here. You understand that, don't you? Otherwise, why call you in Florida? He thinks of this as a prison, and it's a tough place, I grant him that, but I'm sure you've noticed that there are no walls or guards. If you look in the dormitories you won't find any bars. There's just peer pressure. If Alan wanted to, he could have taken off yesterday, the day before, anytime. So why did he wait for you to rush up here?"

"I don't know," Toba said.

"Of course you do," Germaine said.

Toba leaned back against the sofa, folding her arms. "You think it's money."

"I know it's money." Germaine sucked at her cigarette. "Didn't you bring it?"

Toba reddened.

"Without money," Germaine said, "he won't go. He can't go. You think he's a Mohawk who's learned to live off the land? *He* knows he's not. He'd freeze his balls off in a ditch by the side of the road. And Alan doesn't want to die that way, believe me. He uses you. He's clever at it. So clever he may not even realize what's going down."

Alan sprang up and said to Germaine, "Will you please keep out of this?" He faced his mother. "Now, just yes or no, like Dad would say. Will you lend me the goddam money or not?"

I felt myself flush. "Watch your language," I cautioned.

Alan glared at me; I'd never seen that much anger on his face.

"I'd like to talk to you," I said. "Alone, if no one minds."

Toba and Germaine went out the door. I heard the wooden floor-boards creaking, and then the stairs.

Maybe it was the strain of what was happening in that Jacksonville courtroom, maybe it was the stress of all the years of Alan's lies and half-truths. Accumulated feathers, says one Chinese sage, will sink the boat. The boat of my paternal stamina was sinking.

"Is it true that the only reason you called Mom was to get money from her?"

"Probably," he said, a bitter smile twisting his jaw to one side. "So what? I sure didn't ask her to come up here, and I sure as shit didn't ask you to come, either." He talked with wide sweeps of his arms, his body taut, his eyes glaring again. "I asked to borrow money. Big deal! Isn't money the big thing in your life and everyone else's life? What's so terrible about asking for it? Would you rather I tried to steal it or sold drugs to get it, like the people you're always trying to help?"

Alan had never lost his temper with us. He always tried to con us with amiable sweetness and apologies and promises—usually with some measure of success. I knew that other teenagers were more hot-blooded in the season of their rebellions, and for the most part I'd been grateful for Alan's softer nature. In that, I may have been short-sighted.

But that sweetness seemed to have fled.

"I'll tell you something else," he went on. "I've changed my mind about the fucking money. You can keep it, because I don't need it. Germaine's wrong—I won't freeze my balls off in a ditch. I'll leave here tomorrow morning. I've got enough to take a bus to Binghamton and check into the YMCA, and I'll get a job washing dishes or pumping gas and save money to get out to California. I'll be there by summer. On my own! So fuck her!"

His skin turned white as he clenched his fist. I think he wanted to blurt out, "And fuck you too!" I don't know what restrained him.

"Alan, I'd like to explain something to you—"

"I don't want to hear it," he said sharply, raising his open palm. "I want to finish."

I ground my teeth. It had been a long day, and it would be a long night before another long day dawned.

"A few minutes ago," Alan resumed with fervor, "Mom said she had faith in me—you remember? And Germaine said that was dumb, because I was a lying junkie motherfucker. Well, I saw the look on your face, and I knew right away you agreed. And I could see that in some crazy way you were glad she believed that, because it proved you were right all along, and you did the right thing sending me to this hellhole in Siberia. So I want to ask you, why don't you have any faith? Because you always think I'm going to mess up, unless I do it by the rules? Your rules? I say I want to study art and you think that's bullshit because I'm not already an artist, not already practicing. Well, maybe I need help to get started, did you ever think of that?"

I hadn't thought of that; he might have been right.

He kept going. "You think that way about me because I *did* mess up a lot. And maybe I'll mess up again." He shook now with rage. "But who cares if you're right? Give *me* a chance to be right! Or wrong! If I mess up, it *won't* kill me. You can't run my life anymore, that's the bottom line. Let me do it my way! You always do things your way, don't you? I'm getting out of here, Dad. Tomorrow."

I was a stubborn man. When I knew what I wanted, you couldn't stop me. That had certainly been proved in the past year. It began to seem that my son had inherited that trait. It had just taken a while to surface.

Yesterday, when the state had offered him life instead of certain death, Darryl had made a choice. He had turned down the offer and chosen to throw the dice, risking everything. That was a human being's final privilege.

My son's too. He was declining this sanctuary, which he hated, in favor of risk. And he had no advocate to argue for him. He had to do it all alone. I began to respect him.

"Do you want to come back to Sarasota?" I asked.

"No! I'm going out west! On my own!"

"Good luck," I said.

"I will!"

He was hearing words other than the ones I spoke. But we all do that.

I yawned and said, "Let's go downstairs. I'm bushed. I'm hungry too. Would you like to go into town and have a hamburger and coffee with us?"

He took a few deep breaths to regain his composure. He studied my face, looking for hidden motive, but there was none. I was just tired.

"Sure," he said.

"Is there a place that's open?"

"A diner on 17 outside the town of Oakwood."

"Will they let you leave?"

"You heard what the head jailer said. It's not a prison."

We drove through Oakwood and ate at the diner. Alan ordered scrambled eggs and a double ration of bacon, which he claimed he hadn't tasted in three months. After we ate I realized he didn't light up a cigarette, and hadn't done so in the office when Germaine offered him the pack.

"No," he said. "I quit."

"Why?" Toba asked.

"To prove something to myself, I guess, and because I always wanted to. It's a disgusting habit."

"I started again," I said glumly.

"Well, Dad, you always admitted you were a nonpracticing addict." He gave me a tolerant smile.

"I'm going to quit when this trial's over."

"How's that going?"

"It'll be over tomorrow," I said.

"Is this guy going to die?"

"I don't think so."

"I'll bet you feel good about that."

Alan had never made a comment like that before, or showed any interest in my cases.

"Yes," I said. "If he lives I'll feel very good."

Alan went to the men's room.

"What happened?" Toba asked. "He seems so calm. So sure of himself."

"I'll tell you on the drive back. Meanwhile I'm going outside to smoke a cigarette. While I'm freezing my balls off in a ditch, give him a few hundred dollars. Insist on it. He'll take it from you, but not from me."

"But—"

"Let him throw the dice and do it his way, Toba, whatever that is."

I tried to sleep on the drive down to Newark Airport, but at one o'clock in the morning it began to drizzle, and then sleet fell in the mountains. My forehead pressed against the car window; it was like cozying up to the shady side of an iceberg. Toba skidded on a curve and I yelled, "Jesus!"

"Do you want to drive?"

"I want to sleep."

"I'm sure there's a hotel at the airport. You could take a nap for an hour or two."

"If we don't get killed en route."

She hit the brakes. "Drive, Ted!"

By 4:00 A.M., when we returned the car to Hertz, my nose was dripping, my eyes felt ragged and I had trouble keeping them open. But at least, so far, the soles of my feet stayed calm.

"I'll come to court with you," Toba said. "I'd better be there if you fall asleep at the counsel table."

My heart seemed to slow another beat or two. Now my feet itched. "That's good of you, darling, but—"

"Oh, knock it off, Ted. I'm coming."

There was nothing I could do. She would be there, and she would hear my witnesses.

My father had given me two bits of advice I often remembered. Never try to save money on what goes between you and the ground (he meant shoes, tires, and mattresses), and treat yourself to a good steak and a shot of Jack Daniel's whenever you're feeling depressed.

At 5:00 A.M. in the airport restaurant I ordered a medium-rare T-bone and a pot of coffee. The bourbon didn't seem like a good idea yet.

30

OBA AND I changed planes in Atlanta and landed at Jacksonville International just after ten in the morning. The air was warm and crisp. The sun was shining, and the glare hurt my eyes. I kept wiping my red raw nostrils with Kleenex; my stomach had what the Florida crackers of my boyhood called "the whistlebelly thumps."

We took a taxi into the city and reached the courthouse just before eleven. In the elevator I buttoned my collar and tied my tie. A few TV cameramen outside Courtroom Five stared at me. I'd used my suit jacket as a pillow at Newark Airport, and there was a stain on my trousers where a piece of breakfast T-bone had landed. In general, I felt as if I'd been shot out of a cannon and missed the net.

Floyd Nickerson was to have been my first witness, assuming he hadn't left town and risked a contempt citation. He was under a subpoena that Gary Oliver had hand-delivered one evening a week before to Orange Meadow. At first Nickerson had tried to slam the front door. Then he threatened bodily harm to Gary, who stood his ground and said, "Mr. Nickerson, I'm acting as an officer of the court. Touch a hair on my head, and I'll hand you this subpoena tomorrow in a jail cell."

Yesterday after lunch, Gary had gone to Judge Fleming and explained that I'd been called out of town on urgent family business, but that I'd be back the following morning and we would complete our case by the end of that day, as promised—as, in fact, demanded.

In a midnight call from Oakwood, I had prepped Gary on how to examine Nickerson. "Draw it out until I get there. Whatever you do, save the other witnesses for me."

But as soon as I pushed open the courtroom door on Wednesday morning, I realized that Floyd Nickerson was not on the witness stand.

Darryl Morgan, in a khaki jumpsuit provided by the jail, filled a wooden chair at the counsel table. Gary Oliver, seated next to him, was examining a man named James L. Duckworth. In his early sixties, Duckworth was the chief medical examiner in Duval County; he had been my witness in the trial thirteen years ago.

Toba and I passed by Connie and Neil Zide. With a gracious smile, Toba squeezed herself into a seat on the wooden pew across the aisle from them. She hadn't seen Connie since the last time we'd all been together in court, thirteen years ago. Clamping my teeth together, I continued past the bar and to the counsel table.

Gary looked up and spotted me. Without hesitation, he said, "No further questions, Your Honor, and we request a brief recess."

Judge Fleming banged his gavel in agreement.

I sat down, nodding to Darryl. Clutching Gary's arm, I said softly, "Where the hell is Nickerson?"

Gary told me. At three o'clock that morning, Nickerson had killed himself.

Light seemed to fade before my eyes, as in a brownout. I whispered, "I don't believe it."

"Believe, Ted."

"How?"

"Ate his gun."

It was what cops did when they were old and tired and depressed, or still on the job and unable to face the consequences of something rotten about to be uncorked. In his garage, the same garage where I'd seen him saying goodbye to Suzanne Byers—at about the hour that Scott Fitzgerald had called "the dark night of the soul"—Nickerson had put his service revolver in his mouth and pulled the trigger. An insomniac neighbor, hearing the shot, hurried over to find him. Nickerson's subpoena was on the kitchen table next to a copy of the *Times-Union* with its lead story about the hearing, an empty pack of Camels, and an overflowing ashtray. There was also a ground-out butt next to his body in the garage. Gary's report had indicated that

Nickerson hadn't smoked for the last ten years. It was, I suppose, his final pleasure.

Jerry Lee Elroy, now Floyd Nickerson. I could understand how you might think twice about becoming a witness for Ted Jaffe.

Darryl hadn't said a word. He was the only one of us who was calm. "What do we do?" Gary asked. Together we had planned the strategy of this hearing. He knew where Nickerson would have fit, why his presence was so important.

"Does the judge know?"

"Not yet. I thought if I told him, he might call the whole thing off. I called Jim Duckworth just to stall."

The point was, of course, that Fleming had granted this hearing on the basis of my tape recording of Nickerson and the former JSO Homicide detective's promised presence as a witness. Technically, without Nickerson, we had no case of our own except what might be proved through cross-examination.

"Go get Terence," I said. I stood up, brushed past Whatley and grabbed Muriel Suarez by the arm, and made a dash for chambers.

Judge Fleming peered at me with his lizard eyes and said, "Well, I'll be dog. You're not funning me? You lost another one?"

"Yes, sir."

"Off on a stony lonesome, like we say in Clay County?"

I nodded. "Gone belly up."

"You got any other witnesses?"

"Yes, sir."

"Worth my listening to?"

"Yes, sir."

"They in court or close enough to hear you yell?"

"Yes, sir."

It was like a cross-examination where a good lawyer fires a salvo of leading questions that only permits the witness to say yes or no.

"And by the way," the judge said, adjusting his glasses and letting his eyes roam over me, "what in hell happened to you? You look like you just had a root canal."

"That would have been preferable. I had a long night, Your Honor."

"Worth it?"

"Too early to tell."

"Usually is," the judge said. "Well, we're here, we've cleaned the wax out of our ears, we've got a few hours left of precious court time. Seems a shame to send all these snoopy TV folks home early. How long will you take?"

"Not too long," I said.

"Sounds about the right amount of time. Let's get on with it."

Muriel, crowding my elbow there in chambers, protested, but the judge finally flashed me a poisonous smile and said, "Call your next witness, Counselor, before La Bella Cubana comes up with something makes me change my mind."

Back in the courtroom, when his honor had ascended the throne and the bailiff had called for order, I dropped down in a wooden chair next to Darryl and said, "The defense calls Michael Stanzi."

Mike Stanzi, the JSO ballistics expert, was still working at the same job. I had his official report in front of me, as well as the pages of his thirteen-year-old trial testimony. He was a man of forty-five, with curly gray hair, a big mustache, and a pleasant demeanor.

"Mr. Stanzi, tell us briefly what you observed on the morning of December 6, 1978, when you reached the Zide estate and had a good look around."

No secret about that. Stanzi had observed a corpse with two bullet holes. The rounds were from a .38-caliber revolver. A third shot from the same weapon had struck the wall on the far side of the living room from the terrace and embedded itself there in the Swedish oak paneling.

"About how high up in the wall was that bullet hole, sir?"

He glanced at his papers. "My official report says eleven feet seven inches."

"You found no other spent rounds?"

"No, I didn't."

"And you never found the gun?"

"Never."

"Then it's possible that more than three shots were fired from that thirty-eight-caliber pistol, isn't it?"

"Well, I suppose it's theoretically possible, but we didn't find any evidence of that."

"Did you look outside the house?"

"No, because it was just lawn and trees out there, and the pistol had been fired by someone who was facing the house from the direction of the terrace."

"Is that a fact?"

"Yes, sir, that's a fact."

"But how did you know that to be a fact?"

Stanzi smiled, patronizing me. "Because we knew that the perpetrators had been standing on the terrace and fired toward the room. And that was confirmed by the bullet we found in the woodwork on the far wall."

"Mr. Stanzi, think about that a moment. Did you *know* the perpetrators had been standing on the terrace and firing into the room, or did you just assume it?"

"Well, as I said, there was the spent bullet in the woodwork. And I was told by a fellow officer that the bullets had been fired from the terrace."

"Which fellow officer told you that?"

"I believe it was Sergeant Nickerson, when we arrived."

"So you really didn't *know*, you simply took his word for it, right?"

"Yes . . . but there was the evidence of the bullet in the woodwork."

"That evidence," I said, "told you that one bullet had been fired in a specific direction. It didn't tell you that the bullet had been fired from the terrace, did it?"

Stanzi shrugged. "Well, no. All right."

"The bullet in the woodwork didn't tell you anything about the bullets that had struck Mr. Zide, or any bullets that might have been fired from inside the room in the direction of the lawn—did it?"

"There weren't any other bullets out there," Stanzi said smugly.

"How do you know that?"

"Because there were only three shots fired, and those rounds were all accounted for."

"And how did you know *that*?"

"Sergeant Nickerson informed me."

"Did Floyd Nickerson tell you he was there and heard three shots? *Only* three shots?"

Muriel objected. This was hearsay, a statement made out of court that couldn't be confirmed.

"Your Honor," I said, "we're not offering it for the truth of the matter but as to why Mr. Stanzi believed what he believed when he conducted his investigation."

"In that case I'll allow it," Judge Fleming said. He seemed interested.

"Mr. Stanzi?"

"No, Floyd Nickerson didn't say he was there and heard the shots. I can't remember how he knew there were three shots. But he knew it. He was positive."

"Did he say he'd spoken to witnesses who were present when the shots were fired?"

"He may have. I really don't remember."

I believed him. I was sure Nickerson had been deliberately vague. Nickerson! Nickerson was the key, and Nickerson was dead.

"Did you or anyone else conduct a paraffin test of the hands and face of Darryl Morgan?"

"Yes, I did."

"And of William Smith down at the morgue?"

"I did that too."

"With what results?"

"Negative. But that didn't mean that neither of them fired a gun. It's only proof if there *is* paraffin. If there's none, it doesn't really tell you anything. People can wear gloves, they can hold a weapon at arm's length. And we didn't have the weapon, so we couldn't tell if it normally threw off blowback or left residue when it was discharged."

I couldn't stop him from rambling. He was my witness, and theoretically a friendly one.

"Did you do a paraffin test of any of the people in the house?"

"Which house?"

"The house where Solomon Zide was killed."

Stanzi looked puzzled. "No, sir. Why should we? The people in that house were the victims."

I said, "Pass the witness."

Muriel didn't know in what direction I was heading, but she saw that thus far I hadn't done any damage to the state's thirteen-year-old case. I'd only shown that witnesses and lawyers were human and missed out on certain things they weren't interested in and therefore weren't looking for.

"No questions," she said.

When we broke for lunch I looked toward the rear of the courtroom. Connie and Neil were still there. She was dressed in a gray suit today, as she had been when I first met her on that afternoon outside Dillard's, and her son was wearing a cotton windbreaker and baggy white trousers and a Melanesian coral necklace.

Then I also saw Tahaun Powers, Darryl's son. Tall and somewhat solemn, in white Nike T-shirt and bluejeans, he sat squeezed among a group of retirees, jovial courtroom groupies who frequented all the high-profile cases.

I went right up to him. "Tahaun . . . you remember me?"

"Sure," he said. "The lawyer. How are you, man?"

"Good. Where's your mother?"

"I came alone."

"How'd you get up here?"

"Bus."

"Come have lunch with us."

I introduced him to Toba. The least I could do was give some warmth to this son of the man whose life I was fighting for. Maybe, wherever my own son was headed, someone would offer an equal simple kindness.

I ate a grilled cheese sandwich and drank nearly another quart of coffee. When we went back to the courtroom, Toba said to Tahaun, "Please sit with me."

"Sure," he said. He finally smiled a little.

The bailiff called for order as I moved forward to the counsel table. The throng settled into the wooden pews and became quiet.

"The defense," I said, "calls Terence O'Rourke."

How do you set about locating a man of seventy-two, who has disappeared from view, without alerting his former employers that you're looking for him? You put a seventy-five-year-old woman on the job and tell her to be discreet and send you the bill for her expenses when she's finished. I had found him with the help of my mother, whose aid in a court case I had enlisted for the first time in my life.

Sylvia was thrilled to get the assignment. In only a few days she had tracked her quarry to a small rest home only a hundred yards from the ocean on Flagler Beach, south of St. Augustine. It was pricey there, but that wasn't a surprise. Terence had been given a handsome pension.

He was lucky to be alive.

The courtroom door swung open to admit Terence, Gary, and my mother, as well as an escorting bailiff. The previous morning, before I'd flown to the frozen North, I'd asked Sylvia to bring her catch here today and keep him occupied in the Lawyers Lounge until we gave the word. Charm him, I told her. Don't let him out of your sight.

"You're not matchmaking now, are you?" she'd asked me. "Because I can take care of that business myself."

"I have no doubt of it."

"Do you know how many propositions I get, on the average, each week?"

"Tell me another time, Mom."

Terence was a monkey-faced man with sparse white hair, protuberant eyes, and horn-rimmed spectacles, round-bellied now but still conscious of his dignity. He wore a sport jacket and a brightly striped regimental tie for the occasion. He had been a cop in Orlando and, like most cops, had served his time on the witness stand. He knew what to do, and he still had a bit of a lilting Irish brogue.

I had him identify himself and provide some background. Then I said, "Sir, were you a witness in 1979, in *Florida v. Morgan*?"

"No, I was not."

"You were neither subpoenaed nor asked by either side to testify?"

"No, sir, I was not."

"Were you ever interviewed by any police officers or anyone from the state attorney's office?"

He related to the court that Sergeant Floyd Nickerson had talked to him on two or three occasions, had tape-recorded one conversation with him, and had finally thanked him and explained that since Terence's story corroborated what everyone else said, he wouldn't be needed as a witness. And no, not a soul from the state attorney's office had ever come round to talk to him.

And I remembered why. A few weeks before the trial, Nickerson, in response to my query, had said, "O'Rourke? Waste of time. He was asleep. He barely remembers the whole fucking night. He's a lush. He's unreliable. What do you need him for?"

I hadn't argued with that. I had been a busy man, winding up my affairs in more ways than one, and I wasn't at all keen then to put on a witness who might have fixed his ex-cop's eye on me and remembered that I'd come calling on Mrs. Zide when Mr. Zide was in Hong Kong, and had ended up in the swimming pool with all my clothes on.

"Mr. O'Rourke," I said, "did you follow the Morgan trial in the newspapers and on television?"

"No, I was on vacation around that time."

"Where did you go for that vacation?"

"I have a married daughter, Claire, who lives in Colorado, and a married son, Dennis, who lives in Manhattan Beach, which is near Los Angeles. I went out west to visit both of them."

"Do you recall anything unusual, Mr. O'Rourke, about that vacation?"

"Well, the way it came about was a little unusual, you could say, if you had a mind to think that way, which I don't mind telling you I did not, for the Zides were fine people to work for."

He had made his point and established his loyalty.

"Nevertheless," I said, "tell us what might have been considered unusual."

"It was that I had a week due me in summer, but Mrs. Zide came to me one night in February—poor lady still had her face all bandaged up from that awful night—and she said she'd prefer I take my holiday earlier, in the spring, for reasons that I don't at this moment recall. And because it might be an inconvenience, she said, I could take longer than was due. She indicated she was pleased with my work too, which accounted for her generosity. I thanked her and said I surely wasn't going to turn down a kind offer like that."

"How long were you away from Florida?"

"She gave me three weeks off with pay, she did. I was half the time in Denver and half in California. I have a total of seven young grandchildren out there."

"And so you missed the Morgan trial?"

"I was away for all of it, yes, that's what I'm telling you."

"The Colorado and California newspapers didn't cover the trial?"

"I read something about it, but I can't remember where. I believe I read that Morgan had been convicted and sentenced to death. But that was all."

"Mr. O'Rourke, I have to ask you some questions that may embarrass you, and I apologize in advance."

He flushed a little; he knew more or less what was coming. I'd talked to him at some length out on the porch of the rest home at Flagler Beach. But I hadn't coached him—I didn't believe in it, because it tended to make witnesses sound stiff—and that lack of certainty as to exactly what I might ask was making him a little nervous.

"That's all right, sir," he said.

"Do you have a drinking problem?"

"I don't now, but I did. I want to say that I owe my success in licking my problem to the Flagler Beach chapter of Alcoholics Anonymous and to the divine intervention of our Lord Jesus Christ."

I let him enjoy the silent respect of the courtroom for a minute, and then said, "Did you have a drinking problem back in 1978 and 1979?"

"I took a wee drop now and then."

"On the night of December 5, 1978, the night of your employer's murder, were you drunk?"

"That is not a fact, sir. That is definitely an exaggeration. It would be accurate to say I'd a drop taken."

If there were a jury I would have pressed the point and pinned him down, but I had only to worry about Judge Fleming, and when I glanced up I could see by the look in the judge's hooded eyes that he understood completely the euphemism that Terence had elected to use.

"Mr. O'Rourke, cast your mind back and tell us—as best you recall, for it was a while ago—what happened on that night of December 5, 1978."

He was on duty, he said, down at the main gate. There was a party. A good many cars moving in and out, and classical music was played out on the lawn by an orchestra.

"You were alone at the gate?"

No, he had help: a young fellow, the day man. But that young fellow left at midnight after they'd checked their in-out sheet and were sure that all the guests and caterers had departed.

"And then you were alone at the gate?"

"Yes, I was alone."

"You stayed awake?"

"Not all the time. I must have been dozing at one point."

"What woke you?"

"A shot."

"You heard a shot?"

"Indeed. At least, I knew later that it was a shot. And I know now. At the time I wasn't sure. It sounded like a shot, but in the middle of a dark night, and not expecting it, who was to say? I'd been dozing, and the shot woke me. I told you that. I'm not proud of it, but I'm human, and by God it's a fact."

"I understand. So you woke up at the sound of what you thought was a shot, but you weren't absolutely sure it was a shot." I paused. "By the way, when you say 'a shot,' do you mean, literally, a single shot, or many shots?'

"A single shot is what I meant."

"When you woke, were you wide awake or dazed?"

"I'd a drop taken. I told you that too."

"But try to answer my question, please, Mr. O'Rourke. We're human too, and we understand. Were you wide awake or dazed?"

"Not wide awake. Not dazed. It would be correct to say I was awake but a trifle sleepy."

I had to settle for that; he was already pink with shame. "And what did you do in response to hearing what you believed might be a single shot?"

Terence O'Rourke sighed a bit mournfully, a bit bravely. "Nothing. I waited."

"How long?"

"It would be fair to say . . . a minute or two."

"And after that minute or two, did you hear anything else?"

"I heard more shots."

"How many more?"

"Three or four, I believe. If I had to choose, I'd say three."

"The three shots were together or spaced out?"

"Close together. One after the other. Like *bang bang bang*."

"And these last three bangs occurred a minute or two after you heard a single shot?"

"That's correct."

"You're sure of that?"

"Yes, sir."

"When you heard the three shots, what did you do?"

"I took my pistol out of my holster, and I went up to the house."

"You walked up there?"

"With a flashlight in my hand, I did indeed."

"Were you frightened?"

"Yes," Terence said quietly.

"Did you run up there?"

"I was close to sixty years old then, sir, and a little woozy from sleep, and frightened, as I've admitted. No, I did not run."

"Did you walk rapidly?"

"It would be fair to say no, I did not. Not really."

"You strolled?"

"No, sir. I walked at a normal and cautious pace through the darkness, with my flashlight."

"How long did it take for you to get to the house?"

"Maybe three minutes."

"And did you go in?"

"First I shone the beam of my flashlight around, to see if any prowlers were about, and Mr. Zide must have seen it, for he came out to meet me on the gravel."

"Mr. Zide?"

"Young Mr. Zide. Mr. Neil, him as what's here in the courtroom with his mother. Not Mr. Solomon. He had passed on." Terence crossed himself.

"Did you know Mr. Solomon was dead—had passed on—when you got to the house?"

"The terrace faced the beach. I came up the driveway to the front door. What I'm saying is, no, I didn't know Mr. Solomon was dead, and no one told me he was dead until a great deal later that night. What happened is, when I reached the house Mr. Neil came out and said to me, 'Terence, a terrible thing has happened. We've sent for the police. Go back to the gate and wait for them.' "

"And did you do that?"

"First I asked him if he was all right, and if there wasn't anything I could do. He looked pale and he was shaking. He said, 'No, go back to the gate, man. Do as I say.' And I did that."

"And did the police come, as Neil Zide had said they would?"

"Yes, indeed they came."

"How much later?"

"Thirty-five minutes later."

"Thirty-five? Not ten, or twenty, or forty?"

"No, sir, it took them thirty-five minutes to arrive."

I pretended to be puzzled, and to think about what he'd said. "Mr. O'Rourke, how can you be sure of the time interval?"

"We kept an in-out list, a log. I wrote down the times."

"I see. And did anyone else come before the police got there?"

"One person. Mr. Neil called down to the gate a few minutes after I got back there. He said a man would be arriving shortly and I should let him in and not talk to him."

"Do you remember the name of that man?"

"I do now, sir."

"Explain to the court what you mean by that."

"I didn't remember it when you asked me last week, but then you offered a few names to me, and one of them seemed right, and I remembered it."

"The name of that man?"

"Gambrel, it was."

"And the man named Gambrel arrived approximately when?"

"About fifteen minutes after I got back to the gate."

"Twenty minutes before the police?"

Terence mulled that over and then said, "That would be correct."

"You're sure of these time intervals?"

"Yes, I am sure."

"Because you wrote all this down on what you call your in-out list? Your log?"

"I did indeed."

"What happened to that log?"

He sighed. "I gave it to the detective who talked to me."

"That would be Sergeant Floyd Nickerson?"

"Yes."

"Did Sergeant Nickerson ever give the log back to you?"

"He did not."

"Was anyone else present when you talked to Sergeant Nickerson, or when you gave him your log?"

"We were alone. First at the house that night, after the ambulance came flying up, and then later down at the sheriff's office downtown."

"Did you ever tell Sergeant Nickerson that you'd heard a single shot, and then three evenly spaced shots a minute or two later?"

"I told him that, sir. Indeed I did."

"Did he write that down?"

"I believe he did, and in any case he had his machine running."

"A tape recorder?"

"That's what it was."

"Did you ever tell Sergeant Nickerson that on the night of December 5 there had been only three shots and that you heard them all together, in succession, one after another?"

"I did not tell him that. It wasn't so."

"Were you aware that at the trial, back in April 1979, Mrs. Zide and Mr. Neil Zide testified that there had been only three shots fired by the accused, Darryl Morgan? And that they had all been fired at the same time?"

"No, sir, I've told you, I was in Colorado and then in sunny California with my children and grandchildren."

"How soon after the death of Mr. Zide was your employment terminated?"

"About five years later."

"Can you tell us the circumstances?"

"Mrs. Zide came to me and told me she wished to reward me for faithful service. She knew I had another daughter down in Daytona Beach, which you may know is not far from Flagler Beach, and that I thought of retiring there. She said the time had come, and she would take care of me."

"Did she give you severance pay?"

"Yes, she did."

"Tell the court how much."

Terence hesitated, then said, "Two hundred and fifty thousand dollars."

I was silent a few moments to let that sink in for the judge's benefit. Then I asked Terence if he thought that was a lot of money.

Predictably, he did.

"Do you also receive a pension from the Orlando Police Department?"

"Yes, I do."

"Was Mrs. Zide aware that you would receive that pension?"

"I told her, of course."

"And in addition to that pension, and above the quarter-of-a-million-dollar lump-sum payment she gave to you, Mr. O'Rourke, in the past eight years has Mrs. Zide paid you any more money?"

"She has not, but I receive a check from one of Mr. Neil's companies, every month, for four thousand dollars."

"Health insurance and major medical?"

"I have that from them too."

"Did you ever expect such handsome retirement benefits?"

"No, but I've told you, they are good people."

"Pass the witness," I said.

This time it was Muriel who jumped up to do the cross. She and Beldon thought highly of young Whatley, but Muriel wanted Terence O'Rourke for her own. She beat at him, she insulted him, she questioned his sobriety and his mental capacity and even his loyalty to his former employers, tried to twist his words and hammer at his memory and degrade his story in any way she could—as any lawyer would have done had he or she been standing in her shoes—indeed, as I would have done had I been the prosecutor.

Like infidelity, the law is a cruel sport.

I held Muriel in check as best I could by objecting to just about every other question. It was unnecessary: Terence wouldn't budge. He was telling the truth, and the more Muriel tried to twist the knives of ridicule and doubt, the more certain he became. Finally she said, "I have no more questions," and I thanked Terence, and the court told him he could leave.

Judge Fleming looked down from his lofty position on the bench. He was king and emperor and court jester. "Is that all?" he asked me. "You look like death on a cracker. Are you ready to go home and get some sleep?"

"No, Judge, I'm just fine, and I have one more witness. And possibly a second one."

"Can we get them done this afternoon before we close up shop?"

"Yes, sir," I said, somewhat recklessly. "They're both here in the courtroom."

"Let's hear the first one."

"The defense calls Constance Zide."

31

"**Y**OUR HONOR, I would like to declare Mrs. Zide to be a hostile witness."

"Objection!" cried Muriel Suarez.

"State your reasons," Judge Fleming said, clutching his coffee mug and peering down at me.

"I'm going by Rule 90.62 Subsection 2," I said, "of the Florida Criminal Code. Mrs. Zide has already been a witness for the state in the jury trial and in this hearing. That makes her adverse by any standards. If she's *my* witness now, and presumed to be friendly, I can't ask her leading questions. And I don't believe I can get her to speak the truth other than by leading her."

"You want to cross-examine her, Mr. Jaffe? Is that what you're telling me?"

"Yes, Your Honor. But with some latitude."

"You could have cross-examined her day before yesterday, when she was a witness for the state. You said you had no more questions."

"But I asked to have her stay on call."

"And she has." He pointed with his bony hand. "She's here in the courtroom, isn't she?"

"Yes, Your Honor, she's right here."

"So I'll let you cross-examine her, but the cross has to be limited to those matters she discussed under direct examination by Ms.

Suarez. Those are the rules of evidence, sir, and they're my rules too. Don't you consider them fair?"

Yes, but they weren't what I wanted. I wanted to open up new territory, and I couldn't do that under his rules.

"Your Honor, I understand your point. And therefore I repeat my motion to declare this witness as adverse and hostile."

The judge smiled at me as if I were a backward child. He sipped his coffee, then leaned forward toward Muriel in a gentle, inquiring fashion. "Madam Prosecutor, what say you?"

"There's no indication at all of hostility on the part of Mrs. Zide," Muriel fired back. "He asked her to stay on call, and she did. Defense counsel wants to go on a fishing expedition. Let's have a proffer. Then we'll know what kind of fish he's after, and what he's using to bait his hook."

The judge added a nod and a twinkle to his smile. Fish-and-bait was his style of metaphor. Muriel had also learned how to deal with him.

A proffer was an offer before the court, in the presence of opposing counsel, as to what you planned to do. In this instance, a proffer seemed like a logical request—there were no jurors present to be confused by what was going on. Moreover, a proffer would quickly tell the judge if Connie was what I claimed her to be: a hostile witness. But it would also prepare Connie, and alert Muriel to my intentions.

"A proffer's a good idea," the judge said. "Mr. Jaffe? Tell us what you're going to try to prove."

Muriel gave me a soft, smug look. Still friends, sweetie?

"I withdraw my motion, Your Honor"—I tried not to look too hangdog—"although I reserve the right to renew it. I'll take the witness on direct, and we'll consider her to be friendly."

Muriel swooped in for the coup de grace. "I want to remind opposing counsel that if she's *his* witness now, he vouches for the truth of what she tells us."

I spread my hands as if to say, "Win some, lose some," and turned to Connie, who had sat there in the box with hardly a change of expression during this entire colloquy. Her eyes were quiet and dull; she almost seemed drugged. And I began:

"Do you recall, Mrs. Zide, that when your son testified I asked if I might call him Neil? Because we'd known each other socially for fourteen years?"

"Yes, I recall that," she said calmly, "and if you're going to ask me the same question, the answer is of course yes. Please call me Connie."

"Actually, Mrs. Zide, I wasn't going to ask the same privilege of you. I was going to ask if you'd tell the court how I met Neil."

She looked briefly flustered, a little hurt. She clasped her hands together in her lap. "You met him through me, I believe."

"And how did you and I meet?"

From the corner of my eye I saw Muriel open her mouth to object. She could have done so on the grounds of relevance, although I would have battled her. But she closed her mouth. Surely no danger lurked in such a question, she must have thought.

Connie smiled gently, and briefly related to the court the story of her mugging by Alejandro Ortega in the parking lot of the Regency Plaza Mall. Enter her hero. All's well that ends well.

"I asked you a question that day, Mrs. Zide, and I imagine you've forgotten it. But I'll ask it again, if you don't mind. When you ripped the gold chain off the young man who had attacked you outside Dillard's, weren't you frightened that he'd retaliate?"

Muriel still looked puzzled, and so did Judge Fleming. And Muriel still held back.

"No," Connie said, "not really. I was just acting on impulse, as I recall. Not thinking clearly."

"Were you armed?"

A little nerve in Connie's cheek twitched. She said, "Armed?"

Now Muriel jumped up swiftly to object. "Where's this going, Your Honor? It's certainly an odd line of questioning. What's the relevance? Can we have a proffer on *that*?"

The judge looked at me, shrugged, and nodded his approval.

"Of course, Your Honor," I said. "Mrs. Zide told me on that occasion that she *was* armed. That, indeed, she carried a pistol in her handbag and was prepared to use it in an emergency."

Muriel nearly exploded. "Your Honor, that's out of line! *He's* not testifying!"

"You asked for a proffer, Ms. Suarez," the judge said. "And he gave you one."

She'd been bushwhacked, and she saw it immediately. She stepped back, sighing. Even though no jury was present and it wasn't necessary to act, she rolled her eyes heavenward.

Judge Fleming focused again on Connie. "I'll allow the question," he said. "You may answer, Madam."

"Shall I repeat it?" I asked Connie, when still she hesitated.

"Yes, please."

"Were you armed that day in the parking lot outside Dillard's, fourteen years ago?"

"Yes," she replied.

I was over the first hurdle. She could have said no. There was no way I could have proved it.

"Armed with what, Mrs. Zide?"

"A pistol."

"Where you did you carry it?"

"In my handbag."

"What kind of pistol was it?"

She hesitated, twisting the rings on her fingers. "I don't really remember." That, of course, was why she felt safe in admitting she'd been armed.

She was my witness; I couldn't hack at her without incurring the wrath of the court. I couldn't impeach her by questioning her veracity.

But I could nibble at the edges of it.

"Are you sure you don't remember, Mrs. Zide?"

"Objection!" Muriel said angrily. "Asked and answered!"

"True," the judge responded. He gave me a stern look. "Go forward, Mr. Jaffe."

"Was it a revolver or an automatic, Mrs. Zide?"

"Asked and answered!" Muriel cried again. "She said she didn't remember!"

"Withdraw the question," I said. "Did you have a license for that pistol, Mrs. Zide? Or were you carrying it in your handbag, as a concealed weapon, illegally?"

"Objection!" Muriel cried.

"On what grounds?" the judge inquired.

"Relevance!"

"Seems harmless enough to me. You may answer, Mrs. Zide."

Connie had little choice. In a trembling voice she said, "I don't remember." She had good instincts; "I don't remember" was the safest place to hide, and it was exactly what I had feared.

I turned to the judge. "Your Honor, on this specific matter of her carrying a weapon, since the witness is evasive, I ask her to be declared adverse and ask permission to cross-examine."

Muriel almost danced up and down in anger. "She's not being evasive! It's fourteen years ago, and she doesn't remember! He has to accept that!"

Judge Fleming, looking almost sad at the decision he felt he was forced to make, said to me, "I'm afraid that's so, Mr. Jaffe. Her memory isn't fresh, and we have to live with it."

"Perhaps I can refresh her memory," I said.

"You may do that, sir, but not by cross-examining her."

I reached into the folder in front of me on the counsel table and took out a cream-colored document. Gary had dug for me in the deepest recesses of the county's files. But it was too long ago; no record of Connie's pistol registration existed, not even on microfilm.

I said, "I would like to place this in evidence, Your Honor, and then have my witness examine it."

Connie blanched. She looked at Muriel, waiting for an objection, but now none was forthcoming. There were no grounds for one, and Muriel, like the court, was waiting.

Connie blew out her breath and said quietly, "Wait. I remember now. It was registered. I did have a permit, of course. I wouldn't carry a pistol illegally."

"And now that you remember that you had a permit for the weapon," I said, waving the piece of paper at her, "does that jog your memory to remember what kind of pistol it was, Mrs. Zide?"

"Yes, I think so."

"Objection!" Muriel barked.

"She's answered!" I barked back.

"And the objection is overruled," the judge said.

I raised my voice but tried to be calming, composed. "Would you be kind enough to tell us, Mrs. Zide, what kind of pistol it was?"

"A Smith and Wesson Chief Special."

"Do you recall the caliber?"

She hesitated, and the muscles of her face seemed to sag. I waved the paper in my hand slightly. She said, "I believe it was a thirty-eight-caliber."

"And it fit in your purse?"

"It was only a little gun."

"With a two-inch barrel?"

"That's possible. It was small."

"May it please the court," I said, "that this document in my hand be marked defendant's 'A' for identification?"

I walked to the bench and handed the cream-colored piece of paper up to Judge Fleming. He stared at it in puzzlement, blinked a few times behind his tortoiseshell spectacles, then cocked a shaggy white eyebrow.

"Mr. Jaffe, this paper is your sworn affidavit that Mrs. Zide told you she carried a pistol in her handbag. It's not a registration permit to carry that pistol."

"I never said it was, Your Honor."

"Damn you!" Connie cried at me, before Muriel could intervene.

It was all I needed. "Your Honor, this witness is demonstrably hostile! And this witness *has* been evasive. I can't get her to be responsive other than by frightening her or by asking her leading questions. I don't want to frighten her—that's not fair. I renew my motion to cross-examine."

Muriel said angrily, "That business with the affidavit was sheer trickery! There's no basis for the renewal of the motion!"

"Why?" the judge inquired. "He didn't make any statements that it was other than an affidavit. He even showed it to us. Who did he trick? Or whom? There's no jury. You're too smart to be tricked. And the witness had her memory refreshed."

"It's cheap, Your Honor!"

"Flashy, maybe. Not what I'd call cheap. Kind of like a Rolex as opposed to a Timex. I'm going to grant his motion to cross-examine." He turned back to me and wagged a crooked finger. "No more stunts, though, Counsel. We've been entertained, but once is enough. Just ask proper questions."

"Yes, sir!" I said, as if he were a general and I were a lieutenant.

"May we have a ten-minute break, Your Honor?" Muriel said sharply.

Connie came back to the witness stand. Her anger had waned. Her eyes were clear and her gaze steady, as if she had been through something and had triumphed over it. The buzz in the courtroom subsided, and I began again.

"Mrs. Zide . . . you've been in this courtroom during previous testimony, haven't you?"

"Yes, you've seen me here."

"On Monday, you heard the testimony of your son?"

"Yes."

"And this morning, the testimony of Mr. Stanzi, the ballistics expert?"

"Yes."

"And also, this morning, you heard Terence O'Rourke, your former security guard?"

"Yes."

"You heard certain contradictions between what those last three witnesses swore to and what you and your son said here in this courtroom under oath, didn't you?"

"Contradictions?"

"Disagreements as to facts, if you will."

"I'm not sure what you mean. There were some differences of opinion, but that's natural, isn't it? We're talking about events that occurred many years ago."

"What were those differences of opinion, as you call them?"

"I was generalizing. I don't recall offhand."

"Do you recall Mr. O'Rourke saying that on the night of your husband's murder there was a single shot, and then, a minute or two later, three more shots?"

"Yes, I believe he did say that."

"But thirteen years ago you swore under oath"—I glanced down at my notes and lifted a sheet of paper from the table—"that 'there were three, four, five shots.' Is that correct?"

"Yes, I believe so."

I kept looking at the sheet of paper in my hand. "And didn't you say, just two days ago, in your testimony here in this court: 'The shots came one after the other. Then I rushed out to the terrace.' Didn't you say that under oath, Mrs. Zide?"

She had been bluffed and hurt once; she wouldn't allow it to happen twice. That was where her calmness came from. "I don't recall saying that on Monday, Mr. Jaffe. I did say there were a total of three or four shots, and of course I said I rushed out to the terrace. But that's all I recall saying."

"Is it your testimony *now*, Mrs. Zide, that the shots did *not* come one after another?"

"I'm not sure what you mean."

"I'll put it another way. Was Mr. O'Rourke telling the truth when he said there was a single shot, and then, a minute or two later, three more shots?"

"I don't know." She sighed. "It was so long ago."

I handed her the piece of paper in my hand. "Would you identify this, please, Mrs. Zide?"

She stared at it for a moment. "It seems to be part of a trial transcript."

"And the date, as notarized by the court clerk?"

"It says April 14, 1979."

"And who is asking the questions?"

"I believe you were," Connie said softly.

"And who is testifying?"

"I was."

"That testimony took place in this same courtroom in which we sit today, did it not?"

"Yes."

"When you testified here in April of 1979, a man was on trial for his life, was he not?"

"Yes."

"Before a jury of his peers?"

"Yes."

"The same man who sits next to me today?" I laid my hand on Darryl's hot shoulder.

"Yes."

"You identified this man as the one who shot your husband, did you not?"

"Yes."

"And at that trial in April of 1979, there was a judge sitting on the bench, as Judge Fleming sits today, wasn't there?"

"Yes."

"Cloaked in black?"

"Yes."

"Symbolizing the gravity of the occasion and the majesty of our law?"

"Yes, I suppose so."

I frowned. "You weren't sure that the trial of a man for murder was a grave occasion?"

"I'm sorry—yes, I was sure."

"And on that occasion, before you testified, the clerk of the court

311

asked you to raise your hand to God and swear to tell the truth, did she not?"

"Yes."

"And did you tell the truth to that other judge and that jury?"

"Yes."

"Read what you were asked and what you told them, Mrs. Zide, if you please. The part marked in yellow ink."

She read:

> "Q: You heard the shots?
> "A: Yes, there were three, or maybe even four. Shots, I mean. They came one after the other. I ran outside."

I said now, "You still stand by that statement, that the shots 'came one after the other'?"

A trickle of sweat appeared at Connie's temple. "Yes," she murmured.

"Mrs. Zide," I said, "did you, back then, identify this man sitting beside me as the murderer of your husband?"

"Yes."

"How did you do that?"

"I don't recall."

"You don't recall?"

"I mean, I did it because the police arrested him, I think . . . and they showed me photographs . . . and I knew him. He was the man who shot my husband, and he had worked for us. A handyman. He cleaned up after the dogs. I was told that he had a criminal record, that he was violent—"

"Who told you that he had a criminal record and was violent?"

"I don't recall."

"Did Sergeant Floyd Nickerson tell you that?"

"He may have. I don't recall."

"Did your son tell you that?"

"I don't recall!" Her voice rose shrilly. "Can't you understand what I'm saying? Don't you believe me?"

Muriel sprang to her feet. "Your Honor, may we have a break so that the witness can compose herself?"

"I'm going to object to that," I said forcefully. "We're in the midst of a line of questioning. If opposing counsel has any objection to that line, let her state it. Otherwise, I ask the court's permission to continue. Time is limited, and by the court itself."

Judge Fleming thought it over. It was nearly three o'clock in the afternoon.

"Is this your last witness?" he asked me.

In a sense Neil was more vulnerable, but I decided to roll the dice and stay with Connie.

"Yes, Your Honor."

"We *don't* need a break," the judge said. "Keep going."

Connie moaned softly.

"Mrs. Zide," I resumed, "let's get back to what Terence O'Rourke said about the single shot and then, a minute or two later, three evenly spaced shots to follow. That's what he said, isn't it?"

"I think so."

"And by the way, do you at all dispute Mr. O'Rourke's figures about the money you gave him when he left your employ?"

"Not at all. He was a faithful servant."

"How about his vacation to Colorado and California? Did he tell that story accurately?"

"I think he may have exaggerated. He wasn't a young man, and he was looking tired. My recollection is that he was owed those three weeks holiday and the time had come."

She'd had a while to think that over, I realized, and she spoke with a renewed confidence.

"So you didn't, in any sense, send him away to visit his family so that he wouldn't be present in Jacksonville during the trial?"

"Of course not."

"And when he left your employ, you didn't give him that considerable bonus in order to ensure his continued loyalty?"

"He *was* loyal. I didn't need to ensure it."

"Did you know that Neil was sending him four thousand dollars a month for the past eight years?"

"I believe Neil and I discussed it once."

"And that money wasn't meant to keep him quiet either, was it?"

"Not at all."

"Did you ever consider having Terence O'Rourke killed?"

"I beg your pardon?"

"Would you like the court reporter to read back the question to you?"

313

"No, I heard the question," Connie said, her lip quivering. "I was just a little shocked by it. Killing him? Having Terence killed? No, Mr. Jaffe. *No.* Definitely *no.*"

"You never discussed that possibility with your son?"

"No!"

"Did you discuss with Neil the idea of having Victor Gambrel killed?"

"*No!*"

"Did Neil elect to do that on his own?"

"Objection!" Muriel, her face inflamed, jumped to her feet. "There's no predicate whatever for this insinuation. This is bizarre!"

"Objection sustained," Judge Fleming said. Normally he would have told the jury to disregard the question and any answer. But since there was no jury, he was the only one required to disregard the so-called insinuation—if he could. He wagged a finger of admonishment at me.

"Mrs. Zide"—I stood up and began to prowl by the counsel table —"how many servants do you employ at your house?"

"Seven or eight. It varies."

"How many did you employ back in December 1978?"

"Perhaps a few more than that."

"The seven or eight you employ now have been with you since 1978?"

"No, there's some turnover."

"The ones who've gone, have they all been fired?"

"Of course not."

"Some have quit?"

"A few."

"Some have left by mutual agreement with you?"

"Yes."

"Of those who've quit or left your employ by mutual agreement, how many received a bonus of a quarter of a million dollars plus a retirement payment of four thousand dollars a month?"

She had no way out.

"None," she said quietly. "But Terence was special."

"I'm sure he was. Let's go back to the night of December 5, 1978," I said. "The night of the murder."

She nodded; she seemed almost relieved.

"Do you want me to tell you again what happened, Ted?" she asked.

Oh, poor Connie.

It was as if we were going to have a conversation on her living room sofa, or in my office as we had done thirteen years ago. And as if we were still what we once had been: lovers, then careful friends.

"No," I said, smiling sadly. "I want you to answer my questions, Mrs. Zide, if you don't mind."

Connie clasped her hands like a child and nodded obediently.

32

"M<small>RS.</small> Z<small>IDE</small>," I said, "on the night of the murder you had a party on the grounds of your house, is that correct?"

"A musicale," Connie said eagerly. "You were there."

"Yes, I was definitely there. With my wife."

"The party ended about eleven o'clock, I'd say—"

"No, Mrs. Zide, I didn't ask you that. Tell me this, please. That night, the night of your husband's murder, what *first* alerted you to the presence of burglars—or, let's say, intruders—on your grounds?"

A blotch of color appeared on her pale cheek. "An urn crashed on the patio," she said. "We heard the noise of its breaking. Solomon got up from the backgammon table—"

"Mrs. Zide, stop." I wanted to be casual at this stage, but I had to control her. "Just answer my questions. Don't volunteer information. Do you understand?"

"Yes, I thought . . . " Her voice trailed off. She wanted to be friendly, to defuse me.

"So the first thing that alerted you to the presence of burglars was the sound of an urn breaking, is that correct?"

"Yes, that's correct."

"Didn't you have what you once referred to as 'a state-of-the-art security system'?"

She offered a rueful smile. "We thought we did."

"Didn't that security system include a number of spotlights called

First Alert, which would snap on if anyone broke the path of their ultraviolet beams?"

"I'm not sure what they were called. But yes, that's what was supposed to happen."

"It didn't happen? None of the lights went on to alert you?"

"I don't think so."

"When Darryl Morgan and William Smith entered your property in the dead of night, you're telling us they didn't break any of those First Alert beams? Didn't trigger *any* of the spotlights?"

"Objection," Muriel called, rising. "Calls for speculation. She doesn't know if Morgan and Smith broke any of the beams or not. All she remembers is that the lights didn't go on, and she's said so."

"Objection sustained," said the judge.

I could see that Connie was feeling confident again. This was all polite, friendly, and bearable. Muriel was protecting her.

"Do you recall, Mrs. Zide, when your son took the stand here on Monday, that I read aloud some of his testimony from the trial thirteen years ago?"

"Yes, I believe so."

"Do you recall what he said in response to my asking him: 'Did you see the intruders clearly?' "

"Not really."

"You don't recall his saying"—once again I read from the transcript in my hand—" 'the spotlights on the lawn had finally been triggered, I assume by these two men'? Didn't you hear that, Mrs. Zide?"

"I'm not sure. I think so."

"Isn't it a fact, Mrs. Zide, that you *did* see the lights go on outside—while your husband was still alive—and that you then went outside on the terrace in your bathrobe?"

"Objection! Asked and answered."

"Sustained."

I pointed my finger at Connie like a pistol. "And that's also about the time, isn't it, that you heard the Lhasa apso puppies barking?"

"Objection!" Muriel was still on her feet. "There's no predicate for any barking Lhasa apso puppies."

A murmur of laughter flowed through the courtroom.

"Objection sustained."

"And therefore, Mrs. Zide," I said, with as much righteous anger and conviction as I dared—since it was all speculation—"you got up from the backgammon table and went outside *before* any shots were fired?"

"Objection!"

"On what grounds, Ms. Suarez?" the judge asked.

"Argumentative, and when he says 'therefore' he's assuming a fact not in evidence."

"I don't think so. Overruled. She can answer yes or no."

A couple for you, and now one for you, the judge seemed to be saying to Muriel and me. No prejudice in *my* court. He smiled benevolently at Connie.

"No," Connie said to me. "Whatever you say happened, that didn't happen."

"Isn't it a fact, Mrs. Zide, that you came outside in your bathrobe and saw Darryl Morgan on the lawn or on the terrace?"

Connie waited for Muriel's objection, but none came. Muriel played by the rules. I didn't intend to do that. I had more at stake than Muriel had.

"No, it's not a fact," Connie said.

"You didn't see Darryl Morgan?"

"I saw two men. I didn't know then that one of them was Darryl Morgan."

"Isn't it a fact that you saw the other intruder, William Smith, kick one of the puppies as he ran away toward the beach?"

"No," Connie said. "I didn't see anything."

"Are you telling us that a puppy wasn't taken to the vet later that morning by one of your servants, a woman named Martina Vargas?"

Terence had told me about this, but Martina was long vanished to her native León, and Gary hadn't been able to find her. And when Terence was on the stand, I'd forgotten to ask him about it. I was tired; I'd managed about an hour's sleep on the plane from Newark. There was nothing I could do now except try and jam it through.

But Connie couldn't afford to lie blatantly; she didn't know what other pieces of paper I might pull out of my conjuror's hat.

"I'm not sure," she said, placing her hands protectively across her breasts. "It's hard to remember."

"Try, Mrs. Zide."

"I can't remember."

"Did the puppy live?"

"Oh, yes."

"So you remember *that*. Were any of its ribs broken?"

"I don't remember."

"Any of its legs?"

"I don't know."

"Either of its shoulders?"

"Objection!" Muriel tried. "Badgering the witness!"

"Overruled," the judge said. "He's just asking questions."

"Mrs. Zide," I continued, "what's the name of the vet who takes care of your dogs?"

Her scalp was rivering perspiration over her forehead, causing her to rub both palms over her eyes. She didn't know if I knew the name of the vet or not. If I knew, I might have checked with him.

"Dr. Merrill," she said. "I remember now. Harry Merrill. He's still my vet. I have a black Labrador now, and two golden retrievers. One of the puppies was hurt that night. Broken leg, I seem to recall. Yes, he was probably kicked by one of the men when they ran away. How foolish of me not to remember it."

It was a small point, but it loomed large. She had lied about the pistol and now about the kicked puppy. She could have admitted the story of the puppy at the very beginning and then could have disclaimed having seen what happened. It wouldn't have hurt her at all. But she didn't know what I knew or didn't know. Didn't know where each lie would lead. Didn't know what was coming next. She and Neil had woven a tangled web; now it was coming undone. She hadn't been in any real danger, but she had let herself stumble and appear counterfeit. She looked beseechingly at Muriel, but there was nothing Muriel could do . . . and maybe by then, for all I knew, nothing Muriel really wanted to do.

Connie looked quickly up at Judge Fleming. He was studying her with great curiosity.

I rose from the counsel table and moved two steps closer to the witness stand. I wasn't in Connie's territory, but I must have loomed larger to her, as if suddenly she'd trained a telescopic sight on me. But she was not the hunter, and I was not the hunted. And she could see the look in my eyes. There was none of the mercy she was looking for. Pity was there, but no mercy.

The courtroom was completely silent. No one coughed.

"Mrs. Zide," I asked, "what happened to the Smith and Wesson thirty-eight Chief Special you carried in your handbag fourteen years ago?"

"The what?" She seemed confused. "You keep changing the subject, Ted."

I knew that.

"Your pistol, Mrs. Zide. You told us about it earlier, don't you remember? I ask you: What happened to it?"

"I don't know."

"Do you still carry it?"

"No."

"Do you still own it?"

"No."

"Do you carry another pistol?"

She hesitated. "Yes. This is a dangerous city. I have a permit."

"What kind of pistol do you carry now?"

"It's called a Llama. An automatic."

"What's the caliber?"

"I'm not sure."

"How about a thirty-two? Does that sound right?" I knew the Llama Blackhawk; it was a woman's gun. Muriel carried one too.

"Yes. It may be a thirty-two."

"You carry it for protection?"

"Yes, of course."

"You threw the Smith and Wesson thirty-eight away?"

"No, I didn't."

"Neil threw it away?"

"Neil did what?"

"I'm asking *you,* Mrs. Zide. Did Neil throw it away?"

"I don't know."

"If Neil didn't throw it away, what happened to it?"

"I don't know."

"It just vanished? Disappeared?"

"I think so."

"Soon after the death of your husband?"

"I think so. I mean, no. I don't remember."

"Didn't it vanish the night your husband died? Didn't Neil throw it in the ocean, or the Intracoastal?"

"If she knows." From behind me I heard Muriel speak quietly, dutifully.

"Yes, excuse me, Mrs. Zide. If you know."

"I don't know."

"Neil didn't tell you?"

"No."

"Did you shoot your husband, Mrs. Zide?"

"No, I didn't, I swear that to you."

"But on the night of December 5, in the early morning, *someone* fired your pistol, your Smith and Wesson thirty-eight, isn't that so?"

She didn't answer. Her lips twisted into a skeletal grimace. She had been licking them constantly, and the lipstick was gone, so that they seemed colorless. Her blue-green eyes had sunk deep into their sockets.

"Your husband was in a rage that night, wasn't he, Mrs. Zide?"

She nodded her head up and down, slowly. "He was angry at me, yes."

"After the party?"

"Yes, after the party. You were there."

"I was at the party, I wasn't there afterward. Your husband took your pistol out of your handbag and fired it once, didn't he?"

"No."

"And the bullet lodged in the Swedish oak paneling on the far side of the living room from the terrace, isn't that so?"

"No, not so."

There was a half-smile on her bloodless lips and a cunning look in her eyes that at first I couldn't define. But it slowly resolved itself into an expression of superiority. Then I understood. She knew something I didn't know, and she was reveling in it.

"There in the living room, Mrs. Zide, after the party, Solly was in a rage?"

"Yes."

"At you?"

"Yes."

"And he screamed at you?"

"Yes."

"He frightened you?"

"Yes."

"And then Neil came home?"

Her eyes grew stony, darker. "I don't remember."

"You testified under oath, at the trial, that Neil came home from a party while you and Solly were playing backgammon after the musicale. Do you remember that now?"

"Yes."

"Was Neil drunk?"

"I don't think so."

"High on drugs?"

"I don't know."

"Solly was screaming at you when Neil came home?"

"Yes."

"Isn't it a fact, Mrs. Zide, that before any shots were fired from your pistol, you heard the puppies barking, and you went outside and surprised two black men on the lawn, and they ran away?"

"Objection. Asked and answered," I heard Muriel say, but without the vigor of a short time ago.

"Withdrawn," I said. "And when you came back into the living room, the argument with Solly grew worse?"

"I don't remember."

I had it now. "And *you* took your pistol out of your handbag, Mrs. Zide, and you fired a shot over his head, into the woodwork, as a warning?"

"No." But that look of cunning fled her face. She would have made a poor poker player.

"And then Solly broke a bottle and cut you in the face, didn't he?"

"No." The cunning look returned.

"And you shot him, didn't you?"

"No."

"He was on the terrace, and you were just inside the living room, isn't that a fact?"

"No."

"You shot at him three times. One shot missed and went outside —the other two struck him and killed him. Isn't that what happened, Mrs. Zide?"

"No," she said, and the cunning look didn't fade. Because, I realized now, that *wasn't* what had happened. My mind swerved from one possibility to another. If Solly hadn't cut her, who had? Not Neil. I believed the worst of Neil, but not that.

"And then," I said, "Neil took over, didn't he?"

"Took over?" Connie looked frightened, paler than before. "No, he didn't take over. Took over what?"

"You were hurt and couldn't think, so Neil took over and arranged matters, isn't that so?"

"Asked and answered," Muriel said.

"Strike the question," I said. "Neil made a telephone call to the home of Victor Gambrel, chief of security at Zide Industries, didn't he?"

"No, not then."

"Then who did call Victor Gambrel?"

"Neil did, of course," she said, confused. "I'm sorry."

"Victor Gambrel lived close by, in Ponte Vedra, didn't he?"

"He may have. I don't remember."

"And Victor Gambrel arrived before the police did, isn't that correct?"

"Yes, I think so. Does that matter?"

"Victor Gambrel helped Neil move your husband's body so that it looked as if he'd been shot by someone standing *outside,* isn't that so?"

Again, from behind me, Muriel said, "If she knows."

"Yes," I said, "*if* you know."

"I do know. The answer is no. That didn't happen."

"Victor Gambrel helped you and Neil work out the story you needed to tell the police, didn't he?"

"No. There was no story we needed to tell."

"You decided to blame the murder of your husband on the two black men who'd bungled the burglary of your house, isn't that so?"

"No, I didn't do that."

"When you saw Darryl Morgan outside the house that night, you didn't recognize him as a man in your employ, isn't that so?"

"That's true. Yes, that's so."

"Neil deliberately gave to the police a vague description of the two men, didn't he?"

"I don't know."

"You didn't know who they were—*you* hadn't seen them clearly, and Neil hadn't seen them *at all.* Isn't that correct?"

"I don't know," she said, as if by rote.

"And that's why no one described Darryl Morgan as tall, or big, until *after* he was arrested, isn't that correct, Mrs. Zide?"

"I don't know."

"And then, that night, after you'd cooked up your story, Neil called the Jacksonville Beach police, a good twenty minutes after Victor Gambrel had arrived, and Gambrel called his friend Floyd Nickerson at JSO Homicide. Isn't that what happened? *If* you know."

"I don't know."

"And the reason Nickerson sent Carmen Tanagra down to the cabanas to see what happened to the dog was so that he'd have the time to listen to an offer from Gambrel on behalf of Neil. Isn't that what happened? *If* you know."

"I don't know."

"And to your surprise, after Nickerson and Carmen Tanagra picked up Morgan and Smith at the Lil' Champ food store, you found out that Darryl Morgan worked for you as a handyman, isn't that so?"

"I don't know."

"You had no idea he and Smith would be caught, did you?"

"No."

"You didn't want Darryl Morgan to be blamed for the murder of your husband, did you?"

"No."

"Because he hadn't murdered him, isn't that the reason?"

"No, that's not why."

"When you were in Baptist Hospital, the police showed you Morgan's photograph, didn't they?"

"Yes."

"You had to identify the man in that photograph, didn't you?"

"Yes, I think so."

"Because Neil told you that Nickerson had captured a man who admitted trying to burgle your house—Darryl Morgan, a man who worked for you—and the police were going to show you a photograph of him, and you had no choice: you *had* to identify him. Isn't that what happened?"

"No."

"Neil told you Morgan was violent, a career criminal, right?"

"No, I don't remember that."

"And by then it was too late to back out, wasn't it?"

"I don't understand."

"In the end, what did it matter if Morgan was blamed for a murder he didn't commit? He'd do the time anyway, for one crime or another—isn't that what your son, Neil, and Victor Gambrel, told you in Baptist Hospital?"

"No."

"And so it was a choice between Darryl Morgan, an uneducated, violent black criminal who wasn't fit to do more than pick up your dog droppings, taking a fall on a first-degree murder charge, or you taking a fall on a manslaughter charge that might easily turn into murder if they found out how you hated Solly . . . and that was hardly a choice, was it?"

"It's not true," Connie said.

"But you didn't want Morgan to die in the electric chair, did you?"

"I didn't want that at all, Ted."

"You wanted me to go easy on him in the trial, didn't you?"

"Yes." She brightened suddenly; she saw a glimmer of salvation. "I did. You knew that. You remember."

"During the jury selection, we went for a walk along the river, and you told me you didn't want Morgan to die, isn't that right?"

"Yes, darling."

I felt a terrible chill, and my heart fluttered like a torn wing. Toba was there in the courtroom. Toba had heard. But I had to go on. "You knew Morgan wasn't guilty, didn't you, Mrs. Zide?"

"No, Ted."

"Wasn't that why you begged me the way you did?"

"No, Ted."

I switched gears again, as much to save myself as to trap her. "The argument with Solly, before he died—that final argument—that was about Neil, wasn't it?"

"No, Ted."

"And then Neil came in at two o'clock in the morning while it was taking place, didn't he, Mrs. Zide?"

"He came in, yes."

"Solly was violent, wasn't he, Mrs. Zide?"

"Please, my sweet, don't call me that. You know my name."

My wife was hearing all this. I wanted to turn and look at her, to say, "Toba, it was then, not now. It's you I love and cherish." But I didn't dare. I remembered Beldon's hard warnings to me last spring in his office . . . *something makes me feel you shouldn't be involved.* . . . He had known. He had tried to stop me from moving too far into the past, where dragons lived.

But for Darryl's sake I had to go back. And then go on.

"Solly threatened you, Connie, didn't he?"

"Yes."

"Somehow, in this argument, you enraged him to the point where you feared he'd do you bodily harm, isn't that true?"

"He hit me, Ted."

"In the face?"

"Yes. In the face. He cut my cheek."

I realized now that she was telling the truth. She had turned a corner and was racing down a track and couldn't halt herself.

You try not to ask a question where you don't know the answer, but we were beyond that now.

"What was the argument about, Connie?"

"You."

Oh, God. I couldn't back out of it.

"He knew," she said. "And he hated you."

But I could step aside, and I had to, once again for Darryl's sake.

"He slashed you with a knife, Connie, didn't he?"

She wouldn't let me. *She* was in control now. "I couldn't stand him anymore," she said. "I wouldn't let him touch me. I told him I loved you. You never believed that, did you?"

I wanted to shut my eyes. I wanted to run away. I felt Darryl, at my side, staring up at me. I could see the wide wondering look of Judge Fleming. I felt Toba's presence in the courtroom as a red-hot iron searing my flesh.

But I went forward, because there was no choice.

"What did he do to you, Connie?"

"I told him all that had happened. I taunted him. I told him about Cumberland Island."

I felt my nails digging into my palms. When I unclenched my fists I half expected to see blood. "He broke a bottle and struck you with it?"

"No."

"What did he use?"

"I told you, Ted, he hit me with his hand."

"You grabbed your pistol out of your handbag and fired a shot over his head, didn't you, Connie?"

"Yes."

"It hit the woodwork on the other side of the room, isn't that so?"

"Yes."

"And then?"

"He hit me again. He knocked me down."

"So you shot him and killed him, to protect yourself, didn't you?"

"No, my darling, no."

I became aware of a commotion toward the rear of the courtroom.

My back was turned to it. Then I saw Connie's eyes shift that way, and the judge suddenly reached for his gavel. At least I thought it was his gavel; I realized afterward that it may have been a pistol hidden under his robes. All I could think of was: *Toba*.

Neil Zide was in the aisle, and he had wrenched free of the bailiff, a man forty pounds heavier. Neil hurtled down the aisle into the well of the courtroom. His lips had collapsed inward against his teeth, and the blood had fled from his cheeks as if he had been struck. His hair flowed behind him like a lion's mane.

"You swine!" he yelled at me.

Connie was crying his name, trying to stop him. The judge was shouting, "Bailiff!" Connie rose from her seat in the witness box and reeled forward toward us as Neil's body slammed against mine and we tumbled back together against the counsel table.

The tumult subsided. The bailiffs held Neil, while the judge rapped his gavel continuously against the oak bench in order to quiet the courtroom. The muscles in Neil's face twitched; saliva foamed at the edges of his lips.

Connie's eyes looked stony and unfocused.

"I think this is the right time," Muriel said to Judge Fleming, "for a short recess."

"No!" I cried. "She wants to tell us!" I looked up at the bench, pleading. "Judge!"

Thank God, he understood. He simply nodded at me, and I turned on Connie, whose hands searched the air like the claws of a wounded animal.

I pointed at Neil. "He took the pistol from you, didn't he?"

"Yes," she murmured.

"And he shot your husband."

"He didn't mean to."

"Neil was enraged because Solly had hit you, isn't that true, Connie?"

"Yes, he's my son. He loves me. He despised Solly."

"Connie"—I approached her without asking permission from the judge, but I thought I had the right—"who cut your face?"

"I did," she said. "It was cut when Solly slapped me. I had to explain that. They told me to do it. I knew it would heal."

"Who is 'they,' Connie? Do you mean Neil and Gambrel? Did they tell you to cut yourself?"

327

She just nodded, and that was good enough, or terrible enough.

"What did you use?"

"A piece of glass . . . it was just my cheek . . . I knew it would heal."

How brave. How desperate. How insane. To keep her son from a manslaughter charge that might have turned into murder, she would scar herself and send another man to his death.

But she didn't know they would find Darryl, I realized. She hadn't planned it from the beginning. That was just bad luck: Nickerson was good at his job.

Nickerson . . .

I asked, "Did Neil pay off Floyd Nickerson, Connie?" And I added, gently, "If you know."

Neil screamed, "Con! Shut up!"

A broken word rose to her lips, but she was unable to utter it. And it no longer mattered.

33

WE STAYED IN Jacksonville for a week after the hearing. Toba was in a form of shock. The revelations in Judge Fleming's court-room, which the media took such pleasure in relating for the next several days, were like poison for her to absorb. I realized later that I knew what Bill Clinton felt like in the early part of his candidacy; I decided I'd never run for President.

I wanted to say to Toba, "Darling, it's been fourteen years. That's a lifetime ago." But, wisely, I didn't. For one thing, the word *darling* was definitely out of favor for a while. For another, infidelity of that sort doesn't have a statute of limitations.

Toba forgave me in time, because not to do so would have crippled our lives. She thought things over and decided she loved our marriage as it was: whole. It gave her security and freedom and love, and it had a history; what better combination is there?

She was silent and tearful for that week in Jacksonville and scowled at me for the next month in Sarasota, but then one Sunday I persuaded her to go with me out in the boat. On the bay I said, "Who's your best friend? Tell the truth."

"You are."

"So let's drop anchor and do what friends do."

She laughed at that, and the worst was over.

For us, but not for me. Day after day, when I was alone, I relived that moment in the courtroom when I had asked Connie the subject of the argument.

You.

That argument had led to Solly's death and the malignancy of Darryl's thirteen years on death row. Each time that realization flashed clear to me, my heart beat violently, my stomach throbbed with pain.

How much blame did I deserve? That evening when Connie had toppled into the pool, I had ended the love affair as cleanly as I knew how. I'd had no ulterior motive in going to the party; Connie had asked me with Toba, and in view of Solly's sudden interest in my career, it seemed fair to go. By recommending me to Royal, Kelly, he had been trying to get rid of me. I saw that clearly now.

I told him I loved you. . . . I told him all that had happened. I taunted him. I told him about Cumberland Island.

How could I have stopped her from doing that?

There's a price to pay for every act. In this case, the wrong man paid.

And now Connie and Neil would pay their small share. They were not arrested right there in court, but once the court reporter had delivered the transcript of the hearing to the state attorney's office, Muriel Suarez filed charges, and the wheels of public justice began to clunk slowly forward.

The charges that could stick were only second-degree murder and perjury. Neil hired lawyers from both Tallahassee and Washington, and the feeling around the Duval County Courthouse was that he would eventually cut a deal for fifteen years pen time, of which he'd serve two or three, and Connie would walk out the door with a suspended sentence. After all, Neil contributed heavily to both political parties, he was on the cutting edge of land development (without which Florida couldn't survive these hard times), and he and Connie were white.

Neil's great fear, I heard, was that he might not survive prison. There were men at Raiford who identified easily with someone who had lanquished on death row for more than a dozen years, and had little to lose by meting out vengeance to a white man who had done that to a brother. So be it.

As for Connie, it was rumored that she would leave Florida, and even the United States, and I believed it instantly. She had earned that ravaged face; her agony and shame weren't feigned, and she couldn't look anyone in the eye who knew what she had done. I imagined her growing old in some Mediterranean hideway, sitting at a table on her terrace with a drink in her hand and a confusion in her eyes as if somehow life, which once had promised so much, had failed her, cheated her. Enough people would be fond of her but she would never be sure what they knew or really thought, and she would die not knowing.

So that left Darryl.

In court that memorable day, I made a motion for his immediate release. But even Horace Fleming, unusual jurist that he was, couldn't comply without flagrantly breaking the law. Leaning down into the clamor, he said, "Mr. Jaffe, get the transcript of this last bit from my court reporter, and make a formal motion in writing. You look a little on the ragged edge—it shouldn't take you more than all night. The Morgan man's got to sleep somewhere, so let him go back to the jail and bunk down one more time. It won't kill him, and we know some things that would've—ain't that right?"

He turned to Muriel Suarez. "You want to oppose that motion, State, go right ahead. I can tell you, it'll be a hard crop to grow."

"The state will not oppose, Your Honor," Muriel said in a barbed voice.

I sat down with Darryl for a while in the judge's chambers and explained the whole procedure and what his options were. He was still in handcuffs.

"You can probably sue the state and win," I explained, "but you'll grow a beard to your knees before it's over. On the other hand, you file suit against Neil Zide and Connie Zide, and my blind old dog, if I had one, could win that case."

Darryl laughed deep in his belly. "You a lawyer to the end, ain't you. You gonna do that suit for me?"

"No, my friend, I am not. But Gary Oliver will. He'll make you rich."

He mulled that over. "Then I send that boy to school. His sisters too, if they wants to go. If they's enough money."

"I placed my hand on the meat of his shoulder. "Darryl, if Gary does it right, you can go over to the high school playground in the Blodgett Project, round up every kid in sight, and you can send them all to FSU and Grambling and Tuskegee Institute and even Princeton, to keep Tahaun and the girls company."

The next morning, in Judge Fleming's court, Gary filed the motion for release, and the state attorney's office nolle-prossed it, dropping all prosecution.

At noon, Darryl was formally released from the county jail and the Florida state prison system. Gary, Tahaun, and I were waiting for him outside, in the mercy of the warm winter sunlight. His son approached Darryl with an outstretched hand. After thirteen years in a cage on death row, Darryl could fit his worldly possessions into a battered twelve-by-twelve cardboard carton, which he carried under his arm like a purse. His clothes, his two decks of worn playing cards, and his toothbrush were inside it. He sniffed the air as though it were honey.

My eyes misted, but I said, "You want to go somewhere for a beer?"

"Hey," Darryl rumbled at me in The Jury Room, where he slowly sipped a Heineken, "you remember that day you come see me at Raiford? Day I put these round your neck?" Setting the beer bottle down, he raised those huge hands. "Remember what I try to do to you?"

"Yes, I remember."

"Lucky for me you was such a tough little fucker."

That was as close as he ever came to thanking me. And I understood: he knew I had saved his life, but he knew too that it wouldn't have needed saving if the world I lived in hadn't first put him in chains, degraded it and imperiled him.

Toba and I flew home to Sarasota.

A storm howled in from the Gulf that evening. During the night the rain overflowed ditches and gushed down the fairways of Longboat Key. The leaves of banana trees bowed under the lash of water. At dawn the rain stopped; the planet still spun, therefore the sun appeared to rise. I looked out the window where our garden seemed to have soared three inches during the night. A stray cat fell out of a palm tree and cried for food. Birds rushed about the beach, a little crazed. The flying fish in the bay began to surge.

With carnal intent I stroked the back of my slumbering wife. Later I scratched the stubble on my jaw. Should I let my beard grow? It might come out even grayer than my hair, but so what? Yes, I will. I will, therefore I can.

I called Kenny Buckram's office and asked him if he thought the public defender's office in Sarasota would have a place for me, and if so, would he put in a good word?

"Are you serious?"

"Of course."

"I meant are you serious that you think you need a good word from me?"

"Well, the Bar Association is still after my ass—last night I heard the hoofbeats of the posse—and Diaz over in Miami would like to string me up from a cottonwood tree."

"Don't worry about it, Ted."

That's what my mother said too. More important, Judge Ruth said it. I received copies of his letters: one to the Bar Association, one to the state attorney in Tallahassee. To the Bar Association he wrote: "This court would look unfavorably on further harassment of Mr. Jaffe for any—the court repeats, *any*—actions of his in this jurisdiction." And to the state attorney, he said, in effect: "I personally will intervene with the governor if you don't get that little fuck Diaz off my buddy's back."

Within a month I was offered a job in the special defense division of the public defender's office. I would be based in Sarasota County but would travel all over the state. The salary was not quite a third of what Royal, Kelly guaranteed me.

"What do you think?" I asked Toba.

"I think it would be crazy," she said. "Cathy's talking about graduate school. Alan's out there in art school, and he may want to go on to college. What if we lose this lawsuit to the spider woman? We just can't afford it."

"We won't lose the lawsuit," I said firmly. "And I can't afford *not* to take the job. I want it. It will make me feel I'm a useful human being instead of a parasite."

She had seen that look in my eye before. But she didn't back off or sulk. She hugged me and said, "Do it, Ted. We'll work things out."

I took the job. Toba and I went to services at our local temple that Friday evening, and a line from the prayerbook struck me and stayed with me:

There will we serve with awe as in the days of old.